50p

KITTY

By the same author
　The Episode
　Journey to Guyana
　Going Down

Margaret Bacon

Kitty

LONDON : DENNIS DOBSON

Copyright © 1972 by Margaret Tuckwell

All rights reserved

*First published in Great Britain in 1972 by
Dobson Books Ltd., 80 Kensington Church Street, London, W8*

*Printed in Great Britain by
Bristol Typesetting Co. Ltd., Bristol*

ISBN 0 234 77695 1

PART I

CHAPTER ONE

SCHOOL smelled of furniture polish and disinfectant. It always did at the beginning of term, before the influx of girls, clothes, books and trunks dispelled it. The dining-room had its own special aroma compounded of boiled eggs and oranges, which was what they always had for supper on the first night of term.

The eggs were too hard, the whites rubbery and the yolks pale and dead. But the girls were still chastened by the return to school so they only grumbled quietly as they sat at the long tables in the dining-room, heavy with the atmosphere of boiled eggs and oranges, furniture polish and homesickness.

Kitty did not feel exactly homesick, just uneasy and not yet resigned to being only a two hundredth part of a community and to never being alone except in the lavatory, that blessed sanctuary where she had spent hours when she was new, three years ago. There was one particular one, up on the top floor above her bedroom, that had been her special refuge from noise and bells. It had a very high window with bars but by standing on tiptoe on the seat and stretching up, holding on to the overflow pipe, she had been able to see a thin strip of flat country at the other side of the town, beyond the alien streets, and to imagine that not far beyond that there might be fields and streams and bracken-covered hills.

When she had a letter, she used to take it there, sometimes after carrying it around unopened for most of the day, for letters were handed out at breakfast and she was afraid to open it in the presence of those hundreds of eyes lest her own should disgrace her. High up in the cold lavatory she could read and cry alone.

As the weeks passed she sought the refuge less frequently and by the middle of term was opening her letters like everybody else at the breakfast table. Still occasionally she climbed up to her refuge and stared out at the bleak line of green, trying to see beyond it fells marked with outcrops of limestone and the long meandering lines of dry-stone walls. She would strain her ears as if to hear, beyond the hum of the traffic, the distant bleating of sheep on the fellside and the wild, free cry of the curlew.

She would climb down, stiff and cold, and return inexplicably strengthened to face the noise and hustle and shut-in life that everybody else seemed to take for granted. By the end of term she realized with some surprise that when she was behaving cheerfully she was no longer always pretending.

It seemed a long time ago now: she had only been eleven then and the war was just over. But it still returned mildly at the beginning of each new term, that feeling of being lost, and it was inseparably bound up with the smell of disinfectant and polish and oranges, but she knew now that if she could keep it at bay for a few days it would vanish and the cheerful community atmosphere would wrap her around with blinkered security. For she was aware that she was cheating, that she did not really belong to the innocent society which took happy homes for granted and thought that hatred and evil were words out of good literature. The knowledge made her feel lonely, marked out. She felt herself to be years, years older than the children who were her companions. But she found that she could act as if she were one of them and join in the pretence life of school just as if it were real. She could let herself be comforted by its warmth and its everyday problems, pressing and soluble. At the end of term she had to return to reality, but then there were the hills for comfort.

It was Saturday; for half an hour after lunch everybody rested, except girls who were going out. There was no official half-term but once a term they were allowed out with their parents. In the unnatural stillness of the cloakroom Kitty changed her shoes and put on her coat and savoured the marvellous sensation: after ten weeks of term to be going out. Weekend after weekend, she had watched the others go and now, so near the end of term, it was her turn. She had not exactly envied them: they were going out with ordinary parents. She was going out with her father. It was enough just to say the words quietly to herself. All the week she had not let herself think about it, terrified of making the endless lessons and games and preps seem even longer. They were great chunks of time to be got rid of. If she had let herself feel excitement they would have retaliated by prolonging themselves. So she had kept her guard. But now she flung it off. If she shut her eyes she could hear her heart beating.

She was in fact standing with her eyes shut in the middle of the empty cloakroom when the head girl looked in and said, 'Are you all right? Your visitor is in the reception-room. Have a nice time.'

For a moment Kitty stared, loving her passionately. Then she ran up the steps and into the corridor. It stretched out before her, long and green. It was called Silence Corridor because at the other end, at a sort of crossroads, there were short corridors leading off to the Head's room and the staff room which must not be disturbed. She began to run down it, taking great leaps and singing, 'I'm going out, *out, out.*' She seemed to have the great rambling building all to herself, all its streets and alleys were hers, all its by-roads and highways. All the same she stopped singing when she approached the staff corridor and prepared to run in silence for the last two hundred yards that lay between her and the reception-room door. She began to imagine the feel of the handle in her hand.

'Catherine! What do you imagine you are doing?'

Miss Roland stood, slight, grey and terrifying at the junction of the staff corridor. Kitty could have said, 'My father's in the reception-room,' and Miss Roland would have softened instantly. The staff always did when a parent was known to be nearby. The girls thought it was proof of their beastly hypocrisy but possibly it was only because they were momentarily reminded that this was somebody's child.

She did not say it. A wave of hatred smashed over her, taking her breath away. She stood silent and sullen.

'I repeat, what are you doing? Why are you not resting?'

Kitty made a great effort.

'I am going out this afternoon, Miss Roland.'

'Indeed. And at what time do exeats start?'

'Two o'clock, Miss Roland.'

'Precisely. That is the time at which your parents will be expecting you. What is the time now?'

Kitty looked at the great round clock on the wall.

'Ten minutes to two, Miss Roland.'

'Precisely.'

'But I thought . . .'

'Will you never learn, Catherine, that it is your duty not to *think*, but to *conform*?'

Kitty stood aghast. The girls divided the staff into two groups: the Enlightened and the Efficient. Miss Roland was one of the latter, but this succinct and reactionary statement was shocking even from her. It seemed to bounce back off the walls and echo in the air all around them. But Miss Roland did not appear to notice anything.

'You will return to the cloakroom. At precisely two o'clock you will *walk* to the front hall and await your parents.'

She turned on her neat heel and walked briskly away.

Kitty stood for a moment trembling and then turned and walked slowly back to the cloakroom. The golden moment was lost for ever.

The week had gone so quickly, it now seemed, as she sat on a bench in the cloakroom. All one hundred and sixty eight hours of it had simply sped by, but now there were these endless minutes to get rid of. She left the cloakroom and began to walk down the Silence Corridor carefully placing the heel of one foot against the toe of the other. Even so it was not quite two by the round clock on the wall. Once past the clock and seeing that the staff corridor was deserted, she ran out into the hall. It was paved with big square stone flags. The sandstone had worn in the centre of each, hollowing it out. She loved these stones. They were warm and friendly and compassionate, anyway compared with people.

The handle too was an object of affection. It was a great round wooden ball of a thing, needing two hands to turn. All the other times she had opened it, knowing that her father was on the other side of the door, came back to her, all the excitement and love.

He was standing at the far end of the long room, his back to her, as he stood looking out of the window. It was cold and he was wearing a black overcoat. A tall, sombre figure he seemed from the back. It was disconcerting to look at him like this; she wanted him to turn round quickly so that she would see the cheerful, boyish, reassuring face.

He turned, not realizing she was there and his face, unguarded, looked vulnerable. He seemed older, much older and somehow hurt. Although he held out his arms, expecting her to run to him as she usually did, she could not move. As he walked towards her she noticed that he limped. Since the war he had always had a very slight limp, imperceptible to most people, but she had been aware of it when she walked arm in arm with him; he moved not quite evenly, one side seemed to go up and down more than the other. But now anyone could see it. It was almost as if he were lame. By his hat, on the chair, was a stick.

She stared at it; then he was lame. She seemed to stand for a very long time, as he walked towards her, old-looking and sad and, though he smiled, his eyes did not seem to change. The world was doing this to him, the world outside, that she was cocooned away from in here, learning to ignore. When at last he reached her he felt somehow less substantial and his face was very cold. Her head reached almost to his chest, but it felt different there, thinner, narrower. She was filled with terror for him, cold fear in her stomach, in her throat so she could not speak.

'How's my funny girl?' he asked and she managed a gruff hello and a hug. He took her shoulders and tried to hold her away from him and look at her face, but she knew that he would instantly realize that she had seen a change in him which terrified her, so she looked down and said, 'Oh, I'd forgotten—I've got to wear a hat.'

'Then run along and get it, you chump.'

She ran out, relieved to have an excuse to go and hide while she got control over herself. As she reached to get her hat off the peg, great dry sobs seemed to rise out of her stomach of their own accord and hot gusts to tear at her throat, and she leaned among the rows of heavy navy blue overcoats, fighting against tears, biting at her knuckles and getting some kind of comfort from the familiar, dusty smell of school uniform.

Suddenly a bell clanged and from all over the building people began to move. There were distant scraping noises, rumblings of voices and above all the sound of feet. They converged on the cloakroom as people came to change for games or get their coats for walks. On the far side was a flight of steps leading to a tiled cloakroom with a row of lavatories on one side and basins on the other. People ran down the steps and the air was filled with the banging of doors, loud flushings and slammings, running of taps, laughter and shouting.

'Hello, Kitty. I thought you'd gone out.'

'I have, but I forgot my hat.'

'Wicked. Have a marvellous time.'

She elbowed her way to the large glass and pulled her hat on her head. She was not pretty at the best of times, she thought, and now her skin was blotchy and she looked slightly mad.

'Going out, Kit? Lucky you. With your marvellous Dad?'

'He's not *really* her father. They just pretend because the Head won't allow exeats with followers.'

Kitty laughed.

'Honestly, though, Kit, he really is the best of all the fathers. I mean mine looks about ninety. I don't mind, I suppose, but it must be wonderful to have a really young one like yours. I mean you can talk to him as if he was a human being.'

'Yes,' Kitty said. 'He is rather nice; I quite like him really.'

CHAPTER TWO

THEY walked slowly along the railway embankment. The trees were bare but gales had blown the leaves off the path, usually ankle deep and rustling at this time of the year. Now it was only wet and a bit slippery under foot. A mist was beginning to creep in across the meadow beyond the comfortless trees.

The woman coming in the other direction smiled to herself, pleased with the picture of the father bending down to talk to the little girl, telling her a story, perhaps, or hearing some girlish confidence. As she passed she heard him say, 'You see, it was a question of Gresham's law coming into operation; the bad money driving out the good.' Her indulgent smile changed to a look of surprise as she said, 'Good afternoon,' rather sharply as they moved into a single file to let her pass.

Alone, they always talked of economics and history and politics and religion first and at length. Later they talked of the all-important domestic topic—the divorce. It had been so for as long as she could remember.

The woman's passing had broken into the conversation; it had come just when he had finished explaining why England had gone off the gold standard in 1931. They were silent for a while, as she waited for him to move on to the pressing domestic issue. He did not. The mist came nearer. She felt the unevenness of his walk and watched the mist approach. Both gave her a sense of foreboding. Their talk of history and economics had soothed her, for it had all seemed so normal, and her tearing anxiety at school seemed over-dramatic and she felt ashamed when she remembered it, grateful that nobody had seen her crying in the cloakroom among the dusty overcoats. Now, as she waited for him to speak it began to return.

'Daddy?'
'Yes?'

It was no good; he was not ready and she could not ask. So she only said, 'Shall we go and have tea?'

'All right,' he replied, and laughed. 'No need to sound so desperate about it. You're such a dramatic little object, aren't you?' Then, when she did not reply, for that was just what she had been accusing herself of, he went on, afraid that he had hurt her, 'I'm sorry, I didn't really mean that, but you do take things to heart, sweetie, don't you? I'm afraid you're going to suffer horribly when you're older.' He put his arm rather clumsily round her shoulder and then added, 'Well now, tea. The station hotel, I think.'

She was about to object; they never went there. It was expensive and pretentious and frequented by the richest of the visiting parents. Then she realized that it was also the nearest and knew that he had chosen it because he was tired. She wanted to ask him about the limp, she wanted to ask him about the strain and anxiety that had settled on his face and why he was worried and looked old, but she could not. Wives, she supposed, could ask such direct questions, but not daughters. They had to find more devious ways. Certainly once they were through the heavily studded front door of the station hotel they would never be able to talk properly. So she sat down on a damp wooden seat and he sat beside her. A goods train clattered past, throwing up smoke and steam. He took her hand as the grey cloud rose and enveloped them and waited until the noise disappeared into the distance and the smoke began to clear, before he said,

'I'm leaving the Bar.'

It was as if he had said he was going to stop breathing.

'You can't,' she said, automatically and at once.

'I can, you know. In fact, I have.'

It was suddenly absolutely still. After the train, silence. After his words, silence. Only the long fingers of mist moved menacingly towards them across the field.

For as long as she could remember, which was all the years she had known him, the Bar had been his life. Last time he had come to take her out, at Whitsuntide, they had talked about his taking Silk and how he would be one of the youngest K.Cs in the country. He had written about it in letters to her since, though—come to think of it—he had not mentioned it recently. And now he was giving it all up, just like that, without even consulting her. Her eyes smarted. Little schoolgirl daughters do not get consulted. She knew that she could not help him: only watch him suffer.

'You see, darling,' he began to explain, 'there's Gwendolen at the University still and you at school, and it all adds up to an awful lot of money. Then there's your mother's house to keep up and my digs. If I take Silk I'd earn almost no money for at least a year and wouldn't be back to anything very much for perhaps three. It's a gamble. I've thought about it hard and I can't afford a gamble. I used up all my capital during those first years at the Bar. It just can't be done. Perhaps if things had been different and with a wife's help . . . But there it is. It just can't be. So when I had this offer from a firm in the City I knew I must accept it.'

She began to interrupt but he took her hand and insisted on going on.

'It makes sense, darling. Perhaps next year I'll get a flat in London, a proper one, and when Gwendolen has finished her B.Litt we are hoping that she may get a University appointment in London. Then she can live with me and keep house and you'd be able to come and live with us in the holidays and it would be your first real, proper home. Surely that makes you happy? It makes sense, doesn't it?'

'But it doesn't make sense. It means that you are giving up everything. You *know* you are. All this flat thing, it's really just for us, isn't it, for Gwendolen and me? And really it doesn't matter. We'd manage. But once you've done this, you've given up your whole life, don't you see?'

'You're a funny one,' he said lightly. 'Here was I thinking you'd be so pleased at the idea of having a proper little home for the three of us and you don't show a glimmer of pleasure.'

'Please, Daddy, it's not that. You know I'd love it—if it could just be done some other way. It's just that it's not worth the sacrifice. I suppose,' she went on hopefully, and aware that she sounded childish, 'that it couldn't be done some other way? I mean we couldn't do that and you still take Silk?'

'No. Believe me, my pet, I haven't done this lightly. I've thought round and round it—and in and out of it, too.' He paused and then added, 'Gwendolen thinks it's a splendid idea.'

She thought of Gwendolen, the apple of his eye. Gwendolen

with her success at Oxford, her suave boy friends, her poise. Yes, Gwendolen would think it a splendid idea, to transfer her little world to London. Gwendolen would think it was a bit of a pity about Daddy giving up Silk, but she was practical and would accept the benefits therefrom. Besides, she did not merely approve of all sacrifices made in her interests, she immediately convinced herself and everybody else that they were not really sacrifices at all.

'And you see,' he was saying, 'if I do ever get a chance of a divorce, it's much easier with a fixed salary. One knows much better where one stands financially with this kind of job. It has greater security and goodness knows you need all the security I can give you.'

This took them back to the divorce which they discussed until mist and train smoke and a faint drizzle drove them from their wooden seat. Still talking about it they walked to the station hotel and there, absently-mindedly lifting chrome teapots and hot water jugs and passing each other buttered teacakes and fruit cake, they continued to discuss it. Talk came easily, for the divorce was always there, just below the level of consciousness, ready to be brought out and discussed, every detail familiar, every hope of a change in the law gone over, possible moves suggested, her mother's counter-moves anticipated. It was like some perpetual game of chess which they brought out and pored over every time they met. Put the pieces back in the box; time to say good-bye.

As they turned off the main road into the avenue the street lights were on, making the slippery pavement shine, turning the mist yellow and forming great circles of soft, drifting light. The mist was thickening, turning to fog. They reached the front door.

'What are we going to do about Christmas?'

She had postponed talking about it, for it was a reminder of her childishness, her dependence. There was this problem, this divorce, this edifice for the future which they planned and discussed so sanely, so matter-of-factly—and the whole thing crumbled at the word Christmas.

Christmas when the pain and the pretence was greatest.

'I'll come up to your mother's,' he said.

He kissed her, and she opened the front door into the main stone-flagged hall, then suddenly turned to give him a last hug before going inside. Through the glass door she watched him, a tall, dark, solitary figure, standing still for a moment on the door-step looking in. Then he turned, picked up the stick which he had propped against the pillar and walked, unevenly, out into the fog.

CHAPTER THREE

THEY did not sleep in dormitories; it was felt to be more homely to have bedrooms with only six or eight girls in each. To make it seem even more like a natural family unit they were of varying ages too.

When Kitty went up to bed therefore the two youngest, the third formers, were already trying to get to sleep, and when she was in bed the fifths would come up and they would all be trying to get to sleep by the time the sixth formers came up and fumbled their way around in the dark. Like many of the Head's other progressive ideas it presented practical problems for the staff; to minimize the loss of sleep everybody had to be in bed by nine o'clock, a fact which caused constant complaint from the sixth form.

That night, as they undressed, Amanda, who was also fourteen, said, 'Funny thing about your parents; they never seem to come at the same time.'

'No.' Kitty seemed to be trying to remember, then went on casually, 'No, I don't think they ever have. Whenever they've arranged to come together, Daddy suddenly seems to have an important case.'

'You're jolly lucky to have a father that things happen to. Mine goes to work on the 8.47 every morning and comes off the 6.5 every evening and if I say anything he says, "Now where would we be without routine?" Just think of it!' she went on, piling up her clothes on her chair. 'Can you think of a worse sentiment than that?'

Kitty climbed into bed, shivering at the cold touch of the sheets, for the bedrooms were unheated. 'Yes,' she said. 'How about, "Your duty is not to think but to conform"? That's what Roly said to me this afternoon.' But she spoke absently, for she was really thinking that if her father left the Bar, this habitual excuse for the failure of her parents ever to appear at the same time would be taken away from her.

Jill and Susan, the fifth formers, strolled in, wearing their seniority casually. Even after nearly a term, it still made them feel very adult to come into the bedroom and find four young ones in bed. They talked in a sophisticated way about their boy friends as they undressed. Then, wearing her bra and pants and fluffy pink slippers, Jill went and stood in front of the big looking glass at the end of the bedroom and did her hair. She divided her scalp into rectangles with a long-handled comb and pinned up each section very methodically. Sue waited impatiently; it was their bath night.

Felicity Snow, whose parents had sent her away to school on the arrival of a long-awaited baby son, watched them enviously. Small and underdeveloped, she seemed much younger than the other third former, a buxom girl called Polly, who was already half asleep. In fact, she was nearly thirteen. She sat up suddenly.

'Jill,' she said, 'I've got a new photo of Philip, my baby brother, you know.'

She took it out of an envelope and began putting it in a leather folder frame on the little dressing table beside her bed.

Jill gave it a cursory glance as she picked up her sponge bag. 'My mother isn't having any more babies,' she remarked casually to Sue as they went out of the door. 'She's had her tubes tied.'

After they had gone, Felicity turned to Polly.

'Polly? You're not asleep, are you? What did she mean about her mother having her tubes tied?'

'I think it's some kind of doctor's slang. They call their intestines tubes, I believe. Sometimes they call them guts.'

'Oh, I see. Then you mean if you don't want to have babies they tie your intestines in knots?'

'Yes, I suppose so.'

'But what happens to it—the baby, I mean?'

'Well, I suppose it can't get out, so it just disappears.'

'But it must be agony—having your intestines tied up.'

'I expect you have an anaesthetic. Anyway, I shouldn't worry,' she added consolingly, 'it's probably not as much agony as having a baby.'

There was silence for a while, then, 'So really,' Felicity

insisted, 'when you get married you have to choose between being knotted up and having babies all the time?'

'Yes, that's why it's important for a girl to have a career; in case she doesn't want to do either, you know.'

The fifth formers came back.

'Of course,' Sue was saying, 'from a medical point of view'—she brought the phrase out slowly and impressively. She was a doctor's daughter and consequently looked to as something of an expert.—'I really do think that your mother was ill-advised. I have so often heard my father and his medical friends agreeing that it is much easier for men to be done than women.'

'Why?' asked Felicity, relieved but still curious.

'Goodness, are you babes still awake? Well, it's obvious really,' Sue went on rather vaguely. 'It's all *outside* with men, so it's easy to get at, whereas with women it's all *inside* so you have to cut them open before you can even make a start.'

'Yes, of course, yes, I do see,' Felicity agreed, not wanting to seem young and ignorant and then there suddenly appeared a dreadful vision of her little baby brother all knotted up into a most horrible bundle. 'Oh, *no*,' she almost yelped and plunged under the bedclothes, pulling them over her head.

There was a short silence.

'I really think,' Sue said to the room at large, 'that if the little ones are going to get so upset about it, we should not discuss sex.'

Jill noted the patronizing tone and resented it.

'We were not discussing sex,' she contradicted. 'That would be immature and vulgar. Obstetrics is different.'

'Are different,' Sue corrected her.

They were interrupted by the arrival of Miss Theswell, always known as Thesby the Lesby ever since her first night at the school when, as a result of an unfortunate misunderstanding of the House Mistress's instructions, she had gone round kissing all the astonished girls good-night.

In the silence which followed the closing of the bedroom door the sound of her high heels clattering down the stone corridor sounded louder than human. As always their thoughts as they settled themselves to sleep were punctuated by the sound of doors closing and the familiar chorus of good-nights which marked Miss Theswell's progress round the bedrooms.

'What are they?' Felicity whispered across the eighteen inches of darkness which separated her from Polly's bed.

'What are what?' Polly answered with a yawn.

'Those things Jill said are different. Obs—something.'

'I'm not sure. I think it's where male animals keep their sperms. We had it in biology last term.'

'Oh, yes, I did know—I'd just forgotten for the moment. Good-night.'

'Good-night.'

Kitty lay awake. Soon the sixth formers came in and crept about, whispering and dropping things, going off to wash, tiptoeing in again and creaking into bed. She thought over her conversation with Amanda and wondered what she could find as an excuse for her parents not coming to see her together, as the others usually did, now that there would be no more unexpected important cases to blame. She was ashamed that this trivial aspect of the sacrifice should worry her at all. She knew that it didn't really, but at night all kinds of things became immensely and disproportionately important. Cold and wide-awake, she lay and thought about Christmas and the divorce and the dark-coated figure going out alone into the fog. She took all the pieces out of the box, moving them about in her mind, contemplating moves and counter-moves, never finding a solution, the dark king always in check.

Gradually sounds of heavy, rhythmic breathing began to come from each bed until she could distinguish seven separate sleepers. She heard the clock on the landing strike midnight. The mists began to swirl in her mind, the pawns and kings started a slow, mesmeric dance around a Christmas tree and she slept.

CHAPTER FOUR

GRACE DEEDES did not like unpleasantness. All her life she had ignored it and avoided the places which it might inhabit. To her success in so doing she attributed her smooth plump skin and calm, unruffled gaze. She talked gently and she moved slowly. She liked to think of herself as serene.

She liked, too, to think of her life as one of service, both to her fellow men and women, with whom she felt that, despite occasional little misunderstandings, she enjoyed truly meaningful and warm relationships, and to her Maker, with whom she had similarly always been on the best of terms.

She sat comfortably back now in her seat on the bus with her basket beside her. She liked this feeling of going a-marketing on the funny little country bus. She herself did not drive and her husband, Walter, was usually away during the middle of the week, for he had an office in Sheffield, where he owned property. Dear, dear Wally, she thought, always so dependable. He was not a man, she reflected, who would immediately impress a stranger and certainly he did not have her gift for human relationships, but such patience he had and such reserves. He had an undoubted talent for making money too, though on reflection she decided that that sounded rather horrid and that what she really meant was that he had business acumen.

It was nice to think that, wealthy though she was, she could still sit here on this little bus, her big straw basket beside her, and a peasant-like scarf on her head, chatting affably to the village folk as they climbed in, exchanging pleasantries in their humorous Yorkshire voices. A car, she thought, cut one off so from one's fellow creatures. There were surely enough barriers without that. Fortunately dear Wally never minded running in to town on a Saturday morning to get all the heavy shopping.

The bus was filling up now. Last to get on was Martha

Langdon, parcels and baskets and string bags hanging from every finger. She paused beside Grace who considerately moved her basket on to her lap so that she could sit down.

'All ready for Christmas, Martha dear?' she enquired as she watched Martha pushing various bundles on to the rack. A good soul, Martha, she thought, very active and always ready to help anyone, a hard worker and a real pillar of the church, but not serene. No, nobody could call Martha Langdon serene.

'Goodness, no! I shall still be hard at it on Christmas Eve.'

'You'll be coming down to see us on Christmas night as usual, won't you? We've done it for so long that I'm afraid I don't invite you properly any more. My big boys come home on Tuesday. What about your girls?'

'They'll be here on Wednesday. Gwendolen is staying with a friend at Oxford for a few days and then she'll meet Catherine and they'll travel up together. Charles comes on Christmas Eve for three days.'

'Oh dear, that's not very long.'

'Well, he only has the weekend off,' Martha replied defensively.

'Of course, he works so hard; such a distinguished career,' Grace reassured her, in her serenest tones.

Martha was scrabbling about among her parcels and found her purse just as the conductor came alongside. Grace smiled up at him apologetically. 'I *am* so sorry, I shall have to keep you waiting while I find my purse, right at the bottom of my basket under all these bits and bobs.'

'I'll get a ticket for you,' Martha offered irritably.

'Would you, dear? How kind. I won't forget to repay you.'

'It's not fair to keep the man waiting,' Martha replied.

'I really must pull myself together about money. I never seem to have any on me when it's needed. I suppose I've always been spoilt, having Wally there to provide. But really I've always been bad at pennies—I've no excuse,' she said and smiled forgivingly at herself.

The bus wound its way out of Pendlebury, lumbering along between the grey walls of its narrow streets. Then it made its way up the long steep hill beyond the town very slowly and with much changing of gears: it seemed to slow to a standstill to change down more frequently than was technically possible. At the top it waited for a few moments as if to draw breath, and then with renewed energy began the long descent into the next valley. It stopped often not only to drop off passengers at the lane ends of farms, but to pick up or hand out parcels to lone figures who signalled from the roadside.

Grace smiled indulgently at this.

'You don't get this sort of friendliness in the towns, you know,' she remarked proprietorially.

They turned off the main road now and drove slowly between the dry-stone walls of the lane which led to Beckgate.

'You see this cottage here on the right,' Grace said, pointing to it. 'A little while ago I remember the bus stopped just here as it was beginning to rain. Then the driver jumped out, ran into the garden, took in the washing and came back and drove off. He lives there, evidently. What a thoughtful husband!'

'I know the one you mean,' Martha retorted. 'And a real lazy slut his wife is too. *I* never had anyone to take my washing in.'

'And another time,' Grace went on, tactfully ignoring this comment, 'we stopped near here and the driver jumped out, climbed over the wall and came back carrying three enormous mushrooms. He gave them to the passengers and said it was his good deed for the day. Which reminds me of a very charming thing that was said to me by the old Bishop. I signed my name on some subscription list he had brought down and he said with that lovely smile of his, "G. Deedes, it could be Good Deedes, my dear. Good Deedes by name and good deeds by nature." I thought it very charming.'

She gazed for a moment out of the window, lost in pleasant thoughts.

'I hear he is helping you with the nativity play this year,' Martha interrupted sharply.

'Yes, he will take the service. It must be such a help to our young vicar to have a retired bishop in the parish to help. He is so charming and so willing. We are fortunate indeed. We hope to have real lambs again too. The children loved them last year.'

'We are there,' Martha said, beginning to gather up her parcels.

'So we are,' Grace said. 'How quickly the journey goes if one has a little chat.'

The bus rounded the last corner and stopped by the village

green. The driver got out and lit a cigarette. They were running behind time, but the engine was a bit over-heated. That was what he would tell the Inspector, anyway.

Grace got down off the bus slowly and turning to Martha said kindly, 'I do wish I was going your way, Martha dear, and then I could give you a hand with all your burdens.'

'It's all right. I'm used to managing.'

'And I won't forget those pennies I owe you for the ticket.'

'It's all right,' Martha said again, knowing that she would.

CHAPTER FIVE

THE station clock struck eleven as Kitty waited for her sister Gwendolen on Platform One. She had left school after breakfast and travelled to Gradby with all the Northern girls. The Irish girls had left the night before, the Scottish ones had an early breakfast and left by 7.30 a.m., to be followed soon afterwards by the London girls and then the Northern girls. A few local girls were collected by car. Thus the school was emptied of its inhabitants in relays until by a gradual process of attrition only the staff were left. Kitty supposed that they had then to pretend to be ordinary people travelling on public transport. It was hard to imagine them, pushed and ignored, having to accustom themselves to all the minor discourtesies of life. Meanwhile, all alone in a school emptied of children and bells and trunks and even staff, she imagined the Head walking alone down hollow corridors, a lost soul among the catacombs. Or perhaps she enjoyed it and skipped like a young ram.

She wished Gwendolen would come; for weeks she had longed to see her, the only person who could understand exactly what it was like at home, the only person who had lived through it and in it as she had. Compared with this sharing, other differences seemed trivial. They would get a compartment to themselves and talk and talk and somehow by talking they would make it all come right. Gwendolen had a way of making things simple and never seemed to have any trouble with decisions. It was very comforting.

Suddenly Kitty saw her coming under the station arch. Tall and confident, Gwendolen walked with a kind of purposeful grace. She seemed to know exactly where she was going, but she never hurried or got flustered. She was wearing a new red coat and boots and little white fur hat. Kitty was overwhelmed with pride in her. She wanted everybody in the world to know that this was her sister, this marvellous, poised beauty actually was her sister. She ran forward, calling to her excitedly, holding on with one hand to her school hat which kept trying to blow off and with the other dropping and then retrieving first her case and then the sponge bag which she had been unable to fit into it.

Gwendolen turned and watched her, smiling indulgently.

'All right, all right. No need to knock me over. Goodness, what a sight you are!' she said, straightening Kitty's school hat and flattening her collar. 'We'll have to cure those spots—I expect it's all the rotten carbohydrates they feed you on.'

Together they walked across to the platform where the train was waiting and easily found an empty compartment. Kitty put her shabby old case next to Gwendolen's elegant pale grey one on the rack.

'And how has school been this term?' Gwendolen asked.

'All right,' she said, suddenly aware that Gwendolen, always good at managing people, had been a renowned Head of School, while she herself had never been considered suitable material for anything more responsible than Form Ink Monitress. Gwendolen in the sixth form had spoken of the staff in terms of respectful equality and of the girls as easily manageable youngsters. Really it was no good trying to talk about school to Gwendolen; it must have seemed an entirely different establishment to her. She had not even been frightened of that terrifying extrovert Miss Bulley, the Games Mistress.

A few minutes later they had moved out of the station sidings and warehouses into open country for Gradby is one of those industrial towns that people pay the doubtful compliment of calling, 'easy to get out of'. Soon they were following the winding track through undulating green fields and then the fences and hedgerows gave way to dry-stone walls and they moved into a land of green and grey, of short grass and stocky sheep, of craggy hillsides and turf so thin that the limestone kept breaking through it. Kitty gazed at it through the window; even the way that the winter sunlight moved up and down the sides of the hills felt like home.

'A penny for them,' Gwendolen broke in.

'I was thinking,' she said slowly, trying to be honest, 'that it would be marvellous to have a real home—I mean the house and family kind—that was in a place—I mean the sort of country—that was home like this is to us. I mean this sort of dales scenery will always be the real sort of country for us, but it's not associated with the other sort of home. It's a kind of refuge, but it's not exactly a happy feeling. I don't really know, but I think I was thinking something like that, only it felt a bit more sensible than it sounds.'

'Well, that's a consolation,' Gwendolen replied briskly, but then went on more gently, 'but I do know what you mean really. There'll never be any other place like it.'

For a while they watched in silence as the green and grey country moved past the window and the sun slid up and down the hillside as if pushed this way and that by the shadow. Kitty was filled with relief; of course Gwendolen understood, she should never have doubted how she would feel about their father leaving the Bar. In all the things that mattered they would always be on the same side. Yet at the same time she was afraid to risk breaking this harmony. It would be so much easier to say nothing. She made herself speak in a great rush.

'Gwendolen, when Daddy came to see me at school, he said he'd leave the Bar and he can't, can he—I mean we just can't let him, can we? You will stop him somehow, won't you?'

Gwendolen turned slowly away from the window and looked at her. It was a long, hard look of the kind that a mother might give a wayward child, concerned but not approving. Kitty felt her sense of equality dwindling and began to feel suddenly much younger.

'It's the only sensible thing to do, Kitty dear,' Gwendolen said. 'You must see that.'

Kitty stared at her, dumbfounded. Sensible! If she had said it was heart-breaking but essential or something like that, but *sensible*: she felt panic rising, a terrible feeling of boiling over inside.

'But, Gwendolen, he *loves* the Bar—you can't want him to give it up . . .'

'It's not a question of what we *want* but of doing the most sensible thing for all of us,' Gwendolen interrupted. She allowed a deliberate note of impatience to edge its way into her reasonable voice. 'Really he should have done it long ago; I've advised it ever since I was old enough to understand these things.'

The implication that Kitty was not old enough to understand these things was clear, but she persisted.

'But it's not fair; he's giving up the only thing he really cares about. Gwendolen, you must see, it's his life and we c-can't ju-just ca . . .' she began to stammer, as she always did when it was important not to.

Gwendolen let modified impatience give way to exasperation.

'Now look here, Kitty,' she said severely. 'I am not having you causing trouble over this. It is all settled. He has accepted a job with a firm in the City and he is perfectly happy about it. As I said, it's much the best thing for all of us so don't you start getting all emotional and selfish and upsetting everybody.'

Kitty knew that Gwendolen had turned everything inside out and that she was utterly and absolutely wrong. She also knew that Gwendolen was strong and quite unshakeable in support of anything which she had decided was in her own interests. She herself, she knew, was anything but strong—even now her eyes were beginning to smart as she remembered the times she had heard him say cheerfully, 'My life's in court; I just love being on my feet in court. It's the whiff of grapeshot to an old soldier, that's all there is to it, my love,' and the smarting turned to tears as she saw again his patient, resigned face, his defeated look, the last time she had seen him, as if he had begun to die. As she stared out of the window the green and grey scenery became blurred. She made one last effort, born of desperation, to reach her sister.

'Gwendolen, please just listen, just for a minute. You said it would be best for all of us, but really you mean all except him, don't you? No, please let me say it and then I'm sure you'll see what I mean. You're almost qualified, I'll leave school soon and do something or other, and Mummy hates him anyway so really all that matters is that he should do what makes him happy. He is the only one of us with something to lose.'

She was afraid she was going to cry and knew she was making a bad case. She could tell by the look of incomprehension on Gwendolen's face.

'Really, Kitty, you are absurd. You carry on like a child. It's so typical of you to say you'll leave school and "do something or other"! You've no idea what life is like outside those four walls. I have, so leave it to me to do what is best.'

Kitty thought how heavenly it would be to do that; just leave it all to Gwendolen and not quarrel any more.

'I've always had to take all the responsibility, you know,' Gwendolen went on plaintively, 'and it hasn't been easy and I was hoping that now you are older you would be able to help, but it seems I was a bit too optimistic.'

This was awful; she had let her father down and now she had disappointed Gwendolen. She always seemed to let everybody down.

'But never mind, that's all in the past,' Gwendolen said with determined cheerfulness. 'It's all settled now and we'll make it work, won't we? Now that he has this job arranged, we'll get a flat in London and I'll make a proper home of it. That's something he's never had, you know.'

And fill it with your friends so that he'll be lonelier than ever, Kitty thought, but said nothing.

'So please, Kitty, do try to help me by being grown-up and sensible. I know you can be when you try. To tell you the truth, I think Daddy was a wee bit disappointed that you weren't more pleased when he told you about the new plans when he came to see you. So from now on, try to help. Promise?' and she smiled winningly.

Kitty hesitated, half won over, longing to be accepted and at peace, knowing how easy and pleasant life was when she was in accord with her sister, but knowing also that it was always on Gwendolen's terms and still certain that these were the wrong terms.

'But it was awful when he came, Gwendolen. He had a stick,' was all she said.

Gwendolen laughed. 'Kitty, really! Whatever has that got to do with it? He was told that his leg would be likely to play up a bit as he got older. It's only to be expected that, if he's tired, he'll limp slightly as the years go by.'

They were interrupted by a steward coming round with cups of tea on a big tray. Gwendolen paid for two of the thick white cups full of the steaming dark orange liquid. As he pulled the door closed behind him, Kitty took a sip. 'Ugh, it's got sugar in,' she said, spilling some down her coat. She held the cup away from her and when the train lurched it splashed down on to her shoes.

'Oh dear, what shall I do with it?' she asked helplessly.

'If you can't drink it for goodness' sake throw it out of the window,' Gwendolen told her impatiently.

Kitty stood up to throw it out of the narrow sliding ventilator at the top of the window and only after it had left her hand did she realize that the ventilator was closed. Astonished and splashed all over with sweet tea, she watched the orange lines streaming down the window.

'Oh God, how typical,' Gwendolen exclaimed and took a handkerchief out of her bag. Then as she mopped and wiped she began to laugh. 'You're absolutely hopeless,' she said.

Kitty found herself laughing too. The awful panic, the feeling of impending tragedy which had filled her only a few moments ago, vanished. Of course it was true, she was quite hopeless. She began to feel that if Gwendolen thought it was right for their father to leave the Bar, then of course it must be. Gwendolen was so capable.

CHAPTER SIX

GRACE DEEDES looked with beaming affection at her little husband. Walter Deedes was in every way a contrast to his wife: small and spare of frame, his face was narrow and pinched. Where she was suffused in serenity he had only a kind of dogged resignation. Grace cheerfully accepted the fact that she had enough joy in life for both of them.

'I do *so* enjoy Saturday morning breakfast, Wally dear,' she said, as she took another piece of toast. 'It really makes up for all those horrid lonely breakfasts during the week. Come on now, you have another piece and we've finished it all between us.'

Her husband shook his head in silence.

'No? No wonder you're one of the lean kine. Do you know when I was giving one of my Marriage Guidance lectures the other day I was talking about Complementary Characters in a Happy Home and I said that my husband and I are a real Mr and Mrs Jack Spratt.' She helped herself liberally to butter and laughed, her face creased with amusement, her stomach gently rising and falling with mirth.

Wally Deedes smiled his doleful smile.

'The next talk is on the Wider Family. I have for so long wanted to have my little say on the importance of three or even four generation families. It is so sad nowadays the way families are just parents and children. It gives such support to have all the grandparents and aunts and uncles and nephews and nieces the way it used to be here, and still is I believe among the dear unspoilt peoples abroad.'

She popped her last piece of toast into her mouth, wiped her lips slowly on her table napkin and, leaning forward, took his hand affectionately.

'Do you know what was quite the nicest thing anybody has

ever said to me, Wally dear?' she enquired of him. 'It was your mother when she came to see us a year or so after we were married and she said, "Wally has grown into a much *nicer* boy, Grace dear, since he married you." I have always thought that that was a very lovely thing to hear from one's mother-in-law.'

There was a plop as the post fell through the front door. Wally withdrew his hand and went to bring in the letters. He handed three to his wife and kept a fistful of bills for himself.

'I thought, Wally dear, that perhaps after breakfast you wouldn't mind just driving into Pendlebury to fetch a few little bits and pieces for me? Here is the list.'

Her husband took it and observed that it was long and that the first item was a sack of potatoes and the last an ironing board. He put it carefully into his wallet without comment. Then he began to open his bills.

'And then, Wally dear,' his wife went on, 'when you get back I'll have a nice cup of coffee ready for you. Then while I am preparing lunch perhaps you wouldn't mind seeing to a few odd jobs in the garden? I've made a little list and left it in the tool shed.'

'Yes, dear.'

'Or perhaps,' she added a little absently as she began to read her letter, 'it would be a nice little treat to go out for lunch, just this once, Wally dear? That is, if we can afford the pennies. Or do you think I'm being too extravagant—perhaps you would rather bring something home? Oh—No . . .'

For a moment, as she read, she feared she might lose her serenity. Her cheeks, already highly coloured, flushed angrily, and her eyes filled with tears of exasperation. 'It really is *too* bad.'

Wally looked at her but made no comment.

'It's from John,' his wife went on, almost striking his brother's letter with her plump right hand. 'Just listen to what he says: "The doctor thinks that Jo should go into hospital now and stay there for four weeks until the baby is born, so I may take up your original kind offer to stay. At least take up part of it and ask you if you can have the twins for Christmas so that I can stay up here in Edinburgh and keep Jo company. She's very cheerful at the moment but it would be a bit depressing for the poor girl to be devoid of all her family at Christmas." '

Wally looked bleakly across at his wife.

'Well, dear, if you *did* offer,' he began.

'Of course I did, but I never for one moment thought they would accept.'

There was silence.

'After all, they are relations,' Grace went on rather defensively, 'so one had to make a polite gesture. Anyway I thought that, even if they accepted, the parents would be here to look after those dreadful twins.'

Wally prepared to listen. He knew that his wife's intense dislike of his younger brother was overshadowed only by her disapproval of his sister-in-law, and that she had strong views on the way in which their children were brought up.

'For years,' Grace began, 'I have let Jo know my feelings about the way she has brought up those children. It's ridiculous, never having a proper nanny to discipline them or even making the slightest attempt to do so herself and now when they are quite unmanageable to expect me to have them at the busiest time of my whole year! Really, it is too bad.'

She held up her hand as her husband began to speak. 'Yes, I know, dear, just what you are going to say. We are very fortunate in our boys who are so amenable and placid and have such serene natures while the twins are both highly strung and wilful.'

Although this was not in fact what he had been going to say, Wally made no comment.

'But I think I might take just a little credit for that, Wally dear, don't you? They have been brought up in a very calm atmosphere. Apart from that, as far as the twins are concerned, I'm afraid it's a case of heredity will out.'

Wally poured her out another cup of coffee and moved the toast rack towards her. She smiled up at him.

'Thank you, dear. I begin to feel calmer. What can't be cured must be endured,' she added, striving nobly to build up her morale. 'Perhaps Mrs Wall won't mind giving up her holiday to come in over Christmas in the circumstances. It's lovely to have children at Christmas,' she went on bravely but without much conviction, 'though perhaps not such *little* ones. After all, we are almost middle-aged now and it is a long time—oh, well, never mind,' she said with sudden resolve, 'I mustn't be selfish and keep you away from your tasks.'

She smiled up determinedly at her husband. Martyred she might be by his brother and sister-in-law, but she would not complain. She kissed him warmly and forgivingly on his cheek, patted the thin shoulder that rested momentarily against her ample bust and hustled him out of the house. She waved to him as he drove down the drive and then returned to her coffee and letters. The grandfather clock struck ten and from upstairs she could hear the familiar, soothing sound of Mrs Wall hoovering the bedrooms. She began to feel calmer.

CHAPTER SEVEN

THE platform at Beckgate station had been built with a happy disregard for the height of the train. The station master carried a mounting block to the carriage doors so that the passengers could descend. The task was not arduous for not many people used the line.

The station was manned only when the trains were due, as strangers ringing up to enquire about train times found to their chagrin. The station master dealt with everything; he was ticket collector, guard, clerk and porter. He was in charge of the mounting block and looked after the little oil lamps which lit the station. In the summer he tended his garden in the hope of one day winning the prize for the best kept station garden in the dales.

He carried the block now to the door which Gwendolen had opened and greeted them both as they climbed down. Then, 'Comin', comin',' he called to an anxious old lady who was peering down at the platform from the great height of the train. 'Don't jump, lass, whatever you do.'

Immediately she got out of the train, Kitty took a deep breath. If she had been blindfolded she would have known when she was home. The air everywhere else was just a nothingness, but here it was positive, tangible, with a sharp edge to it. When she went back to school she used to take a deep breath in the hope of carrying some of it back with her in her lungs. She took another gulp now as she watched the little train set off, pushing its way up the long, winding dale and finally disappearing round the edge of the hill.

Gwendolen looked at her pityingly. 'Could you possibly stop doing your deep breathing exercises and come on? The station master's waiting, and I expect the car is too.'

They crossed the line and handed their tickets to the station master who was standing by the gate to receive them. In the yard behind him they could see the black car waiting. Young Drinkwater ran the village taxi service. His father was the village shopkeeper but Tom was not interested in groceries and running about fetching things for people. With a taxi it was different: he was less aware of serving people when he did it by car.

The station had been built two miles outside the village by special stipulation as a result of protests from the villagers in 1853 when a Private Act of Parliament had allowed it to be built. The villagers had opposed the dangerous innovation which would terrify the sheep, dry up the cows and poison the air. They had failed to stop it being built but they had succeeded in preventing it from coming any nearer than two miles. It was a victory which their descendants much regretted. Only young Drinkwater with his passion for the motor car found any profit in it.

'Afternoon, Gwen, afternoon, Kitty,' Tom said as he put the cases in the boot; he had developed a kind of teasing matiness of speech in reaction to the solemn obsequiousness with which his father treated his customers. 'Been expelled, have you then, the pair on you?'

'No such luck,' Gwendolen replied. 'Why aren't you serving in the shop then? Did your dad sack you?'

Gwendolen could always respond in good part; all things to all men, she even affected a slight Yorkshire accent when talking to village people.

Tom laughed. 'You won't catch me weighing out tatties for t'old girls in village,' he said, setting off with bravado, but he went carefully all the same for the road was narrow and twisting. Years ago it had been a sheep track, then a lane, and slowly men had improved its surface but had not thought to straighten its route, until finally it had been tar macadamed and was now the main road to the village. There was another way over the hills, almost dead straight, for it had been laid down by the Romans, but it was quite unfrequented, only a broad, grassy lane. Some people said that this was the lane that should have been made into a road but Kitty was glad it had not. It was a lovely, wide path between the hills which she did not want to share with anyone except the ghosts of the Romans.

'It's perishingly cold,' Gwendolen said. 'Can't you afford a rug for the car, then, Tom?'

'I'll get one next winter, when I put the fares up.'

'Get away, you charge enough already. Anyway, you ought to have a meter instead of just guessing. You'll have the police after you.'

They talked and laughed and Kitty gazed up at the hills and was surprised to hear Tom say, 'Well, here we are, safe and sound at your Mam's house. That'll be four shillings.'

Kitty felt herself go hot; it was awful talking money like that after all the teasing and being friends. But Gwendolen only laughed and handing him some coins said, 'And have a merry Christmas with the change,' and got out.

They stood at the top of the drive, not moving even when he had driven out of sight. It was a forbidding house, which had grown old without becoming mellow. Small-windowed, it seemed to look in on itself and be embittered by what it saw. Its grey stone had been partly rendered and partly re-pointed with cement. The tiles of the roof were mossy, for the overhanging trees kept it always damp. The door and window frames were painted a dreary, serviceable dark green. It was a four-square, uncompromising house, which seemed to defy affection as it defied the elements. It always seemed to Kitty an appropriate building to house her mother.

Martha Langdon must have heard the taxi drive away, for she opened the front door as they were walking up the drive. This was a relief to Kitty who never knew, when she first arrived, if she was supposed to ring the doorbell or not.

Tall, grey and forbidding as the house itself, Martha Langdon stood in the doorway. Her long, grey face was as hard as the surrounding stone and the pale, thin lips as uncompromising. She did not move; the only sign of life was in her restless, censorious eyes, for ever looking for something to condemn.

'So you've come, have you?' she said, her hard voice turning the statement into an accusation.

She gave each of them in turn her characteristic sharp, suspicious gaze, equally disapproving of her elder daughter's elegance and her younger daughter's untidiness. As they entered the house she pecked them both severely on the cheek and then turned her cheek to each of them in turn to be kissed. Then she began to talk.

Martha Langdon was not one to make enquiries of newly-arrived people about their journey or their health or to offer refreshment to the travel-weary; this would have been to pander to their weakness. She believed that they must take her as they found her and that would be working. Their arrival, therefore, was only a momentary interruption in her day and she went on almost as if they had not come, except that she talked without pause in a shrill, toneless monologue which they did not attempt to follow as they stood in the kitchen watching her bake. Eventually she broke off from what she was saying about the arrangements for the Mothers' Union party in January to say sharply, 'Well, aren't you going to unpack? It'll be tea time soon.'

Inside the house was as gloomy as outside. It faced north and indeed had no windows at all on the south and west. Low ceilinged and full of dark corners it might have been made homely, but it was furnished in a depressing, haphazard mixture of large, uncomfortable Victorian pieces and graceless pre-war veneer furniture which might have looked more at home in a semi-detached house in the suburbs. Nothing seemed to weld them together; each room contained a selection of objects which at one time or another Martha had found convenient to put there. It was instantly apparent that nobody had cared about the overall effect and nobody had put any love in it. Each room had the uncompromisingly forbidding look that the outside of the house promised and each one was cold and uncomfortable.

Kitty unpacked quickly. She did not have much in her case. Her trunk would come later; usually it spent a large part of the holiday getting to her and arrived just in time to be repacked. One Easter it had not arrived until the day before the end of the holidays and her mother had been furiously angry with her as if she was responsible for the way her trunk was journeying to and fro on the railways. She hung up a few things, tipped the rest into a drawer and went into Gwendolen's room. It was larger and well placed over the kitchen fire, so one wall felt, if not exactly warm, at least less glacial than the others. Kitty leant against it.

'Don't they ever put anything on those chilblains of yours at school?' Gwendolen enquired. 'They look horrible.'

'Yes, but it doesn't seem to do any good. One of the new girls had one on her toe and she went to tell Sister—still the same deaf old Sister Henley you know—and when she said she'd got a sore toe The Hen said, "Go and gargle, child", so she did. And it got better, so it just shows.'

'She ought to be made to retire—she must be years past sixty,' Gwendolen said, but she laughed all the same. Then she took one of Kitty's hands and looked at it disapprovingly. Kitty was not surprised. It was a purple colour, blending to mauve at the tips of the fingers which were either swollen with incipient chilblains or lined and crusty with the remnants of old ones.

'We'll get some stuff for them in Pendlebury,' Gwendolen said kindly, as if moved by the sight of the podgy, mauve object in her own neat, white hand.

It had a marvellous, motherly sound and Kitty suddenly put her arms round her sister's neck and hugged her gratefully.

'That's enough now,' Martha's voice cut in sharply behind her. 'If there's one thing I hate it's sloppiness. Tea's on the table.'

She was a surprisingly generous cook; there was apple pie and cream, scones and girdle cakes, parkin and fruit loaf, freshly made tea-cakes and home-made jam. It was the kind of tea you might have expected a plump and motherly farmer's wife to produce. Kitty pondered this inconsistency of her mother's as she began to eat. The doorbell rang. It usually did at meal times.

'Oh, God,' Gwendolen said as soon as her mother had gone out of the room to answer it. 'Just look at all this carbohydrate. Typically Northern. I wonder what's the least fattening.'

'You haven't eaten anything,' Kitty remarked, helping herself to parkin. 'Aren't you starving?'

'Yes, but honestly, Kitty, no wonder you're so fat and spotty. Do you always eat like this? Here, you can have the pastry off my apple pie.'

Their mother returned. 'It was just the vicar's wife,' she said, 'wanting cakes for the Jacob's Join Tea in aid the church hall, tomorrow. I'll have to bake again.'

Kitty spread raspberry jam on her tea-cake and reflected on this curious trait in her mother: that she would go to endless trouble for anyone outside the family. She would exhaust herself baking for the young or the needy or the elderly. She did it all without any feeling; indeed she did not seem to like any of the recipients of her good works and of the poor she was always particularly scornful. She was generally regarded in the village as a good woman, one who would always lend a hand. Perhaps it was out of a sense of duty, since it wasn't from love, Kitty thought. But surely a sense of duty could not inspire quite such compulsive good works, such frenetic activity. For as long as she could remember, her mother had always been far too busy to have any time for her, beyond seeing to her basic physical needs. She had no time to waste on listening or interest to spare. If goodwill had anything to do with her mother's good works surely a little bit would have spilled over on to her family. Perhaps it was just that the opinion of her family was less important to her than that of her neighbours.

'How is the new vicar doing?' Gwendolen asked.

'Oh, he's a poor bit of a thing,' her mother said contemptuously. 'And his wife's not much help to us either. He's weak, not a man you can get a decision out of at a Parish Council meeting. Mabey, he's called. Maybe by name and maybe by nature, I say. We've tried all sorts since old Pritchard retired. He'd been here about twenty years. The council said they wanted a younger man for a change. I told them a little country parish like this was no place for a young man; he'd not have enough to do and only get into mischief. Which young Feather did, of course. As for that Dr Jones, he was way above everybody's head. It was just as well he decided to go back to teaching at theological college when his wife died. Then they said they wanted somebody less remote, a working man, somebody more like one of themselves and we got Patterson. He'd been a miner and given it up to get ordained. But that didn't work either—they don't really want their vicar to be one of them. Anyway, the climate didn't suit his chest so he went last summer.' She paused for a moment to take a drink of tea. 'Some people say it was really only for health reasons that he had to get out of the mines in the first place, but fair's fair and I daresay he had a calling.'

Kitty caught her sister's eye and looked down quickly. Sometimes her mother was dreadfully and unintentionally funny. They saved such episodes for bath time.

The bathroom was the best room in the house, Kitty thought. A previous owner had converted it from a bedroom, so it was big and had intricate mouldings on the ceiling. The bath was old and shapely with four dear little claw feet. There was a full-length mirror on the wall, about four feet wide and two yards high with a carved frame painted white. The bathroom was the only room in the house where everything seemed appropriate, perhaps because there was no furniture in it, apart from a couple of white-painted chairs and a wicker laundry basket.

On one wall was a big, walk-in airing cupboard in which Kitty always crouched to change her clothes. She was sitting in it now while Gwendolen, naked except for her fur boots, was having a thorough wash at the basin. There was not enough water for a bath, their mother had said before she went out to her meeting. If she had been in, Kitty would not have dared to sit in the airing cupboard with the door open talking to Gwendolen, for it was one of her mother's rules that the door must be kept shut in case the heat escaped into the bathroom.

'What sort of mischief did that vicar get into?' Kitty asked.

'Not much, not as much as he'd have liked to,' Gwendolen replied, washing her neck.

'I can remember old Pritchard, you know. I loved him.'

'Nonsense, he went years ago when you were tiny.'

'But I do. He used to stand up by the altar and give the blessing like this.'

She jumped out of the airing cupboard, picked up a white bath towel, climbed up on the side of the bath and spread her arms out wide. 'He did it with his arms spread right out, as if he were really sheltering everybody and it was marvellous. I used to watch him through my fingers and feel—I don't know, just a lovely, safe feeling.'

'You're barmy,' Gwendolen said, without malice, 'and if Mummy catches you standing on the bath with your shoes on heaven help us. Aren't you ever going to get undressed? She'll be furious if you're not in bed when she gets back. I've nearly finished washing. I've just my feet to do.'

Gwendolen was a thorough washer; she cleansed her body systematically, dividing it into sections and keeping separate flannels for her face, her body and her feet.

'You're like Gaul,' Kitty said suddenly. 'Divided into three parts.'

Gwendolen laughed, put on her nightdress and dressing gown;

both warm and glamorous, and began pinning up her hair. She had put on her fur boots again; there were too many icy draughts chasing each other across the green linoleum to let her risk keeping them off.

Kitty watched her for a moment, and then, still crouching in the airing cupboard, eased her way out of her skirt and jumper and into her pyjamas in such a way that she was not simultaneously deprived of both. Then she crept out and over to the basin, found that Gwendolen had used all the hot water, so made do with splashing her face with cold water.

'You'll start to smell if you only wash like that,' Gwendolen said, through her hair pins.

'I'll have a proper wash in the morning.'

'You know you won't. There's never any hot water in the morning.'

'There isn't any now either—sh, wasn't that the gate?'

They heard the click of the gate and their mother's footsteps coming down the drive. Kitty flung her towel on the rail, kissed her sister, ran down the corridor and was in bed before her mother opened the front door.

CHAPTER EIGHT

EVERYTHING seemed to be going wrong with Christmas, Grace Deedes reflected, and this really was the last straw. Her special children's nativity service was to be deprived of its real lambs because of foot and mouth disease. She would not have minded so much, but, as she had tried to explain to that really rather exasperating old farmer, the foot and mouth disease was only one small outbreak on the other side of the Pennines. But he was adamant; he not only refused her the lambs but insisted that she stepped into a tub of disinfectant although she explained that her new winter boots were not waterproof.

The old Bishop had been quite charming about it.

'Well,' he had said in his sweet, fatherly way, 'I feel it may be a blessing in disguise. The sheep might have presented problems—droppings, don't you know?'

It was so like him to find a word of comfort and she had left him feeling much consoled.

This made it all the worse that the twins had virtually broken up the outdoor service which the Bishop had arranged for the turning on of the Christmas tree lights on the village green. She had tried hard to avoid bringing the twins but there seemed to be a positive conspiracy to make her do so. Their father had only delivered them that morning and she had suggested they should go to bed early, but Mrs Wall had carried on about the 'Poor wee mites, away from their mummy, and every other child in the village going to it,' so that she had felt obliged to bring them with her.

It was a lovely setting, the tree on the green in the stillness of the evening, for what little traffic went through the village had been diverted, the choir boys and girls processing with their candles on sticks and the Bishop in his robes at the end. She was no snob, Grace told herself, but it was nice to have a retired bishop among them; it lent such tone to all their little celebrations which might otherwise have seemed quite ordinary.

Unfortunately the twins had mistaken the Bishop for Father Christmas and began loudly demanding to know the whereabouts of his beard and sack of presents. They soon had the village children rioting. Then the twins, who were town children, had suddenly realized that they were standing in the middle of a road. Disregarding her efforts to explain that the traffic had been diverted, they had begun noisily moving the village children on, warning them that they would soon be 'squashened' by cars. Suddenly she gripped each child round the upper arm, rather more tightly than was strictly necessary, and dragged them off home, grateful for the dark.

She was quite determined not to bring them to the nativity service two days before Christmas, but again there seemed to be some kind of conspiracy to make her; everyone assumed that she would, and offered to sit next to them in the congregation while she was in charge of the play. In the end Wally had agreed to take charge of them and she had instructed him to bring them as late as possible and sit at the back of the church.

The little church was gratifyingly full. Parents who never came to church had come to see their children act, for the vicar had wisely suggested that the cast should be as big as possible in order to bring in the maximum number of parents.

His wife, Caroline, came in quickly and sat in her usual pew near the back; she looked and felt ill-at-ease. As she knelt down she caught sight of the Bishop helping to arrange the crib. She would not have shared Grace Deedes' opinion that it was good to have a retired bishop in the parish, so eager to help. The Bishop had for a long time had a holiday cottage outside the village and in the 'days of his greatness' as he mockingly referred to them, he had loved to escape from his palace and take a turn at being a parish priest, among the villagers and their children. Now that he was retired it was natural for him to want to help; he enjoyed it and the village began to look to him for anything a bit special. He was a great help, everyone agreed. But not much help, Mrs Mabey thought, to her already nervous husband. Of course, to be fair, she reflected, looking at him through her fingers, he was a very nice old man, benign and friendly, and very charming. Thank goodness he is a widower, she thought suddenly. Then she checked herself, said a quick 'Amen' and sat back in her pew.

Her husband was standing in the choir; he looked abstracted, his lower lip moving slightly, as if in silent prayer. Actually he was counting the congregation. It was a nervous habit he had developed shortly after his induction. Usually he did it after getting into the pulpit, during the last verse of the hymn, gazing abstractedly at the back of the church, his mouth slightly ajar and his eye moving almost imperceptibly from pew to pew. When she realized that people were smiling indulgently and children beginning to smirk, she made herself raise the subject with him.

'I can't help it,' he had said. 'I am so afraid numbers will go down. They have, in fact, quite steadily ever since I came.'

'Of course, they're bound to. I expect they always do as the weather gets colder and the vicar less of a novelty. There was quite a bout of sickness in the autumn, too.'

'I know, but one must make a success of one's first appointment. It is a question of the trust invested in one.'

'But you can't *count* success like that.'

'No, of course not, but then how else can one tell?'

She said no more, but made a mental note that she must find a good moment for mentioning to him this dreadful self-deprecatory habit of calling himself 'one'. Somehow it was always like this; she tried to help him with one problem and only succeeded in finding another.

She tried to concentrate on Christmas, but her thoughts began to wander again. 'Please God make me pregnant,' she murmured, and then added wearily, 'because if You don't, I'm sure I don't know who will.'

In the vestry the children were nearly ready. Grace Deedes smiled benignly at them and at all her willing helpers busy pinning up skirts, adjusting haloes and beards. The Bishop was standing by Jimmy Ackroyd, who was tucked into a rather shabby old sheepskin rug. The Bishop patted his head, 'Now you do your best, young fellow,' he said. 'Remember you are Mrs Deedes' answer to foot and mouth.'

Grace Deedes smiled up at him serenely. It was really a very lovely little occasion. 'We're almost ready,' she assured the Bishop. 'By the time the first hymn is over.'

'Then I'll give the sign to the organist,' he replied. 'I don't see your little ones yet, though.'

A look of unease touched her face momentarily. Then she said with determined cheerfulness, 'Wally will be bringing them in when the hymn starts.'

As the congregation rose to the strains of 'O come, all ye faithful,' she saw, as she peeped through the curtains, Wally coming in with the twins. Dear Wally, she thought, he had probably been waiting in the porch so patiently until they were allowed in. He was looking anxiously at the unexpectedly crowded pews. She had forgotten that people unaccustomed to church-going always huddle towards the back of the church. Wally had to walk more than half-way up the aisle before he found a place to install himself and the children. It was in the pew in front of the Langdons, Grace noted. The twins looked about them with interest. Certainly they were bright little things, she thought. No denying that.

At the end of the hymn, the Bishop stood in the centre of the aisle. 'Let us pray,' he said in his deep rich voice, which in a layman might have been described as fruity.

'No, don't let's,' Grace heard Claire say very clearly.

'Let us take off our welly boots,' her sister Zoe counter-suggested.

The Bishop paused, but only momentarily, before starting his prayer. His voice was powerful but did not quite cover the shuffling and snorting noises that Zoe made as she prised off her boots. Then she was quiet and Wally must have been lulled into a false sense of security for Grace saw him make a sudden lunge, but too late. There was a pitter-pattering sound of bare feet on polished floor boards and Zoe took off up the aisle, boots in one hand and socks in the other, looking for some safe place to put them.

Grace prayed that Wally would not follow her; if he came creeping up behind the child her shame would be complete. Wisely he stayed with Claire. Zoe, after what seemed hours, reached the top of the aisle and stepped in front of the improvised stage in the choirstalls. There she placed her boots carefully side by side in the centre, and having stuffed a not very clean sock into each boot, walked unconcernedly back to her uncle. The Bishop concluded his prayer, the congregation murmured a ragged Amen and lowered its corporate self back into the sitting position.

The play consisted of a series of scenes from the Scriptures, made more comprehensible by lines inserted by the vicar though, as the Bishop had jocularly put it, the story-line was after all fairly well known. Grace Deedes ushered in the first performers, listening sadly as she always did. After all these weeks of rehearsal they still sounded so flat. Week after week she had spoken the lovely words in her own melodious, warm, expressive voice, and made the children repeat them slowly after her. Yet, well-drilled though they certainly were, they still sounded like this. It was not the accent—she was no accent snob, she hoped—but the flat, expressionless tone of voice. Phrase by phrase, even now, little Joan Gramble was intoning the Magnificat as if it was a shopping list.

Joseph, on the other hand, had almost too much expression. He was a born improviser, which was just as well as he appeared to have no memory, something which she had not realized when, delighted to find one child who could act with gusto, she had chosen him for the part, and then written in a lot of extra lines so that he played a more dominant role than is usually vouchsafed to Joseph in the story of the nativity.

He stood now confronting the congregation and proclaiming, 'So I says to the Lord.' He paused. 'Now then, God, I says . . .'

'No, dear, I prayed to the Lord . . .'

'No, dear, I prayed t'Lord,' Sam Drinkwater repeated obediently, before continuing with his improvisation.

Mary, fortunately, had nothing to say after the Magnificat, for though a beautiful child, with an ethereal, heart-shaped face, she was very adenoidal. The tableau looked very attractive with Mary and Joseph and the child. It was a pity that Mary had carried the baby in upside down. He was in his shawl on her knee now with only his feet showing. Grace signalled to her, but she appeared to be in some kind of trance and when Joseph gave her a poke and pointed at the baby and said, 'T'other way up, 'e oughta be', she only picked up the whole bundle and turned it round. Thereafter the shepherds and kings addressed all their remarks to the soles of the small china feet.

A small shepherd, giving Jimmy Ackroyd in the sheepskin rug a final pat, approached and addressed the feet. Pulling a fluffy animal from his shirt, he piped up, 'I have a lamb in my bosom,' and laid it gently down on the floor.

It was a touching moment. Grace smiled, reflecting that they could not have had that little scene if they had had the real lambs. Suddenly from the middle of the church she heard Zoe, who had not been paying much attention but had suddenly heard her favourite word, shout 'Bosom, bosom, bosom,' with the full joy of recognition. She was still shouting it as Wally picked her up and set off down the aisle, carrying her under one arm, her bare feet thrashing. At the door it changed to 'I'll be good.' She prayed he would stride on, but to her dismay, after a brief conversation in which he presumably tried to extract some kind of promise—as if that would be much help from a three-year-old like Zoe—they both returned to the pew.

However, she had to admit to herself that the child was good thereafter. Shepherds and wise men came and went, extracts from the Bible were read, hymns and carols sung without any interruption from the congregation. They did all look rather hot; the vicar had stoked up the boiler very enthusiastically to reassure people who did not usually come to church that it was a comfortable place to come on winter Sundays. The day had turned out to be wet and muggy and the atmosphere in church was now very hot and steamy. From her vantage point by the curtain Grace could see that Claire was beginning to undress. It was nearly over; the final tableau was complete and, apart from the unusual position of the Infant Jesus in his shawl, everything was perfect from the sheepskin-covered Jimmy Ackroyd at the front to the fairest and tallest angel at the back.

Grace Deedes looked at them with satisfaction; she forgot her irritation with the flat voices, the adenoids, the joylessness. It was very moving how much beauty one could create from such poor—well, at any rate *simple*—material. Her heart sank when the Bishop, obviously moved too, said, 'Let us look upon this tableau and meditate in silence.' Claire, she knew, was not at her best in silence. She could see her now, scrabbling around in an effort to remove her clothes.

The congregation stood, heads down, faces serious. Shepherds, kings and angels stood or knelt very still. Mary in the centre, her beautiful little face framed in blue, gazed down at the Holy Baby's feet. The silence was deep and moving. Grace Deedes began to feel the peace of God descending upon her as she looked at the village children, 'her' children as she called them to herself at times like these. Really and truly, she thought, I give so much of myself when training them that they are in a sense mine. She was full of love and grace as she stood, head bowed, by the curtain. Suddenly this intense and moving silence was shattered by Claire's deafening and triumphant revelation: 'Do you *know*, there's a *hole* in my *knickers*?'

CHAPTER NINE

ON Christmas Eve, Kitty was so afraid that she might not be allowed to go to meet her father at the station in the evening that she spent the morning trying to placate her mother by being helpful. As usual she succeeded only in irritating her.

'You're always under my feet, child,' her mother snapped as she helped with the washing up after an early lunch. 'I can't get on with my baking with you around this afternoon. For goodness' sake go out for a walk and get a bit of fresh air.'

Gwendolen was busy writing letters to her boy friends, so Kitty set off by herself. She walked through the village, past the smithy and the inn and Drinkwater's shop. The church was on the far side of the village and the vicarage was the last house she passed. The only building after that was the school.

She paused, looked both ways, and since nobody was about, climbed up the few steps, pushed open the little iron gate and walked slowly up the path. It was here that she had been sent when she was five and the war had removed them from the town to Beckgate. She had bitterly resented the war for depriving her of the marvellous grey uniform of the little private school in town where she had only spent one term. The hat, which had a ribbon and a badge with a rose on it, was particularly beautiful even though it did make it a bit difficult to see where she was going.

The grown-ups had suddenly turned very kind because of the war: in gentle voices they kept telling her that the village school was a lovely little place and that Miss Singleton was so sweet and that there were only twelve children in her class. They did not realize that twelve seemed an enormous number to her: all the years she had lived only added up to five.

She looked at the school; now that she was fourteen it seemed astonishingly small, even though a concrete and glass wing had been built on. The old school had been virtually gutted and rebuilt. When she had first gone there it had been a little grey stone building with long narrow windows set deep and high in its thick walls. There was a very heavy wide door over which was carved in stone letters, 'INFANTS', which had pleased her and made her feel like Jesus. Inside there was a cloakroom which smelled wet, and beyond that a big room with a great black stove in the middle, enclosed in a tall fire-guard like the one they had had in the nursery in the house in town. They all sat in a semi-circle around the stove and when it was very cold Miss Singleton used to stand between the stove and the fire-guard, leaning forward on the shiny brass rail, her cheeks flushed. When she turned away the backs of her legs had pretty pink patterns on them. Kitty had loved Miss Singleton, who was old and kind and never shouted. She had soft, round cheeks and was indeed round all over. If you were tired at the end of the afternoon when she read a story she would let you sit on her knee and she was soft to lean against like a pillow. Even if you fell asleep she did not mind, but just told you what had happened in the story in her own words when you woke up.

Sometimes she took the children into the stationery cupboard to get rubbers or pencils. Its walls were stacked high with exercise books and sheaves of paper, lovely, shiny, unused paper. The war made the paper very special and they were only allowed to use it in very small amounts; when they wrote in the exercise books they had to try to write twice between the lines, which was very difficult. She used to watch, awestruck, as Miss Singleton stood on a chair and removed a few sheets of the precious paper for them to draw on. There were also little drawers with labels that said 'paper clips' or 'elastic bands' that Miss Singleton would let them pull in and out so that they could see how smoothly they moved on their runners because the village carpenter had made them so carefully. On the floor there were two huge glass bottles, covered with straw. They had old and wrinkly corks in the tops, like round walnuts, and they were full of ink. Once a week Miss Singleton poured ink from one of them into a white enamel jug and allowed the biggest girl to fill all the little white ink pots, which were then dropped carefully into a blue-rimmed hole in each desk.

In the yard at the back where they played there was a hutch

with a white rabbit in it called Softy, which they fed with lettuce leaves and were allowed to stroke while it lay, trembling violently, in Miss Singleton's arms. Up a flight of stone steps was the little garden where once a week they dug with forks and trowels and weeded and planted and made stone edgings and little paths. Miss Singleton wore bright orange garden gloves and her hat. On her feet she wore something she called her brogues which looked just like shoes.

If it was too cold for gardening they went for a walk instead and Miss Singleton told them the names of the flowers. She pointed out the hills to them too; Arbenside, pretty and wooded, Southerby, green and sunny with dark patches where the shadows of clouds chased across it, and Thornborough, highest of them all, most dark and least friendly. They all knew the names of the hills which ringed the village, of course, but she repeated them just the same. They took it in turns to walk next to her holding her hand.

Suddenly disaster struck. Incredibly Miss Singleton was going to leave them to get married. Kitty had not known such betrayal before; she had not thought it possible. She was sure that the parents—who could do anything—would stop this foolishness of Miss Singleton's, but they behaved very strangely and seemed to approve her treachery. They even gave the children pennies to take to school to buy a present for her as if she had been good and deserved a prize. Inexplicably they arrived one day with things to eat and drink and gave a parcel to the youngest girl to hand to Miss Singleton.

She was going to marry a farmer, but she did not belong to a farm. She belonged in the schoolroom, most particularly she belonged in the little cage between the fire-guard and the stove. Kitty knew that the farmer was very big because she heard Mrs Bates who cleaned the school saying to one of the parents, 'I'm right pleased for 'er; farmer Sanderson's a *grand* 'un and t'lass must be knocking on thirty; it's time she were settled.'

Miss Singleton let them look at the present which the parents had bought but which she, for some reason, kept thanking the children for; six little spoons, fruit spoons she called them, in a dear little box of their own. They were bigger than teaspoons and not plain round but with little ridges like shells. The box had a furry lining and each spoon slipped into its own little groove. They were made of real silver and were very, very valuable. When nobody was looking she picked one up out of the box. It felt delicate and precious. On its back it said E.P.N.S. which she supposed were Miss Singleton's initials.

She could never feel the same about Miss Singleton after this betrayal nor forgive her for preferring a strange farmer to the children who had loved her without rival. But she did sometimes think of her: a rather sad picture of Miss Singleton and the tall farmer sitting one on each side of a table eating fruit with three spoons each. She knew that Miss Singleton was filled with remorse at leaving them, it could not be otherwise. Sometimes she wished that she could go and seek her out and tell her they all forgave her and she could come back to her place by the stove, leaning on the brass rail of the fire-guard.

She often conjured up this vision in the bleak and miserable days of Miss Timms, sharp-nosed and always angry. Miss Timms' eyes were little brown slits and she hissed when she was cross, like a snake. For the first two days she was kind to them and they waited, suspicious, uncertain and watchful to see what would happen next. Thereafter, she began to shout and hiss. The nature walks stopped and Softy disappeared from the yard.

The other disaster which shook her world was the arrival of the evacuees. They appeared, quite unheralded, in the village hall one evening and ate soup at long tables. They stayed for a while in the village, coming to school, and then some moved on and more came before finally they settled down. For almost a term they came and went, huge, red and noisy, terrorizing the playground. Yet there was a dreadful fascination about them, these beings, big and wild, from another planet. They came from wonderful far-away lands with exotic names like Wigan and Bradford and 'Uddersfield.

The places they came from were much superior to little Beckgate, they said, for there they had great streets and picture-houses and the milk came in bottles. Kitty began to be ashamed of the way Mr Pollard took the milk round Beckgate every morning in his cart. Until now she had loved to watch him tipping up his can to fill the two big white jugs her mother left on the marble slab in the back kitchen. It was frothy on the top and over the jugs were white muslin covers, their edges threaded with little green beads that made a tinkly sound if there was a breeze.

Most of Miss Timms' wrath was now directed against the evacuees, especially the big boys who wore heavy boots and thick grey socks that lay in great coils around their ankles. They spoke a strange tongue and used words she had not heard before.

It was a church school; in Miss Singleton's time old Mr Pritchard had come to teach them scripture twice a week; now he had gone and young Mr Feather came instead. He had a big girl and a boy who was now six, like Kitty. She remembered how Tom Feather had gone home one afternoon and said to his mother, 'Mummy, don't you think bloody bugger's a nice name?' His mother had not said a word, just looked at him and fallen unconscious to the floor. There the vicar found her sometime later, lying concussed on the cold slabs of the kitchen floor when he came to find out why tea was so late.

There was further excitement, she remembered, when the nurse came. She was a grey, anxious-looking lady with a nasty smell. She had with her a case and a little enamel bowl full of smelly water and an odd assortment of queer combs. She stood behind each one of the children in turn, combing their hair, parting it with her fingers and peering into the spaces. Then they all had to take notes home to their mothers. After that each night her mother combed her hair, parting and peering as the nurse had done. Kitty enjoyed this for she liked having her hair fiddled with and though her mother clucked angrily and muttered words like 'slums' and 'brats' and 'disgraceful', she always concluded with, 'Well, you're all right, thank goodness,' which made Kitty feel she had done quite well.

Mrs Feather (who Kitty had heard had some secret illness called highlystrung) again reacted violently. When her daughter Jane, pale and long-haired, came home with her note, her mother shrieked, 'Fleas! the child must go to hospital!' and drove her at once twenty-five miles to the local infirmary. There had been ugly talk in the village about her using her husband's petrol ration intended for visiting the sick. Kitty could still remember standing in the village shop, holding her sweet ration card and sixpence (she had very rarely had sweets before, but the war had made all children have them), hearing Mrs Drinkwater, who always spat when she talked, say to another lady, 'Mis-use of pastoral petrol, that's what it is,' and the phrase *pastoral petrol* had lodged in her mind for ever. It was always linked with the powdery smell of the village shop and Mrs Drinkwater, huge and very wide in her flowered overall, and the fine spray that issued forth from her lips as she talked.

Soon afterwards the vicar had conspicuously laid up the car and taken to a red bicycle. Kitty remembered how she used to see him swooping down the steep lanes, big and black and terrifyingly handsome like an archangel so that she would wonder if God had sent him, especially when she began to sense that the grown-ups did not trust him. She wanted to tell him that she knew who he really was and that she was on his side and that he mustn't worry because people never welcomed God when he came on a visit anyway, but he too disappeared and the elderly Dr Jones, whom nobody could understand, came instead. She used to imagine young Mr Feather cycling the lanes and swooping down the hilly roads of that strange land inhabited by all the people who suddenly vanish out of a child's life, without explanation or reason or proper warning.

Miss Singleton had taught her the catechism. At the beginning it was deceptively easy, 'What is your name?' asked Miss Singleton on behalf of God. 'Kitty,' she had replied the first time. 'Catherine,' Miss Singleton had gently corrected her. Kitty had demurred. 'God prefers us to use our full names,' Miss Singleton had explained.

After that it got progressively more difficult with strange expressions to remember like sinful lusts, which meant things like birthday parties, and adultery which meant having babies and the sacrament which was too difficult so must be left until later on.

Coveting was difficult too because it meant you must not be jealous, but God was a jealous God and surely He should understand. But perhaps He was only teasing. She never feared Him, for that reason. He had His little ways, like not liking birthday parties, babies and nicknames. Eccentric perhaps, but never terrifying, like Miss Timms and the evacuees.

The evacuees were all right in class; they seemed harmless enough as they sat, big and puzzled at their desks, but let loose in the yard, they became demons. She dimly remembered the old days when Miss Singleton had stood with them, holding Softy, and they had played gently around her, bowling hoops and bouncing balls and trying to skip. Now Miss Timms stayed inside, leaving them alone in the yard with their tormentors. Chief centre of terror was the row of lavatories at the top of the yard. They were great round earth closets; the girls' were divided by a wall from the boys', but the boys used to climb up and shout threats. It was dark inside, so she used to leave the door open just a little. Even with the threatening boys outside she was afraid to be shut in alone with the deep hole, and the smell and the spiders. When the evacuees realized this, they would reach down with a stick and push the door wider open and throw in a frog or a worm. So she never went near the lavatory in the playtimes, but waited until they were back indoors, and then asked to be excused.

Once Miss Timms refused and after an hour of agony she found herself sitting, to her shame, in a puddle on her chair. When it was time to go, to lift the chairs on the top of the desks so that Mrs Bates could sweep round them, and sing the evening hymn, she refused to get up. She just sat, paralysed with shame, while Miss Timms got angrier and shouted and hissed. Everybody else put up their chairs, stood around the piano with folded hands and screwed up eyes and sang, 'Now the day is over' and went home, and still she sat, defiant, sure that Miss Timms, who was watching her with her tiny snakes' eyes filled with hatred, would soon kill her.

At last her mother arrived and the dreadful truth was discovered. With the utter inexplicability of adults, Miss Timms said gently, 'Well now, why didn't you tell me? Poor little lamb. Don't worry, Mrs Langdon, I always keep a spare pair, in case of such emergencies,' and her mother and Miss Timms had kept nodding and smiling at each other so that both their faces were scarcely recognizable. Miss Timms had said, 'The little ones are probably a bit upset by the evacuee children, you know,' and her mother had said, 'Yes, it's dreadful, but with you in charge I'm sure everything is under control.' During the weekend she wondered if this strange, new Miss Timms, who smiled and nodded and always kept a spare pair, would be there again on Monday morning. But on Monday she was back to normal and remained so until Kitty left the school and went to what she had hitherto called 'Gwendolen's big school' in Pendlebury.

CHAPTER TEN

ONCE past the school the road deteriorated rapidly. For half a mile or so it was surfaced and then it became a stony lane visible a long way ahead as it climbed steeply and lost itself among the hills. On one side lay Southerby, green and patched with bracken, and on the other the dark and craggy Thornborough. She walked between them with her head down, for the way was steep and the wind was sharp despite the protection of the dry-stone walls on each side.

At the top she stood and looked back, leaning on the wind. She always stopped here for it was a dividing line; below her lay the village and on each side the familiar, homely hills. Once over the brow of the hill the lane descended and rose again in different country. It was wilder, grander, and less marked by human hand. The fells were more distant, remote and awe-inspiring. She loved them both, the wild fells and the friendly hills.

She could see her mother's house from here, a grim reminder of bitterness and argument, yet all about her she had the unchanging hills for solace. For as long as she could remember she had come up to these hills for comfort. Sometimes she would leave the lane here and climb up Old Saul, whose green and gentle lower slopes led to a grassy cliff topped by a single cairn. From the lane it was the profile of an old and craggy man. In the summer she would lie on the short and springy turf, smelling the sweet, warm earth just below the sheep-cropped grass. Sometimes, hurt and bruised by her mother's tongue, obstinately refusing to cry down there in the valley, she had lain on her stomach on the hillside, watching the tears run down on to the grass beneath her chin, while the sheep grazed round about her unperturbed. This was the comfort of the hills; they made no demands, just let you come and take comfort from them and go on your way. They never let her go uncomforted, she always walked back to the village calmed as if a little of their timeless strength had somehow been absorbed into her body.

She leaned against the wall, fingering the stones. It was a live thing, this dry-stone wall. She could hear the breath stirring in it, sighing in all the tiny crevices. In the winter when the snow drifted up against these walls the sheep that sheltered beside them would live, breathing the air that reached them through the spaces between the stones. Up against a solid wall they died. She did not like mortared walls, all joined up with concrete. Dead things they were, not like these grey and friendly walls that climbed all over the dales and lay, like a net, over hills and valleys.

She felt the stones under her hand. They were rough, encrusted with lichen, tiny raised circles of intricate grey and green patterns. She leaned her face against the stones and gently moved her cheek, feeling the rough surface. When they were little, she and Gwendolen, they used to go into the bathroom to watch Daddy shaving. 'Give us a scratchy kiss,' they would say and he would scrape his chin gently against theirs and they would squeal at the roughness of it. Then they sat on the edge of the bath and watched fascinated as he stood, in his blue and white striped dressing-gown, a towel round his shoulders, lathering his face. He had a small metal box into which he put the razor blade and they were allowed to turn the little handle, which was bent out at right-angles like a mangle. When turned it made a champing sound and somehow sharpened the blade inside. They watched as he replaced it in the razor and scraped smooth channels through the lather on his face, dipping the razor into a jug of water which steamed on the window sill. As he scraped and dipped and stretched his face up to catch the light, she marvelled at his courage in having such a dangerous thing so near his neck. When he had finished they would jump off the edge of the bath and ask for a smooth kiss and then his face felt all soft and moist. It was more like this damp and mossy stone by her knee than the lichen-covered one against her cheek.

She turned from the wall and walked on over the brow of the hill, leaving Old Saul and Thornborough and moving up towards the wilder fells. Overhead a curlew shrieked. It must be a lone bird, for the others would have long ago made for the dalehead tarn, rested there and flown to join a flock beside the Irish sea. There they would spend the winter, returning next spring when the hills called them, filling them with a longing they could not resist. Perhaps this one too would follow when the frosts began to cut more keenly or perhaps it would stay here alone throughout the winter. It seemed to cut great circles of flight out of the sky as it wheeled overhead, filling the world with its wild and lonely cry.

The lane finally ended in a field, a big field, which lost itself up the fellside. Here in the lee of a line of wind-swept trees was a farm. Old, weather-beaten and low lying, it looked from a distance like an outcrop of stone.

The farmer was standing by the gate at the end of the lane, clearing the bracken with a sickle.

'Good afternoon, Mr Boothby.'

'Takin' a walk, arta lass?'

'Yes, just up to the source.'

'Ah reckon nowt on t'source. Tha'd do better to come in and tak a cup o' tea wi' missus.'

He laid down the sickle and looked at her seriously and she knew he was going to make his usual joke.

'One day they'll mak' a right grand road up 'ere and city folks'll come in cars wi' picnic baskets and flasks of tea.'

'Then you can start a restaurant and paint CAFE in big letters on the farm roof.'

'Ah'd mak' more brass that road than Ah does on t'farm,' he said, always ready to grumble.

Mrs Boothby came out of the farm and joined them.

'Comin' in, love? Stop and 'ave a bite? Kettle's boilin' on t'hob.'

'I'd better not, thank you. My mother'll worry if I'm not back before it's dark.'

'Ay, it's dark betimes now. But Ah've summat to show you. Ah'm right set up wi' a tap in t'kitchen.'

'Oh, you haven't got rid of the pump in the yard, have you?'

It was a dreadful blow, for this was one of her most precious memories; years ago, it seemed now, when they had first come here, they had walked up this lane. She had been tired and thirsty and her legs had ached. She had grumbled a lot and at last Daddy had said he would carry her and she had ridden high up on his shoulders and she had been able to see right over the high walls. Usually she couldn't see much except the path in front of her feet and felt cheated of the sights that the adults referred to over the wall in the fields or on the hillsides. Now she could see it all—much more than they could see. There were sheep that were dotted about the hillside like grey boulders, streams rushing down into the valley, foamy and white like milk, cows chewing and staring, and once a horse. She felt that she owned it all, every animal, every stile, every blade of grass. But still she was thirsty. They had promised earlier that they would ask at a farm for a drink of water. Then suddenly she had seen it.

'There's a farm,' she had called down to them from her look-out.

'There can't be,' they had objected. 'Not right up here. They couldn't farm right up here.'

'She probably means a *barn*,' Gwendolen had said superciliously.

They were all wrong. There was a farm. They said they would knock at the door and ask for a drink of water for her. Gwendolen had objected to this; she said you couldn't just knock at doors and ask strangers for drinks, but Daddy said it was different in the country. And it must have been because the farmer's wife had said, 'Of course, love. Wouldn't she rather have milk?' and she had said, 'Oh no, I hate milk,' and immediately sensed that they were all ashamed of her. But the farmer's wife didn't seem to bother about manners and just said she didn't care for the stuff herself either. Then she had brought a glass and led the way to the pump. Kitty slithered off her father's back and stood holding the glass while the farmer's wife moved the great pump handle up and down. A little water trickled down, and then suddenly a great cascade gushed out, splashing over her hand and the glass, sparkling, dancing, marvellously alive. And she, who had expected ordinary, tame water out of a tap, was suddenly so delighted by this wild stuff that she had started to laugh and laugh at the joy of it. In her excitement she almost forgot to drink it, but when she did it was ice cold and crisp and unlike any water she had ever drunk before.

After that she had been many times and had a drink from the

pump and always loved to see the water toss itself out, many-coloured in the sun, as it gushed from the pump's mouth, but it had never seemed quite so brilliant as that first time. In the war, the grown-ups had complained about the water and said the limestone made it hard and grumbled because the war had for some reason taken most of the soap away, and they said they ought to have more soap coupons because of the hard water. But she would not have changed the water for anything. All her life she never tasted water to compare with the water that came out of these hills.

She could not bear to think that the pump had gone.

Mrs Boothby was laughing. 'Nay, lass, that pump'd take a bit of shifting, it would. Besides,' she added confidentially, 'Tap's all right, but it's a bit fiddlesome like. Ah still go out to pump when Ah'm in an 'urry.'

Kitty promised to come and see the tap next time she was up and set off again. Back in the field the farmer was still chopping away at the bracken. 'Sometimes Ah wonder Ah bother,' he remarked as she passed. 'Ah might as well gie up and let t'cursed bracken take over.'

The cursed bracken was brown and sharp now. In the summer it was soft and green and waist high. When she was tiny the bracken had been a jungle of dense, sweet-smelling foliage as tall as herself. Later they had come up with Ben, the white mongrel who had been her seventh birthday present from her father, and he used to lose himself among the bracken, emerging occasionally as a white curve as he bounded up only to sink and be lost again. Where the bracken was shorter they would see his white tail moving like a sail on the green sea. When she went away to school her mother had said Ben did not get enough exercise and had had him put to sleep. She said it was kinder than letting him get fat and old. Kitty forced the memory of Ben down, down out of her mind, down among the other buried memories.

It was strange to think there could be farming up here among all this bracken. And even where there was none the soil was so thin that the rocks broke through it and surfaced in great outcrops. Elsewhere you could feel them just below the thin layer of matted grass. You could pull the grass off like peeling skin and see the rock below. Even the sheep did not find anything up here. They nibbled a little and then moved on tasting here and there. They jumped among the rocks, these stocky sheep, as if they were goats.

She climbed on until she saw the little bent tree that marked the source of the river, for here the village beck first saw the light of day. In this remote place it emerged mysteriously from a dark underground cave. She ran the last few yards and then stood leaning against the gnarled old tree breathing hard and looking down, hearing the rippling of the water. Then she climbed down the few steps that nature seemed to have provided for her and sat on a big flat stone by the water's edge. They had often explored, Gwendolen and she, in the days when Gwendolen still enjoyed it, as far as they could go into the cave, always mystified by this endless supply of water which the hills provided to make the village beck. They could not go in very far; huge boulders blocked the way after five or six yards and it was very dark and cold and frightening. She peered in now and thought that if there should be another war she would come and hide here. She imagined herself crouched behind the rocks watching men parachuting down on the fell, heard their voices, guttural and menacing, coming nearer. German, of course. To one who was five when the war broke out the enemy would always be German.

At school Miss Singleton had told them that the Germans might come tumbling out of the sky on the end of parachutes and then pretend to be English. They would not know where they were, for all the signposts had been removed and there were no maps for sale in the shops. She told the children not to answer if they were asked the way by strangers. Once, when she had been about seven years old, an old couple in a car had asked her the way to the village and she had pointed in the opposite direction and they had smiled and thanked her and driven off towards Pendlebury. She watched them go and felt very excited and patriotic; it was the first time she had taken a direct part in the war.

Once out of the cavern, the water scarcely moved but lay flat and calm in a shallow pool, then it dropped in a miniature waterfall and so fell in stages, pool and fall, pool and fall, until it disappeared into the next field. All the way down to the village it grew, fed by a thousand hillside streams, meandering through fields and hamlets and under little packhorse bridges. Sometimes it hurried under bent rowan trees and gnarled old hazel bushes until it found its way under the gentle willows down to Beckgate. By the time it flowed under the old bridge in the village, it was a wide and dappled stream with quiet corners and shady pools where old men fished for trout.

After that she knew that it joined becks from other villages, and became a river and went out to sea, but by then it was something on a map and not part of the real world at all.

She sat and gazed at the water creeping out of the cold dark cave into the pale light of the winter afternoon. It flowed as it had always flowed and would always flow, winter and summer, world without end. Gwendolen, who had a scientific mind, had several times tried to explain to her why the water rose just here. Evidently the streams met underground, sinking through the porous limestone and then were forced up by the millstone grit. Gwendolen knew the reason for everything; if she did not, she made it up. Nothing was a mystery to Gwendolen. Kitty both pitied and envied this quality in her sister which made her immune from both wonder and horror.

As she sat and gazed at the water, mesmerized by its magical continuity, she thought of nothing. She felt nothing. She seemed not to exist except as part of nature like the rocks and the grass and the water and the old stunted tree which bent with the wind above the cave. Overhead the curlew cried.

CHAPTER ELEVEN

'TOO cold to snow,' Tom said, as he banged the car door behind him. 'No white Christmas for you this year, I'm afraid.'

It was intensely cold; the night was still and frozen, so that when they had walked down the drive the sound of their feet and voices had seemed to crack the air around them. The sky was stretched tight between brilliant stars.

'Oh, nonsense!' Gwendolen said. 'The barometer's falling: it could mean snow tomorrow.'

'The barometer didn't change until Mummy put the paraffin heater into the hall.'

'Honestly, Kitty, you're hopeless. Don't they teach you the difference between temperature and pressure at school?'

'I think they did try once,' Kitty said, trying to remember. 'But it's bound to matter to the barometer what kind of atmosphere it's in.'

'Well, they've changed the atmosphere up at Beckgate Hall,' Tom said. 'Ma Turton—you know her that does for them—came rushin' into me Dad's shop the other day all flustered. "They've got sensual 'eating up at 'all," she says, "and it's got them right flummaxed."'

The girls laughed.

'Who lives up there now?' Gwendolen asked.

'Oh, another of them steel chaps from Sheffield. Made a packet in the war, they say. They comes and goes, always 'ave, Dad says, but Ma Turton goes on for ever, bin there since she were a lass, before Great War, or maybe Boer War. But she's never seen such carryings on as there are now. Modernization that's what it is. She says it were like a furnace up there with the central heating, every room an oven. And the old girl from Sheffield 'ad sweat running down her face and were gasping,

"But can't we turn it off, love, like the gentleman told us 'ow to?" and the old boy, red as a turkey cock, shouting, "You said you wanted central heating and now you've got it, you'll bloody well put up wi' it." '

Gwendolen was sitting in front with Tom. Kitty liked this arrangement. She could lean back, hearing them talk and laugh but not obliged to join in and then slowly let herself withdraw as she gazed at the stars in the hard, black sky. Warm, black skies were quite different, velvety soft, as if the stars must be sunk deep into the folds of blackness. But these stars stood out sharp and brilliant from the unyielding sky, all millions and millions of years away. Yet so close that she felt herself spinning among them.

She came back to earth with a jolt as Tom swung the car into the station yard. She was lucky to be here at all; her mother had been very angry with her for being late for tea after her walk, and Kitty knew that if she had let her see how much she wanted to go to the station she would certainly have prevented her. So she had feigned indifference and offered to stay at home and help to cook, so that her mother had said, 'I'd rather you were out of my way. If you can stay out on the hills all that time a bit of fresh air at the station won't hurt you. Go and get your coat on.' So with secret jubilation she had gone and got her coat on.

'You'd best wait in the car,' Tom said. 'You've got ten minutes before the train comes in and it's perishing cold on that platform.'

She was glad when Gwendolen said, 'It can't be any colder than your car,' and got out, for now that she was here she was suddenly excited and wanted to be as near to the train as possible. Tom just laughed, settled himself comfortably back in his seat and lit a cigarette.

The station master had not arrived yet and the platform was deserted. The little station lay empty and silent under the night sky. They went through the gate quietly, like trespassers. As they crossed the line their footsteps echoed.

They stood by one of the oil-lit station lamps, feeling the tiny warmth through the glass. The flame flickered as a slight draught of air touched it through the little glass door.

'It's perfect, this station, isn't it?' Kitty whispered, feeling as if they were intruders.

'Oh, it can't last much longer,' Gwendolen replied. 'Why aren't you talking properly; is your throat sore?'

'No. Why shouldn't it last?'

'It just can't be economic; it's hardly used at all. They'll have to close it one day.'

'But they *couldn't*—not our station. It's been here for years. It must be one of the oldest stations in the world and it's the only one I've ever seen with oil lamps. Oh, and all the lovely little bits of ironwork; it looks like lace round the shelter, but when you touch it it's all hard and strong.'

'You can't keep stations just because they're pretty. You look, when Daddy comes he'll probably be the only person on the train. There—it's signalled.'

They heard the gate bang. The station master had left his cottage over the road and was now crossing the line, swinging his storm lamp.

'Evening,' he said. 'Sharp night, isn't it?' Then he went on rather grandly, 'We've got a waiting room, you know, young ladies,' and led them hospitably into the tiny, ice-cold shelter. 'You might as well be comfortable; there's a few minutes yet.' He looked around as if making sure that everything was in perfect order and went out.

They managed to keep quiet until he was out of earshot and then they both collapsed on the bench and roared with laughter. The shelter, a small stone shell with neither doors nor windows, was much colder than the platform, for it contrived to feel damp also. They never went into it unless it was pouring with rain.

'The way he ushered us in,' Kitty said, recovering first, 'as if there was a huge, roaring fire blazing away in that.' She pointed at the little broken grate in the corner.

'It wouldn't be so bad if we could see properly,' Gwendolen remarked.

'Ah, but can't you see the great glittering chandeliers hanging in the middle of the ceiling? And just look at the moulding, goodness, what cornices! And, Gwendolen, the curtains, the lovely rich velvet curtains with shutters behind to keep us snug.' She pretended to stroke them and smoothed her cheek against them until Gwendolen was laughing helplessly.

'Oh, do stop, Kitty, it hurts. You really are an ass. But I feel warmer for all that laughing anyway. Is that the train?'

But it was only the station master dragging the steps along ready for the passengers, and they had to stand in the waiting room stamping their feet and clapping their hands until at last they heard the train.

It only had two coaches. Every compartment was, as Gwendolen had prophesied, empty. In sudden panic, Kitty felt sure he had not come. She felt sick. And then there he was, in the last compartment, leaning out of the window. And the station master was putting the mounting block ready and they were standing and waiting and it was a perfect night and Christmas Eve.

The door swung open and he climbed rather awkwardly down the mounting block. He hugged Gwendolen and held her back for a moment. 'And how's my lovely girl? I like your Mother Christmas hat. And Kitty, how's my poppet?' He hugged her and the black overcoat was rough against her face and smelled of smoke.

When the train had gone, the station master took the case and led them across the line, his lamp swinging so that she walked now in darkness, now in light. She held her father's arm and could feel the unevenness of his walk, up and down. She noticed that he had not brought the stick.

He sat in front with Tom, while Gwendolen and she sat in the back. Tom, she observed, was less talkative now, more deferential, and Gwendolen did not make provocative remarks but treated him somewhat distantly as if he were a proper taxi driver. It might have been prearranged the way they all adjusted their characters like jackets, she thought. She always felt excitement at the way people shifted about like this, altering all the time and changing with the people they were with and what they were doing. She thought suddenly that she did it herself; when Gwendolen appeared she played a younger sister role, assing about and being even more inefficient than . . .

'I said what is the dreamer dreaming about?' he asked, apparently not for the first time.

'Oh, nothing, nothing really. Just people and things.'

'People and things! That adds up to everything, not nothing.'

There was silence and she was grateful to him for not making her go on and sound silly.

'And how is your mother?' he asked politely.

'All right,' Gwendolen replied equally politely. 'Very busy, of course, with Christmas.'

'Of course.'

They were all sobered by this conversation and scarcely talked for the rest of the way, until Tom drew up carefully at the gate and jumped out to open the doors for them. They waited while he was paid and drove off and then the three of them turned and walked silently down the drive. Gwendolen opened the door and they all began to talk at once. Their mother heard the door and came out of the kitchen. She stood surveying them from the far end of the passage. 'No need to stand there letting the cold in,' she said sharply. 'It costs enough to heat this house without that.'

Kitty, standing close to her father, could feel him forcing himself forward. 'Hello, Martha,' he said. 'How are you?'

Her mother gave him her usual hard, suspicious stare and said, 'As well as can be expected, Charles,' and held up her cheek. They kissed.

The stone hot water bottle spluttered and sizzled and beads of water oozed out from around the stopper. Kitty wiped it on her skirt and slid the bottle carefully down the bed.

That was the last of them; she had carried up her own and Gwendolen's and her parents', for they were always put in before supper. Her father was sleeping in the spare room next to Gwendolen and opposite to her own. Her mother's room was at the far end of the corridor, next to the bathroom.

The spare room was bleaker even than hers. There seemed to be even more dark brown paint in here than in the other rooms. Its twin beds were draped with mauve and purple bedspreads and the floor was covered with green linoleum. Texts and samplers hung above the beds. Against the opposite wall was a Victorian wash-stand with a marble top and next to it a pre-war dressing table with a shiny veneer finish. Above it hung a reproduction of the crucifixion in moribund greys and sickly pale greens. She liked the old grandfather clock that stood in the corner, even though it did not go. Its face was the only cheerful object in the room.

Her father had unpacked his few possessions: on the table by the bed was his brush and comb and the blue and white sponge bag in which he kept his shaving things. On the bed were his pyjamas. She picked them up and rolled them carefully around the bottle and replaced it in the bed.

Then she sat down on the other bed. She looked at his little pile of belongings; he seemed to have so few things. She stared at them, these pitiable, transitory possessions, until they seemed to have some intense significance. Ordinary things caught in eternity, like objects in a still-life painting.

She remembered the kiss. How odd it was, this grown-up world, which made a man and a woman who hated each other make themselves, against all their instincts, actually kiss each other. And all for the sake of the children who were not for one single moment deceived by it.

Suddenly she remembered the time she had stayed with Amanda last Easter. One evening as she and Amanda were getting into bed she remembered she had left her book in the drawing-room. She ran downstairs and across the hall. The drawing-room door was open and Amanda's parents were sitting by the the fire. She was just going in when Amanda's mother put down the paper and said something and her father looked up and smiled. For a moment they looked at each other. Nothing happened; they just looked at each other. She stood in the dark hall looking in, but not able to move, so strong was the sense that there was something there which she had never known in her own family that it shocked her. They were happy and thought it quite normal and ordinary and Amanda took it for granted. She could not make herself go in, but stood in the dark hall looking in at them in the light. Then she turned and ran upstairs and told Amanda she did not want that book after all.

They had only looked at each other and a whole world of warmth and love had surrounded them, so safe and strong that she could remember it all these months later. It had nothing to do with the wretched little ritual of the kiss which she had watched for years at home. The kiss was merely a necessary preamble; once it was over all the rest could follow; all the Christmas rituals and celebrations. It was the price agreed upon so that everybody could enjoy the rest.

But it was not worth the price and the children did not want it to be paid. It was the whole army of grown-ups who ordered this pretence and then made a virtue of hypocrisy by saying it was for the children's sake. They ought to try asking the children, Kitty thought, getting up off the bed. But then, she reflected, most children are incoherent, as she had always been when it was a question of anything she cared about. They have no one to state their case for them—except the abundant self-appointed misinterpreters.

'Just because we can't explain about things,' she said suddenly to the grandfather clock, 'they think we don't feel—and we do feel, more than they do. When I'm grown up I'm going to remember how it feels. I'm going to remember for ever and ever.'

'Supper's ready. Have you put yourself to bed with those bottles?' Gwendolen called from downstairs.

'Just coming,' she replied, but she repeated her vow slowly to the grandfather clock before she did so.

Supper was laid in the cold dining-room: cold meat, and the cutlery felt cold even on cold fingers. She shivered.

'Go and put another jumper on,' her mother said. 'We can't afford electric fires all over the house, not on the pittance I get for housekeeping.'

She reappeared with a green cardigan over her blue sweater, avoiding her sister's eye. 'That's better,' her mother said. 'You'll get no sympathy from me if you catch cold; I hear you were seen mooning round the school this afternoon when you were supposed to be out getting exercise. Charles, cut some bread, please.'

Her father began to cut the new loaf. It crumbled and the slice broke.

'Here, give it to me,' her mother said scornfully, taking the knife from him. 'You sit down. Really, you'd think cutting bread would be a man's job. Like using a saw.'

'You get more practice,' Kitty put in.

'Needs must. And don't leave that fat, miss. When I was a girl we had to eat everything on our plates. We weren't allowed to leave a scrap. Anything we left was served up next meal, even if it meant cold cabbage for tea.'

'If you always had to eat everything how could there be anything left for the next meal?'

'That's enough; don't answer back. Charles, that child is

getting impossibly cheeky. I don't know what they teach her at that school you chose for her but it certainly isn't manners.'

'Well, what do they teach you, Kitty?' her father asked her, to divert the conversation.

'Oh, pressure and temperature and things like that.'

'When I was a girl we were taught Honour Thy Father and Thy Mother and we never dared to do otherwise.'

'Perhaps your parents honoured each other,' Kitty said innocently. Martha drew in her lips sharply and said nothing. Her father had deserted her mother soon after she was born, whereupon her mother had left her in an orphanage and emigrated to Australia, where she lived to a ripe old age. Kitty was not supposed to know this.

Gwendolen looked at her furiously and when they took the plates into the kitchen, hissed at her, 'You must not say things like that. For goodness' sake let's get through Christmas without one of their ghastly rows.'

'Well, it's so stupid; how can you make yourself honour anybody? It's instinctive. It's like the quality of mercy—not strained.'

'Oh shut up and stop being such an idiot. Bring that baked custard in, and don't you dare go stirring up trouble and provoking her, do you hear?'

She was so angry that Kitty suddenly felt frightened and said, 'I'm sorry, Gwendolen.' But she wasn't sorry really; sometimes she felt that if she didn't fight against the illogical rubbish her mother talked she might end up believing it. She had believed it for so long. When she was little she always believed her mother when she said that her father was away because he did not love his children; only when she was about ten did she realize that the war had taken him away and not other fathers in the village since they were mostly farmers. When he did occasionally come on leave, she had, therefore, treated him with great coldness, which he had always found very puzzling.

As she carried the baked custard down the cold corridor, she could hear her mother's voice, 'mooning about, dreaming, lazy, wasting time. Then the minute you appear she's quite impossible.'

Her father did not reply; for the rest of the meal he scarcely spoke except to add a remark when her mother paused for breath in the course of her monologue. A look of great weariness seemed to settle upon him; the weariness of one exerting self-control by an almost intolerable effort of will. I wonder why he's never killed her, Kitty thought.

After supper her mother went into the kitchen to cook and she helped her father with the decorations. As they pinned up holly and put up the Father Christmas frieze that always went round the drawing-room she began to feel excited, almost despite herself. They began to laugh and joke as she handed up tacks for him to hammer in, the fire crackled when they threw on bits of holly they didn't want and then they went down the garden and she held the torch while he dug up the Christmas tree. It smelled of every Christmas she had ever known. They took it inside and she held it upright in the old copper boiler while he packed soil and then coal around its roots to make it firm. She sniffed at the branches of the tree, smelling the wonder of Christmas.

Her father brought down the box of decorations and she sat by the fire unpacking them. There was something reassuring about the familiar glass balls, the stars, the yellowing tinsel and rather tatty angel. She took the year-old newspaper wrappings off them carefully, recognizing each in delight. She had almost forgotten the humming bird, with its shiny turquoise body and long, sleek tail. She fastened it carefully on to a branch, suddenly sure that it was a symbol and that calamity would follow its breaking.

She sat on the rug gazing into the fire and remembering how obsessed she had once been by symbols. The fire itself had been one: it would suddenly become imperative to feed it with tiny pieces of coal. At other times it was vitally important not to walk across the virgin snow on the lawn but to plod round by the wall, or to touch every third tree in the avenue on the way to church. Otherwise the god of the fire or the snow or the wood would be offended and obliterate her.

Her father was watching her. 'What are you thinking of all so serious gazing into the fire?' he asked, sitting down on a chair and taking her hand.

'About when I was young,' she replied.

She was aware that something in the reply troubled him. 'Is it so very long ago?' he asked sadly. Then he went on lightly,

'Well, up you get and help me climb to the top of this tree and fix the angel on. Then you'd better see if there is anything you can do to help your mother.'

In the kitchen her mother was working frenetically, chopping parsley and pounding stuffing. She interrupted these operations to say briefly to Kitty, 'We'll go to early service tomorrow. That'll leave the morning clear for cooking. The Mabeys and Mrs Harbinger are coming to dinner, don't forget.'

Kitty stood fascinated and watched her mother, pummelling and banging and slapping at the sweetmeats and viands in preparation for the love feast on the morrow.

CHAPTER TWELVE

IT was dark the next morning when they set off for church. It was exciting to leave the house in the frosty morning, hardly awake, unfed, and the village so silent that their footsteps sounded like an army. The church bell uttered its single clang, clang, clang, leaden in the leaden air. It stopped as they went in; the vicar always waited for her mother.

She followed her mother into the pew. Gwendolen followed her. Her father was still in bed.

It was marvellous, she thought as she knelt, the suppressed excitement of knowing that it was Christmas morning and yet going on quietly with the communion service as if it were an ordinary Sunday. It heightened the tension that always seemed to Kitty to mount at each prayer and response. Sublime phrase followed sublime phrase, striking and poignant, though familiar. For the service had grown very familiar throughout the years she had sat and listened after Matins, watching first her mother and later Gwendolen go up and take communion while she stayed alone in the pew, as did all the other children of the devout. She used to watch her mother come back down the aisle from the altar, a faint and knowing smile on her thin lips, which were still damp with the communion wine, and wonder what mystery had touched her, up there at the communion rails.

For from the time she had gone to the village school and learned the Catechism from Miss Singleton, Kitty had understood that her mother had gone up to the altar to meet the strange and inexplicable God who did not hold with parties and babies and nicknames. Her mother even had a holy smell when she returned to the pew. The fact that some of the mystery and awe had rubbed off on to her mother made it impossible to question her. Kitty knew that she would just have to wait until she was older and able to go up there and find out for herself. Sometimes she felt she could not bear to wait all that time until her own confirmation.

It was about the time that she went to school in Pendlebury that her affection for Miss Singleton's God began to wane; she could no longer make allowances for Him. She felt sure that there must be some explanation of it all which would be revealed to her in due course. She was glad when it was decided that she should be confirmed early and set out for her first class, having rushed through her tea and homework, full of anxious questions. But Dr Jones did not seem to welcome questions; he preferred to impart each evening a great truth—sometimes two, if they started on time—and let them meditate upon it.

Dr Jones would keep on about suffering; he kept inviting them to contemplate Christ on the Cross. He did not seem to understand the horror of watching the innocent suffer, the awful guilt and misery of it. If you could not help, she asked, what good did it do to contemplate suffering? Dr Jones pointed out that Christ was suffering for her sake. That only made it worse. Anyway she had not asked Him to. Some instinct prevented her from actually saying this; she knew that it was a wicked comment to make upon the crucifixion and not less wicked for being truly felt. She began to suspect too that when Dr Jones talked about contemplating the crucifixion he was talking about something more casual than the intense sharing of suffering that she herself endured.

In the middle of the classes Dr Jones left and was replaced by Mr Patterson. She felt that this would somehow give her a new start, for Mr Patterson was younger and talked in everyday language. From the first he told them that he wanted to talk about religion in just the same way as anything else. This was marvellous; there would be no more double meanings and no slithering over difficulties, Kitty thought. One would be able to get it all cut and dried: one would be able to be reasonable. Being reasonable was very important to her at that time.

But it soon created difficulties between Mr Patterson and herself.

'But I don't understand your problem,' he said at last. 'You believe in other things that you can't prove.'

He looked at her with a conspiratorial smile and she knew that a homely comparison was on its way.

'Take electricity,' he said. 'You accept it on trust, don't you? But you don't understand how it works. Why can't you believe in God in the same way?'

'But that's a reason for believing in just anything,' Kitty objected. 'It's not a reason for believing in Christianity especially.'

'If only you would accept, Kitty, just accept like the rest of the class.'

She began to notice that whereas at first he had almost encouraged her to argue, quoting amiably, 'There lives more faith in honest doubt, believe me, than in half the creeds,' he began after two or three weeks to be less tolerant of her questions. An edge of impatience would creep into his voice; she realized that doubts are only respectable once they have been vanquished.

'It would be so much easier, Kitty, not just for me—that is the least important consideration—but for you, if you could just believe, just accept. Why not try it? You will find that all the rest falls into place, once you have accepted.'

Finally she decided that that would be the simplest thing to do. For the purposes of confirmation she would suspend her disbelief. She did not exactly feign belief, just assumed it as a kind of intellectual exercise. She found that it was true, once the basic belief was accepted, the rest followed. She felt guilty about it, especially as thereafter the vicar treated her as one who has seen the light. Her only hope now was that some revelation would happen after her confirmation to justify her hypocrisy. But when she herself walked down the aisle after her first communion all she had had was the bitter taste of the wine in her mouth and disappointment that nothing had happened. There had been no revelation, no drama up there by the rails. It was no more than she had expected, but she was disappointed all the same.

That autumn she had gone away to boarding school and it had ceased to matter. Religion there was a topic to be discussed, services were attended, like lessons, because they were part of the curriculum. The need to understand ceased to be so burningly urgent; the fire had gone out. It flared up again, during the holidays, kindled by the clash of feelings towards her gentle, agnostic father and harsh, church-going mother.

It was nearly time to go up now for her Christmas communion; the marvellous 'comfortable words our Saviour Jesus Christ saith,' were being read: 'Come unto me all that travail and are heavy laden and I will refresh you.' She truly believed that He had said it; nobody could have made up words like that. Had He really meant, though, that all this was to come of it, she thought, as she followed her mother up the aisle, so that nearly two thousand years later she should be kneeling here like this, accepting a neat little square of factory-made wafer, chasing it nervously round the palm of her hand with her tongue?

It was really quite simple, she thought as she walked back down the aisle. It was just that she could never see any connection between Jesus Christ and all the elaborate rituals performed in His name. It would have been so different if only they had taken a bit of notice of all He had said about love and forgiveness instead of making such a fuss about the very few things He had said about rituals. Why had generations of grown-ups had to latch on to the least important, why had they made institutions, why had they had to make a religion out of Him? Could that really be what He had intended? She suddenly felt guilty in case it was. So, as she knelt for the final blessing she added quickly, 'I'm not being critical, God, just wondering.'

The organ struck up a joyful Christmas anthem and they began to move towards the door. The church was crowded; the vicar stood in the porch wishing everyone a happy Christmas, counting them again. He noticed that his estimate at the altar had been correct; there had been sixty-two in the congregation and he had had to consecrate a second lot of bread and wine. Of course, some would be women who usually came to Matins but would be too busy cooking later this morning. Still it was very satisfactory. This and the prospect of a big Christmas breakfast with grapefruit and bacon and egg and coffee made him feel, as he shut the church door behind him and strode down the road to the vicarage, a strange, unusual elation, almost akin to confidence.

He strode into the kitchen, where his wife was turning the bacon over in the frying pan with a carving fork, and stood behind her. He held her to him, pressing her back into his chest, as he held her breasts and stomach, while she carefully laid down the fork and stared at the bacon in some astonishment. Then she turned round in his arms. The bacon spluttered and spat and the milk began to rise in the saucepan. Regretfully he released her. If it could only be now, he thought, it would be all right. But there was only an hour for breakfast and the preparations for Matins and all kinds of people might call. He prayed—no, that would be a sacrilege—he hoped anxiously—that the confidence would last until tonight. At the same time he could not repress the ominous thought that since so many had turned out for Early Communion, numbers at Evensong were likely to be depressingly small. He kissed her again, without passion, and said, 'Happy Christmas.'

'Happy Christmas, Charles,' Martha said with the formality of one who says 'Good Morning' when it is raining.

'And to you too, Martha,' her husband replied, kissing her upturned cheek. Then they all sat down to their grapefruit.

By tradition they always kept their presents until after their Christmas dinner. In the morning Kitty offered to help in the kitchen.

'Much help you are, dreaming about the place,' her mother replied. 'Better go out for a walk with your father. He's the only one who hasn't been to church; it might do him a bit of good to be out among God's creatures.'

Animals, *en masse*, Kitty thought, were God's creatures, to be respected, but individual ones were as unlovable as human beings and had to be put to sleep like Ben. She tapped the barometer as she went through the hall. It was very high. 'So it *was* the paraffin heater,' she remarked to nobody in particular.

They walked away from Old Saul and Thornborough, down the village street and over the bridge and along a wide green lane. The mud was hard and in the ruts made by the farm carts lay tiny pools of frozen water. The ice crackled as she stepped on it; her father walked on the flat part in the centre and she herself, holding his hand, walked in the ruts. The hills were still and distant. It would not rain or snow. She breathed deeply.

'Happy?' he asked. When she did not reply he added, 'How are the holidays going?'

'All right,' she replied guardedly. 'It's much better with Gwendolen here.'

He did not reply for a few seconds and then said apologetically, 'She wants to come back with me.'

Kitty stopped and stared at him.

'You mean you're *both* going the day after tomorrow?'

'Yes, I'm afraid so. She wants to have some time in London before next term. But don't worry; I'll have a talk with her and see if she won't change her mind. You know that I hate leaving you up here alone, don't you?'

'Yes, I know.'

She made herself go on talking, and disguise her misery with peevishness.

'Whatever does she want to go to London for?'

'London's fun when you're Gwendolen's age.' He took her hand and tucked it into his arm. She could feel the slow up and down unevenness of his walk. 'By next holidays—certainly by the summer—we'll have a flat and you'll be able to come too. You'll like that, won't you? It will be a real home for you at last.'

She couldn't say that this lane, these hills and fields were home, yet she could not deny them. She said nothing.

'It's natural, you know,' he said gently. 'Where you are when you are growing up feels like home for the rest of your life. The sea calls back people who were born by it and the streets of towns too. Think how the streets and squares and odd corners of London that Dickens grew up in, were with him all his writing life. It is part of you, you can't help it any more than you can help your bones growing.'

She laughed, partly with relief at the way he always understood without having to have things explained.

'It must be marvellous to have both—a happy home in a place that feels like home, I mean.'

'I know. I'm sorry.'

'It isn't your fault. Except for marrying her in the first place. Why did you?'

She had never dared to ask before, but now it had been easy.

'Pity. Beware of pity.'

'Why? Because it creeps up on you and doesn't seem dangerous?'

'Yes, and especially because it's not a very good reason for marrying someone.'

'I shan't marry anyone for any reason.'

He stopped. 'You don't really feel that?'

'Yes, I do,' she insisted, though wishing she had not said it and so added to the things he blamed himself for. 'It hasn't done *you* much good.'

'Yes, it has. It has given me you and Gwendolen.'

'But if you hadn't had us you wouldn't have known what you were missing. Is it true about not missing what you haven't had?' she asked to divert the conversation.

But he would not be side-tracked. He took her hand again.

'Look, darling, I know it must puzzle you. I made a mistake and I must take what follows; what is hard is that *you* have to take the consequences of something which wasn't your fault. Above all, I don't want you to feel that all marriages are like this.'

'You still haven't said why you did it.'

'My own parents were parted. I wanted a home of my own. The girl I loved wouldn't have me. I met your mother and she had such faith and ideals. She was lovely then, too, rather like Gwendolen though less sophisticated. I thought I loved her. There was something very appealing about her, a kind of simplicity. She was remote and hard too and I knew that. But I was very young and quixotic and I thought I could somehow or other soften her with love and bring out all the good qualities that are in her. It was much more my fault than hers.'

'Why?'

'Partly because I'm a man. I did the pursuing and the asking. But mostly because *I* should have known it was a mistake. I knew even then that people who haven't been loved will never be able to love; I knew it was hopeless but I had to try. I had this yearning for a lost cause, I suppose. Then again, I'd read more than she had and thought more, so I should have known better. She didn't see the dangers, she doesn't look ahead or speculate; it isn't her nature, but it was mine. In fact I *did* know better but I just blundered on all the same.'

The lane narrowed here and they walked in single file until it had rounded the bend and widened again before crossing the beck. They stood together on the packhorse bridge. Where the water met the bank it turned to ice, imprisoning a few brown and shrivelled reeds.

'I suppose you won't have had a chance to talk to your mother about the divorce?' he asked as they walked together again up the lane.

'No, not this time. But when I did in the summer she said something odd. You see, she seems to have all the arguments; she can throw any bit of the past at me and I don't know if it's true or not.'

He said nothing, sickened at what he had involved her in. At fourteen.

'She said,' she went on, not noticing this, 'that you could have had a divorce years and years ago if you'd really wanted it, and the truth was you were too weak to manage without her.'

'It's true that she did offer me one when you were three, but then I'd have had no control over you two at all. I was desperately tempted. I thought she was driving me mad and went to a psychiatrist. At first he didn't seem to think it was serious but then he met her and listened to her and told me he was sure I must get away from her before she undermined my health and work. It was tempting; the thought of being free of her and the endless, nagging, arguing, justifying, self-righteousness—well, you know what it's like. But then, I should have had to be what's called the guilty party and that would have meant I'd have lost you both. That was really what she wanted. She'd have been without me, whom she disliked anyway, I'd have been branded as guilty, she proclaimed innocent, which fits in with her black-and-white scheme of things and I'd have been deprived of you children, which would have been the greatest triumph of all for her. I did consider it, but then I thought of you two being brought up alone with her, without tenderness, and I couldn't do it.'

'I wish you had.'

He wasn't exactly expecting her thanks, but was hardly prepared for that reaction.

'It was for your sake—yours and Gwendolen's. I couldn't let you be brought up to be bigoted, unappreciative of good and beautiful things, unloved until perhaps in the end you were incapable of giving love.'

'I know, but you don't understand. You made the wrong sacrifice. We should have managed somehow, Gwendolen and I, but you lost your only chance to be free. Now you might never, never be free of her.'

'Don't say that—why do you say it?'

There was agony in his voice; she was silent, wishing that compassion had silenced her before.

'Kitty—please, she has said more to you, hasn't she?' he insisted.

'Well, she just said she'd nothing to gain by divorcing you. Then she carried on about her religion and how marriages were made in Heaven and I said yours was made in Hell and . . .'

'Kitty!' he laughed an outraged laugh. 'Oh, well, it's true I suppose, but somehow not quite the sort of thing one expects from one's little daughter.'

She looked at him keenly.

'Now what have I said wrong?' he asked.

'Just the little daughter thing. You know I understand it all—people of my age do if they are brought up in certain situations—but it isn't possible to turn us back into dear little children, like something on a chocolate box, just when it's convenient.'

'Yes, I know. Forgive my few illusions. I wish you had a few more yourself sometimes. All right, don't say it, I know whose fault it is that you haven't.'

This was better, much better, well away from the dead end misery of a few minutes ago. For she was fairly sure that her mother would not give him a divorce now.

'You were saying, Kitty?'

'Well, that was all really. I can't think why she wants to hang on to you when she doesn't like you anyway. She really seems to hate you more than you do her.'

'She has strong emotions. No feelings, but very strong emotions, which is why she hurts people like us because our feelings make us vulnerable. But no, I don't hate her; I terribly want to be free of her, that's all. More than anything in the world I want to be free of her.'

The yearning in his voice frightened her. It seemed more than human. She thought suddenly of the curlew filling the world with its lonely cry as it wheeled over the fells. She pushed the image away: if she was to help him she must be practical, she must keep her feet on the ground down here in the valley.

'She says you just want to be free of her so that you can carry on with other women.'

'If I was made that way I could do it now, couldn't I? No, I don't even want to marry again, not for years and years anyway. But I can see your mother's point of view. It would be bad enough to have a husband who wanted to divorce you for somebody else, but to have one who just wants to be free of you for the sheer joy and relief of it, that's much worse. Besides, it leaves her with no one to blame.'

They had come to another packhorse bridge. A weather-beaten hawthorn bush stood like a bunch of old sticks by the side. They automatically snapped off a few dry twigs and dropped them into the water. Then they stood on the bridge and waited until they came out on the other side, where a stronger current bore them rapidly away. He watched them go.

'Sometimes,' he said in a voice of complete resignation, 'I know that it doesn't really matter at all. Life will flow on just the same, divorce or no divorce, freedom or no freedom. It is really all quite trivial.'

His resignation filled her with the fear she had felt when he came to school last term. It was like death. Better that he should struggle and suffer than resign himself like this.

'It's not trivial to me,' she said stoutly and with almost deliberate childishness.

'No, I know it's not, my pet. And I'm grateful. I'm sorry about the mess you were born into. As I say, it was mostly my fault. I'm sorry for her too; she has some good qualities and if she'd been happier, who knows how differently she might have lived.'

'You sound as if you're pleading for her,' she accused him angrily. 'She never finds anything kind to say about you, so there's no need to invent good things to say about her.'

'Kitty, it's not a question of inventing things. They're there. Perhaps she isn't good, I don't know. Who can judge? But she does good. She was a good mother to you when you were little; it was only when you began to grow up and have a mind of your own that she grew harsh towards you, as she is towards me. But she has helped many people and always been ready to take in the weak or ill or helpless.'

'Who can't fight back.'

'Don't be bitter, little one. She has great virtues; I think you have inherited some of them.'

'Thank you, but I'd rather inherit your vices than her virtues.'

'God Almighty—what have I done?'

'And may God Almighty help us to remember the hungry,' Mr Mabey concluded grace as they sat down to their Christmas dinner.

Kitty, who had felt ravenous when she got in from the morning's walk, suddenly remembered them—the hungry, hollow-eyed and pot-bellied. Her appetite vanished. The table laden with food, the turkey, golden and crisp-skinned, suddenly seemed a mockery. She looked resentfully at the vicar, as he tucked into a plateful of turkey and ham, bright green sprouts and buttered carrots, bacon rolls and sausages, stuffing and bread sauce. She wondered if he was really thinking of the hungry as he ate. She hoped not; it was a gratuitous insult to the hungry to remember them as you ate a superabundant meal. It was not bearable to have too much when they had nothing. She sent up a counter-prayer to be allowed to forget them just for now.

Gwendolen caught her eye and nodded towards her plate. She picked up her knife and fork, but not before her mother had said sarcastically, 'Isn't it good enough for you then, Kitty?'

She murmured something and began to eat.

'Young people nowadays are very particular,' Martha went on to Mrs Harbinger. 'When we were little it was very different, wasn't it?'

Mrs Harbinger was Martha's good deed for the day. A widow whose children were married and lived far away, she would otherwise have spent Christmas Day alone. She was a pale, plumpish little woman, the colour and texture of risen dough. Only her nose did not seem to belong to the rest of her. It was a large chunk of a nose, bony and aggressive. Its purple colour did not match the rest of her face. Somewhere, Kitty thought, there must be a General, mauve-complexioned and very bossy, wearing the soft little button nose that belonged to Mrs Harbinger.

'Oh dear me, yes, Mrs Langdon,' Mrs Harbinger said. She was clearly much in awe of her hostess.

'I expect you were like me,' Martha pressed on. 'Not allowed to argue about whether you liked a meal or not.'

'Kitty wasn't arguing,' Charles put in mildly. 'Just dreaming.'

Martha began to reply, but then, inhibited by the presence of guests, said nothing. She contented herself with glaring at Kitty.

After lunch they went into the drawing-room for coffee. Martha looked at her watch and said suddenly, 'Three o'clock; time for the royal message,' and switched on the radio.

When the National Anthem began, Mr Mabey suggested that they should all stand up. Kitty, embarrassed, glanced round at the others. Her mother and Mr Mabey stood with their heads bowed as if in prayer, Gwendolen looked supercilious, her father quietly amused and Mrs Harbinger rather pleased and patriotic, the nose held high. Mrs Mabey was in the lavatory.

When the speech was over the Reverend Mabey looked at his watch. 'All good things must come to an end,' he said. 'We have to be at the party at the children's home in Pendlebury at four.'

'What a shame; no rest from duty even on Christmas Day,' Martha said.

'We are glad to go along, Mrs Langdon. We like to share other people's children, having none of our own—yet.'

He patted his wife's shoulder reassuringly as he helped her into her coat.

'Oh yes,' Martha said, as they stood at the front door seeing them off. 'Christmas is a time for children, I always say.'

Kitty looked at her in astonishment.

'I must be getting along too,' Mrs Harbinger said nervously when they returned to the drawing-room.

'Nonsense, you've nothing to go home to,' Martha told her brusquely.

'Well, I—er.'

'And there might be a parcel for you on the tree,' Martha said, to clinch the matter.

The presents were still piled around the Christmas tree, for they always waited until the afternoon before opening them. When she was little Kitty used to creep in and out all day, feeling the nobbly parcels, guessing what their strange shapes contained. They still excited her, even though she knew that, once opened, the mystery was lost for ever and inside there were only objects which would grow familiar before spring came.

This year there was one great luxury: it was a torch, big and silver, from her father. She turned it on and off and when nobody was about turned out the lights in the hall and went upstairs by torchlight.

'Whatever are you doing?' Gwendolen asked, coming out of her bedroom. 'I thought the lights must have failed.'

'Isn't it time to get ready to go to the Deedes yet?' Kitty asked.

'We can't very well until Mrs Harbinger goes. Looking forward to it, Kitty?'

'I can't wait,' Kitty replied, almost shivering with excitement. Going to the Deedes was the highlight of Christmas Day. They had done so ever since they came to Beckgate, and it was always warm and homely, and fun, with marvellous games and lots to eat.

'Well, I really must be going,' Mrs Harbinger was saying to Martha as they went back into the drawing-room. Diffidently she raised herself an inch or two out of the armchair. Then to Kitty's dismay, sank back again.

'It has been a pleasure having you,' Martha said.

The note of dismissal was clear enough. Mrs Harbinger raised herself again more purposefully and this time completed the operation and stood up.

'Thank you very much, Mrs Langdon,' she said as they stood in the hall.

'We couldn't have let you be all alone—not on Christmas Day,' Martha said.

'You are very kind.'

'It is what we are here for,' Martha informed her.

They watched as the plump little figure made its way up the drive. Mrs Harbinger walked slowly at first and then more quickly. She was longing to get back to her empty little house. The fire would be out and the room cold, but she would have it all to herself. For years she had had to work hard at Christmas, looking after her family, cooking huge meals though she herself was not interested in food, arranging games for the children although she did not really like noise. Then her husband had died and the children had all gone away. This year she had resisted their efforts to come and cheer her up, for she just wanted to be left alone in peace to enjoy Christmas all by herself.

For the first time in her life, she had decided, she would spend her Christmas in the way she herself liked. But Martha Langdon she had been unable to resist. She sighed and hurried on her way.

Martha shut the front door.

'A poor bit of a thing,' she said to Gwendolen.

'Oh, I think she's rather sweet, Mummy. She's shy, and I expect she found us a bit of an ordeal.'

'I'm sure I don't know why anyone should find me an ordeal.'

'No, I meant . . .'

'Never mind that now. Our Lord said we must comfort the widow, and I've done my duty. Now we must get ready to go to the Deedes. It is rude to be late.'

They all went upstairs. As they prepared to go to the Deedes' party, Mrs Harbinger, happy at last, was squatting in front of her own hearth. The room was very cold, so she still had on her coat, as she lifted the husks of dead cinders out on to a newspaper and prepared to light another fire.

CHAPTER THIRTEEN

As they walked through the village to the Deedes' house for the annual Christmas party, Kitty shone her torch into the sky. 'Just think,' she said, 'if I had done that three years ago, Old Phipps would have had me cast into a dungeon.'

Old Phipps had been in charge of the blackout during the war. Every night he and his band used to creep about the village, in and out among the darkened houses to see if a glimmer of light might be detected. If so much as a chink appeared from under the blackout boards or between the heavy curtains he would bang on the offending window and shout, 'Don't you know there's a war on? This bloody place looks like Crystal Palace.'

At first Kitty had thought that the enemy was Old Phipps; all the fear and tension of the grown-ups seemed to concentrate itself into the need to darken the house at night because of this terrifying, powerful little man who only appeared at dusk. If they allowed a chink of light to escape from their refuge she understood that they would be in his ruthless hands. Later, when she realized that the danger was not this intensely personal one but only from remote enemy aeroplanes, she felt tremendous relief; she had imagined something far worse than a few bombs.

'There's no need to have that thing on,' her mother said sharply. 'It's a clear night and anyway, you've managed without a torch for fourteen years.'

Kitty flashed her torch in a great arc across the sky as a final act of defiance to the memory of old Phipps, who since the end of the war had turned into a harmless old man with arthritis. Then she did as her mother said and turned it off.

The Deedes' house was ablaze with light. There were lanterns up the drive, floodlights on the lawn and an illuminated Christmas tree by the front door.

'No wonder there is an electricity shortage,' Martha said as they climbed up the steps, and rang the bell.

Grace Deedes flung wide the door and held her arms open. 'Welcome, welcome,' she said in her deepest and warmest tones. 'A very happy Christmas to you all. God bless us every one,' she added, in a somewhat inappropriate echo of Tiny Tim.

She kissed Martha, shook hands with Charles, kissed Gwendolen and embraced Kitty. She felt soft and downy, Kitty thought, and smelled a bit sweet and stuffy, like custard powder. When she had finished welcoming them, Wally was revealed standing behind her, ready to take their coats.

'You all know our Bishop, of course,' Grace said as she led them into the drawing-room. 'And this is his son, Mark, and his daughter-in-law, Beatrice, who are spending Christmas with him. We all prefer Christian names, don't we?'

They shook hands. Mark, who was a schoolmaster in a northern public school, was a less worldly edition of his father. His wife Beatrice was tall, beautiful and distant. Her remoteness was due as much to deafness as to natural inclination. She did not, as some deaf people do, develop a habit of agreement for fear of having misunderstood, but rather cultivated a certain aggressiveness of speech which, combined with deafness, often lent baffling illogicality to her pronouncements. As the years passed, her husband found this increasingly irritating; what had at first struck him as amusing now seemed embarrassing. Unworldly though he was, he realized that it was not a characteristic that any board of governors would consider helpful in a headmaster's wife.

'Now I must get you good people a drink,' Grace said. 'Wally dear, you will see to that, won't you?'

As Wally withdrew, Grace explained to Martha, 'The Charlesworths have been so kind. They have had the twins for the afternoon so that I have been able to make a few little preparations for tonight.'

'They were no trouble,' the Bishop assured her. 'They spent most of the time with young Satan up in the loft.'

'My father-in-law,' Beatrice cut in, 'is referring to my son Matthew, whose name he seldom uses, although he himself gave it to him in baptism.'

'My dear Beatrice,' the Bishop replied, 'I should hesitate to use the name of a blessed apostle in such a connection. You see,' he said turning to Charles, 'my grandson goes to a very free kind of school.'

'He uses the word in its libertarian, not its financial, sense,' Beatrice explained.

'They will understand that,' her husband said. 'It is an accepted educational principle that as far as discipline goes the more you pay the less you get.'

'So in return for large sums of money,' the Bishop went on, 'he is taught to call adults by their Christian names, beat up junior masters and use expressions which one expects to encounter only in the Bible.'

They laughed.

'So you're having a rough Christmas, are you, Bishop?" Charles asked.

'I keep my strength up by remembering what a horrid child I was myself. Boys will be boys; one grows philosophical.'

'My father-in-law fails to distinguish between generalizing and philosophizing,' Beatrice commented.

'You all know my two boys, of course,' Grace said as her husband and sons came into the room carrying the drinks. Thomas and Gerald Deedes were so much alike that it was hard to believe that they were not twins. Although there was eighteen months between them, they were of similar build, medium height and both had dark hair and obliging expressions.

'Would you like a drink, sir?' one of them asked the Bishop.

'I'll have a dry sherry, thank you, my boy. I only hope that it will not happen to me as it did in the story.'

'What was that?'

'A bishop arrived at a party and was offered and accepted a sherry. Later a second bishop arrived—one of the teetotal sort—and he stepped back in horror when offered the sherry, saying, "I would sooner commit adultery." Whereupon the first bishop looked up rather regretfully and said, "I did not know that we were being offered an alternative." '

They all laughed; even Martha smiled, since it was Christmas and he was a bishop.

Kitty listened to them.

'Would you like to go up to the twins, dear?' Grace asked her.

'Matthew is up there with them. Or would you rather stay down here with the grown-ups?'

Kitty hesitated, knowing that she did not belong anywhere. Then, 'Please can I stay here?' she asked humbly.

'Of course, dear,' Grace said. She took her by the hand. 'Wally dear, we must think of just the right drink for this young lady.'

'Orange juice will do for her,' Martha said, raising her long nose from a gin and lime.

In the end they gave her tomato juice with a few drops of sherry; it spoiled the taste but she enjoyed the sensation. Even more she enjoyed standing among the grown-ups, moving from group to group, ignored but absorbed, listening and watching, but not having to participate.

'Well, Charles,' Grace was saying to her father, 'what great case are you working on now? Or should I not ask? Wally dear, Charles' glass needs filling.'

'Well, Grace, now that I . . .'

'You see, I'm sure it's wrong of me but I always feel a little glow of pride when I read your name in the paper. That's right, Wally dear, and I think I noticed Beatrice's . . .'

'I have left the Bar,' Charles said firmly. 'So I am afraid that you won't be seeing my name in the papers so much.'

'Oh, how *sad*. Martha didn't mention it. I am so sorry, though of course I am sure that you are going on to even greater things.'

'Different things, certainly.'

Martha was talking to Beatrice Charlesworth.

'I hear you are coming to stay for Easter, Mrs Charlesworth?'

'No, I was not a teacher, Mrs Langdon. I was a nursing sister.'

'A great public service, nurses do,' Martha replied imperturbably.

'I did private nursing. In fact, I met my husband when I was nursing his father, who had a severe illness shortly after his wife died and required to be nursed at home.'

'And very hard she worked, too, Mrs Langdon,' her husband said, coming up, as he often did, aware that his wife's conversations could disconcert the uninitiated. 'In the end she was running the house, cooking for me, nursing father, even washing all kinds of vestments and regalia.'

'The male genitalia is a triple absurdity which we will not discuss,' his wife said and walked away.

The Bishop came up to Martha. 'And how has Christmas been, Mrs Langdon?' he asked kindly.

'Hard work, as usual, Bishop.'

'You are well named. I always feel poor Martha gets short shrift in the Bible. If it weren't for you Marthas, the Marys of this life would find themselves short of a chair to sit on.'

'Well, I must say I don't find much time for sitting, except in the sermon, of course.'

'We must ask young Mabey to make them longer in that case.'

'Well now,' Grace interrupted. 'Now that we have all had a drink, shall we start the games? Are you sure that you won't stay, Bishop?'

'Quite sure, my dear Mrs Deedes. My old bones won't stand for too much dashing about; I shall take them off home to bed. But I have enjoyed this happy time with you all. Mark insists upon driving me home, but he'll be back shortly. Don't let me disturb the party.'

'Not at all. But first of all the twins have a little surprise for you. Come along everybody.'

The guests all followed her out of the drawing-room. In the hall Matthew joined them; a quick, bright-eyed boy with dark, curly hair, there was indeed something Pan-like if not actually Satanic about him. The twins had followed him as far as the landing.

Everything was going according to plan; Grace beamed at her guests. The Bishop and his son, ready coated, stood with the others in the hall.

'Now the twins are going to sing us a carol before they go to bed,' Grace said. For the first time since they had arrived, she was feeling truly well-disposed towards the twins, for she had hardly seen them all day and they did make an enchanting pair as they stood there on the landing. It was a wide, deep landing, almost like a stage. On it the twins waited patiently. With their long, fair hair and big blue innocent eyes they looked indeed like angels. Each wore a blue dressing gown over her nightie and each held a white and fluffy toy lamb. When their aunt gave the signal they began to sing 'Away in a Manger' in sweet, high voices.

When they had finished, Grace turned to the Bishop, her big brown eyes moist. 'Forgive me,' she said, 'but it is so touching to hear these childish voices. I always feel that Christmas is for the little ones, don't you? Bless them.' Then she raised her voice and sang out, 'Now my little darlings, run along to bed. I'll come up and we'll say our prayers and then I'll tuck you both up in your little beds for the night.'

Claire smiled back. 'All right, auntie,' she said obediently. 'We'll just go and have a piss first, shall we?'

There was complete silence in the hall. Gerald and Thomas looked stricken and their mother's face lost its serenity. For a moment Kitty, watching her, hoped that she might bawl out something like, 'Shut up or I'll tan your backsides,' but she said nothing.

The silence was broken by Beatrice, who asked, 'Why are we waiting here? What did the small girl say?' Then, in the business of finding paper and pencils and preparing to play games, the dreadful moment was lost.

Outside it had started to snow. In the fine white flakes the Bishop was leaning against the gate post heaving with pent-up laughter. ' "We'll just go and—" oh, my goodness, and such an angel child too! Oh, poor dear Grace,' and he began to gurgle and roar again, tears pouring down his smooth plump cheeks.

'Oh, come, father, it wasn't as funny as all that,' his son put in, afraid that he would have a heart attack.

'Oh, yes it was, just as funny as all that,' the Bishop replied, getting into the car at last. 'The trouble with you is that you're losing your sense of humour. I wonder what else Matthew taught them.'

'Matthew? Oh Lord, I hope not.'

'I expect Grace is in for a lively time,' said the Bishop, beginning to laugh again, as his son drove anxiously through the snow.

Grace Deedes was good at entertaining. Her Christmas party always followed the same pattern. There were games at first which necessitated running into every room of the big warm house, rushing up and down stairs, bumping into each other and apologizing and generally getting everybody mixed up and friendly. Kitty revelled in it all and in the luxury of the fitted carpets and central heating and huge fires. Wally had spent the morning carrying buckets of coal and baskets of logs about the house and fires blazed in most of the rooms, even in the bedroom where they went to tidy themselves before supper.

In the dining-room the tables were arrayed with plates of cold turkey and ham and baked potatoes and dishes of salad and great bowls of trifle and cream. They took up plates and forks and helped themselves while Grace encouraged them to take more, assuring everybody that there was much more waiting in the kitchen. She always produced lavish amounts of food; even in the war she had managed to do it. They had always marvelled at it. Stories circulated the village of how she exchanged coal from Wally's business friends for turkeys from local farmers for whom she obtained pig food in return for hams. She had organized a black market with such homely innocence that nobody had questioned her methods. Kitty could remember her mother's strictures upon Mrs. Deedes. Martha herself had not been above going to a certain farm for eggs which she brought home in a basket covered with sticks and rhubarb leaves, in case they should meet anybody as they walked back across the fields, but even that was done with resentment and secrecy, without Grace's bland assurance. Grace always seemed to assume that she was doing God's will and somehow feeding the five thousand.

After supper they always sat around the fire in the drawing-room and played what Grace called 'our quiet games'. Tonight the quiet game consisted of sending out pairs who had to act historical couples, whose identities the rest then tried to guess. Matthew and Kitty were sent out first.

'I know,' Matthew said, immediately they got outside the door. 'We'll be the brides-in-the-bath murderer and his victim. I expect they've got an old bath somewhere.'

Though not altogether delighted with the idea of being Matthew's victim, Kitty joined in the hunt for a bath. In the kitchen they found a washing basket which the murderer thought would be too small. Rushing into the scullery he almost crashed into an old tin bath hanging on the wall.

'Just the thing, just the thing,' he called out in delight. 'I know, we fill it with water and drag it into the drawing-room and you get into it and I come in and hold your nose and push you under and keep you there until you're dead.'

'But I can't get undressed in front of all those people.'

'Blast it,' Matthew said impatiently and then with inspiration asked, 'got a swim suit with you?'

'No. Not with me.'

'I know. Wait a minute.'

He rushed back into the drawing-room. The guests were sitting round the fire.

'Have you a swim suit, Mrs Deedes?' he asked.

'Well, yes, Matthew dear.'

'Could I borrow it?'

'What, now? Do you mean for you to wear?'

'No, Kitty, of course,' he said with ill-concealed impatience at the slowness of comprehension of the adult world.

Grace went upstairs and reappeared with a large red, white and blue swim suit.

'Thanks,' Matthew said briefly and rushed back to the kitchen.

Kitty held it up doubtfully. 'But it's ridiculous,' she said. 'It looks as if she was expecting to be drowned. And anyway, we can't drag that great heavy bath full of water into the drawing-room; it'll slop all over the carpet. Couldn't we do this act dry?'

Matthew hesitated; he felt the weight of the bath and found he could only just move it even when it was empty.

'I know,' he said. 'I think I've got it. I'll just take a jug of water and pour it into your mouth and so drown you symbolically.'

When eventually they reappeared in the drawing-room, Kitty was wearing a trousseau dress made of an assortment of cloaks and overalls, on the arm of Matthew resplendent in a bowler hat, gym shoes and a butcher's apron, which Wally used for washing up. They stood arm in arm smiling, then climbed up imaginary stairs and, while Kitty removed a cloak or two, Matthew, with looks of diabolical cunning and many conspiratorial glances at the audience, turned on the taps for her at the top of the rusty old bath. Then Kitty stepped in, feeling the water carefully first with her toe and then her elbow, smiled gratefully at her husband and stepped into the bath.

'Marvellous, both of them,' Grace murmured to Beatrice. 'Your son is a natural actor.'

'Your sons seem fond of their parents and that is a nice characteristic too,' Beatrice replied.

Kitty lay with what she supposed to be an expression of married bliss on her face until Matthew reappeared with the jug and leering villainously. Then he grasped her firmly by the nose and poured the water down her open gullet. She began to roll her eyes and choke.

'Sh, it's a silent charade,' Matthew hissed at her as he poured.

'Stop it, you young idiot—or you really will kill her,' Charles suddenly shouted. But Matthew was so carried away by the drama of the role that he continued to pour and gloat until his father strode on stage and removed the jug from his hand.

Kitty spluttered, rubbed her arm across the face and climbed out of the bath. 'Have you guessed what we were?' she asked.

'You nearly weren't anyone, except a corpse,' her father told her cheerfully.

'That was the whole point,' Matthew said, partly exasperated and partly delighted that somebody was getting warm at last.

'Crippen, dear, and er—Mrs Crippen,' Grace suggested.

Wally was looking gloomily at the trail of dirt and cobwebs that marked the path of the old tin bath across the carpet.

'Wasn't that the bath we kept half a pig in during the war?' Gerald asked; it was his one indiscretion of the evening.

'Nonsense, dear,' his mother said with unusual asperity.

'Yes, you're right. There's salt around the rim,' Matthew remarked, scraping some rusty crystals on to the carpet. 'No, not Crippen, Mrs Deedes. He just poisoned his wife and put her under the floorboards. I never thought of that,' he said regretfully to Kitty. 'We could do that next year.'

'Were you perhaps Henry VIII and one of his wives?' Thomas asked.

'Nonsense, boy,' Mark Charlesworth said, forgetting for a moment that it was not term time. 'There was nothing so personal about Henry's methods. He did it at one remove. No, I know who you were meant to be, Matthew. I wish I could remember the chap's name. My memory is getting awful.'

'Your mind is furring up, Mark,' Beatrice remarked absently. 'It needs scaling, like a kettle.'

'I think he was just called The Brides-in-the-Bath Murderer,' Gwendolen said. 'I don't think he had a name.'

'Of course he had a name. Everybody has,' Matthew objected. 'His parents would give him a name like an ordinary person. They couldn't know he was going to be so successful.'

Beatrice, who appeared to have opted out of the game, suddenly said, 'George Joseph Smith, commonly known as Brides-in-the-Bath Smith. I have seen him at Madame Tussaud's.'

Everyone made the sort of noises that people make when they discover what was on the tip of their tongue, and then applauded.

'Well, you were splendid, anyway,' Grace said. 'We'll put you both on the stage when you are grown up. Wally dear, perhaps you would help Matthew to take that bath back?'

Wally removed the bath and swept up the rust and cobwebs from the carpet while his wife announced that they would now play charades and they started to pick sides. 'Then we'll have some mince pies and wind up with Murder as usual,' she said. 'Oh dear, I think the fire's getting a bit low, and the scuttle is empty.'

'I'll see to it,' Charles offered, picking up the coal scuttle.

'Oh no, don't you do that, Charles. You are far too good to be spared from the charades. Wally will see to it, won't you, dear?'

It seemed to Kitty that Wally, as he took up the coal scuttle and log basket, cast a look of hatred at her father, before making for the door.

For Kitty, charades were the highlight of the evening; there was something reassuring about this predictable, funny world they created. Christmas after Christmas they chose words, dressed up, astonished each other with their ingenuity. Year after year there were operating scenes in which her father drew yards and yards of sausages out of somebody's body as it lay rolled up on a table cloth on the tea trolley. Year after year Grace Deedes appeared in one of her sons' school cap and blazer inexplicably and gloriously funny, so that it was almost a relief when she finally skipped out of the drawing-room at the end of her Billy Bunter act because it had begun to hurt to laugh so much.

As usual, Gwendolen played parts like Helen of Troy, Mary Queen of Scots and Jane Grey. Thomas and Gerald performed straightforward but necessary roles like pall bearers and male nurses. Her father was both producer and chief actor, creating characters, tossing off witticisms, improvising whole scenes, casting people with genius: her mother and Wally Deedes, for example, with tricolor scarves on their heads and ancient spectacles on their noses, made a marvellously evil-looking pair of tricoteuses at the foot of the guillotine, which was a saw suspended on two rather flimsy bits of string and manipulated by Matthew, who, as he let it drop, simultaneously tossed a cabbage into a pillow case and shrieked, while Mr Charlesworth did his Sidney Carton act. Mrs Charlesworth was surprising too; beautiful, detached, as if disdaining to play such childish games, she would then join in with remarks which showed a complete disregard for what the rest of the characters were doing or saying, but which were always funny and somehow apt.

'My goodness, it's nearly tomorrow,' Grace said at the end of the second round. 'We must have some coffee and mince pies. Wally dear, perhaps you could help me? Thank you, boys. Yes, you two run along with your father. You know where the mince pies are, don't you, Wally?'

'In the oven,' said Wally, who had put them there twenty minutes before.

Kitty sat on a stool by the fire, watching the pink and glowing world that was within it crumble and reshape itself. The mince pies were hot and spicy and exciting, her coffee sweet, and life was good; this year she would not be frightened during Murder. It was only a game.

Grace was explaining the rules. 'Now let me see, what happens. We need a pack of cards, I think. Wally dear . . .' But Wally was already out of the door before she could ask him.

When he returned with the pack she began to look through them.

'Now, we need—oh dear, I can't remember. Charles, you must explain—you're the legal expert.'

'Here are twelve cards,' Charles began. 'Now we must each take one. If you find you have the ace, you must admit it and you are the detective, but if you have the king, say nothing. You are the murderer. Then we all go away to any part of the house and hide or move about quietly and the murderer kills somebody. When the victim screams nobody may move except the murderer. The detective then turns on all the lights and inspects the scene of the crime. Then we all come back here and the detective asks questions. Everyone must tell the truth except the murderer, who can lie unless he is asked outright if he did it. The detective can only ask directly if someone did it three times. All clear?'

It was. The twelve cards were fanned out. As always Kitty prayed she would be allowed to be detective or murderer, and not have to creep around in the dark waiting for it to happen. She picked the three of clubs. Charlesworth confessed to being the detective. Kitty looked around at the others: one was now to be feared. She began to feel cold. She wished she knew which, but they were all looking nonchalant. It's only a game, she said to herself as they all left the drawing-room, it's only a game.

Every light was off. She groped her way towards the stairs, felt the banister and began climbing up. Once she touched a hand and nearly cried out in horror. She reached the landing where the twins had sung. She could hear somebody breathing as she crept past. She felt her way to the next flight of stairs. She knew that the first door on the right was a lavatory. If she could lock herself in there she would be safe. Suddenly, as she looked up, she saw a tiny circle of light, a red glow at the top of the stairs. She froze. It was waiting for her, somebody with a cigarette. Her heart thumped; it's only a game, she told it, but it went on thumping. Suddenly the light vanished. He had put it behind his back, she thought. Or perhaps it was a she. She tried to think who smoked, but could no longer identify these shapes that crept about and breathed and could not be seen in the dark, as anybody at the Christmas party. She moved forward again, feeling each stair with her hands to see if anybody's feet should be in the way. There was nobody. She reached the top of the stairs. She felt for the door. It was slightly open. She pushed it gently and slid inside. Very quietly she shut the door behind her and, feeling for the bolt, as silently locked it. Then she turned round leaning against the locked door, her eyes closed in relief. She opened them to see the red tip of the cigarette in front of her, like an eye watching her. It moved towards her. She heard herself scream again and again.

'Lights on,' somebody called, and all the lights were turned on.

'That's very odd,' she heard Gwendolen say. 'I'm the murderer and I haven't killed anybody yet.'

They all converged on the drawing-room.

'There seems to be some confusion,' the detective remarked. 'A death wish on the part of some eager victim.'

'I'm so sorry,' Kitty said miserably. 'I thought I was going to be murdered.'

It seemed so silly now. They were all friends and it was only a game.

'Well, I was the only one near you and I didn't touch you,' Beatrice remarked, throwing her cigarette into the fire.

'Well, I suggest you pick again, but I shall go on being detective, because it's a nice comfortable job,' Mark Charlesworth said.

'Honestly, you are a chump, Kitty,' Matthew said. 'You mustn't scream until you're murdered. Don't you know the rules yet?'

'Charles,' Martha said, 'it's ridiculous to let that child play—look at her face. She's as white as a sheet. She must stay down here with the detective.'

'Oh no, I love it. *Please* let me play. I'm not a bit white, really I'm not.'

Her father took her hand. 'We'll stay together,' he said quietly. They chose cards again and once more moved out into the hall. 'Let's go and hide in the bathroom,' she said. 'I know, there's a nice little corner by the airing cupboard behind the door.' She took his hand and led him with great confidence up the stairs and felt for the second door. They went in and sat with their backs against the airing cupboard and feet pressed against the door. 'There now,' she said, feeling quite safe as she pressed herself up against his shoulder, 'now nobody can get in.'

'Listen, Kitty,' he whispered back. 'I want you to be sensible. Stay here by yourself for a moment. I'm going out just for a second and I'll tap the first person I bump into on the shoulder and come straight back. The lights will be on by then.'

'But why?' she said, clinging to his arm.

'Because I picked the king, goose.'

'You mean you're the murderer—' she asked, pushing his arm away in horror.

'It's only a game, darling. I just picked the card. Now I'm off.'

But it was too late. The horror of finding that the one she

had clung to for protection was the murderer himself overwhelmed her and she began to scream.

'All right,' he said. 'We'll say I murdered you,' and he switched on the lights.

Mark Charlesworth raced up the stairs, all the lights were on now. Kitty lay down on the floor obediently.

'Well, my task is easy,' Charlesworth said as they reassembled in the drawing-room. 'As I came up the stairs I caught a glimpse of the murderer comforting the victim. A most considerate murderer: he even stopped to turn the light on for me.'

'Honestly, Kitty,' Matthew said furiously. 'You've gone and mucked it again. You're hopeless. I jolly well wish I'd been the murderer and I'd do you in good and proper.'

'That's enough, Matthew,' his father said sharply. 'I'm not surprised you've got her terrified; with you around there might well be a real murder.'

'We must go soon,' Martha said.

'Yes, it's tomorrow already,' Charles agreed, looking at Kitty's white face.

'A last drink,' Grace said. 'Wally dear, you and the boys will bring the glasses in, won't you? Mrs Wall will have washed them and left them on a tray.'

Kitty sat quietly by the fire, wishing she could be swallowed up in its flames. She was still shivering but felt burning hot with shame. It wasn't Matthew that made her afraid. It was the dark and not knowing and the feeling that everybody smiled but nobody could be trusted, that one couldn't be sure of anyone. It just didn't seem like a game when you didn't know who your friends were. She couldn't explain it, not even to herself. She supposed it was just panic.

As they left the house, they were astonished to find that thick snow lay on the ground and more was falling. Kitty looked at it in amazement: all the time they had been playing it had been falling steadily, silently, and they had been quite unaware of the transformation that had been taking place in the outside world. The light shone out of the door and lit up the whole white scene, the thickened branches of the trees, the caps of snow on the tops of the gate posts. They called good night and set off down the thickly-covered road through the village. The air was dense with snow; there seemed to be some link between all the flakes as they hung gauzily in the sky, turning and swirling, falling and rising, seeming never actually to fall to the ground. There was ice under the snow; Gwendolen pretended to skate.

'It was a lovely party, wasn't it?' she said.

'Yes, it's always a good one,' her father agreed. 'Grace certainly knows how to make everyone warm and welcome.'

'She can afford it,' Martha said sharply. She did not approve of central heating; there was something immoral about it.

'It's a comfy sort of house,' Kitty remarked.

'Comfort! That's all you young people think about nowadays. As for those fitted carpets, I wouldn't have them if they were given to me. You can't even take them up for spring cleaning. Disgusting. I hate to think what it's like under Grace Deedes' carpets.'

Kitty knew she was going to laugh, so skated on after Gwendolen. Hand in hand they ski-ed and skidded through the empty village street, the snow stinging their cheeks.

'Oh, it's perfect, perfect,' Kitty said as they paused for breath by the gate.

'And it's Boxing Day,' Gwendolen remarked. 'So really I can say that tomorrow I go to London.'

Suddenly all the joy went out of Kitty's world and the awful reality of the solitude to come seemed to swallow her up. While Gwendolen skated cheerfully back to her parents, she opened the gate and walked slowly down the drive, her footsteps making a lonely track through the snow.

CHAPTER FOURTEEN

IT snowed all that night and in the morning snow was piled up deep against the walls of the house and lay so thickly across the windows that they seemed to have shutters on the outside. The snow was almost blue in the bright sun and she was glad when her mother sent them off to take some things to an old widow who lived on a farm at the foot of Arbenside.

'Let's go across the fields for the first part,' she said to Gwendolen. 'It'll be more fun than going all the way along the lane.' She was determined to forget that Gwendolen was leaving tomorrow.

'Next Christmas,' Gwendolen said as she climbed the stile into the field, 'I'm going to go skiing. I shall take a vac job in the summer and make lots of money, like I did last year. Oh, isn't it heavenly?'

The field lay in front of them, smoothed out by the snow and glittering in the sunshine. Gwendolen began to leap across the field. 'Bliss was it in that dawn to be alive,' she called back, jumping at each word.

'But to be young was very heaven,' Kitty added, jumping into her footprints.

'So they do teach you something at "that place" as Mummy calls it.'

Kitty laughed. 'But it's true, Gwendolen, isn't it? About being young I mean. It must be absolutely horrible being old.'

'No need to sound so tragic; it's a long way off.'

'But to be all stiff and not to be able to jump about. To be thirty.'

'I shall be thirty in nine years' time.'

'And I'll be twenty-three. I wonder why it happens.'

'What?'

'Being so alive when you're young. Then people seem so dead

when they're grown up. Wouldn't it be awful if we just found out that once we were grown up we started to die? Perhaps once you've had children nature doesn't need you to live any more, so you go on walking about but really you're dead.'

'Do you think you could walk a bit more quickly while you work it all out?' Gwendolen enquired, opening the gate into the lane. 'We're supposed to be back for Boxing Day lunch.'

'But I don't know,' Kitty went on, not noticing the interruption. 'It would be marvellous to be grown up, all the same, and do whatever you liked. Goodness, look at the drifts.'

On each side of the lane the snow had been swept by the wind into huge drifts along the walls, leaving only a thin covering of crisp snow down the centre.

'Do you remember how we used to throw Ben into the drifts?' Gwendolen asked.

'And when we got home he used to have masses of tiny snowballs hanging off his coat?'

'And you used to pull them off and he'd snap?'

'Well, if we left them on he'd melt all over the kitchen floor and Mummy would be furious.'

There was silence for a while except for the crunching of the snow as their boots broke through its frozen surface.

'Do you remember that winter in the war when we were snowed up and the buses couldn't go into Pendlebury?'

'And we tried to walk and had to keep to the tops of the walls and if we missed we fell right into the drifts?'

'I was scared. It was all right for you—you were too little to know how dangerous it was. Those drifts were six or eight feet deep.'

'And then the snow-plough came and spoilt it all.'

'I had ten days off school all the same.'

'Wasn't the village on the news because they dropped food or something?'

'Oh yes. I remember that, because it was the time you were so upset because I told you that the man on the wireless didn't make up all the news himself.'

'It was awful. I'd always thought he was so wise and knew everything and just sat and told us all he knew every few hours; all about the Russian salvoes and names like Voroshilov. Then you said he didn't know it at all; just read it off a piece of paper.'

'Poor Kitty; I didn't know it was so important to you.'

'It was worse than finding out about Father Christmas.'

The lane began to climb the hillside and they stopped talking as they made their way up. At the top of the ridge they stood looking back. The village was hard to distinguish under the snow; just a series of humps at the foot of the encircling hills.

'What are we going to do about them, Mummy and Daddy, I mean?' Kitty asked abruptly.

'Do about them? What can we do? Honestly, Kitty, we can't alter them.'

'No, we learned that, didn't we?'

There had been a time about three years ago when they had decided that if they talked to each parent in turn they might persuade them to be reconciled. It seemed naïve now. They had talked very solemnly to their father and he had promised to try again, but then they had not dared to approach their mother.

'But at least now we know that they ought to be parted, so we can work for that.'

'I saw Virginia last term,' Gwendolen said. 'You know she has known them both for years and she says she thinks they are both very good people but it's just that they should never be under the same roof.'

'I know. I wonder how *she* does.'

Gwendolen smiled. 'Most people would wonder how *you* do. You're fourteen; she's about forty.'

'Oh, age! No, I meant without being as close to them as we've been.'

'Well, we think they're special, but grown-ups know that it's quite usual. There are probably thousands of cases just like theirs.'

'*Cases?*'

'Yes, that's all it is. Virginia says there are lots of couples who just bring out the worst in each other—destroy each other—and who should be kept apart. The only trouble is that the law doesn't seem to understand that.'

'Daddy says that they might change the law.'

'The trouble is that it takes so long.'

'Gwendolen, do you sometimes feel that there isn't very long? That he can't go on like this, can't wait for the law to be changed, I mean?'

'All dramatic again, aren't you? Well, he'll have to wait. But I expect it'll change in the end.'

'Gwendolen, why don't people like Virginia say it to her? She might listen to them; she likes Virginia better than us, anyway.'

'Because they know she doesn't want to hear it.'

'How do you mean?'

'Well, she's useful to them. She was with Virginia last term, you know, when Virginia's mother-in-law was ill and the kids had to be looked after, so Mummy went and stayed for a month. Virginia said she was glad of the help but she nearly drove her potty—unliveable with, she said she was. She said it made her realize what it must have been like for Daddy all these years.'

'Well, why doesn't she tell her?'

'Well, it's obvious. If you tell somebody they're unliveable with and therefore ought to be divorced they're less likely to come and nurse your mother-in-law and look after your kids. Be practical.'

'But it's so unfair. Nobody ever tells her the truth. I know she talks to some of them about it, and they all think like Virginia really, but they go on telling her she's a saint and so good and it makes her even more determined about the divorce. She doesn't see it as a problem between two human beings; just good versus evil—herself being the good, of course.'

'Look, Kitty. I know you're right. We both know it and so does Daddy but you can't expect other people not to put their own interests first.'

'Yes, I can.'

Suddenly she took her sister's hand. 'Oh, Gwendolen, must you go tomorrow?'

'Yes. I've masses of things to do before next term. Clothes to get, all kinds of things. Daddy asked me to stay on with you here, but honestly, Kitty, it's quite impossible. Never mind, it's not long now before you go back to school.'

Not much comforted by this thought, Kitty did not reply for a while. Then she said, 'Gwendolen, *please* couldn't you try to talk to her? She'd take more notice of you.'

'She doesn't take any notice of anyone.'

'But you could just *try*.'

'Why should I? She might be useful to me one day.'
'Gwendolen!'
'Only teasing.'

Mrs Braithwaite's cottage was built into the side of Arbenside and under the snow seemed almost to be part of the hill. They left the lane and walked up the little path whose edges were marked by a series of mounds, which were curiously shaped pieces of limestone now buried under the snow. They knocked at the door.

Mrs Braithwaite called to them to come in. They opened the door and pulled aside the thick curtain that hung on the other side of it. Coming in from the glare of the sun and snow they could at first scarcely make out the shape of Mrs Braithwaite sitting by the fire, for the room was dark and musty, with much brown paint and heavy dark furniture. The windows were small and set deep in the walls which were four feet thick. The cottage was designed to keep out the wind and the snow, rather than to let in the light. On the wall opposite the door was a clock with a very loud tick, a warming pan and a big china cupboard whose glass doors were decorated with pressed leaves. The flagged floor was almost covered with rag mats. A kettle sizzled on the hob. Mrs Braithwaite was sitting in the rocking chair by the fire cleaning the brasses. Her teeth were on the table beside her.

She was a very old lady; her black skirt reached almost to the ground and her thin hair disappeared under a little blue and white mob cap. The face beneath it was lively although thin and worn.

'Come in,' she said. 'Don't stand there.'

She reached for her teeth and popped them between her sunken jaws. 'I don't bother with them unless I've got company,' she said. 'They're a bit big.' The teeth, as she talked, made a clackety sound as if in agreement.

'Sit yourselves down, I've nearly done the brasses. Then I'll be making a cup o' tea,' she went on, the teeth echoing each phrase. She gave a final rub to a long brass poker and set it back on the hearth.

'Don't bother with tea, Mrs Braithwaite,' Gwendolen said politely. 'We've got to get back.'

'And 'ow's mother?'

'Very well, thank you. She sent you this mincemeat and some bottled fruit.'

'Aye, she's kind is your mother, she's a grand lass. Tell 'er I'll enjoy them.' As she talked she gathered up her cleaning things. Her hands were black with the polish and moved like little claws among the polishes and cloths.

'Aye, she's grand is your mother,' she said again. 'Last time you came Mr Braithwaite was 'ere, weren't 'e?'

'Yes, he was.'

Kitty remembered him, sitting on the edge of the settle, his hands pressed on his knees. He was a big, very clean-looking old man with fine white hair and a pink unlined face, who always knew what the weather was going to do.

'We 'ad a job getting 'im down,' Mrs Braithwaite said. 'Stairs is so bendy.'

They all looked at the spiral stairs that wound their way up from the far corner of the room.

'They 'ad to up-end 'im,' his widow went on. 'Fair shook 'im about a bit, they did, too. I telled 'em to use drop 'ole but they wouldna'.'

Kitty looked up. In the ceiling just above her head was a trapdoor.

''is Dad came down that way,' Mrs Braithwaite went on, nodding towards the trapdoor. 'And no doubt 'is Grandad too, but I don't recall it. It would 'ave been good enough for 'im too, but that Gabriel's a know-all and wouldn't pay any 'eed to what I telled 'im.'

'Gabriel Cross, the undertaker's son, you mean?'

'Aye, that's t'lad, but 'e's not really in 'is Dad's undertaking shop any more. 'e went to Removal in Pendlebury and fancies 'isself as a hexpert. Aye, that's what 'e calls 'isself, a hexpert.'

Kitty avoided her sister's eye.

''e were only 'elping out at 'ome because it were weekend and 'is Dad were poorly. But I wouldn't 'ave 'im again. Wouldn't listen to ought I said about drop 'ole. Said 'e'd taken pianos down worse stairs than they. By the time 'e'd finished wi' my poor man I bet they both wished 'e'd kept to pianos.'

She suddenly laughed a shrill, merry cackle and thrust the kettle deep into the heart of the fire.

'Nay, but you must 'ave a drink o' tea to warm you up. I know it's cold today; I were out shakin' mats a while back and were nigh frozed.'

Kitty went to help her get the cups out, partly in order to look more closely at the cupboard. She loved all the collection of old things in the cottage. The leaves seemed to have been pressed on to the glass from the inside and then lacquered over, she observed as Mrs Braithwaite handed her the best cups. They were white with a gold band round the rim.

'It's nice to 'ave a bit o' company,' Mrs Braithwaite said, talking as she lifted the kettle off the fire and warmed the pot, then brewed the tea and covered it with a knitted red and brown tea cosy. 'I don't see many nowadays. Folks is all too busy. Your mother brings the church magazine, of course. There was a nice lady used to come in the war collecting war savings, but she's stopped coming now. Died maybe. It was nice, the war. Friendly like.'

The tea was dark orange and very hot. Kitty burnt her lips and spilled some tea into her saucer.

'Never mind, lass. I can see you were looking at my egg boiler.'

She reached up and took it off the mantelpiece. It was an egg-shaped silver container, so well made that the join of the lid was scarcely visible. Underneath was a little silver pan.

'How does it work?'

'You put the methylated into the little pan and set it alight after you've put the eggs in the boilin' water in top and when t'methylated is burnt out, eggs is done. You can put t'pan t'other road up and that's deeper so it takes longer and t'eggs is 'ard boiled. But nowadays folks use these new fangly egg timers instead.'

When they had finished their tea, Kitty carried the tray for her into the kitchen and put it down by the shallow stone sink.

She noticed more teeth in a bowl on the draining board.

Mrs Braithwaite, whose old eyes seemed to miss nothing, must have caught her glance. 'Them's Mr Braithwaite's,' she explained. 'That young Gabriel says, "Will you want me to be disposin' of these for you, since the deceased won't 'ave no further use for them?" ('e talks posh now 'e's in Removal in Pendlebury). "You leave them just where they are," I says. "'e may 'ave no further use for them, but I 'ave." I remember my mum found 'er man's were a better fit than 'er own, when 'e'd gone. It's always 'andy to 'ave a spare pair in the 'ouse. 'e always used my spectacles so I don't expect 'e'll mind if I 'ave a share in 'is teeth,' she ended with another merry, high-pitched cackle, as she showed them to the door.

She drew back the thick brown curtain and lifted the latch.

'Thank you for comin',' she said, 'it's been nice 'avin' a bit o' company.'

'Thank you for the tea.'

'And thank your mother, love,' she called after them as they walked down the path. 'She's grand, is your mother.'

CHAPTER FIFTEEN

KITTY put the bottles into the beds and felt her legs shake as she came downstairs. She felt wobbly and had a headache.

At supper time she looked anxiously at the plate her mother handed her. 'I'm not very hungry,' she said apologetically.

'Nonsense. You need it to keep warm. Good food's better than any central heating,' her mother said, putting another spoonful of fried potatoes on Kitty's plate.

'I went to see Tom about the taxi,' Gwendolen said, 'and he says he's to pick up people for the hall off that train so he's quite pleased to take us.'

'I expect he'll charge full fare just the same,' her mother put in. 'He's a real chip off the old block, he is.'

'Can't I come to see you off, then?' Kitty asked.

'If you're not up to eating supper, you'll not be up to seeing people off at the station tomorrow,' her mother told her.

'I expect they'll be able to squeeze you in,' her father said.

'I can walk back.'

'It's too far to walk by yourself,' he objected.

'Nonsense,' Martha cut in. 'It's less than two miles by the lane. She walks much further than that when it suits her. Of course she can walk back.'

Kitty was so delighted at the sudden switch of opinion that she started again on her supper.

'Don't push the food round your plate like that,' her mother said. 'There's thousands of children would be glad of that food you are so scornful of. Think about them for a change.'

'I'm not scornful. It's just that I've got a headache and don't feel hungry.'

'Oh, it's headache now, is it? When I was your age I was kept too busy to get headaches. Keep occupied, we were told,

Satan will find something for you to do otherwise. There's a lot in what the Christian Scientists say.'

'What do they say?'

'Mind over matter, mind over matter.'

'But what does it mean?'

'If you don't mind, it doesn't matter,' Charles put in.

Gwendolen and Kitty laughed.

Martha flushed angrily. 'Oh, I might have known you would be among the mockers, Charles, of course,' she said and began gathering up the plates very noisily.

'I'm not mocking. It was only a joke, Martha,' she heard her father reply as she carried the plates down into the kitchen. Once there, she could still hear snatches of her mother's reply.

'Bringing them up to mock . . . cynical . . . clever . . .'

'Poor kid, leave her alone, she looks pale.'

'Too much Christmas spoiling,' her mother was saying, as she and Gwendolen returned with the lemon meringue pie and plates.

'And let me tell you, Miss,' she said abruptly to Kitty. 'If you were well enough to play all those games last night, showing off in charades and such like, in front of everyone, you're well enough to sit up at table with your own family and behave yourself decently.'

The pastry seemed to go round and round in her mouth, she could only think that Gwendolen and Daddy were going away tomorrow and she would be left alone. Her throat felt constricted so that the food seemed to stick in a huge lump, and, when she swallowed, her eyes filled with tears. After supper her father said, 'Up to bed, Kitty, and I'll give you a couple of aspirins. We were very late last night.'

To her surprise her mother raised no objection beyond saying, 'And that gets both of you out of the washing up, I suppose.'

'I'll do the dishes,' Gwendolen said, 'and then I'll go to bed too, if you don't mind. We didn't get much sleep last night and I suppose I ought to pack tonight if we're to be off early tomorrow.'

Kitty could hear the excitement in her sister's voice. She turned and walked slowly upstairs.

'It's perishing in this room,' her father said, bringing in an electric fire. 'In you hop, I'll get the aspirins and then I'll read to you. What would you like?'

'You choose.'

He came back a little later with a glass of water, the aspirins and a book. She was in bed hugging the stone hot-water bottle.

'I don't think you've got a temperature,' he said, feeling her forehead, 'just tired. I've brought Dickens—in fact the best, *Tale of Two Cities*.'

She was glad. When he read aloud to her at night, he had a special rhythmic voice, not over-expressive, which suited the long Dickensian cadences and ironic turns of sentence. She lay and listened and the reading seemed to lap about her gently, reassuringly, until she observed with a kind of detached surprise that she was drifting off to sleep. He brought his chair over to the bedside and stroked her forehead as he read and, under the gentle pressure of his hand, her mind seemed to relax and she slept.

When she woke it was to hear voices in the hall; the familiar high-pitched, accusing voice of her mother, counterpointed by his deep, resigned one.

'Fire in the bedroom indeed!' her mother was saying. 'Pampering the child. No wonder the meter was racing round.'

'Now, Martha, you know that she's not pampered,' he replied in his extra-reasonable tone of voice, which was always a sign that his temper was at breaking point. 'And it wasn't on long anyway.'

'Leaving it up there so that I wouldn't know. The deceit of it!'

'Nonsense,' he replied angrily. 'I just didn't think to bring it down, that's all.'

'No, that's the trouble—you never do think.'

'I'll go and get the damned thing,' she heard him say.

She heard the door knob turn and he came quietly in. She lay very still, pretending to be asleep. He took the fire and went out with it. She heard him go downstairs and open and shut the drawing-room door.

She was wide awake now, her mind sharp-edged and alert as she listened to the rhythms of the argument from below. It was a solid, thick-walled old house and sounds did not normally carry from one room to another, but somehow she could always detect the sound of quarrelling, not what they were saying, but the rise and fall of disagreement. Her father at first made quiet, resigned responses, then her mother's attacks grew longer, higher-pitched, louder. Then came her father's longer replies. Sometimes it went on and on. Like the time she had brought it to an end with very unexpected results.

It was when she was still at school in Pendlebury where it had been intended that she should stay for the rest of her school life. She must have been eleven.

There had been a fair at Pendlebury to which her father had taken her, in the summer holidays. She climbed off a red and yellow horse on the roundabout to hear a newspaper man shouting that Japan had surrendered after some new kind of bomb had been dropped on a place with a queer name. Everyone had gone mad with joy and she was taken aback when her father looked grave.

'But they're our *enemies*,' she said.

'That's one label for them, yes. But they are also little children and their mothers who don't know any more about the war than you do. It's not just the ones that have been killed—thousands who were a long way from the bomb will have been horribly burnt and blinded.'

She tried to be sad, but could not. As they walked home she was full of relief, all bound up with the sounds of the fair and the feel of the sun which she had absorbed during the day and the smell of the summer evening. It was only when they got home and she saw her mother triumphant and elated and wearing her hat ready to go to a special church service of thanksgiving for the bomb that the truth of what he had said came home to her. She shut her eyes and imagined how it would be to be blind. Especially for a girl like herself who was afraid of the dark.

That evening her parents had supper outside in the garden and their voices floated up to her bedroom window.

'It's unpatriotic not to rejoice. I'm surprised at you,' her mother said. 'Your country's victory should delight you.'

'But the *price*, Martha. And it wasn't necessary; it could have been demonstrated anywhere. There was no need to incinerate a city. Even if there was, it's not something to rejoice over—and as for thanking God . . .'

'And you're making that child just as bad,' Martha went on as if he had not spoken. 'She's getting quite out of hand, always answering back.'

'I'm worried about her, Martha. She doesn't look happy; when she smiles it's only with her mouth, not her eyes. That's dreadful in a little girl.'

'Little girl! She's eleven. When I was her age nobody bothered about my eyes smiling, I can tell you.'

'I know, Martha, you had a hard childhood, but . . .'

'It did me no harm.'

They moved indoors then, and their voices became muffled. She could just catch the rise and fall, sharper than in friendly conversation, as phrase followed phrase.

'I must make them *stop*, I wish they'd stop,' she said to herself, suddenly feeling she could not bear to hear it a minute longer. There must be some way. No good to go down and ask them: that would only provoke the charge of cheekiness, of impossible behaviour.

Suddenly she knew what she must do: even her mother could not blame her for having a nightmare.

She arranged her pillows tidily and got ready to scream. No sound came out. She was quite surprised; she had not thought it would be so difficult just to sit up in bed alone and yell. She tried to imagine herself in a play, or that a burglar was climbing in at the window, but still she could not scream.

From downstairs the voices continued to rise and fall as the quarrel progressed. They just did not seem to be able to be together without quarrelling even for the few days a year when they met.

Suddenly she managed to produce a scream. Having done so once she was disinclined to stop; piercing scream followed piercing scream. The talk stopped immediately; she heard the drawing-room door flung open and both her parents dashing upstairs. Her father was first into the bedroom, switching on the light as he came in.

Her dramatic sense stood her in good stead; she let her screams subside and lay making little sobbing sounds, looked amazed and muttered, 'What? er—where?' and so on.

Her parents exchanged swift glances, both looking guilty. She had not expected that. They looked like a couple of conspirators caught in the act; they must both be blaming the screaming on their quarrelling.

'It must have been a nightmare,' her father said. He sat on the bed and put his arms around her. 'It's all right, pet, just a bad dream. I used to have them when I was a boy. You get yourself wide awake and then it'll go away and not come back.'

Her mother sat down on the other side of the bed.

'I'll take care of this, Charles,' she said severely. 'The child is shocked and frightened, probably by the sound of your voice downstairs. She needs her mother.'

Revelling in the freedom of being regarded as not quite responsible for her actions, Kitty looked at her mother and said, 'Go away,' and opened her mouth to scream again.

'Go away, Charles. She is hysterical. I'll get her under control.'

'I think you should go downstairs, Martha,' her father said very quietly. Her mother went.

He sat on the bed, stroking her hair and talking softly with inconsequential, soothing words. She could see he was thinking deeply, blaming himself, trying to find some solution. She began to feel guilty; perhaps she ought to tell him it was just a hoax and that she had acted a lie. She dared not; besides she wasn't sure how much it was a hoax. She had really been ready to scream if her mother had not gone away—and it had felt quite involuntary.

Almost immediately afterwards her father had arranged for her to go away to boarding school. Which was why, when she later stood holding on to the overflow pipe in the topmost lavatory of the school, gazing out at imaginary hills between the bars, she knew that she had only herself to blame.

It snowed again in the night and right up until the moment when she heard the sound of a car door slamming and Tom's footsteps, muffled by the snow, coming down the drive, she hoped that they might not be able to get to the station.

She was up in Gwendolen's bedroom when she heard him come. Gwendolen and her father were waiting by their cases in the hall, her mother was already washing their sheets in the scullery and she had hidden herself away in Gwendolen's room. All Gwendolen's belongings had gone, the little jars and bottles had vanished and the bed was piled high with folded blankets and covered with a dust sheet. It seemed as if there had been a death.

When the doorbell rang she went downstairs.

'Good-bye, Mummy,' Gwendolen was saying. 'Thank you for a lovely holiday.'

'Make sure you come at Easter, now.'

'I'll see.'

'Good-bye, Martha.'

'Good-bye, Charles.'

They kissed.

'Put a scarf on, child.'

She ran upstairs to get a scarf, looked all over for it and then remembered that she had put it in the scullery the night before to dry.

'Typical,' her mother was saying. 'You've been hanging about for hours and now you keep everyone waiting while you look for your scarf.'

She wound the scarf round her neck and ran up the drive after the others, nearly falling on the icy snow.

'It's all right; we've plenty of time,' her father called back to her.

'We'll have to take it slow,' Tom remarked. 'The roads are icy—they've only just started gritting them. The trains are running to time though; I was down at the station for the early one. I've got chains, of course.'

He went cautiously. There were very few cars about. They passed a bus creeping over the ice like a nervous animal. The air was very still and cold and there was no sun.

Gwendolen sat in her corner of the taxi and her sister could feel the excitement glowing from her. She looked radiant. She smelled nice too.

'You do stink pretty, Gwendolen,' she said, trying to be cheerful.

Gwendolen smiled. 'A present from Arthur,' she said.

'Makes him sound like a seaside resort. Who's Arthur?'

'Oh, one of the swains. You haven't met him. He's rather nice, really.'

116

So much for Arthur. She would have liked to have obliterated him, not from dislike but simply because he was a distraction which would be better annulled. He would preoccupy Gwendolen when she should be doing something about the situation at home, when she should be concentrating her affection, not dissipating it.

As they slowly ground their way into the station yard, the station master was sweeping the snow.

'It's nobbut scraping the top off,' he remarked, as he brushed the fresh layer of white powder off the frozen snow beneath. Then he threw down some crumbs for the birds, leant his brush against the wall and looked at their tickets.

'You've not long to wait,' he said, handing them back the tickets. 'She's just signalled.'

The station looked even tinier under its covering of snow. It seemed to merge into the countryside, as if folded away for the winter. When the train—dark and noisy—appeared, it seemed far too big for the cold little station. Indeed it seemed to break it in pieces as it bustled in, shattering the silence and blowing out steam in all directions.

The station master carried his mounting block to the back of the train, and began helping passengers out. Gwendolen and her father got into the front, Kitty followed them and watched them settle themselves in, lifting their cases on to the rack, looking about them in the proprietorial way of people who are going to spend a few hours of their life in a place, even if it is as temporary as a railway compartment. She would have given much to have been sharing it with them.

'You'd better get off now,' he said gently. 'I'll jump you down.'

As she stood on the platform she was aware of a lot of bustling going on behind her. Fur-coated women and bowler-hatted men, all stout and middle-aged, were laughing and chaffing, converging on Tom's taxi, squeezing into the seats. Car doors slammed them safely in.

Her father and Gwendolen leaned out of the window to talk to her. There was nothing to say. Soon they would move slowly out and leave her alone. She wanted to beg them not to leave her behind. She shut her mouth tightly.

'I wish we could take you with us, little one,' her father said.

'It's all right.'

She took off her woollen glove and stretched up to put her hand on his as it rested on the top of the open window.

'Oh, goodness, I was going to do something about those chilblains of yours,' Gwendolen said, looking down at the bumpy mauve hand. 'I meant to get some stuff in Pendlebury. You'd better get it yourself now.'

'Have you any money?' her father asked.

'No.'

He put a ten shilling note into her hand. She put it into her coat pocket.

The station master shouted a warning, the train began to jerk slowly forward. They both leaned out of the window and she walked alongside it, smiling, until she reached the end of the platform. Then Gwendolen withdrew into the compartment and her father continued to lean out, waving a white handkerchief. She stood, waving and smiling, at the end of the platform, watching until the train and the fluttering white handkerchief disappeared round the hill. Only then did she realize that tears were running down her cheeks.

At first she walked quickly along the wide path which the Romans had made between the hills, but when she had rounded the nose of Old Saul and the village came into view, she began to go more slowly. Southerby was green and white, with great drifts four or five feet high against the walls and bare patches of grass in the middle of the fields, where the gusts had swirled all the snow away. The drifts had been sculptured by the wind into marvellous shapes; some were deeply undercut, with a great overhang of snow which would fall off in huge chunks when the thaw came. She crossed the little bridge; the beck was iced right across but she could see the water flowing underneath the ice. Water plants with long green leaves like ribbons were drifting in the current, mysterious and strangely elegant under their glass cover.

She could see her mother's house now: she let herself imagine what it would be like to return to a real welcome—a smile and a hug and a hot drink and warmth and—she did not even dare think the word—love. She must not weaken. She was alone, without allies as she used to be when she was at school in Pendlebury after Gwendolen had left.

'So you're back, are you?' her mother said as she came in the door. 'Just in time to make yourself useful. You can help me fold these sheets. The vicar came when you were out to ask for help with the Sunday School tea, so you can take these scones along after lunch. It'll only be a scrap lunch anyway; I've been baking all this morning. You can take a few scones to old Mrs Samson on the way. She's almost bedridden and used to be a marvellous cook too.'

Kitty kicked off her boots and put on her slippers and followed her mother into the kitchen.

'And you'd better take down all the Christmas decorations,' she said.

'Already? Can't they stay up until Twelfth Night?'

'I'm sick to death of the pine needles falling all over the drawing-room. I'm for ever sweeping them off the lino. And I can't dust with all those cards to move.'

'I'll do the dusting and sweeping.'

Her mother gave a short laugh. 'A fine mess you'd make of it. If you want to help you can do the potatoes for lunch. And we'll have no more arguing. Christmas is over and there's an end to it.'

She threw some potatoes into the sink. Kitty began to unbutton her coat.

'I've arranged for two of the big lads from Sunday School,' her mother went on, 'to come and take the tree away tomorrow morning, so it must be stripped down by tonight.'

'All right.'

'Put your boots by the stove and give me that coat. Gloves in your pocket! Think, child, however will they dry? And what's this—a ten shilling note?'

'Daddy gave it to me. It's to buy some ointment for my chilblains.'

'Then he'd no right to. Fancy giving a child like you ten shillings. And to buy some stupid cream. He hasn't the sense he was born with. I'll put it in the housekeeping.' She took a green purse out of the drawer and put the note into it.

Kitty wanted to protest that it was hers and that the chilblains hurt, but her eyes began to smart so she said nothing.

'When I was a child we used to rub our chilblains with meths. I can remember sitting and rubbing my toes with them. It was enough to make you cry the way it used to sting,' her mother reminisced. 'Now, get on with those potatoes, Miss. No, not the hot tap—no need to waste hot water when cold will do. And if you make a good job of it I'll give you some meths tonight to rub on your hands.'

In the afternoon, after she had gone on various errands, she began to take the decorations down. She unwound the tinsel and carefully removed the balls and ornaments, gently wrapping them in newspaper and packing them away in the cardboard boxes. It was very cold in the room; there was no fire like the one in which they had burned pieces of holly on Christmas Eve, nobody to talk to, no feeling of excitement. Even the smell of the Christmas tree was different, sad, poignant, reminding her of Christmas Eve. It was silly, really, she thought; she looked forward so much to something like decorating the tree, treasured the moment anxiously when it came and, when it was over, was sad as she remembered it. Yet it was the same event whichever way you looked at it, from the past, present or future. So really it made no difference. Perhaps happenings weren't always there but disappeared when nobody thought about them, as she used to feel that the hills disappeared when she wasn't there to see them. When she was little she had often tried to catch them at it; she would shut her eyes and open them suddenly: sometimes she was sure she had caught a trace of movement out of the corner of her eye as the hills settled back into their places.

She held the humming bird in her hand, stroking her cheek gently with its silky tail and then wrapped it carefully in a piece of soft tissue paper. 'There, now, nothing happened to you after all,' she said, leaning forward to tuck it into the box.

'What a time you have been with one small job,' her mother said, opening the door suddenly.

Kitty jumped guiltily and the humming bird slipped from her fingers, escaped from the tissue paper and crashed to pieces on the hearth. The tissue paper fluttered uselessly after it.

'Goodness, child! I've never known anyone so clumsy. Don't you know that these decorations cost a lot of money?' her mother asked as she picked up the brush and shovel and with brisk, angry movements swept the shattered glass from the hearth.

'You young people have no idea of the value of anything, that's the trouble,' she went on. 'Life's too easy for you. Easy come, easy go,' she concluded, as she carried the remains of the humming bird out of the room on the shovel.

Kitty packed the rest of the decorations as quickly as she could and stowed them away in the box. 'I won't think,' she kept repeating to herself. 'I won't let myself think.'

CHAPTER SIXTEEN

IT was the last night of the holidays. Her trunk was packed and despatched. All within a week it had arrived, been unpacked, its contents washed and repacked. Only the books which lined the bottom had not been disturbed.

Somehow the rest of the holidays had been disposed of; she had helped in the house, gone on errands, delivered cakes and jam to old ladies and, whenever she could escape, walked on the hills in the snow, returning in the evenings so cold that her fingers ached as they thawed out and seemed likely to burst their skins.

They sat alone now, her mother and herself, as they ate their supper. The clock ticked loudly and slowly and with great deliberation, as if passing judgement, as it looked down on them and the table spread with a yellow and orange checked tablecloth and the remains of a pie, dirty plates, cream crackers and the cheese board. The details of the scene seemed very sharp and clear, as if they had been carefully chosen like the properties on a stage. The scene was set. Outside the snow had cleared but a cold wind was blowing and she could hear it growling among the trees near the house.

'Have you everything packed? I've no time to spend wrapping up parcels if you forget anything.'

'I think I've got everything, thank you,' Kitty said politely. She was being very careful about being polite. She had decided that she could not go back to school without raising the question of the divorce again and wanted to do it in a civilized and adult manner. She had tried several times but each time her nerve had failed her at the last moment.

'Then I'll see you again at Easter.'

This was the chance, she thought, remembering what her father had said about the flat.

'I expect so,' she said cautiously.

'Expect? Aren't you sure, then?'

Her mother spoke sharply; she always wanted them back. She didn't seem pleased to see them when they came and made it clear that they were a great nuisance while they were with her, but still she seemed to want them to come back.

'The Deedes boys always come home every holiday,' her mother said.

Children must be seen to come home, Kitty thought: keep up the pretence for the sake of the parents.

'I expect Gwendolen will be gallivanting off for part of the time,' Martha went on. 'And your father will most likely be staying in London with that woman he lives with.'

This was the way she always referred to Mrs Wedgwood, her father's elderly landlady. Kitty said nothing. More than ever before, her mother had these holidays thrown out bitter accusations against her father, but she had refused to rise to them.

There was silence for a while; only the sound of the wind and the trees creaking and the grandfather clock's tick of judgement. Now or never.

'He may get a flat if Gwendolen gets a job in London after getting her B.Litt.'

'Oh, that! He did mention something about it. I've never heard such rubbish. If he can afford to squander money on flats I'm sure I don't know why I have to scrape so.'

Now or never.

'You'd get much more money if you had a divorce; you get given a third of your husband's income, you know.'

Martha stared at her. She stared back. She was not going to be afraid of her, she was just going to argue this out on practical grounds. She was going to make her mother see sense and even for once in her life be reasonable. So she stared back.

'How dare you, Miss?' Martha said, but her voice lacked that uncontrolled, unbridled fury which Kitty had expected.

'Dare what?' Kitty said innocently. 'I'm only trying to help. You said you hadn't enough money. That way you'd get more.'

Her mother hesitated. Then she said, 'I happen to have a conscience. I'm a God-fearing woman and I've kept my marriage vows.'

'To love and to cherish?' Kitty said, and then regretted it for she had decided not to follow her mother's side-tracks. 'But that's not the point,' she went on hastily. 'It's a question of if you'd be better off.'

'It's a question of my religion,' Martha said angrily. 'Besides, I'd be better off *without* a divorce, *if he died.*'

So that was the real reason; Kitty felt herself go cold as her blood seemed to leave her and she felt dizzy. So Martha had noticed whatever it was that she herself had sensed in her father last term; it was a terrifying confirmation of her fears. Hatred had seen what love had seen, both of them always on the watch for weakness.

She was surprised at how calmly she could reply. 'That's a long way off; think how much richer you'd be now.'

'Oh, he won't make old bones. Men living like he does never do. It's not natural. He needs people. Loneliness will finish him. He should be like me, always doing things for people, surrounded with gratitude.'

'But he does have friends, heaps of friends. Other people love him. People love you for what you are, not for what you do. It's just family life he hasn't got—' Kitty's voice trailed off. She was aware that she had lost her determination not to be side-tracked, and that her mother had been quick to notice the panic in her voice.

Martha looked at her shrewdly. 'And that's what will finish him,' she said, piling up the dirty dishes with finality. 'As his widow I'll get everything. Divorced, I wouldn't. No divorce for me.'

Kitty made herself push away the thought that they were talking about his death. She had resolved to be practical, to see it from her mother's point of view, to argue it from her side. Money, evidently it was a question of guaranteeing money for Martha.

'If you could have some kind of document, guaranteeing the money, would that be all right?'

'Wouldn't trust him. And anyway why are you so keen on getting your parents divorced? What do you think you'll get out of it? Shame, that's all you'll get, shame. It should be the last thing any decent girl would want, to see her own mother dragged through the divorce courts.'

'Gwendolen and I both think it would be for the best.'

'Oh, you do, do you? Best for your father, you mean?'

'No, it would probably be more expensive for him,' Kitty said casually. 'But we think it would be best for both of you to be apart and not have all this pretending.'

She could see that the point about expense had gone home. Martha was always interested in anything which might create difficulties for her husband.

'He probably wouldn't be able to afford school fees,' Martha said thoughtfully. 'You'd end up back at Pendlebury, I shouldn't wonder. Of course, I'd have the custody of you, so I could see to that anyway.'

Kitty could see that she was warming to the idea. She saw also that it was going to be conditional upon her surrendering her life to Martha. She thought of the years in this bleak, unloved, unloving house and shivered. But it was only fair. If going to live with her mother was the only way she could help her father, then she'd just have to do it.

Martha put her head on one side and looked up at the clock.

'I'll consider it,' she said. 'Yes, it's definitely worth considering. I'd have to be sure of you and Gwendolen of course.'

'We'd stay with you,' Kitty said firmly. 'We'd support you.' She meant it; the only thing really hateful in her mother was the ill-will with which she pursued her father. Once she had stopped her mother inflicting suffering on him, she could view her as the rest of the world did: hard, cranky, unpredictable, sometimes funny and always full of good works. She would be able to forgive her for any unkindness to herself.

She leaned across the table, as if clinching a deal. 'You see, really, there's only the divorce thing between us,' she said. 'Once you've agreed to that, it's out of the way and I promise I'll do whatever you like. You give him the divorce and then we can respect you, Gwendolen and I, but we can't . . .'

Suddenly Martha thrust her face forward. 'How dare you talk to me like this?' she shouted, and for a moment Kitty thought she was going to slap her face. 'A child of fourteen telling her mother to get divorced.' Martha's voice cracked with rage. 'I know who's put you up to this: that horrible man, your father.'

Kitty, who a few seconds before, had seen her life all smoothly arranged, herself sacrificed, maybe, but her father free, fell back in her chair, horrified.

'And I'll tell you why I won't divorce him,' her mother raged on, 'because I'm pretty sure he'll die if I don't. And don't ask me how I know; when you hate people you get to know things.'

Kitty just wanted to get out, to escape this fiendish thing. When her mother gave full rein to her emotions vileness seemed to pour out of her and the sight was sickening beyond belief. Certainly nobody outside the family would have believed it if they had been told. The veins in her neck protruded and throbbed. Her cheeks were flushed and her hard eyes were lit with brilliant malignancy.

'I'm looking forward to widowhood,' she said.

Kitty got up.

'And where are you going?'

'When I go to school tomorrow, I'm never coming back.'

'Brave talk. Who else do you think will have you?' Martha said angrily, but there was uneasiness in her voice, as if she had caught the determination in her daughter's voice.

'I know I'm only fourteen, but if I have to kill myself I'm not coming back here.'

Suddenly Martha crumpled. 'I didn't mean it, Kitty,' she said. 'The trouble is, I'm not really very happy.' She began to cry. 'I don't want to lose you and Gwendolen.'

'You can have us and the divorce or neither,' Kitty replied, contempt making her impervious to her mother's emotions. Strong emotions, her mother had, but no feelings. Wasn't that what he had said?

'All right, dear, I'll do that, provided you promise. It's really been my religion, you know. But I'll sacrifice that provided you and Gwendolen promise to stay.'

She drew a large khaki handkerchief out of her knicker leg and blew her nose.

'And provided your father makes an immediate financial settlement,' she concluded.

'How and how much?'

'Through his solicitor.'

'You know he can't. It's called collusion.'

'Well, an agreed third party then.'

'Do you promise?'

'I promise. I'll write tomorrow.'

'Now.'

'Oh, very well.'

Kitty went out and brought writing paper, envelopes, a postage stamp, and her mother's fountain pen. With the dirty dishes still piled around them and the crumbs still lying on the checked tablecloth and to the sound of the grandfather clock's steady judicial ticking, they composed a letter to her father.

She posted it the next day on her way back to school.

CHAPTER SEVENTEEN

'I REALLY had it out with my mother in the holidays,' Jill said as she pinned up her hair in the big looking glass at the end of the dormitory. ' "If I can't go to the flicks and come in at ten o'clock without you treating me as if I was a harlot," I said, "I'll jolly well go into digs next holidays." '

'What did she say to that?' Amanda asked.

'She asked me what I'd use for money.'

'Honestly, parents! I had mother trouble too.'

'Boy friends?'

'No. It's her clothes. You just can't believe how badly my mother dresses. Last term she came to take me out in a ghastly suit that she'd had in the war—great padded shoulders, it had, and a ridiculous bit of a skirt. Honestly, she might have been a dame in a pantomime. I told her that if she came in that again I'd kill her.'

'What did she say?'

'Oh, she just laughed and said it might be safer not to come then. Daddy backed her up of course and said she looked smashing in that suit.'

'Parents always gang up on one.'

'The trouble with my mother is that she's got absolutely no dress sense at all.'

'I don't think that any of that generation had.'

Kitty lay and listened to them, trying to imagine what it must be like: fancy daring to tell your mother what you thought of her clothes, fancy teasing her, fancy having parents that ganged up on you!

Felicity Snow had been doing her history test paper under the bedclothes. She slid it out on to the bedside table.

'Would you mind just looking at it for me?' she whispered to Kitty. 'Polly's asleep.'

Kitty slid it off and read it under her sheet. There were two questions for revision. 'What is the penal code?' was written in Miss Taunton's purple, stencilled handwriting. Underneath Felicity had written, 'The penal code is the male organ of reproduction in the rabbit.' The second question was 'What was the industrial revolution?' This was harder and it had taken Felicity longer to think out the answer which, ill-spelt and blotchy, was, 'It was the change from reproducing in cottages with the whole family joining in to reproducing in factories which was more efficient but less fun.'

'I think you've done it again,' Kitty said kindly.

'What?'

'Muddled up history and biology.'

One of Felicity's problems was that history was followed by a double period of biology on Friday afternoons and she was inclined to confuse the two subjects.

The fifth formers returned before they could say more, so Kitty slid the paper back on to the bedside table and pretended to be asleep. Working in the dormitories was strictly forbidden.

Everything was going very well though, Kitty thought, as she lay in bed after lights out, listening to the whispered conversation of the sixth formers who had just come in. She had heard from her father that her mother had promised the divorce in return for an agreed proportion of his estate if he died and a sum of money now which was to be settled with the Deedes until the divorce was through. The Deedes were to act as referees; they were to be the agreed third party. He thought them a good choice of Martha's, for Mrs Deedes did marriage guidance work and Wally's business gave him a certain knowledge of the law. Anyway he could think of nobody more suitable and there could be no question of involving a solicitor. Mrs Deedes was coming to see him next week, he wrote, after visiting the boys at school. He would be coming to take Kitty out soon this term and would tell her all about it. She had written in her letter back that she was a bit worried about the Deedes, she just had this funny feeling of not trusting them, but he had written telling her not to be so gloomy and his letters were so cheerful now and so full of life and so funny that she felt quite guilty for even trying to raise a doubt in his mind.

Gwendolen knew all about it too, of course, and she was quite confident that it would all work out, but then she was full of her own plans now: no wonder she had been so excited when she left Beckgate. Kitty lay with her eyes shut and remembered. It had been the second day of term that she had been summoned to see Miss Roland. Her sister, Miss Roland said, was on the telephone in the office and had asked, as a very special concession, to be allowed to speak to her. Since she was a former head girl and there seemed something important to communicate, the Head had agreed. Miss Roland led her to the office, indicated the telephone, said the call would be put through in a moment and ostentatiously withdrew.

'Hello, Kitty?'

'Oh, Gwendolen, yes, it's me. Whatever's happened?'

'Nothing dreadful. I've got some important news for you. I wanted to tell you myself so I thought I'd ring you up.'

There was a pause while Kitty wondered whatever could merit this quite unheard-of course of action.

'I'm engaged, darling.'

'You're what?'

'Engaged. To Arthur—you remember, I told you about Arthur?'

'You mean the one who gave you the stuff that made you stink pretty? No, you didn't tell me about him.'

'Of course I did. He's the one I met first when I was a fresher and he was doing a final year at Law. He had been interrupted by the war so he was quite a lot older than me—six years in fact. Then he went away to London to be articled and we happened to meet at a party and he's come up to see me quite often at weekends and things. You know how it is.'

'Yes,' said Kitty, although she did not.

'But I didn't really think he was very interested in me really and then suddenly it has all come to a head because he has been offered a partnership in a firm of solicitors in Oxford and also a house!'

'A house? Did you say a house? It sounded as if you said a house.'

'I did. Honestly, Kitty. Is it you or the line that's blocking communication? His family are quite disgustingly rich and own property all over the place, and his uncle wants to get rid of this old place in north Oxford. It's a lovely old house, needs a lot doing to it, but very sound, Arthur says. It seems a bit silly for me to be in digs in one part of the town, Arthur says, and him in digs in another, so we thought we might as well get married quickly and move into the house.'

'But, Gwendolen, what about the flat?'

'What flat?'

'The one Daddy was going to get in London and you were going to look after. You know, he gave up the Bar partly so that you and he could have a flat and you said you'd make a home . . .'

'Oh my,' Gwendolen said, laughing, 'for a moment I thought you meant a *real* flat.'

'I thought it was going to be real.'

'If you're worried about not having a home, pet, Arthur and I will love you to stay with us whenever you like.'

'Thank you,' Kitty replied almost in a whisper, 'but I didn't mean me.'

'What? I've told Arthur about you—he's simply longing to meet you. He thinks you sound ever so quaint. You'll love him, he's got a terrific sense of humour. He can make funny voices too—it's killing. We'll have some wonderful times when you come to stay and there'll be lots of undergraduates for you to meet—well, I suppose there won't be any in the school holidays, but . . .'

'Gwendolen—you didn't say *when* you were getting married.'

'Oh, didn't I? We thought next month. I shall arrange it all myself and we'll have it in Oxford of course and you'll be a bridesmaid.'

'What—in term time?'

'Yes, I've spoken to the Head and she says it will be all right. Oh Lord, there are the pips again. I'll write it all down, darling, but I just wanted to tell you myself first in case it was too much of a surprise by post. Good-bye, darling.'

'Good-bye, Gwendolen. And—Gwendolen?'

'Yes?'

'I'm very pleased, really I am.'

She had come away from the office hardly able to think or even move. Of course she could not really be pleased; it was a calamity.

She tried to feel pleased now, as she lay in bed, for Gwendolen's sake she must try. But she could only think how catastrophic it was for her father. Thank goodness it was now, anyway, when the divorce was all arranged. At least he had that on the credit side, now that he was being left for this Arthur. If only she herself were older, if only it wasn't years and years before she would be able to make a home for him in the way that Gwendolen could do now if only she would concentrate on the things that mattered instead of going traipsing off to live in Oxford with Arthur.

It was the end of part of her own life too, she thought sadly. No more long talks in the bathroom, no more hairwashing sessions. Arthur could hardly be expected to make it a threesome. She would be outside; their voices and their laughter would be on the other side of a closed door. She was ashamed of herself for thinking of the trivial differences it would make for her. They were nothing compared with what it would do to her father's life. Besides, it was nice for Gwendolen to have Arthur. She had sounded very pleased with herself. She concentrated on thinking of the wedding.

Gwendolen's letters were full of the arrangements; it was fantastic how much work went into getting married. She had chosen invitations and sent them out, she had ordered flowers and cars and booked hotels in advance. She had had two fittings for her wedding dress. She had even written to the domestic science mistress and asked her to take Kitty's measurements so that her dress could be all ready. She had explained to Kitty that once the measurements were taken she must not put on any weight. Heaps of people at school remembered Gwendolen and everyone kept asking her about her wedding. The domestic science mistress was particularly deferential as she took the measurements. Despite herself, part of Kitty had begun to bask in the reflected glory and to feel really quite pleased about Gwendolen's wedding. Everyone seemed to assume that weddings were something to be pleased about.

She lay and thought about it; there were three other bridesmaids; Virginia's little girl and two of Arthur's nieces. She imagined Gwendolen coming up the aisle, but then she saw her father walking beside her, supporting her on his arm, so that Gwendolen would feel the gentle up and down movement of his uneven walk as he took her up the aisle to give her away. Suddenly Kitty's eyes filled with tears, knowing that now he only had her left and she was a poor substitute for Gwendolen.

Polly began to snore. Kitty realized that everyone else was awake.

'Poor Polly,' Felicity said, 'we ought to stop her. Nobody will want to marry a girl who snores.'

'Just think of making love to a girl who made a noise like that afterwards,' Jill said in disgust.

'But of course they wouldn't know, would they, until after they'd married her?' Amanda asked.

'After the first night they would,' Jill told her. 'Next morning she'd be packed off home to her mother. She'd just have one glorious memory to live on for the rest of her lonely life.'

'She could marry lots of people for very short times.'

'No, they'd tell on her. Men are fearful gossips, Mummy says.'

'You can be cured of snoring,' Sue put in. 'I read an article about it actually in the holidays in one of my father's medical journals. Definitely you can cure them.'

'You mean rolled in salt like bacon?'

'Honestly, Felicity, you are a *muddler*. Of course I don't mean that kind of cured. Cured like diseases, you idiot. My father feels that most things will be cured within the decade. I expect a course of injections would put Polly right in no time. Within the decade, certainly.'

As always they were overawed by Sue's inner knowledge. There was silence for a while, punctuated by Polly's prolonged and rattly snoring.

'It's all very well talking about courses of injections,' Jill said, 'but what we need is something to stop her now. Has anybody got anything to throw?'

Kitty groped along the top of her table. 'I've got a pair of scissors,' she said.

'For goodness' sake, Kitty! The poor kid will have even less chance of getting married if she's only got one eye!'

'I'll throw my shoe at her,' Amanda offered and there was a scraping sound as she pulled her outdoor shoes from under the bed. She sat up in bed, ready to throw it.

'If you're thinking of throwing that size eight clog of yours at

Polly,' one of the sixth formers said, 'I absolutely forbid it. You could break her jaw.'

The door opened suddenly.

'Do I hear talking?' Miss Theswell enquired rhetorically. They all pretended to be asleep. The silence was suddenly broken by Polly who awoke with a loud snort and said, 'What—what's that?'

'Well, I, er—I'm sorry if I disturbed you. Good-night everyone,' Miss Theswell replied, backing out and shutting the door softly behind her.

They began to giggle. 'Sh, you know she always listens at the door,' the sixth former hissed at them. 'Now shut up the lot of you and go to sleep. Polly, lie on your side; you've been snoring.'

'What me? I never snore.'

'Shut up. Good-night.'

They murmured good-night and one by one their breathing became slower, more rhythmical until only Kitty lay awake. She was trying to remember what it was that made her feel uneasy, unable to share her father's optimism that everything was going to work out, his confidence in the Deedes. There was something, she knew there was something, if only she could remember. She let her mind whiffle about, seeking memories of Wally Deedes, following little tracks of thought, prodding at scenes in the past, hunting out each occasion she had watched him. Her mind seemed to be behaving like Ben when he sniffed and hunted about to get the scent of a rabbit. Suddenly she recognized it. A very clear picture of Wally came into her mind; he was carrying in one hand a log basket and in the other a coal scuttle. He moved, a small, spare, somewhat spider-like figure, across the drawing-room carpet and towards the door. As he went out of the room he suddenly cast back a look of unexpected malignancy. Somewhat out of place at a Christmas party had been the look of hatred which Wally Deedes had shot back at her father.

CHAPTER EIGHTEEN

GRACE DEEDES sat back in the corner of her first class compartment. She was smiling and felt at peace with the world. The school concert had been extremely enjoyable and all the masters to whom she had spoken had seemed very pleased with her two boys. The Housemaster had used a very charming phrase; he had referred to their 'unfailing courtesy and helpfulness'. She liked that: all one's virtues should be unfailing.

In chapel that morning she had given heartfelt thanks for the way her two boys had turned out. One only had to look around to realize how fortunate—how blessed—one was. Yes, she felt she could, without vanity, claim to have done a good piece of work with her boys. It was very worth-while, she reflected, bringing up children to think and to act in a way which was pleasing to the Lord—and to oneself.

Wally had not accompanied her. He had some business affairs to see to. Besides, really and truly he did not enjoy the school concerts as much as she did. Music and poetry did not do for him quite what they did for her. Dear Wally, feet so firmly on the ground, whereas hers, she had to admit, were always a little inclined to float up among the clouds. There were so many uplifting experiences in life.

She took out her wallet, reassured herself that there were plenty of those useful five pound notes, and settled back to read her magazines. Rubbishy things, of course, she thought, as she folded one back, but then if one couldn't indulge oneself on a train journey once in a while the world would be a sorry place. She popped a piece of chocolate into her mouth and settled down to read the serial.

The journey passed quickly. Indeed it seemed no time at all until she was in London, getting into a taxi, giving Charles' address to the taximan. In the taxi she powdered her nose and adjusted her hat. She was quite looking forward to this visit; almost an ambassadress, she felt herself to be.

Of course, she reflected, as she climbed up the stairs to Charles' digs, it was all very sad, very sad indeed. A man alone like this, such a successful, distinguished man. Sad for those girls, too. Sometimes it was good to remember how fortunate one was and to compare one's happy lot with that of other people. She often looked at all the misery there was in the world in order to remind herself that one should not grumble.

Mrs Wedgwood opened the door. An elderly person, Grace noted, comfortably round and very respectable-looking. She was holding a little boy by the hand.

'Mr Langdon is expecting me,' she said.

'That's right, Mrs Deedes, isn't it?' Mrs Wedgwood replied observing her with, Grace realized, rather more interest than circumstances merited.

'I've just come on a little matter of business,' she said, unable to keep a defensive note out of her voice.

'I see, but I expect you'd like some tea, all the same,' Mrs Wedgwood replied, showing her upstairs. 'I'm Mrs Wedgwood, by the way, Mr Langdon's landlady.'

'How do you do? Yes, tea would be lovely, thank you.'

'It's this door, that one is his bedroom.'

'Oh, yes, I see,' Grace said, turning away from it, flustered. She allowed Mrs Wedgwood to tap at the other door and open it for her.

'Well, Grace, how nice to see you,' Charles said, getting up from his desk and coming across the room to shake her by the hand. 'Do take off your things. Would you like to go into the bedroom?'

" I'll just leave them here, thank you,' Grace said rather quickly. 'What a very lovely room.'

Mrs Wedgwood's flat, of which Charles had two rooms, was at the top of an old Victorian house. His study had dormer windows which looked right across London.

'It's very pleasant—above the noise level and nice and light. It gets a bit overheated in the summer and would be cold in the winter, but Mrs Wedgwood is very generous with the heating.'

'She seems a nice person.'

'Oh, yes, she is. It suits me very well, really. She lets me have all my own bits and pieces in the rooms, and she'll always put up one of the girls in her attic room for a night or two in an emergency; it's been very handy for Gwendolen in the past when she's wanted to have a couple of days in London.'

'And how is dear Gwendolen?'

Charles laughed. 'Fantastic, Grace, really fantastic. She's arranging everything for the wedding herself and yet seems to fit in quite a lot of work for her thesis too. Mind you, I expect she burns the candle at both ends as well as in the middle. But she's a remarkable girl; she is so practical and yet so academically gifted.'

'I expect she combines Martha's busy, practical nature with your brilliant mind,' Grace said sweetly.

There was a silence; it was not a particularly fortunate remark to make, Charles reflected, when on an errand such as Grace's. He tried to think of something to say quickly to save poor Grace from embarrassment, but Grace was happily unaware of anything amiss; she was thinking that perhaps poor little Kitty combined her mother's brain with her father's practicality, or rather lack of it.

'And how do you like your future son-in-law?' she asked before Charles had time to speak.

'A very nice fellow,' Charles said. 'I don't like the hurry; I'd sooner she had had some time to be free and look around and so on, but there it is. It's her decision and certainly she couldn't have chosen a nicer person.'

He spoke with finality; he wasn't going to discuss his future son-in-law, so kind and well-meaning, so unequal in brain power to Gwendolen, with Grace Deedes.

'And your new job, how do you like that?'

'Different, of course. It takes a bit of getting used to, being in an office, you know.' Again he tried to speak with conviction, but was aware that he was less successful this time.

'You must miss court life, I'm sure. Though for my part the very idea of a law case and unpleasantness makes me feel quite wretched.'

For a moment the whole atmosphere of court, the tension, the excitement, the controlled drama of it, overcame him. He longed for it with the terrible, insatiable yearning of homesickness for a land to which there can be no hope of return. It was a relief to be interrupted by Mrs Wedgwood bringing in the tea.

They talked of other things as they handed buttered teacakes and sugar to each other and drank tea. Charles wondered how, amid all this, they were going to approach the purpose of Grace's visit. However, when they had finished eating and she had poured them each out a second cup of tea, she said, 'Well, Charles, I must say you are looking remarkably well. I was afraid that the change of job and the worry over the wedding would have made you rather harassed, but really you look even younger than at Christmas and nobody would have thought you old enough to have a grown-up daughter even then!'

Charles laughed, and seized the opportunity. 'Well, it's been a great help to get this business of the divorce settled. It is very good of you and Wally to involve yourselves in our rather messy family affairs. I don't need to tell you how much I wish we didn't have to.'

'You forget, Charles, that it is My Work,' Grace said, suddenly solemn and pouring all the conviction that she could into the words. It was so very important, she always felt, that people in need of help should feel one's utter sincerity and single-minded determination to serve them. 'Your problem is by no means rare; it sometimes helps people a great deal to know that. There is always somebody worse off.'

Charles, who had never found the fact that other people had troubles too anything but depressing, remained silent.

'Just one thing I want to be quite, quite sure of, Charles,' Grace went on earnestly. 'You are quite sure that there is no chance of a reconciliation?'

'None.'

'It sometimes happens and how marvellous it is!'

'Look, Grace, you know Martha and you know me. Greater incompatibility you are unlikely to meet.'

'Yes. I do see that. But with God all things are possible.'

'Even mistakes?'

'Well, I—what I meant was—no, really I do see that you have *very* little in common, but I just wanted to be sure, you know. Now, I have one or two papers here . . .'

She opened her bag and took out an envelope.

'Here is the agreement which Wally drew up. You will settle

£1,000 immediately and then here is the draft for the will.'

'That is correct.'

She hesitated. 'Martha confided in me, Charles, a little fear that she had that you might alter it afterwards, so we thought perhaps some signed statement which Wally could keep? I think it would reassure her poor anxious mind.'

Charles swallowed. 'Agreed,' he said quietly. Humiliation had been part of his marriage: it was fitting that it should be part of the ending of it.

He took the papers to the desk and signed them.

'I've made out the cheque,' he said. 'Do I get a receipt for it?'

Grace hesitated.

'Well, Charles, you place me in a quandary,' she said. 'We did not think you would have the money available immediately so we haven't anything like that prepared.'

Charles smiled. 'Flat money,' he said. 'It's the last of my capital. I had it set aside ready for the flat which Gwendolen and I were going to have, but now that her life has changed course it won't be needed for that.'

'Of course not. You'll stay here?'

'I don't know if I shall be able to. Mrs Wedgwood had a married son who was killed in a car accident a year ago. His little boy spends a lot of time here with his Granny now.'

'That would be the little boy I met as I came in?'

'Yes, Christopher. Nice little chap. He and his mother live nearby. Really it would be more sensible for Mrs Wedgwood to go and live there with them so that her daughter-in-law can go out to work; she's a trained teacher so can make much more than her mother-in-law does letting these rooms. Mrs Wedgwood asked me about it last year and I agreed I'd be willing to move out as we were going to get our own flat anyway, but of course I'd rather stay here now.'

'Oh dear, and it isn't easy to get somewhere else like this in London nowadays.'

'I don't think Mrs Wedgwood really wants to give up her flat here. I'm rather afraid that later on her daughter-in-law—who is very young—may marry again and then Mrs Wedgwood would have no home of her own. I think really she'd be better to keep her own place, but of course I'm not the one to say so since I obviously have an interest in her staying here. But it would be very sad for her to have to leave her daughter-in-law's home if she did marry again. They get on well but she's the kind of person who would feel she should leave even if she had no place of her own to go to.'

Grace looked at him thoughtfully.

'Dear Charles,' she said. 'You take everybody else's problems to heart so. Just like me.'

'Well, to get back to our own problems then,' Charles said briskly. 'Presumably you will guarantee that Martha goes ahead with the divorce?'

'If you keep your side then she will certainly keep hers.'

'Excellent. Then I will arrange for the hotel bill to be sent in evidence and all that. It's a silly fabrication, but that's the way the law is at the moment so we must go along with it. My only fear is that she will change her mind at the last moment and try to back out.'

'She won't do that, Charles. She is a very upright person, you know.'

Charles pondered on this view of Martha.

'We're all very upright in some matters,' he said at last, 'and less so in others.'

Then, as Grace waited for him to go on, he added, 'You see, Grace, I've had a certain amount of cat-and-mouse treatment in the past and that is really why I need you and Wally to make sure it doesn't happen again. As you know, the law being as it is, it's no good trying to think in terms of legal agreements.'

'You can rely on us,' Grace said, again putting all the conviction she could into the words. 'You can both do so. We want you both to feel that we are your friends.'

'Thank you. I do.'

Suddenly a shaft of sunlight lit up the January sky. It flung itself through the dormer window, throwing a beam of sunshine across the room, in which particles of dust instantly appeared and began to dance. It lit up the little table as if in a floodlight. They smiled at each other, pleased with it and with the success of their negotiations.

'A symbol, Charles,' Grace said serenely, leaning forward to finish a piece of teacake. Charles, who felt suddenly relieved as if a physical burden had been lifted from him, was in no mood to disagree.

CHAPTER NINETEEN

'IF I were you, Felicity, I should ask Greta Humphreys,' Polly said. 'She knows an awful lot.'
'Why does she?'
'Because of being an orphan.'
'Oh, yes, I see, of course,' Felicity said and began putting the new photograph of her baby brother into the leather folder by her bedside table. It was not easy in the dark.
When she had got it in, she said, 'But how exactly does being an orphan . . .' her voice trailed off. She hardly ever finished a sentence nowadays.
'Well, it's obvious really. She says everyone thinks, "poor child, she hasn't a mother, so nobody will have told her the facts of life". So they all think they'd better tell her. She says she's been told the facts of life more times than anybody else in the world.'
'Whatever are you two talking about?'
'Greta Humphreys. She says nobody has been told the facts of life more times than she has.'
'Yes, I heard that. But there must have been somebody to tell her; I mean who brought her up?'
'Her grandmother, but of course she'd be too old to know about things like that.'
Kitty lay half listening to them, but really rehearsing in her mind everything that she would do from the moment she woke up next morning. Her train ticket was in a brown envelope in the pocket of her school coat. She was to get up immediately the first bell went, get dressed, put on her hat and coat and go quickly down for an early breakfast all by herself at the staff table in the corner of the dining-room, walk to the station and travel alone to London. She shivered with excitement at the thought of it. There her father would meet her off the train and

they would cross London to the other station and go together to Oxford.

'She says it's surprising how little what they say varies from person to person. I mean, you'd expect there'd be a few variations.'

'I don't see why. It's the same thing, whoever tells you.'

'Oh, I don't know, you'd think they might each have some sort of slant of their own.'

'Do you remember that doctor last term?'

'Oh, golly, it was funny. Kitty, you were awful, do you remember? She can't be asleep, can she? Not when she's going to Gwen's wedding tomorrow. Kitty!'

Kitty's picture of herself and her father on the platform slipped away. She remembered the red-haired doctor who came to speak to the middle school on the facts of life. A large and hearty lady, wearing a baggy tweed suit, she was obviously the Head's idea of a thoroughly sensible person to talk to the girls. Kitty remembered her standing with one leg on the bar of her chair, proclaiming with great heartiness, 'The modern girl is sensible. The modern girl takes sex in her stride.' Kitty, sitting at the back, had said quietly, 'Well, where else could she take it?' and everyone had started to giggle.

'Yes, I remember,' she said shamefacedly; it seemed rather awful now, especially with Gwendolen getting married the day after tomorrow.

'I say, isn't it lovely without the sixth form?' Amanda said. 'It's so civilized to be able to talk after lights out.'

'Just for a little while,' Sue said. 'Remember that Jill and I are in charge tonight.'

'I wish they went out to lectures in the town every night. It's jolly good for them; it should be a regular part of their education.'

'Go and tell the Head. I bet they wouldn't mind. It must be marvellous just to get out of this place in the evening.'

'They're not as lucky as Kitty,' Amanda said. She stretched in the bed. 'Oh, Kitty, just think—a whole weekend away! You are lucky. I'd give anything, absolutely anything, to be getting out of here tomorrow even if it wasn't for a gorgeous wedding with handsome ushers and best men and all that.'

'I think there's only one best man,' Kitty said.

'I hate this term. The autumn term has Christmas at the end and the summer term has tennis and swimming, but this one is just foul and cold and beastly. Nothing but work.'

'I wish the staff would go on strike.'

'Polly, what a wonderful idea! They jolly well ought to; it's disgraceful the way they're underpaid.'

'I'd want to keep up woodwork though.'

'Mr Flynn wouldn't strike. He doesn't count as staff; anyway he wouldn't hear about it down there in the basement.'

'I'd hate them to go on strike,' Felicity said. 'I wouldn't know what to do. You don't really think . . .?'

'My father says that teachers ought to be badly paid,' Sue told them. 'Otherwise they will start going in for it just for the money.'

They were silenced: it was always the same with Sue's father, whose expert opinions now seemed to be spreading from the medical to the economic field.

'You'd get the wrong type going in for it,' Sue said to clinch the argument.

'But you get the wrong type now anyway,' Amanda objected.

'Hear, hear. Look at Roly and Thesby.'

'I'd rather not.'

'Oh, Roly's all right. She's poisonous, of course, but she isn't *embarrassing* like Thesby.'

'Don't be unkind,' Kitty said piously. 'Some of my best friends are lesbians.'

'Oh, Kit, you are a clown. When you leave school you ought to go into a circus.'

'I am. It's all arranged. I'm going to the Head's old circus.'

'Seriously though, I wonder what any of us will do?'

There was silence as they thought about the future and grew depressed.

'I just want to grow up and have a happy ending,' Felicity said at last.

'I'd like to do something that sounds marvellous when people ask you what you do at a party. I mean, it can't be very nice for Thesby when they ask her, can it?' Amanda said.

'My sister says she'll just go on saying she's a student even when she's teaching. She says that if you admit at a party that you teach, men just walk away.'

'How awful. Honestly, Jill, I don't know what we'd do without your sister to warn us about things.'

'She went ski-ing last year and she went up in one of those railway things that go up in the sky and there was just one other passenger, a Frenchman, and at the top they got out at the foot of Mont Blanc and it was so beautiful, she said. Anyway, they talked a bit and he asked her what she did and she said she was a student and, being polite, she asked him and he said, *"Je suis inséminateur artificiel."* She said it was awful; there just wasn't anything to say.'

'I'd like a job like that; that when you tell them what you do, nobody knows what to say.'

'So would I. It doesn't really matter what you do; it's what it *sounds* like that counts.'

'What are you going to do, Sue?'

'As a matter of fact, I talked it over last holidays with my father and a careers gentleman who happens to be one of his patients and I'm going to be a Government Social Security Investigation Officer.'

'A *what*?'

Sue repeated her choice of career.

'But what does it mean?'

'You go about making sure people don't get more benefits and things than they should. My father says it is very important now that there is so much welfare about.'

'Miserable old scrooge,' Polly said under her breath.

'Like being a spy, you mean, but without the foreign travel?'

'Really, Kitty, you are ridiculous. Anyway, it's time we went to sleep.'

'I don't feel a bit sleepy. Nobody does tonight. We don't get enough fresh air this term. Anyway, it's important to discuss our future. I'll do anything but teach and then I'll get married.'

'I'm going to marry late; in fact, I'm not marrying until I'm twenty-five.'

'You mustn't leave it too late, Polly. You might have to marry some horrible old man with no hair and that doggy smell that men get after forty.'

'Do they, Amanda? I didn't know.'

'My aunt says it's very difficult to meet men once you're thirty.'

'Well, my mother's aunt got married when she was fifty.'
'How disgusting! Honestly, I do think grown-ups are foul.'
'How did she do it, Jill?'
'She went to Oberammergau—before the war, of course—and met a man there. He was a solicitor and even older than she was.'
'Had he gone to look for a wife?'
'No, he was an executor for six religious ladies so he took them all there. Then he met my aunt.'
'What did they do with the six religious ladies?'
'I dunno. Had them for bridesmaids, maybe.'
They laughed so loudly that they did not hear the door open.
'Do I hear unseemly levity?' Miss Theswell asked.
There was no reply.
'Since it is my birthday,' she went on, 'I shall say no more about it.'
'Thank you, Miss Theswell. Happy birthday, Miss Theswell. Good-night, Miss Theswell.'
'Thank you, girls.' She giggled and added skittishly, 'The staff are only human, you know,' and went out.
'You could have fooled me,' Polly murmured.
'Sh, don't be so unkind,' Jill said. 'She's sure to be listening.'

To Kitty's relief they stopped talking and settled themselves to sleep. When the sixth formers crept in shortly afterwards, she was the only one left awake. At last she could indulge in the luxury of imagining tomorrow, knowing that she would not be disturbed. She let her mind drift back to the station. She saw her father and herself boarding the train, looking around the carriage and settling in, their cases on the rack over their heads.

Gwendolen would meet them at the station at Oxford and take her to the dressmaker's to try on the frock. It was all ready, apparently, hanging on a coat hanger at the back of the door of the dressmaker's workroom. It was ice blue lace over deep blue satin, with a big bow. It would be suitable for dances afterwards, Gwendolen had said, probably forgetting that Kitty never went to dances. Kitty shivered again with pleasure when she thought of the dress. Gwendolen said that the dressmaker had promised to set aside the whole evening in case the dress needed altering. But it wouldn't, Kitty was sure of that, not after the hours it had taken the domestic science mistress to measure her and the way she had kept not eating this term. It might even need taking in a little bit. She shivered again, partly with pleasure and partly because it was cold, this early February night.

She awoke at intervals during the night, imagining the blue dress hanging on its coat hanger behind the door and hearing the sounds of the station. She dreamed that she had missed the train, that the dress was brown and made of sacking and that she had lost her father, was hunting everywhere for him and nobody would listen or care. When at last the rising bell clanged, she was stiff and weary. She got up and walked over to the door to turn on the light. Nobody stirred.

Her hand on the switch looked funny, her arm looked funny too, dotted all over. She lifted up her nightdress and her legs had dots all over them as well. She took off her nightdress and in the cold dormitory stood naked in front of the long mirror. By the light of the unshaded bulb which swung from a long flex from the ceiling, she surveyed herself. She stared in disbelief; her body was covered all over in spots. Some of them were neat little spots, some big with white blobs on top. Her face was blotchy with big, messy-looking spots. She thought of the blue dress hanging limply on its coat hanger in a strange room, waiting for her. Big tears began to roll down her blotchy cheeks as she climbed back into bed.

CHAPTER TWENTY

'AND I'll have that chap,' Kitty said, taking the last but one of her father's pawns.

'And I'll have yours,' he replied, placing his black knight on the square where her white pawn had been.

'You shouldn't have done that,' Kitty said, racing her bishop up from the far corner to take his knight.

They played with speed and gusto and a technique more suited to the draughts' board. Indeed it was because they had played draughts together for so long that when they turned to chess they could never get away from the idea of trying to take as many of their opponent's pieces as possible.

Sister Henley came in to take Kitty's temperature. She was very apologetic about it, Kitty noticed, casting benign glances all over the place and then standing with her hands primly folded on her stomach as she waited by the bed.

Kitty stared in front of her, frustrated by the glass rod which made her feel such a ninny, but even that could not spoil the joy of the day. It was being an absolutely perfect weekend, and she would remember it for ever. A week ago she could never have believed that she would ever be happy again. She had been aware, in a kind of nightmare, of being removed to the sanatorium, of somebody saying it was only—yes, *only*—a bad case of chickenpox, of telegrams being sent to her father and Gwendolen, of the Hen standing by the bed and saying, 'Never mind, better you than the bride,' in a voice that was obviously meant to be encouraging and cheerful.

After three days she began to feel better and then a telegram came from her father saying he would come for the weekend and she was cured. She had a little room to herself because she was infectious.

So all yesterday afternoon he had sat in the armchair by the bed and they had played games and talked about Gwendolen getting married. At least he had told her all about the wedding; all the things that did not matter, like who had been there and what they had worn and said. Not the things that really mattered like how it had felt walking up the aisle to give away the irreplaceable Gwendolen.

The Hen had behaved extraordinarily. All the staff were inclined to be pleasanter when there was a parent about, but the Hen had a great partiality for fathers.

She had sustained him with cups of tea and coffee and had even given him supper and had clucked in apologetically to take Kitty's temperature and pulse and had not bustled or snapped once. She beamed at Charles and nodded in agreement with whatever he said, smiling the agreeable smile of the very deaf, and then standing with her hands demurely clasped on her starched apron.

She removed the thermometer now, looked at it critically, her head inclined so that she made herself an extra chin, said 'Excellent, excellent,' and shook it down. She gave Charles a glance that was at once pleased and modest as if to show that, although delighted with his daughter's improvement, she would not dream of taking all the credit for it. Charles thanked her and she said, 'Well, I'll leave you in peace now,' and left them alone together.

He pulled the table up to the bed again and after a few quick turns there remained on the board only two kings.

'It's a draw,' Charles said, as he took Kitty's queen in exchange for his own.

'Is it? Surely if one of us was really clever we could still put the other in check—like so?' she indicated two squares.

'Yes, but we're not clever, so we can't. Our kings would just go waltzing round the board together for ever.'

She laughed and stretched in bed. 'I love being bad at chess,' she said contentedly.

'Yes, it would be awfully worrying to be good at it.'

'Having to think before every move—ugh!'

'And not being able to have a game unless you had two hours to spare.'

'I like anemones best of all,' she remarked inconsequentially.

They both looked at the bowl by the bed. He had brought

them the day before and now they were opening out in the warm room, wide, soft petals of glowing blue and purple and powdery black.

'You deserved them.'

'Why?'

'You didn't fuss.'

'It's a bit negative. I don't think I'd like to have "She didn't fuss" on my tombstone.'

'I'll see that you don't.'

She laughed.

'Happy?'

'Yes. It must be awful to have a sensible father.'

'No more flowers for you if you say things like that. By the way, I talked to the Head yesterday and she's rather pleased with you.'

'Pleased with *me*?'

'Well, don't sound so surprised. She thinks you've got a bit of brain hidden away somewhere.'

'Very penetrating of her, I must say. Nobody else has ever noticed it. I've been a late developer for years.'

'No, I'm being serious.'

'Well, I think I'll go on being a late developer for a few more years. It suits my way of life.'

'Kitty, shut up or I'll smack your bottom for you, spots or no spots. She says you've done very well this term and she thinks it's because you're happier. I think so too, and—' he paused and took her hand, 'I just want you to know that you're to stay happy and not to worry and that everything is working out all right.'

'You shouldn't say things like that. It's tempting providence. You ask the Hen—she's good on Providence.'

She was terrified that he would be serious; if they could just drift along until it was all settled, then there might be a chance, but if they were solemn and talked about it as if it was all definite, fate would be obliged to intervene.

'Please, Kitty. Be sensible. It is important, you know. You just don't seem to believe it will all be all right, do you?'

'Of course I do.'

'You've done marvellously. I don't want you to be the loser by this divorce.'

'The loser? It'll be a gain for everybody,' she said briskly.

'I wish I could make a home for you. You know that I would if I could, don't you?'

'Yes, I know, but I don't mind. I'll go up there in the holidays. It's all right, really.'

He stroked her hand and said nothing.

'It's not for ever,' she added.

Still he said nothing.

She would have liked to have told him that she really meant it; that she wasn't just being brave, but could not think of the right words.

'Can you stay at Mrs Wedgwood's?' she asked.

'No, I don't think so, not for long, anyway.'

'I wish you could have stayed there until I left school and then we could have had a flat together. We must make it really lovely so that if you get married again you'll have a proper home ready for her.'

Charles looked at her, startled.

'Well, what a little schemer you are! And you say it as if you wouldn't mind.'

'Mind? Why should I mind?'

He might marry someone very clever whom he could really talk to, or someone very beautiful and kind or someone very good at making everything homely. He might marry somebody who was all of those things. But just one of them would be wonderful, and enough to make him happy.

'You're a funny little object. Most girls would mind a lot if they made a home for their father and then he married again.'

'Why? Daughters are only daughters.'

Once in Art Appreciation the art mistress, giving them a talk on 'mother love' with slides, had shown them a picture by some Renaissance artist of a woman suckling at her breast not a baby but her aged father. The art mistress had found it very moving; it had made Kitty feel rather sick. Daughters are only daughters.

'You're right, Kitty. I suppose I'm so used to the idea of love being possessive—and even hate being possessive, if it comes to that—that I'd forgotten that the love of a child for a parent need not be. I'm sorry,' he said humbly.

It was awful; she said the first thing that came into her head.

'You don't mind too much about losing Gwendolen?' she asked, and instantly regretted it.

She willed the words unsaid, but he replied quite matter-of-factly, 'No, not so long as she's happy. Children mustn't mould their lives around their parents.'

How simple he made it sound, she thought. She imagined him leaving Gwendolen with Arthur at the top of the aisle, taking his place in the pew next to the bride's mother. So Gwendolen had been bound to Arthur in holy matrimony and they had watched it together, Martha and Charles.

'Kitty,' he said suddenly, 'I am grateful to you, you know. I do realize that it's all due to you and I want to tell you how marvellous it is, like a great weight being lifted from me. I was beginning to despair; even now I can hardly believe that I really shall be free—thank you, little one.'

'I didn't do anything.'

'Didn't you? Truly?'

'Well, we had this little chat at the end of the Christmas holidays, of course.'

'Of course.'

'And now shall we play another game of chess? We've got five minutes before tea, so we should just do it.'

He looked at her for a moment, began to speak and then thought better of it. With a characteristic shrug of helplessness he shook his head at her and began to arrange the chessmen.

CHAPTER TWENTY-ONE

LOOKING back, Kitty always remembered it as her happiest term at school. Perhaps it had something to do with the kudos attached to being Gwendolen's sister and the compassion which being unable to go to the wedding aroused in even the most hardened breast, such as Miss Roland sported under her good twin set and pearls. Work had suddenly become more interesting too and some of the staff began to turn into real human beings. Most remarkable of all, however, was a sense of being one of the crowd. She seemed to be part of the life of school, not just an observer of it. She joined in and no longer did every chance remark seem to bounce off the walls with echoing absurdity or sinister repercussions.

She decided that now that work had become interesting she would solve the problem of the holidays by working really hard. In future the books would not remain undisturbed in the bottom of her trunk, she resolved, as she packed twice as many as usual. Now that it was all settled, she would go to her mother's in the holidays, be as good and uncritical as possible and work hard. She pictured herself, wrapped in layers of sweaters and a rug, at the table in the arctic dining room. If her mother went out in the evening she would take her books up to the airing cupboard and work in that. She almost looked forward to the holidays. When she was given a message on the last day of term telling her that her father had rung up to say that he could meet her for half an hour in the buffet on Gradby station as he had been on business up north, her cup of happiness was full.

Even Miss Theswell's unfortunate remark did not spoil it. Before leaving school they all had to be checked by one of the house staff to see that they were tidy enough for the outside world. Miss Theswell, clicking her tongue in distress, pulled

Kitty's coat collar out and straightened her hat. 'Really Kitty,' she said jocularly. 'You look like a child with no mother and two fathers.' Then she paused, looked as if she wished she had not spoken and turned away. Kitty realized that she was thinking of her parents. So they did know at school, then. But she did not mind. Better that they should, now that it was all going to be settled legally and finally. No more being tactful, no more pretending.

A lot of them travelled together as far as Gradby and then dispersed. She and Amanda had a compartment to themselves. She opened her case and took out the wedding photographs that Gwendolen had sent her to look at and then take to the Deedes, who had been unable to go to the wedding. As they sat with the contents of the case strewn along the seats commenting on everybody at the wedding, Kitty found herself almost forgetting that she had not been there herself. Then she replaced them carefully at the bottom of the case to keep them flat, and repacked her belongings on top.

'What are you going to do these hols, Kitty?' Amanda asked as they drew into Gradby station.

'Work; I've got so many books in my trunk there was hardly any room for my clothes.'

'Horrible old swot!' Amanda said amiably.

'What are you doing?'

'I've got to go away with my parents to some boring old hotel by the sea. We've been before; there's nothing to do and in the evening the parents dance; honestly at their age! It's disgusting.'

She jumped off the train while it was still moving and disappeared into the crowd. Kitty, who was less athletic, waited until it had stopped before getting off. She made her way towards the buffet.

The air was cold and foggy and damp. It struck chill after the pleasantly stuffy train. She could scarcely see the face of the clock in the middle of the station through the thick mixture of fog and smoke. She shivered and almost ran to the buffet. She pushed with her case against the swing doors and felt the warm steaminess of the restaurant rush to welcome her. It smelled of tea and people and warmth and damp clothing.

It was early and there were not many customers. The woman

at the urns looked up expectantly when she came in. Kitty hesitated; she didn't want to get her coffee before he came, but on the other hand she was not sure if it was allowed just to sit at a table without buying anything. She was tempted to go back outside but told herself that she was nearly fifteen and not to be ridiculous; just march up to a table like a grown-up would. Then she stood by the door and ostentatiously looked at her watch so that the woman at the urns would know that she was waiting for someone.

The man at the far table lifted his head and looked bleakly at her, then smiled suddenly and waved. She had to superimpose this picture of her father, drained, tired, waving wearily at her, on the image she had had of him laughing, striding in, full of life. For a moment everything was misty, blurred so that she felt dizzy. Then she walked towards him; he kissed her somewhat absent-mindedly and smiled at her with a poor attempt at cheerfulness and asked if she had had a good term. She watched him, every movement, every flicker of expression. He put a coin into her hand. 'Off with you to get a couple of coffees,' he said. 'And then we'll have a talk.'

She took the money and went across to the counter where the urns hissed and steamed like engines. The woman behind them looked at her disapprovingly, and squirted coffee and milk into two cups.

Kitty carried the cups back to their table and sat opposite to him. The little marble-topped table was somewhat apart from the others, in a corner. There were some tea stains and crumbs on it. A fat, slow-moving woman in a dirty floral overall approached and they watched in silence as she smeared a greasy dishcloth over the surface of the table and removed an over-flowing ash tray.

The coffee was scalding hot. She felt it blaze a trail down her throat, and then fan out in her chest.

Her father looked down at his watch.

'Well, I suppose I had better start,' he said. Then he paused. 'It's failed, Kitty. They went back on it.'

'They?'

'Yes. I don't know where to start.'

'Begin in the middle,' she said. 'I know the first part.'

'You know how Mrs Deedes came to see me and it was all

arranged? Shortly afterwards I sent off the necessary evidence and waited for your mother to act. Nothing happened. After a while I wrote and she did not reply. So I wrote again and then she did reply, just a short note saying she had no intention of doing anything. So I wrote at once to Mr Deedes—I didn't believe it really. I thought she was just wanting to get me worried, you know how she is. I had an absolutely unbelievable letter from him saying how pleased he was that I'd made this recent financial settlement on my wife, which would ease her house-keeping problems!'

'No, no, he *couldn't*.'

'But he did. No mention of the divorce. So I wrote again reminding him of the agreement. I wrote to your mother too. She wrote back saying that for religious and financial reasons she had changed her mind.'

'Religious and financial reasons!'

'Yes. It's marvellous isn't it? Funny—at least it might be in any other context.'

'But it's stealing—it's like taking money for something and then not giving it.'

He smiled wearily. 'Well, it is and it isn't. You see the whole transaction is illegal, which makes it impossible to get redress. Wally Deedes knows this, so he knows that they have the upper hand.'

'But why should he do it? What's his motive?'

He looked at her seriously. 'That's what puzzles me, Kitty. I keep asking myself why. You see, I knew it was the way Martha might behave—she's played this cat-and-mouse game before—so that was why I wanted to involve the Deedes; I thought they'd see fair play. They quite categorically said that if I kept my side of the bargain they'd see that she kept hers.'

A picture of Wally Deedes came into Kitty's mind. A Wally Deedes walking spider-like to the door, holding a log basket and a coal scuttle, a Wally Deedes carrying the kicking Zoe out of church, aware of suppressed laughter when the twins made their gaffe on the stairs, a Wally Deedes constantly humiliated by his wife's social aspirations, always bearing the brunt of her ambitions, doing the work while she basked in the glory, a Wally Deedes goaded into furious resentment as he went to fetch coal and logs, stopping by the door to throw back a look of hatred at a flattered and admired and distinguished guest, who was treated as a being superior to himself.

'Can you think, Kitty, why he should do it?'

'No,' she lied, knowing that she could not explain.

'Well, I still thought he would see sense, so as I had to come up north for a conference two days ago, I wrote and told him I'd ring him at his office. I did, yesterday. A secretary answered and said she would put me through. Then she called back and said he wasn't available. In short he refused to speak to me.'

'He couldn't face it! the beastly, horrible little man! I'd like to kill them both.'

'Don't, love—it doesn't help,' he said wearily, taking her hand, and unclenching the fingers one by one. 'Well, it just means we're back where we started, only poorer and wiser.'

She knew that school fees were a source of constant anxiety. 'Would you like me to leave school?' she asked hopefully.

For the first time he smiled spontaneously.

'No such luck, my love. We'll manage the fees somehow or other.'

He sat in silence for a while, and then he said, 'Of course, to be fair to the man, goodness knows what your mother has said to him. It was probably a mistake on my side to part with the money so easily. It was the last of my savings, which I'd earmarked for a deposit on the flat, but to him it probably seemed that if I could just toss off a cheque for a thousand pounds without any hesitation I must be very rich and able to repeat the performance any time. Your mother always likes to give the impression that I'm a rake, so maybe she's made out that I'm a very rich, mean one as well. He may well have felt that it was justifiable to hedge and repeat the thing next year.'

'But, surely you wouldn't . . .'

'Don't you worry; they won't catch me twice. Even if the money existed, which it doesn't, they wouldn't manage to play the same trick on me again.'

It was the first time she had ever heard such bitterness in his voice. In all these years he had managed to laugh, to be tolerant, to make excuses for her mother, to be unembittered even in the face of her bitterness and railing. She hated them for doing this to him. She looked at the stricken face; how changed since he came to see her in the sanatorium, yet really it was only that the cheeks were hollower, the eyes deeper, with dark rings around them; but it was more than that, there was this deep resignation behind the features and the change of expression changed the face. Only the hair remained incongruously buoyant and cheerful. She wanted so much to comfort him. If only she had been a wife, say, she'd have been able to stroke that hair, murmuring comfort and endearments. Or if she had been a mother, mothers can comfort; she had seen them do it. But daughters cannot. Daughters are powerless to help, especially if they are still schoolgirls, a bit fat, a bit spotty and rather plain.

'How can they do it?' she burst out suddenly, wanting to fight them there and then.

'The combination of Wally's financial acumen and your mother's religious convictions could do anything,' he replied in the same bitter voice.

She knew she was only making things worse by asking questions, going on about it. But what else would a daughter do?

'Can't you threaten him with something or other—after all you've got the law on your side?'

'That's just what I haven't got—this thing is collusion.'

That wasn't what she had meant, but she didn't interrupt to try to explain.

'But you've got a point,' he went on. 'In fact, I did think of threatening to put the whole thing, all the evidence, the agreement, which was collusion, in the hands of a group of MPs who are lobbying for the reform of the divorce laws. They would use it as evidence in favour of reform or at least to get a Royal Commission set up. Of course everybody already knows what goes on but it would be further evidence for them of the way the present law is abused. But, you see, Wally Deedes knows that he has nothing to lose, compared with what I have. For a start, any hint of collusion could lose me the chance of divorce later on, and furthermore, I'm in a profession where such a taint would be very harmful to my career, and he isn't. Though I suppose it would matter less to me now than it would have done at the Bar,' he concluded sadly.

Her eyes began to smart; from his voice she knew that he was aware of the mistake he had made in leaving the Bar. He had done it for their sake, for Gwendolen's and hers, and now he alone would suffer.

'Once you've left the Bar, can you go back?'

'No. I made my decision, Kitty, and I must stick by it. I think I knew when I did it that it was probably a mistake,' he added almost to himself. They were almost exactly the words he had once used about his marriage. With his marriage, so with his career. Was he doomed to go wittingly into disaster as people born for tragedy do?

He realized immediately that he had said more than he had intended and looked briskly at his watch. At the same time over the loudspeaker there came a series of booming sounds, loud but unintelligible. 'That might be your train,' he said. 'We'd better go.'

He pushed the chair back and reached for the stick which she had not noticed leaning against the wall. She picked up her case.

'I'm sorry, poppet,' he said. 'You tried so hard to help. It's nobody's fault; just the way life is.'

He put his hand rather clumsily on her shoulder, knocking the brim of her school hat with his arm. She tried to smile and then, her eyes smarting and her hat making visibility even more difficult, she led the way between the little round tables to the swing doors.

He took her arm as they went across to the platform. He had his stick hooked over the other arm which held the case. She could feel the slow up-and-down of his uneven walk. The limp was more pronounced; he seemed almost to be leaning on her. The fog was thickening.

The train was in and almost empty: he put her case up on the rack and she took off her hat and tossed it up on top of the case. Then they went out into the corridor. She leaned out of the window while he stood on the platform. Behind him was a pillar and an empty bench.

'Well, well,' he said. 'I almost forgot to tell you that Gwendolen sends her love.' He put his hand on hers as it lay on top of the open window.

Before she could reply the train gave a lurch forward.

'Daddy,' she said, suddenly afraid that the train was leaving. 'What are we going to do?'

'Nothing,' he said. 'But don't you worry.' The train stopped again. 'You know, one of the consolations of growing older is that you realize that most problems solve themselves if you leave them alone long enough.'

'Oh, you know that's not true. It's just letting yourself get resigned; it's giving up.'

'When you're young,' he went on as if she had not interrupted, 'you rush about trying to put things right and then you learn that most problems can't be solved. But if you do nothing, time has a way of disposing of them. You see, most problems belong to a particular time and once that is over they don't exist any more.' He looked at her with his old, wry smile. 'As you sit on the train, Kitty, just think of some of the things in history that people got so worked up about, huge problems like religious power threatening the state; nobody ever solved them. Time passed, people ceased to care and the problems went out of date. So you see we must just sit it out until this particular problem dies a natural death.'

'You're an impossible old tease,' she said, 'and you know you're talking rubbish.' Then, emboldened by a more purposeful lurch forward by the train, she added, 'and I love you very much.'

He took both her hands for a moment and then, as the train began to move, replaced them on the window ledge and stood back. She leaned out waving to him, but not for long, for he was very soon lost, with the pillar and the bench, in the fog.

CHAPTER TWENTY-TWO

'IF there is one thing I hate it's breaking promises,' Martha said angrily. 'It's a sin, like dishonesty. If you said you would take those photographs to the Deedes, then you must do so.'

'But not today—any time will do.'

Kitty had just arrived and was unpacking her case in the cold bedroom which benefited hardly at all from the brilliant spring sunshine outside. Her mother had come in as she reached the bottom of the case, removing her slippers and sponge bag to reveal the large brown envelope which contained the wedding photographs.

'Any time *won't* do, Miss.'

'Won't you be seeing her at one of your meetings?' Kitty persisted, terrified of having to face the Deedes before she had had time to work out the next move. On the train she had tried to grasp what had happened, desperately wanting to think how she could intervene, afraid that he would just let things happen, resign himself and let them destroy him. But she was confused at the sudden change and her mind seemed to slip about, unable to grasp any of the new facts firmly enough to plan anything.

She understood clearly enough, however, that the facts were not really new, that all the time she had been blissfully happy thinking it was all settled, the little spider-like figure had been there waiting and watching. So it had all been an illusion. The happy memory of last term had been destroyed.

Once, on a windy day when she was walking along by a stream on the lower slopes of Southerby, she had come across a little hollow between the rocks, warmed by the sun and sheltered from the wind. She had lain there, warm and protected, with her eyes shut, listening to the water rippling over the pebbles and hearing the wind among the rocks and trees overhead. It had felt so sheltered, so safe. She had opened her eyes suddenly to see, staring at her, only a few yards away, the idiot son of the farmer who lived down the valley. She knew him; he was quite harmless and simple, but she never forgot the horror of realizing that all the time she had lain there, blissfully unaware of anything but the feel of the sun and the sound of the water, those eyes had been upon her, watching. His presence destroyed even the pleasant memory of the place, for she could not remember the one without the other.

She knew that she would never be able to explain about Wally to anybody; the rational part of even her own mind could not accept it. Even in the fog and wretchedness of the journey out of Gradby it seemed too melodramatic and unlikely. When after half an hour they ran into brilliant sunshine and she saw her first lamb, leaping and prancing on the green slopes, the evil of it seemed impossible to believe in, yet she knew without a shadow of a doubt that it was true.

The snow had all gone, leaving the grass a vivid green against which the lambs showed up almost white next to the grey sheep and outcrops of stone. Her heart seemed to reach out to the green country which slid up and down outside the windows; maybe it housed the enemy, but it was home.

She remembered the feeling as she stood now in this house which did not feel at all like home and heard her mother say suspiciously, 'Anyway, why are you so unwilling to go? You're usually eager enough.'

'I'll go after lunch,' Kitty said. 'There wouldn't be time now.'

'That's better,' Martha said with satisfaction. 'But next time we'll have less arguing before you do as you're told, if you don't mind.'

She paused at the door. 'And don't forget,' she added, 'that when you get back Miss Flute will be here, so mind your manners, please, Miss.'

In the short time since she had arrived, Kitty had heard a lot about Miss Flute, who was coming to stay for two days. She was coming to arrange for a mission to the village in the summer, for which she was the organizer of accommodation and general manager. She was also the reason for a mammoth baking that morning and the need for a scratch lunch.

That afternoon, as she walked slowly through the village to the

F 161

Deedes' house, carrying the photographs, Kitty tried to think what she would say. It depended, of course, on how they received her: shamefacedly, perhaps, with apologies, or defiantly. The way to the house was very familiar, for years ago when they were all children Gwendolen used to go and play with the little Deedes' boys and as she left the house she would say, 'Oh, Mummy, do I have to take *her*?' She meant Kitty, of course, and her mother would say, 'Yes, of course you must, don't be so selfish. You can't leave your little sister behind. Besides, I don't want her under my feet in the kitchen.'

Gwendolen would pull a face, making a clicking sound with her tongue and take her unwillingly by the hand and walk her far too quickly through the village to the Deedes' house, so that Kitty always had a stitch in her side when they arrived. Once the gate at the bottom of the drive was closed behind them, Gwendolen would say, 'Now, you go and play by yourself and don't bother us. Mind you don't go out of the garden,' and leave her.

She used to wander into the vegetable garden and spend hours watching Old Glossop. Mrs Deedes had bought a piece of the field behind her house to grow vegetables in because of the war. She had even acquired a gardener to grow them, when nobody else had gardeners. Of course, Old Glossop was too old for the war. He was really too old for gardening. He was the slowest-moving man Kitty had ever seen. She used to love to meet him when she walked home from school, just to watch his slow walk. He was not crippled or ill or anything like that. He walked quite normally but it was just that he did it in slow motion. Inch by inch he moved along, not quite motionless though he seemed so at first glance. The village children called him 'old greased lightning,' which she did not understand and always meant to ask a grown-up what it meant, but when she remembered about it there never seemed to be a grown-up there to ask.

When he came to work in the Deedes' new vegetable garden, she sat for hours on an edging stone just watching him, while Gwendolen was off playing with the boys. He took no notice of her; he just got on with his digging as if she wasn't there. He dug a deep trench, carting the soil out in a wheelbarrow until it lay in a series of hillocks at the far end of the plot. He dug deeply and very slowly. Between every movement of the spade he straightened himself up and said 'Oooh,' or 'Ahhh,' releasing his breath in long sigh. Sometimes he spat into the trench in a friendly way, as if he was talking to it. She supposed that that was why he later on referred to the trench as 't'spit'.

It took him about a week to dig that trench. Then he started all over again, except that he threw the soil from the next trench into the first one, instead of carting it away to the far end. It seemed to Kitty, sitting on her stone watching him, that it would take him years and years before he got to the end and was able to throw the first lot of soil into his last trench. It must have taken quite a long time, because she remembered that by the time he was ready to do so, the heap at the end of the plot was all overgrown with weeds.

He used to have his tea in the Deedes' kitchen and sometimes she would go in and watch him. He had a big pint mug of tea and dipped everything into it. When he drank he made a very satisfactory slurping sound and then wiped his moustache slowly on his sleeve. It was a big, grey, drooping kind of moustache which seemed to fall into everything he ate or drank.

By the time he had finished, the kitchen had a different smell, compounded of tobacco and old clothes and something indefinable which she later identified as the smell of potting shed. Mrs Deedes used to open all the windows when he had gone out. 'I'm so sorry,' she would murmur, 'but really it is too cold to give the poor man his tea in the garage.'

Soon she had somebody else to watch as well; Mrs Deedes had to have a wall built between her new vegetable garden and the field. Grandad Pickering—so called to distinguish him from his grandson at the limeworks—came to build it. He was said to be the last dry-stone-waller in the district. Farmers and shepherds did bits, of course, mending them, but Grandad Pickering was scornful of the efforts of such 'gap-wallers'. He had been at his trade since he was a lad at school with Old Glossop. All his life had been spent just building walls. Kitty wondered sometimes how many of the walls that straggled all over the hills had been built by Grandad Pickering.

He was quite different from Old Glossop, very talkative and although his craft was a slow one there was something quick and lively about the way he looked and moved. He would bring a great pile of stones from the hills in a cart and then work away at it until there were none left and the untidy heap of stones had been transformed into Mrs Deedes' wall.

He built two walls really, next to each other and then filled in the space between them with smaller stones. Sometimes he would put big key stones across to tie the two sides together, he said. Unlike Old Glossop, he liked to explain everything to her and kept telling her that the wall would be standing there long after he had gone and maybe after she had gone too, though he did not say where. Once he even let her try, but none of the stones she picked up seemed to fit into the spaces. After that she marvelled at the way he always picked up the right stone first time and almost never had to throw it back on the heap and choose another.

He was critical of Old Glossop, whom he had known all his life. One morning when Mrs Deedes had carried out a cup of tea to them he called over to Old Glossop, 'What do you want diggin' so deep? It's God's good earth on top and bloody muck underneath.'

Kitty looked; it was true. She had often noticed that all the nice soft, crumbly soil was going to the bottom of the trench and then being buried under great slices and chunks of heavy grey-coloured clay. Glossop turned his head slowly in Grandad Pickering's direction. 'You didn't oughta use language like that in front of a lady,' he said reproachfully. Then he dipped his moustache down into the mug of tea and began making the slurping sounds which meant that he was drinking.

All her holidays, when she was little, seemed to have been spent watching the two old men, but now, with the greater wisdom of nearly fifteen years, she knew that it could not really have taken more than a few months to build the wall between the field and Mrs Deedes' new vegetable garden. It always seemed to have been sunny then, she thought, feeling the warm knob on the wrought iron gate and remembering how she always used to have a stitch in her side when she reached it.

When she reached the top of the drive she still had not worked out what she would say to Mrs Deedes.

Grace Deedes was lying back in a deck chair in a sheltered, sunny corner by the front door. She was wearing a floppy hat and had the newspaper on her knee. An empty cup was on a little table by her side.

'Hello, Kitty dear,' she said warmly as Kitty approached. 'Wally and I are just doing a spot of gardening.'

Kitty had observed, as she came up the drive, a dark figure down on its knees and hard at work on the other side of the hedge, where the soft fruit trees grew.

'There is *so* much to be done,' Grace went on, 'at this time of the year. All the horrid weeds just bursting forth everywhere and everything to be done in preparation for the new season's growth. There, come and sit beside me.'

With her plump, beringed hand, she patted a kind of garden pouffe near her chair. Kitty remained standing.

'Ah, I see you have the photographs. How kind! I had a note from Gwendolen telling me you would bring them. Now let me see.' She hunted in her bag for her spectacles, put them on and reached for the photographs. Kitty found herself sitting on the pouffe, handing her the photographs one by one, while Grace went slowly through them, commenting on each. 'Charming, charming,' she would say. 'Such a handsome couple they make, don't they? Your parents must have been so proud of their big girl.'

It was astonishing; she was carrying on as if nothing had happened. Kitty had not known what to expect, but certainly she had not expected everything to be just the same as usual. It was very difficult to hate Grace Deedes, Kitty thought, when she burbled on in this motherly way. She must disconcert her somehow or other.

'Such a shame about your chickenpox, Kitty dear,' Grace was saying. 'Never mind, better luck next time.'

'I don't think Gwendolen is thinking of getting married again just yet,' Kitty said.

Grace laughed. 'Well, dear, I didn't exactly mean that,' she said. 'I was thinking of when it comes to your turn,' and she gave Kitty an arch look from under the floppy hat. Kitty ignored it.

'My boys will be home from school tomorrow,' Grace went on. 'Thomas hopes to help the vet in Pendlebury; he is so very fond of animals. And how has this term been with you at your school, dear? I expect you have all kinds of talks and concerts, like my boys do.'

'We had a talk by a vet whose job it was to fit contraceptive devices to the sacred cows in India.'

Grace swallowed. Really it was so difficult to tell if this child was serious or not.

She smiled placatingly.

'Very interesting, dear. Now I'm sure you'll stay and have a little tea with us. I'm just making some. I'll call Wally. No, it would be a shame to take him away from his task a minute too soon. There's such a tangle of horrid weeds among the blackcurrant bushes and as for the gooseberries, I just don't know how he squeezes in between them.'

It suddenly became very important to Kitty not to take tea or anything else from Grace Deedes. It was betrayal enough to have to talk to her but to break bread with her —never.

'My mother said I was to hurry back because she wants me to get tea for a Miss Flute who is coming to stay.'

'Ah, yes. Well, if you're quite sure, dear, I won't keep you from doing your duty. I know you will want to help your dear mother as much as you can when she is always so busy. Perhaps you wouldn't mind calling to Wally as you go down the drive— he is working in the fruit garden beyond the hedge. Just tell him tea will be ready in ten minutes, would you, dear? That will save me a little journey. I do so hate shouting. What was it Shakespeare said? "Her voice was ever soft, gentle and low, an excellent thing in woman." I do agree with that; I hate raised voices myself.'

Kitty picked up the photographs, said good-bye briefly and set off down the drive. At the bottom she called over the hedge, as rudely as she dared, 'Mr Deedes, Mrs Deedes says your tea will be ready in ten minutes.'

The spare figure straightened itself painfully and walked over to the hedge, but she was already out of sight. Wally Deedes glanced at his watch, pulled off his gardening gloves, looked dolefully at the deep scratches that the gooseberry thorns had made on his arms and then sat down on one of the big stones that edged the fruit garden.

As he sat he stared down at his watch, gazing at the hands; the second hand racing round, the minute hand advancing slowly towards four o'clock and the hour hand quite still and yet imperceptibly carrying away his life.

When the ten minutes were up he got off his stone, stretched and then walked slowly out of the fruit garden to join his wife.

'Tea's ready, perfect timing,' Grace called down to him, contriving at the same time to keep her voice soft and gentle although not low. Then she lay back in her deck chair and indicated the pouffe by her side. Wally sat down heavily. She took his hand. 'Isn't it lovely,' she said, 'to enjoy a little break? Nothing like gardening and fresh air to make one long for a nice cup of tea.' She looked tolerantly up into the sky. 'You know, whenever I hear people grumbling at working men wanting tea breaks, I always say to myself, "My goodness me, if I was working in a deep hole in the road all day, I'm sure I'd want a tea break".'

Wally, who had been paying more attention to the pain in his back than to what his wife was saying, looked up at her in some surprise. 'Yes, dear, I expect you would,' he agreed.

'Wally dear, you'll be going indoors to wash handies, so I wonder if you would mind, while you're in the kitchen, just boiling up some more water in the kettle and bringing it out with you? Thank you so much, dear.'

Wally, whose hands had kept remarkably clean under his gardening gloves, hesitated and then got up off the pouffe and walked stiffly indoors. When he returned, his wife was lying back and had finished her first cup of tea. His own, which she had poured out and left by the pouffe, was already cold.

'What a funny little object Kitty is,' Grace mused. 'So jumpy and highly strung. One hardly knows how to take the things she says.'

Wally grunted. 'Has she been then?' he asked. 'I didn't see who it was who called me.'

'Oh, didn't you see her, dear? She came this afternoon to show me Gwendolen's wedding photographs. Otherwise I should have been down with you grubbing out those horrid weeds, of course. But one doesn't like to seem to want to get rid of a little girl in her sad circumstances.'

'I suppose she knows about her parents?'

'Oh, surely not, Wally dear. That would be dreadful. She is only a child. I'm sure that if we had any little ups and downs we should take great care not to let our boys know anything about it, and they are much older than little Kitty.'

Wally did not reply. Little ups and downs seemed a singularly inappropriate way of referring to the troubles that beset the Langdons' marriage.

'Surely, Wally dear, you agree with me?' Grace insisted.

'Of course,' Wally replied wearily.

'Splendid,' Grace said, smiling serenely up at him. 'For a moment you seemed less than sure.'

She leaned forward, her mouth pursed, intending to kiss his forehead.

'I shouldn't,' Wally warned. 'You can't trust those deck chairs.'

'Perhaps you're right, dear. What would I do without you to take care of me? I'll have another cup of tea if you can squeeze one out of the pot.'

He poured it out and handed it to her.

'Wally,' she said thoughtfully as she stirred it. 'You are quite certain that we did the right thing about Martha and Charles, aren't you?'

'Quite.'

'I should like to think that one day they will all be grateful to us.'

'Martha is already.'

'Er—yes. You are not being a little—well—er—cynical, are you, Wally?'

'No, only practical.'

'Like Martha, so practical, such a busy person. Do you know she has one of the mission ladies staying with her? I was going to offer hospitality and then I remembered that we might be going away, so of course I couldn't.' She took a drink of tea. 'Then we didn't go away after all,' she added.

Wally got up.

'I shouldn't think about it any more,' he said. 'It's done now.'

'Of course, the girls are bound to be grateful to us; such a disgrace it would have been to have divorced parents. Especially for a sensitive child like Kitty.'

There was silence as Wally stood, waiting to see if she had finished.

'Back to the toil, dear? I'll join you shortly. I'll just finish up my tea. One mustn't waste good things when so many people are in need. Then I'll clear away these odds and ends and come down and join you. Yes, I think—I pray—that one day all the

Langdons will be grateful for what you did. It's just that sometimes I wonder about poor Charles.'

Wally walked back to the fruit garden. He pulled on his gloves and began to attack the weeds among the bushes. Docks and creeping things were all tangled together; far into the ground they went, wrapping themselves around the roots of the fruit bushes and biting with long white fangs deep into the ground. Wally dug around and under a clump of ground elder, stopping now and then to tug at it, but it seemed to be anchored somewhere out of reach. He dug deeper and the stem got thicker. He put down his spade and heaved on the thick grey stem. 'Poor Charles, indeed,' he muttered to himself sarcastically. 'I don't expect he's spending his Easter holiday pulling up weeds.' He gave an extra tug and the stem broke. He looked at it with something approaching triumph, and then he suddenly spoke out loud. 'Why should he be shot of her?' he demanded with venom.

CHAPTER TWENTY-THREE

MISS FLUTE said grace, which freed them all to start on the steak and kidney pie, and then, 'What a splendid clock,' she said, almost in the same breath as that with which she had addressed her Maker.

'It has been in my family for years, Miss Flute,' Martha replied. 'Of course, in those days such lovely old pieces were treasured, but I am afraid there isn't much feeling for them nowadays.'

'Yes, it is so sad,' Miss Flute agreed. 'There is so much sentimentality nowadays and so little real sentiment.'

Miss Flute made an interesting contrast with her mother, Kitty thought, as she watched them eating their steak and kidney pie and agreeing with one another. Miss Flute had a round, pink-and-white face and a lot of fuzzy fair hair. She had wet, rather sore-looking lips and was short-sighted. Her spectacles were big and thick, and sparkling, so that they hid the expression of her eyes. She seemed very eager to please: more than that, she seemed confident that she could do so. She was short and dumpy. Kitty was intrigued to notice that she hooked her bow legs one on each side of the table leg, as if anchoring herself to it. It was the position in which they had to arrange their legs around the bottom of the rope in gym. She pictured Miss Flute suddenly shinning up the table leg.

'I've had a very useful day,' Miss Flute was saying to Martha. 'I've made lots of contacts and have had several firm offers of accommodation. I always find people are so kind if one just approaches them in the right way.'

'Will you come back yourself?' Martha asked. 'You're very welcome to a bed here, you know.'

'I may return, but really I'm only an organiser, a very humble position. I just go ahead and arrange things; a kind of outrider for the Lord. I think that's the word, isn't it, Kitty?' she added to draw the child into the conversation.

Kitty, who was sitting smiling to herself at the thought of Miss Flute shinning up the table leg, jumped and said, 'What?' Her mother glared at her.

'I was just asking you if the word was outrider?'

'Outrigger, I think it is,' Kitty said vaguely, avoiding her mother's eye. She was hoping to keep in favour sufficiently to be allowed to walk on the hills tomorrow. Clearly it wasn't going to be possible to have any talks with her mother while Miss Flute was here. Her best plan was to go out on the hills and get her strength up ready for the battle.

'Miss Flute,' she said earnestly, 'do you want anything to be delivered? I could take it.'

'Well, now, there's a kind offer,' Miss Flute said. 'We want to send notices to everyone in the parish, but of course it *is* a very far-flung village and I fear I shan't be able to get my Little Billee to some of those hill farms.'

Little Billee was Miss Flute's baby Austin, now in the garage.

'Kitty will take them; it will give her something to do.'

'Of course, I should really like to see the people myself. It is one of my principles never to just push literature through the letter box, but to go inside and talk to the people who live there. I always say to my helpers, "Remember, there are Real People on the other side of That Door".'

There was a short silence after this proclamation and then Martha said, 'Well, in that case, perhaps Kitty could take you to the more remote parts? I would come too, but I don't think I shall have the time this week.'

'Splendid, splendid.' For a moment Kitty thought Miss Flute was going to clap her hands. Then she turned her sparkling spectacles on Kitty and said, 'Would you really do that? Show me all these places? In that case I will do the village on foot tomorrow morning, then in the afternoon we'll take Little Billee and the next day it will be Shanks's Pony and the hill farms. Now, no more shop, that's settled. Tell me, Kitty, how do you like school? What are young people thinking about nowadays?"

She made several attempts to draw Kitty out during the rest of the meal, always by asking some huge and unanswerable question that succeeded in rendering Kitty quite dumb.

Not a very bright little girl, Miss Flute reflected, as she helped her kind hostess clear away the dishes. She really must try to open her up a little, get through that reserve. Perhaps having such an energetic and public-spirited mother overshadowed the poor little mite, she thought as she marched to and fro between the dining room and kitchen, humming 'Onward Christian Soldiers' to herself. She had always had a way with children; not that it was any credit to her, of course, it was just that they sensed she was interested in them. Children are like animals, she always thought, they *know*.

'Come and sit down now,' Martha said, leading the way into the drawing room after they had washed up.

'What a lovely fire,' Miss Flute remarked as she held out her hands towards it.

'Well, it's a cold house,' Martha explained. 'I hope you'll be warm enough. I've had the electric fire on in your bedroom all the afternoon, so I hope you'll be all right, but just tell me if you feel at all cold.'

Kitty had noticed, when she went to put the bottles in the beds, that Miss Flute's room seemed, compared with the others, like a hothouse. It felt almost immoral in there, it was so warm. The feeling was heightened by the amount of feminine clutter which Miss Flute had spread about. On the bed there was a pile of silk scarves and stockings and a big leather pouch marked 'My Nightie'. There were spectacle cases and a shoe horn and some hair curlers with bits of fluffy fair hair attached to them on the dressing table, as well as some little religious booklets and two paperback thrillers, some pink and blue underwear, three pairs of gloves and a hat.

'My cousin was in the mission field,' Miss Flute was saying to Martha. 'But he had an unfortunate experience at the hands of the Muslims, you know.'

An understanding look was exchanged and then Miss Flute went on more cheerfully, 'He is now a very successful chiropodist in Surbiton.'

'God moves in a mysterious way,' Martha said.

'Indeed, yes. He is doing very well at it, too.'

They were sitting next to each other, Miss Flute and Martha, on the sofa and Kitty thought again what a contrast they made: her mother, tall, bony and grey, her clothes and expression equally severe. Next to her Miss Flute, plump, wearing a kind of knitted blouse like a teacosy, her pink face looking up obligingly, her spectacles sparkling and her fair, frizzy hair completing the picture of fussiness and fidget. On her temple she had a mole decorated with what looked like hundreds of fair, feathery hairs. Her mother's mole, by contrast, bore a single straight hair like a length of grey wire.

They were drinking tea.

'The trouble is that people have no sense of responsibility,' her mother said. ' They come to church to be christened, married and buried, that's all. I wouldn't have it; I'd shut the doors in their faces.'

'You don't think, perhaps, Mrs Langdon, that coming just one of these times might start something up in some of them that might make them change their lives?' Miss Flute gave Martha a persuasive little look over the brim of her teacup.

'Well, some say so, but I think it's weakness, just an excuse. The vicars should be firmer, they shouldn't stand for it.'

'Ah, now tell me a little bit about your Vicar; I must go and see him first thing tomorrow.'

'Well . . .' Martha began, glancing in Kitty's direction.

'I quite understand,' Miss Flute said, and turned her attention to the teacup.

'You can get a book, Kitty,' her mother said, nodding towards the bookcase.

As she stood by the shelves of books at the far end of the room, looking along the titles, Kitty was astonished to hear her mother say in kindly tones to Miss Flute, 'Not much fun for a girl of her age just listening to grown-up conversation. I wish she'd go out more, but of course you lose friends if you go away to school.'

Kitty chose *Little Dorrit* and took it to a chair near the bookcase, as far as possible from the sofa.

'Yes, it is one of the disadvantages,' Miss Flute was saying. 'But I always think that education is so important in this day and age.' She took another sip of tea. 'Even for a girl,' she added.

Somewhere in Kitty's mind there floated a remark she had

read somewhere: 'She had every virtue and only one vice; she was intolerable.' She giggled. Miss Flute glanced towards her. She pretended to be laughing at the book. She was aware that Miss Flute was giving her an indulgent smile.

Then Miss Flute turned her attention back to Martha and they fell into quiet conversation. From the sofa, Kitty could hear whispered snatches in which words like 'diocesan', and 'evangelical' and 'very high *indeed*', frequently occurred. The names of past vicars cropped up too and sometimes her mother's voice sank to inaudibility and Miss Flute made clucking sounds.

Soon, however, she herself was lost in *Little Dorrit,* living and feeling with William Dorrit and little Amy in the world of the Marshalsea; that world was more real to her than the room in which she sat and its people more alive than her mother and Miss Flute. She had escaped.

CHAPTER TWENTY-FOUR

'IT'S too silly of me to have upset our arrangements like this,' Miss Flute said, as she limped to the car, 'but really how *providential* that it's not too bad for me to drive.'

'You've done very well,' Martha reassured her. 'There's only the Bartons left and Kitty and I will go there tomorrow. I'll explain to Mrs Barton all about it, don't you worry. If it had to happen, it couldn't have happened at a better time.'

'But it didn't have to happen,' Kitty reflected. If the sight of the new lambs had not made Miss Flute feel so skittish that she had jumped off the top of a high stile as they returned home across the fields from Thornton, it would not have happened at all.

'We are in the Lord's hands,' Miss Flute told her, shutting the car door with a bang.

'Let me know if you get back safely, won't you?' Martha requested.

She can't if she doesn't, Kitty thought to herself.

'Because I really don't like you driving with that foot.'

She can't drive without it, Kitty reflected.

'Don't you worry, Mrs Langdon. You'll be hearing from me; I never forget my bread-and-butter letters! But really I'm sure that this is the best arrangement. It isn't too painful and if I wait until tomorrow I might not be able to get home at all. In the circumstances I can't hope to visit the Bartons anyway, so there it is. Well, Mrs Langdon and dear Kitty, we must be on our way, Little Billee and I. Thank you so much; you have been more than kind.'

'It was no trouble. After all, we are put into this world to help each other.'

'Ah, if only everybody thought that, the world would be a happier place,' Miss Flute said wistfully. Then she added more briskly, 'Well, we must be off,' turned on the engine and pulled the starter. 'He's getting impatient,' she said with a giggle as Little Billee jerked into gear and took a great leap forward.

'Good-bye, good-bye,' Miss Flute called out of the window. Little Billee moved erratically up the drive, stalled by the gate and finally set off noisily down the road in the wrong gear.

'Good-bye. Come again, any time,' Martha called back. 'Don't just stand there, child, go and shut the gate after her. *Think!*'

It was quiet in the house after Miss Flute had gone; for two days she seemed to have filled it with bustle and chat and had spent a lot of time in the kitchen singing hymns as she made sandwiches. Now, for the first time these holidays, Kitty was alone with her mother.

She sensed that her mother was aware of it too and was avoiding all opportunities of conversation; she kept frantically busy, tearing the sheets off Miss Flute's bed, washing and ironing, tossing on dust sheets, cooking and generally working herself into a state of exhaustion.

It was not until they sat down to supper that they were alone and inactive. Now was the time, Kitty thought, for there would be no chatting by a fire tonight. The drawing room grate was scraped bare, the hearth washed clean and the chimney stuffed with newspaper. So it was now or never.

'Your report came this morning,' her mother said, interrupting her train of thought.

'It's early; I suppose they wanted to get them out before Easter.'

'It's better than usual,' Martha said grudgingly.

'Oh, good.'

'No need to sound so pleased with yourself. Any credit must go to the Lord.'

'Then He must take the blame for the bad ones too.'

'Once and for all, Kitty, I will not have this; how dare you speak sacrilege in this house?'

'I'm not, I'm only being logical. If He gets the credit, He must also take the blame. It's only fair.'

'You talk just like your father. We will not discuss it any more.'

There was silence as she poured herself out another cup of tea, took a cream cracker and handed the plate to Kitty.

'We'll go up to Bartons' farm tomorrow,' she said.

'I can go alone,' Kitty offered politely. 'There's no need for you to give up your time.'

'Must you argue about everything? I've told Miss Flute I'll go and speak to them and I will. If there's one thing I can't bear,' she said, snapping the cream cracker angrily in two, 'it's people who break their promises.'

Now or never, Kitty thought again. She shut her eyes, made herself say, 'You broke your promise about the divorce,' and waited for the roof to fall. It felt like the bravest thing she had ever done.

Her mother, however, was obviously prepared.

'I did not,' she said calmly. 'I asked the Lord for guidance and did as He said.'

'Then you mean you were wrong the first time?'

'No, I do not. If we let the Lord guide us we cannot do wrong.'

'So you mean you never blame yourself for anything?'

'No, I do not. If it was wrong, the Lord wouldn't have let me do it. People are so stupid—if only they'd just obey the will of God, they'd find life much easier. The whole trouble with your father is that he has no faith.'

Kitty was silent. She knew it was fruitless to argue. Reason had no place in her mother's scheme of things and she would only get side-tracked. She must counter emotion with emotion. She must cling to the one thing that mattered, which was somehow, at this eleventh hour, to save him.

'And just to confirm my opinion,' her mother went on, 'I took spiritual advice from Mr Mabey.'

Kitty stared at her. For a moment she was afraid she might laugh. The idea of her mother seeking spiritual advice from Mr Mabey was a bit like a cat asking a mouse for advice on its diet.

'I gave no details, of course,' Martha went on. 'I just asked his opinion about divorce in general. His views were very much in accord with my own,' she concluded with satisfaction.

'Of course,' Kitty said.

'So we'll have no more talk of divorces,' her mother said. 'It's a disgraceful way for a child to talk anyway.'

'I don't see why; it affects us as much as it does you.'

'We shall go on as we are. It suits me perfectly. And, as I say, if the Lord has widowhood prepared for me I hope I shall accept His will with a good grace. Indeed I shall welcome it.'

She wiped her mouth with her table napkin as if to demonstrate her preparedness.

'Besides,' she continued, 'I do not intend to jeopardize my own future and my children's by risking poverty as the divorced wife of a dead man.'

'You shouldn't use us as an excuse. Gwendolen doesn't come into it now that she's married, and I don't because . . .'

'Oh, yes you do. And don't try threatening me with leaving home. I know your father can't afford any fancy flats to keep you in during the holidays. As for Gwendolen, I know her well enough and she isn't one who wants to be bothered with a young schoolgirl sister about the place when she's newly married. It isn't as if you're useful and you're not exactly decorative, are you?'

Talking of Gwendolen seemed to start a new train of thought in her mother's mind. She looked at Kitty and a little smile worried the corners of her thin mouth.

'You owe your father no loyalty, you know,' she said with quiet triumph. 'Gwendolen was always his favourite. Everything for Gwendolen had to be the best.' She spoke in short sentences which fell from her mouth rhythmically like blows from a hammer. 'It didn't matter if it was toys or nighties. It had to be the best for Gwendolen. Second hand would do for you. He has never really been interested in you. Of course, he wanted Gwendolen and that makes a difference. He didn't really want you : you were a mistake.'

'Not so much of a mistake as he made when he married you,' Kitty replied, but by the time she had thought of saying it she was alone and in bed. At the actual time she had said nothing and victory had seemed to go to her mother. Only when she was re-living the scene in bed did the argument go her way and the repartee come out right.

It was worse than that. Her mother did not even win a fair argument; she just made forays on her own ground and issued triumphant statements. She didn't understand anything; she didn't understand that of course Kitty always knew that her father must prefer Gwendolen. It only made sense. First-borns are always special, even in books. And then Gwendolen was so clever and so lovely to look at and so capable, so in control of things. She was able to manipulate circumstances somehow, not just people, though she did that too, of course, very well.

Kitty felt almost sorry for her mother for imagining that she could make her jealous of Gwendolen; it had never entered her head even to compare herself with Gwendolen. They were quite different people.

She remembered the hopeless look on her father's face, the resignation, and felt herself stiffen with fear in the cold bed. She wrapped herself round the stone hot water bottle for comfort. She must think; her mother clearly was convinced that the best and quickest way to widowhood was by refusing a divorce. She might even try to go on extracting money by dangling the hope of a divorce in front of him. He had said he wouldn't fall for that one again, but what else could he clutch at but straws? Hope would be followed by disappointment, distress, torment. Her mother was right; it was the quickest road to widowhood.

She mustn't despair, she told herself firmly, moving the bottle as it began to burn her. There must be some way out; tomorrow there would be ample time to talk. She imagined them setting out, walking through the village and climbing up Thornborough, for the way to the Bartons' farm lay just over the crest of it.

They would pick their way among the boulders, limestone and millstone grit, see the new braken pushing its way through the coarse, wiry grass, her mother holding forth incessantly about the mission and the vicar and meetings and village affairs, determinedly avoiding the topic uppermost in both their minds.

Surely, she thought, if there was some way of raising it up there in the hills, her mother wouldn't be able to use all the old false arguments, using herself and even Gwendolen as an excuse? Deception and hate and self-righteousness belonged down here in the valley, but surely truth dwelled among the hills? She jerked suddenly; she must have been nearly asleep. Some half-asleep words like truth dwelling in the hills were still in her mind.

It would not do: she must think clearly and be practical. She pulled the hard bottle towards her again. It would be easier to talk when they neared Funnel Pot, because her mother was nervous of it and usually fell silent as they approached the scree. In fact she rarely came that way. Kitty didn't much like it either, and sometimes tormented herself by imagining how it would feel to slip off the path and scudder down the slope of loose scree, faster, faster towards the great black emptiness.

The far side of the Funnel, as it was usually called by the villagers, was level, but the ground was marshy and, except at the end of a hot, dry summer, was impossible to walk over. There was a little fence at that side to stop anybody who was lost in a mist from falling in, but the scree side was unfenced, for there was no level ground at all. Sheep were known to have fallen in. When a pot-holing team had managed to get to the bottom by crawing along a side passage and then lowering themselves on ropes, they had found a great many sheep bones as well as two human skeletons.

The first time she had been there was soon after they came to Beckgate, so she must have been five or six. She remembered how fascinated she had been by the Funnel that first day. It was a very hot afternoon in autumn and all the long, hot walk up she had wanted to know what it would be like. The grown-ups had tried to describe it to her: a pot-hole. She imagined a little hole in the ground, a bit like a drain perhaps. Evidently a bigger hole than that, but made of pot. Nobody had thought to tell her that it was not really made of pot at all.

The awesomeness of it was unexpected. The curious steam that rose from it, the cold, earthy smell, the blackness and the way it made your heart go thump thump when you looked at it. She had stood holding her father's hand, by the fence. He had thrown a stone into the pit; they did not hear it reach the bottom, hundreds of feet below. They heard it strike first one side and then the other, for the hole was narrow, and then there was silence. It just vanished into eternity. No, it must have landed among the sheep bones and two human skeletons.

Her mother, standing well back, shouted to them that it was

time to go, but they stood marvelling, herself and the father who was holding her hand. At one side an endless stream of water trickled down the side of the rock.

'Fall in if you want to, Charles,' she heard her mother say. 'I don't care. I'll get the insurance.'

His grip on her hand tightened, and he drew her gently away. She didn't know what the words meant, only that something dreadful had been said.

The path above the scree along which they would walk tomorrow was wide and perfectly safe, but her mother always said as they approached, 'Mind you keep well in, lean up against the hillside. Look straight ahead,' and insisted upon going first. If it was at all windy she wouldn't go, which was ridiculous because the hillside sheltered you from any wind that might blow you into the funnel.

Of course, if you slipped, if you tripped up, if you were pushed . . . Suddenly every light in her brain seemed to flash on. She saw it all clearly: her mother, tall and angular, walking quickly ahead, herself following. Suddenly she saw herself slip, grab at the figure ahead, pushing between it and the hillside. After that it would be very quick, the slip on to the scree, the rush down its steep, loose surface of pebbles and stones, the disappearance into the black hole.

Then—then she would go back to the village—or should she go on to the Bartons? No, yes. She'd have to think that one out. There was no problem for herself: grown-ups get so used to arranging the small things for children that they altogether forget that children might arrange important things for themselves. They think grown-ups must be responsible for anything that really matters. She would just need to say, 'She slipped, she slipped,' and they would be so busy comforting her that they wouldn't question her closely. Anyway, adults always seem to want to believe children: it reassures them that innocence is part of the human condition.

The real problem would be her father. He knew her too well. She was not absolutely sure that she would be able to lie to him. There might even come a time when she would want to tell him, would be tempted to confess. It might even haunt her so that she had to go back and look at the place and feel the need to tell. She must vow now, in bed and clutching the stone bottle, that she would never, never, never, whatever she felt, tell him about it. If she did he would blame himself entirely, take the guilt on himself. He would hate the crime and blame himself for being the cause. It was so unfair that he had a conscience, that was what hampered him in the battle with her mother, who had none.

As for herself she had no conscience about it either; it was simply one death to prevent another. It was so simple too, so simple and quick and somehow appropriate. Maybe she had learned or inherited from her mother, this lack of conscience. Perhaps, she thought, as she settled down to work out the details of tomorrow's plan, she was more like her mother than she had ever realized.

CHAPTER TWENTY-FIVE

WALKING through the village with Martha was a tedious business, for she always stopped to talk to everybody they met. They were lucky this early afternoon, however, for most of the village was still having lunch.

They were almost through the village when they saw Miss Clotworthy who took in sewing. She was a pale, thin woman, with rimless spectacles. If she had been alone, Kitty would have accelerated so that she was walking quickly as she passed, calling out cheerfully, 'Good afternoon'. There was always this moment of decision when somebody was coming towards you: if you slowed, all was lost; you had to stop and talk. It was essential to put on speed. She felt her mother slowing down.

'Good afternoon, Miss Clotworthy.'

'Good afternoon,' Miss Clotworthy said, drawing up alongside. At the end of the pinched nose a droplet sparkled.

'Off for a walk, then, are you?'

'Going up to the Bartons' farm,' her mother explained, and went on, as Kitty had feared that she would, with a long explanation of why they were going, about Miss Flute and her ankle and the Bartons' literature, by which she meant a green and black pamphlet. Miss Clotworthy listened, nodding and saying, 'Oh, aye,' and later she would go home and tell her sister. Everyone in the village received news impassively, almost without interest, but retold it with great excitement as if by adding part of themselves to it they had made the news much more important.

'Did you get to the Council meeting?' her mother asked. 'I couldn't because I had this Miss Flute to stay.'

'Aye; they asked about t'Funnel like you said they should.'

'It's disgraceful. It should be fenced off; other pot-holes are.'

'That's what somebody said, but others said it were difficult like, with t'slope being so steep.' She laughed. 'But I can't talk; I've never been near t'place. Bartons were at meeting and 'e said 'e never uses that track now and sheep can't get along t'ledge because they've blocked up t'openings.'

'Well, Kitty and I will have a good look today,' Martha said. 'We'll keep a look-out for dead sheep too. It's scandalous the way they get left when the drifts melt.'

'Aye, it's a job for t'farmers to find them sometimes,' Miss Clotworthy said. Kitty often noticed how her mother's censoriousness brought out charitability in people in whom it was not otherwise very marked.

'And 'ow's little Gwendolen?' Miss Clotworthy asked turning to Kitty. She always muddled up their names. 'Not so little any more, you're going to be tall like your mother,' she observed.

They said good-bye to her and walked on beyond the village and up the lane. Little did Miss Clotworthy know, Kitty thought, what a heroine she would be by tomorrow morning. She would be the last one to have seen them as they set off. She could imagine Miss Clotworthy dabbing with her handkerchief around the perimeter of the thin nose, repeating their conversation, stressing the fact that poor Martha had talked about the dangers of the Funnel, prophetic-like. No doubt there'd be something about the poor little lass setting off too and now an orphan, like as not, since according to poor Martha that man of hers wasn't much good. It was lucky really, meeting Miss Clotworthy; she would document their journey.

'Well, it's a grand day for a walk,' Mr Pollard, the farmer who brought their milk, called to them. Fortunately he was in a hurry to get back to work after his dinner so did not stop to talk, but contented himself with saying, 'Good to be alive on a day like this.'

Once through the village it was unusual to meet anybody. They climbed up the steep lane to Thornborough in silence. Kitty relaxed, sure now that there would be no more interruptions, no more delays. It was a marvellous day. Spring comes to the North with all flags flying; it does not creep up on the world as it does in the South. It was still cold; there were pockets of snow even on the lower hills and no leaves on the trees yet, but there was no mistaking the presence of spring in the air.

'The sap's rising,' her mother said idly.

Kitty looked at her in surprise: that was it. You could feel the sap rising.

It was a long climb, sometimes traversing the hillside along tracks made by the sheep, later climbing between boulders and skirting patches of bracken. At the top they sat down and rested. Above them the bigger hills—mountains really—were blue in the distance and capped with snow. Below them the slopes fell away, tier after tier, down to the village and its outlying hamlets.

'Better get on,' Martha said, once she had got her breath back. 'No point in sitting about here.'

She walked ahead. Kitty followed. She felt almost light-headed with the relief of not having to be finding ways of approaching the subject of the divorce, of thinking of arguments in favour of it, tensing herself against the cruelty of the replies. This perfect day did not have to be spoiled with arguments and hatred and spite. The offering to the Funnel was a good, clean, honest way of settling it all. It seemed right that this straightforward and simple solution should be found up here among the hills where truth and honesty dwelt.

Suddenly a curlew swooped low in front of them.

'It's too early for curlews,' her mother remarked disapprovingly, as she walked on, looking at the ground.

Kitty stopped to gaze up into the sky, watching the flight of the bird as it wheeled and soared overhead. It might be the lone one she had seen at the Source at Christmas. She rejoiced as she watched it cut great arcs of freedom in the sky. Then she followed her mother.

The path was beginning to narrow and soon they were opening the little gate in the wall on the other side of which the Funnel was waiting. She gazed ahead, enchanted. Under the clear blue sky the scree sparkled; there was a haze over it which moved and shimmered in the sun, contrasting with the dark stillness of the mist which hung over the Funnel. How sheer the scree dropped and at its foot how sudden was the plunge down into the earth.

'Come on, come on,' her mother said, irritable in her nervousness. 'I don't like this at all. It's disgraceful the way the Council won't do anything. No dawdling, mind; I'll go first.'

She set off along the ledge and Kitty followed her. The path was almost three feet wide at first but soon narrowed and, which was more alarming, sloped down towards the Funnel. Then it righted itself and widened again. That was the point, this side of the place where it righted itself, where the path narrowed and sloped down towards the scree.

It would be better, Kitty had decided, that it should be done on the return journey. This would give her a chance to make sure that there was nothing new to create problems and to check the exact spot where the path narrowed. Furthermore, it would make more sense for her to run on to the village rather than return to Bartons' farm, which was nearer. Not that she had quite decided about that one yet; it might be better to leave it until afterwards and then do whichever felt right.

Immediately they were through the gate at the other side, her mother broke into a tirade against the Council. 'All the other pot-holes are fenced; it's ridiculous just to have that bit of fence at the other side.'

'But where could they put it on this side?'

'Round the edge, of course.'

'But there's nowhere flat for them even to stand and it's all loose stones.'

'They could build a wall from loose scree. They would find a way if they wanted. Where there's a will there's a way. In the old days men didn't shy off a bit of work just because it was dangerous. There's too much namby-pamby nonsense nowadays, all this welfare state, that's the trouble. It undermines people's morale, that's what it does, undermines the morale.'

'Miss Clotworthy said that it wasn't used nowadays anyway. The Bartons go round the other way; they've got a tractor, you know, and they go down the back way. I've seen them.'

'And as far as the Bartons are concerned, the Devil may take care of the poor sheep.'

'She said the sheep couldn't get through now.'

'That's enough; she was talking to me, not you. Don't they teach you not to eavesdrop at that place your father sent you to school? Pendlebury wasn't good enough. Oh no!'

She stopped suddenly and pointed. Kitty realized that her last exclamation referred not to school but to the tractor which was disappearing through a gate in the field beyond. It seemed to have two or three people on it and careered on despite their shouts, entering a lane and disappearing from sight.

'Well, let's hope there's somebody left at home,' Martha said. 'Or it will have been a real waste of an afternoon.'

A clump of trees hid the farm from view, protecting it from the wind. There were few trees in these dales and it seemed strange to walk under them, suddenly cut off both from the bright sun and the sharp wind.

There was nobody in at the farm except Granny Barton who was stone deaf. Martha tried several times to explain to her about Miss Flute and the mission, but although she smiled and nodded and seemed eager to oblige, she clearly had no idea what it was all about.

'They've just gone,' she repeated. 'It's a shame, you've only missed 'em by a few minutes. They're takin' a pair of lambs over to 'Ollerbridge.'

'That's all right,' Martha shouted at her. 'I'll just write a note on the pamphlet.'

In her neat, slightly backhand writing she added a few lines to the pamphlet and put it into Granny Barton's hand, shouting, 'For your daughter-in-law.'

'Yes, you're right, quite right there,' Granny Barton replied. Then she added confidentially, 'I'm a bit 'ard of 'earing, you know.' She stood, smiling and holding the papers until they left the farmyard.

'Well, that's an afternoon wasted,' Martha said as she shut the farm gate. 'I'll just have to have talk with Mrs Barton after church—not that they come very often.'

'It's a long way,' Kitty said.

'They get down every week to the whist drive well enough. If they can do it for the one they can do it for the other. Fancy leaving that poor old woman alone in the farm. Whatever would happen if she had a fall, she could be calling for hours,' she went on fiercely. 'Nobody cares for their old people nowadays. Just push them into a home out of sight. No respect for age, that's the trouble, no respect at all.'

They were crossing the field before the Funnel. Kitty felt very calm. It was all fitting in tidily. The decision to run on to the village afterwards was made: no point in running back to a deaf old woman. She could see the wall now and the little gate, no more than a flap of wood across a narrow gap in the wall. Once there had been a stile, but the sheep used to climb it.

She opened the gate for her mother. Halfway through, her mother paused. 'Just a minute,' she said. 'Wasn't that a sheep I saw back there, lying near the wall?'

'I expect so.'

'It looked funny, you know, the way it was lying. We'll go back and have a look at it. It might be dead.'

'Well, we can't do anything if it is.'

'Yes, we can. We can report it. It's disgraceful the way these farmers don't hunt out all the dead sheep at the end of the winter. I read somewhere—in the by-laws maybe—that it is incumbent upon the farmers to find all the sheep and bury them. Incumbent upon the farmers, it said.'

She opened the gate again and made Kitty return with her. The sheep was certainly lying very oddly, with its head twisted back at a queer angle. Kitty prayed that it would jump up in alarm when they approached and skip clumsily away. It did not move.

'Can't think why we didn't see it when we came,' Martha said.

'We wouldn't,' Kitty replied automatically. 'We'd have had our backs to it.'

'It must have sheltered here from the snow and been buried under a drift, or I suppose it might have slipped,' her mother observed, looking down at it. 'The poor thing, you'd think they'd have gone out and looked.'

The sheep's body seemed swollen and its legs stuck out stiffly like those of a toy. Something had eaten away part of its face and birds had pecked out its eyes.

Kitty felt sick. 'Come on,' she said, almost in a whisper.

'I wonder who it belongs to? Bartons I expect, but it should have a mark. It must be on the other side.'

She took hold of the horns and tried to lift the animal up to see the other shoulder.

'Oh, look, there's a bit of blue, I can see it,' she said triumphantly. 'Well, that's useful to know anyway.'

She straightened up.

'Goodness, what a colour, child! You've gone quite white. You'd better come away from it.'

Kitty consented to being led away. As they went through the gate her mother said, 'Squeamish, that's your trouble; you'd never make a nurse.'

She stopped where the path began to narrow.

'You'd better go first,' she said.

'No, I'm all right. You go first—you always do.'

'Do as you're told,' her mother said, pushing her ahead. 'I don't want you going dizzy and falling down there, though I suppose it might make the Council hurry up and do something about it. They didn't widen the road near the bridge until a child was killed.'

Kitty tried to think; it was no good pretending to fall forward now. They were nearly at the exact spot; a few seconds more and it would be too late. She must try something; if she stopped suddenly her mother might bump into her and slip to the left. She walked more slowly so that by the time they reached the place where the path narrowed and sloped down towards the scree, her mother was almost on her heels, then she stopped abruptly and pushed herself against the hillside.

Her mother stumbled, caught her by the arm, said firmly, 'Keep going, I've got you,' and frog-marched her to the far side. She did not pause until they reached the safety of the gate.

'Well, and what was all that about?' she enquired grimly. 'Trying to get us both down there or something? Sit on that stone and get your head between your knees for goodness' sake. You're almost green.'

After a while her mother was satisfied with her colour and they began the long walk home. Kitty was aware of being totally exhausted and walked automatically, one foot finding its way after the other between rocks, over stiles, along the coarse green turf. The sun had gone in and the air was cold. It was no longer sharp and fresh, just damp and chill. As they picked their way between the boulders, and traversed the slopes along little ridges which were the paths which generations of sheep had made, she said to herself over and over again, 'I'm sorry I'm sorry, I failed.' The words went through her head all the way back. She was still saying them to herself as she walked with her mother down the lane and into the village. Martha did not interrupt her thoughts for she too was tired.

They made their way through the village together without talking and in silence they reached home.

All that evening, all through the silent preparations for supper and the clearing away, until she lay beside the stone hot water bottle in bed, Kitty could only think, 'I failed, I failed.' If only there had been something else to blame, she thought, something beside herself. Her weakness disgusted her; to feel so sick at the sight of death, just a decomposing sheep—she made a conscious effort not to remember it. Now there would never be another chance. He had been so near freedom and she had failed him; she had let his one hope slip through her grasp. She could hardly believe that it had happened; that she had been so hopeless. What had he done to deserve such a daughter as herself? Gwendolen was so capable. Gwendolen had arranged a great complicated affair like her wedding, but she, Kitty, couldn't even manage a simple thing like killing her own mother.

PART II

CHAPTER TWENTY-SIX

'LIE flat on your back, and bend your knees,' Kitty read out, 'with the soles of your feet flat on the bed. Arms relaxed at sides. Breathe in. Push out your ribs and abdomen.'

'I can't breathe in *and* push out.'

'Well, that's what it says here. Do it five times. And it doesn't say anything about making that rude noise either.'

'I can't help it. I think I took in too much air with that last exercise. You know, that tighten-all-your-stop-cocks one. Anyway, you're allowed to when you're pregnant.'

Gwendolen lay on her bed, breathing in and pushing out while Kitty sat on a chair between the bed and the window looking into the garden. Summer had come to North Oxford: the long garden was green and lush, overgrown and drowsy. It lay below her passive in the sun, as if exhausted by the frantic activity of spring.

'You're not doing it,' she said. 'You've stopped breathing.'

'I've done it five times and the next exercise is how to relax. If you fall asleep in the middle of it you get full marks, so shut up.'

Kitty laughed. 'Good-night until tea time then,' she said.

She picked up her book and settled herself to read. Soon she felt alone and glancing at the bed saw that Gwendolen was asleep. She turned her chair and looked at her.

It always amazed her how beautiful Gwendolen was. Her hair now was spread out behind her head, framing the heart-shaped face. She seemd very young like that, her cheeks flushed and her eye-lashes long and dark. Goodness but she was lovely. When she was awake one did not notice it so much, distracted by the talking. But when she was asleep like this, it just seemed to lie open, all this loveliness, to be gazed at. The bump made her seem more vulnerable; it gave a touch of pathos, of mystery which the waking Gwendolen did not have.

Not that she looked very pregnant, Kitty thought, not six months anyway. In fact when Kitty had come at the beginning of the holidays she hadn't noticed anything at all and was surprised when Gwendolen told her about what she called the honeymoon baby. Gwendolen had laughed at her for not noticing and said it was quite obvious to everyone else. In fact she had thought Gwendolen looked a bit thicker; getting married seemed to have made her somewhat older and solider. She treated Arthur with a kind of loving tolerance that was almost maternal, combined with an excessive deference to his wishes, as if she was playing at brides.

It was strange and rather charming, this new side of Gwendolen. She had always been so knowledgeable and sure of herself and to see her now consulting Arthur as if she couldn't possibly decide upon the colour of the paint in the dinning room without his help was a little unreal, as if she were acting a part, enjoying the relief of pretending to obey while remaining confident in her possession of the power she had temporarily suspended. As for Arthur, he positively glowed under this treatment.

Arthur. Kitty smiled. She always smiled at the thought of Arthur. For some reason she could not quite take him seriously, could not quite believe in him as a separate person, independent of Gwendolen. It was as if he only existed so that Gwendolen could act her role. He was so delighted with life and with Gwendolen, so big and good-natured and handsome and extrovert. He was so pleased to have a clever wife who might have had a brilliant career; even more pleased that she had given it up. With genuine pride he emphasized to his friends that she had a better degree than he had. He was so generous and uncomplicated, he was so cheerful and just *nice*.

He was slow too. Predictable and deliberate, his mind moved methodically, never taking leaps. If he had not been clever, Kitty reflected, one might have thought him stupid. He treated Kitty in a teasing, affectionate kind of way, like a kid sister. She liked him very much, but would never be really close to him. It would be unthinkable to talk to him about something that really mattered, like the divorce. He knew all about it, of course; Gwendolen and he discussed it and then Gwendolen told Kitty what he had said. Arthur predicted that there would soon be a change in the law which would make separation a ground for divorce. It was vital, therefore, Arthur said, that her parents should keep apart in readiness for the change in the law. Keeping apart meant, according to Arthur via Gwendolen, not sleeping under the same roof. Under the same roof. It was an inappropriate little phrase, Kitty thought. It made her think of round native huts with no sides and thatched roofs. It had a happy, outdoor sound, a sunniness which did not go at all well with the word divorce.

Apart from waiting for a change in the law, Arthur said it was obvious that the divorce would be advantageous to Martha, and they would soon get her to see it that way. Kitty remembered her own terrible, dramatic failure up at the Funnel last Easter and felt hot shame again. Arthur and Gwendolen, confident and somehow powerful, would never fail in the miserable way that she had done.

Last term had been horrible; her miserable failure at the Funnel seemed to overshadow everything and cut her off from everybody. Everything she did seemed to be wrong. Yet she had dreaded the end of term with its prospect of the summer holidays. Then suddenly she had been told that her mother was going to help some cousins in Ireland and she herself was to spend the whole of the holidays, the entire ten weeks of it, with Arthur and Gwendolen. She, who had been hoping that at the best she might be allowed to stay with them for a week, could hardly believe it.

It had been marvellous, every minute of it, from the day she arrived. Nothing could have been more different from the awful Easter holidays. She could hardly believe that a sister of hers could have a marriage, a home like this. She looked gratefully across at the bed. Gwendolen looked so relaxed and contented as she slept, as if she had everything she wanted. She had, of course: academic success, comfort, security, even—compared with what they were used to—luxury. It was a lovely house, Kitty thought, solid and spacious and all so light and somehow cheerful. It would be impossible to imagine a house more different from her mother's gloomy, tree-darkened dwelling. They had worked upon it room by room and Gwendolen's mark was on everything. They were busy with the conservatory now; it was a great ramshackle thing on the back of the house, a Victorian addition to the Georgian building, which everyone who came to admire the rest of the house assumed that they would pull down. Arthur had said that they would, but Gwendolen, in one of her spells of being exaggeratedly deferential to his slightest wish, had begged to be allowed to retain it. He had agreed and she had been suitably grateful. Gwendolen was going to make it charming; already her imagination had filled it with vines and exotic plants. She used to sit in the evening doing quick sketches from different angles, to show exactly how it would be. Last night, as she sketched another corner, Arthur had watched her with adoration and Kitty had watched them both. 'She could have been a professional artist too, you know,' he had remarked quietly and knowledgeably to Kitty and she knew from his voice that what he meant was that Gwendolen could have been anything and that he was still baffled by the fact that she had chosen to be his wife.

This baby should certainly be beautiful, she thought, looking at Gwendolen and remembering Arthur. Unless, of course, the poor little thing took after its aunt. She laughed aloud and Gwendolen stirred and opened her eyes. She stretched slowly and yawned.

'What are you staring at, funny face?' she asked.

'Just making sure you get full marks for relaxation. I reckon you deserve about five hundred per cent.'

'I don't care how rude you are; it's just lovely lying here. I can't remember ever being so lazy, Kitty, I'm just basking in being preggers. I've gone very unacademic. I think being pregnant makes you superstitious. Do you know, I found myself not looking in the fields when Arthur and I walked along the lane the other evening in case I saw a rabbit and gave the baby a hare lip?'

'Then you'd better not look at me or the baby will be fat and spotty.'

Gwendolen laughed.

'Will you work afterwards?' Kitty asked her.

'Lord, no. Arthur wouldn't stand for it.'

'You used to say you'd always go on working.'

'Oh, I've lost all my ambitions. I just love being domesticated and making a home and I shall potter about looking after my baby, all as merry as a marriage bell.'

Suddenly it seemed important to get Gwendolen back into reality.

'You won't, not for ever, you know. You'll get jolly fed up with it when the novelty's worn off.'

'You sound like a prophetess, gloomy old thing.'

'You're playing house, you're dramatizing everything, like you always say I do . . .'

'What's that smell? Oh, Kitty, you *did* turn the peaches to low, didn't you? The ones I'm poaching for tonight, I mean?'

But Kitty had already gone, leaping down the stairs and into the kitchen, and put the blackened pan on to the back door step.

'I'm terribly sorry, Gwendolen,' she said as she came back into the bedroom. 'I quite forgot.'

'You're hopeless, Kitty.'

'I know. I really *am* sorry.'

'Never mind, I've got lots more. I bought an awful lot, they seemed so cheap,' Gwendolen said as she began to get dressed. 'I suppose I had better put on stockings.'

She took a maternity corset which seemed to be several yards long and began wrapping it round herself. It was a great white cage of a thing, all hooks and pieces of tape. 'It's still a bit big,' she said apologetically, as Kitty helped her to fasten rows of hooks and tie a great many tapes.

'A *bit*—it goes round nearly twice. Honestly, it would hold Arthur as well.'

Gwendolen laughed.

'There's quite a lot to spare,' she admitted. 'Just think, I'll be that big by November,' she added, holding it out in front of her.

Kitty did not reply for she was suddenly overawed by this strange thing that was happening to her sister, by the mystery of it all.

'You won't be able to see your feet,' she said at last, as casually as she could.

'I've put on one of my new maternity bras,' Gwendolen said. 'Have you seen them?'

Kitty looked. It had hooks up the front.

'It's well designed,' Gwendolen explained, 'and so practical. You just unhook it here and the front opens so you can feed the baby without the whole thing falling off.' She opened the little linen trap door and a large brown nipple popped out. Kitty jumped.

'It's gone a funny colour,' she said.

'They're meant to—it's not sunburn. Don't look so alarmed.'

'Will it go pink again afterwards?'

'No, never. I didn't know either. All sorts of funny things happen that you don't expect,' she remarked, as she pulled a smock over her head. 'This old thing will do for cooking. I know, we'll teach you to cook. It's time you could. Really it's quite simple. So long as you do exactly what it says in the book you can't go wrong.'

There were shelves of cookery books in the kitchen and Kitty began thumbing through them as Gwendolen took out bowls and spoons.

'I don't expect I'll be allowed to stay with you again, shall I?' she asked, as casually as she could, as she stared down at a coloured illustration for something called Faisan en chaud-froid. The poor pheasant still had its lovely tail feathers at one end of the dish, but at the other end the place where its head should have been was filled with hard-boiled eggs in aspic jelly.

'Rubbish, of course you will,' Gwendolen replied. 'Slice this onion for me, will you? Here's the chopping board and knife. Arthur and I were talking about it last night, but I wasn't going to say anything to you until Daddy comes next weekend. The thing is that Mummy is going back to Ireland for Christmas because the family there is emigrating in the New Year so it will be her last chance to see them. So you and Daddy will come here and we'll have an absolutely marvellous Christmas. Arthur's parents may come, but they usually go away and . . .'

'Oh, Gwendolen, is it really true? You're not just pretending?'

'Of course I'm not.'

'Oh, how lovely. I just can't believe it. Just think—no Christmas rows!'

The pheasant suddenly looked very colourful and gay with its long tail feathers and no head.

'No rows at all, my Kitty. Actually it's just as well that it has worked out like this because they shouldn't be under the same roof anyway in case of jeopardizing the chances of a divorce.'

'You think it will be all right then, the divorce, I mean?'

'Of course it will. I've made it quite plain to Mummy: if she wants to see anything of Arthur and me and the baby—when it arrives—she'll have to see sense about this divorce. You know how public opinion matters to her and, besides, she likes babies. It's the best weapon we've ever had.'

'The only one,' Kitty said quietly.

'What? And anyway now that I'm married I can deal with her so much better. You see, once one has had experience of a happy marriage—as I have—one understands even more how dreadful an unhappy one must be and theirs has been that for years. It's a sacrilege.'

She spoke piously; it was not real, Kitty thought. It was all part of the play acting; it would all melt away at the first touch of reality.

'What have you actually said to her?' she asked matter-of-factly.

'Oh, I'll make her see reason, don't you worry,' Gwendolen replied airily. 'I've always been able to deal with her better than anybody else and Arthur's being a solicitor is a help too. Anyway, he can twist her round his little finger.'

Kitty laughed at the picture thus conjured up and looked at her sister, doubtfully, half-believing, longing to be convinced.

'But, Gwendolen, you know what she did before; I just don't see, I can't see, that she'll ever really change.'

'Nonsense, of course she will. I've told her what we feel, you, Arthur and I, and I'll see that she's sensible. Arthur can spell out to her the advantages of her being divorced and getting more money and having it all settled. She'll see reason.'

'But she's so hard, and she hates him, Gwendolen. She wouldn't care about her own interests so long as she could hurt him.'

'I can be hard too; I've let her know that there's no coming here until this thing is settled. You don't think she wants all her cronies knowing that she wasn't even asked to the christening, do you? Don't look so worried, Kitty. Leave it to the grown-ups.'

'I would love to, really I would. I'm not meaning to be difficult, Gwendolen. It's just that it would be so awful if anything went wrong again.' She thought of his face, his stoop, the stick. 'I don't think he would—I mean, there's rather a lot at stake,' she ended lamely, trying not to be over-dramatic.

'I know that as well as you do, Kitty,' Gwendolen said, a note of reproof in her voice. 'There now, let's get on. You can peel these mushrooms. I've seen to the peaches. Then I'll show you how to make risotto.'

They peeled and chopped and sauted and the butter made a friendly noise in the frying pan. Kitty felt anxiety slipping from her as she got on with the necessary routine tasks that belonged to Arthur and Gwendolen's world, to the ritual of the evening meal. The kitchen smelled warm and homely, the results of the cooking were reassuring and Kitty began to share her sister's faith that everything would turn out all right. By the time that Arthur came home, she was sure of it.

It was a round, deal table and the cloth had red and white checks. Matching napkins, shaped into cones, stood on each plate. In the centre was a thick, twisty green candle in a chianti bottle, for they lingered over this meal and twilight would come before they had finished.

Even though she had been here for more than a month, Kitty still tingled with excitement at the thought of this meal. After knowing only the long dark tables at school and her mother's cold, forbidding dining-room, this was romance, heady, almost frightening. Excitement grew from the time when Gwendolen folded the last table napkin and said, 'Now we'll go and change.' It did not take Kitty long to wash herself and put on her good frock; she was soon down again, hovering around the table, surreptitiously feeling the waxiness of the candle, letting it slide up and down in her gently clenched fist.

She wandered into the kitchen savouring the herbal smells that escaped with the steam from the pans. Everything in the kitchen seemed new and matching. Even the pans were all the same, going down in stages through different sizes, like a well-spaced family.

She took the lid off one and peeped inside and then took a new and rather strangely-shaped wooden spoon and began to stir importantly, pretending she was a cook. She was doing that when Gwendolen came down. She had piled her hair up on top of her head so that Kitty stared when she saw her, taken aback by the different beauty, more remote, dignified, somehow very far removed from herself. She stood and stared, letting the spoon she had just removed from the soup drip down her frock.

Gwendolen laughed. 'Do you like it? I thought I'd give Arthur a surprise,' she said, rubbing the marks off Kitty's frock with a dish cloth. 'If you're going to throw food all over yourself for goodness' sake wear a pinny, you goose.'

'You look jolly nice pregnant,' Kitty said, allowing herself to be rubbed.

'It's just a case of keeping your bosom an inch or two in front of your tummy.'

'Yours is about six inches ahead just now.'

'It gets more difficult as the months go by, I'm told.'

They heard the sound of Arthur's car and then of the garage door being closed. Gwendolen looked quickly into the glass and patted her hair. Kitty, suddenly embarrassed and not wanting to be there when they kissed, ran out of the kitchen, but Arthur had come in by the conservatory door and she butted into him in the doorway.

'Hello, Kit,' he said, steadying her, but looking over her shoulder at Gwendolen.

'Darling, you are *ravishing*,' he said. 'Let me see.' He turned Gwendolen round, examining her from all angles, and then held her back at arm's length from him. Gwendolen turned up her face to be kissed, sweetly, dramatically. Kitty watched, as if it was staged for her and then, suddenly embarrassed again, began stirring the soup with great vigour, splashing it all over the cooker.

The air became electric with tension. 'Grub up,' she said heartily. 'Break it up.'

They laughed and Gwendolen looked at her, her head leaning against her husband's shoulder. 'Kitty,' she said patiently, 'would you mind not waving that soup ladle about? There'll soon be more on the cooker than in the pan. Honestly, you're hopeless.'

'No, she's not,' Arthur said. 'She's my favourite sister-in-law, aren't you, poppet?'

He kissed her perfunctorily. At the same time he said, 'Well, I must go and have a wash,' and strode out of the kitchen.

Kitty felt her eyes fill with unexpected tears, moved by a sudden overwhelming sense of gratitude combined with certainty that this state of bliss could not last.

'It's nice of you to have me to stay,' she said. 'Thank you, Gwendolen.'

Gwendolen put her arms round her. 'Funny little scrap,' she said, and the feel of her breast was very comfortable. 'You haven't had much fun until now, have you? Never mind, I'm going to make everything all right now that I have a home of my own. And now let's get this meal organized.'

As she carried the soup bowls on to the little round table with the checked cloth, and piled up the melba toast in the bread basket, Kitty tried hard to believe her, to rid herself of the feeling that this was all pretence, play acting, a kind of dramatic interlude before reality closed in. But even putting the bread basket on the table made her feel as if she was helping to set the stage in readiness for the actors to make their entrance.

'I'm starving,' Arthur said as he sat down. 'Aren't I lucky to have a harem of girls to get my meals?' He beamed at them appreciatively. 'This is good. Whatever is it?'

'It's called potage bortsch. Beetroot soup to you, darling. Don't you like it?'

'It's delicious; it was just a bit of a surprise that's all. I thought it was going to be tomato soup like mother used to make. You know, out of a tin.'

'Not a word against my mother-in-law! I should have warned you. It's what your father calls "some outlandish foreign dish".'

'He rang up the office today, by the way.'

'From London? Is anything wrong?'

'No, just a business matter. They're coming back home tomorrow.'

'We must ask them over for the day on Sunday,' Gwendolen said. 'Daddy's coming for the weekend so it would be lovely to have them all together.'

'No, it would be too much for you. I won't allow it,' Arthur said firmly.

'But, darling, Daddy's out all day Saturday and Sunday; he's coming up for that conference, you remember? He'll be at his college all day and only here in the evenings.'

'All the same, if you have my parents on Sunday in addition to your father it will make a lot of extra work and in your condition you need rest. You'll need more as the weeks go by.'

'But I do rest, darling. I lie down every afternoon because I know you want me to, don't I, Kitty?'

'Yes, she relaxes, pushes, tightens, puffs and blows and then goes to sleep.'

'Well, you can both laugh at me as much as you like. I know you think I'm fussing, but I don't mind. You mustn't overdo it, Gwendolen. I won't allow it.'

Gwendolen looked at him contritely. 'Of course, you're right,' she said. She paused as if thinking out a solution. 'I know, if you let them come, I'll promise to have an extra long afternoon rest the day before. Would that be all right?'

'That's my sensible girl,' Arthur said. 'You know when I have to be firm like this that it's only because I love you, don't you?'

'Yes, I know, darling; I will try to be good,' Gwendolen said, and they looked at each other for what seemed a very long time.

'And you're a marvellous cook, too,' Arthur said at last, returning to his soup.

Then he put down his spoon and said, 'I met Tim whatsisname today in the Broad—your old supervisor, you know.'

'Barraclough? How is he?'

'Very well. He asked after you, of course. Actually, I think he was angling to get you to take a job in Hilary Term.'

'What sort of a job? Not that I'd take it, of course.'

'Of course not. Apparently his junior tutor has had some fabulous offer from the States and they won't keep it open after January, so he's off then.'

'Then he has plenty of time to look for someone else.'

'You'd think so, but as he says people are mostly fixed up now for October; really it's more difficult than you'd think.'

'Poor old Tim.'

'Well, it's his worry, not ours. I must say I was a bit surprised that he mentioned it, knowing your condition. He even suggested that you might be fit and able to go back to work two months after you have had the baby.'

Gwendolen laughed. 'Well, some people do, you know,' she said. 'Heaps of my friends have managed it.'

'Well, in my opinion it's ridiculous,' Arthur said. 'What I mean is—if a girl decides to get married, she decides to get married. If she wants a career, she can have a career, but she must choose.' He paused. 'You can't have your cake and eat it,' he pronounced slowly, helping himself to melba toast.

Gwendolen smiled at him indulgently.

'You're so right,' she said sweetly.

'I'm not old-fashioned but I do think that once a woman's married she's got a job and shouldn't go looking for another. I think a woman's place is in the home, don't you, Kitty?'

'I think her place is where she wants to be,' Kitty said.

'Well, of course I agree with that, but what I can't understand is how these women can hand their children over to somebody else to be looked after,' Arthur went on.

'Our parents did—to nannies,' Gwendolen said. 'Your mother did, if it comes to that.'

'But that was different. She wasn't going out to work.'

Gwendolen laughed. 'You're gorgeous and I adore you,' she said, taking his hand.

He drew her on to his knee. 'It's mutual,' he murmured into her hair.

Kitty picked up the soup bowls. *'Pas devant moi,'* she said, carrying the dishes out into the kitchen.

'She's priceless, your sister. But seriously, Gwendolen, you do agree with me, don't you?'

'Of course I do. I keep telling you. I'm perfectly content to be a wife and mother just now. Besides, from a practical point of view, the nanny breed has died out. I wouldn't be able to find somebody able to look after our baby even if I wanted to.'

'Nobody must, except your darling self.'

'And you after midnight?'

'I don't mind. It's Daddy's babe throughout the night.'

'I'll keep you to that. Oh, Kitty, I am sorry, leaving you to do all the fetching and carrying while I just sit here on Arthur's knee. What a way to treat a guest.'

'Change places?' Kitty offered.

'Where's the wine?' Arthur asked, getting up. 'I'm sorry, Kitty, that wasn't meant to be unchivalrous.'

'It's still in the cellar, darling. I thought we'd have asti spumante, it's such a hot evening, but I didn't bring it up: the stairs are getting a bit steep for me.'

'Of course, darling, you mustn't think of it. Now promise me you'll never go near the cellar steps?'

'I promise.'

'Good girl.'

'I'll go,' Kitty offered.

'No, thanks all the same, Kit. It's a bit awkward to get at. Marvellous bargain, it was: a dozen bottles for the price of eleven. My father got on to it. It makes it a very economical drink.'

'Could you write and tell the school governors? They've got this thing about water.'

Arthur laughed. 'Poor old Kit,' he said. 'We'll put a bottle in your trunk. Do start serving, Gwendolen. It's right at the back of the cellar behind the crates—I meant to move it forward last time I got a bottle out, when your mother came.'

There was a silence. Kitty stared at her sister but Gwendolen had turned and was leaning over the serving table. In the silence Arthur's retreating footsteps sounded very loud.

'You like everything, don't you, Kitty?' Gwendolen said, busy with serving spoons.

'Did he say Mummy had been here? You never told me.'

'Didn't I?' Gwendolen said vaguely. 'I quite forgot. It's a while ago. She just arrived one evening. Literally landed herself on the door step so I had to ask her in.'

'But you said . . .'

'Now be reasonable, Kitty. I couldn't very well just leave her stuck there on the doorstep, now could I?'

Kitty began to reply, but Gwendolen came and sat down wearily at the table, resting her head on her hand. 'I don't feel awfully like food,' she said forlornly. 'But you won't tell Arthur, will you? Probably just a touch of blood pressure, but we mustn't worry him about it.'

Kitty hesitated and then dropped the subject, fearful of upsetting her sister or doing some irreparable damage to the precious child she carried.

'There now, we'll just carry on as if nothing had happened,' Gwendolen said, with cheerful forgiveness. Kitty was not sure if she was referring to her own health or to her mother's visit.

CHAPTER TWENTY-SEVEN

'IT'S a perfect time of day for a walk,' Kitty said as they climbed down the steps to the tow path.

'Well, it gives Gwendolen and Arthur an evening to themselves.'

'I think they quite like having me to stay,' Kitty said rather defensively. 'Gwendolen says it's company during the day.'

'I'm sure they do,' her father assured her with a smile. 'It must be lonely for a girl when she's first married, especially if she's used to having people around all day as Gwendolen was.'

They stood still for a moment, looking at the barges and houseboats. In one they could see a couple sitting talking, eating and drinking while the water lapped about the boat, slapping gently against the sides, rocking them in their home.

'It must be lovely to live on a houseboat,' Kitty said suddenly.

'You make it sound as if it would solve every problem you've ever had,' her father said, taking her arm and beginning to walk again.

'Well, it feels as if it would.'

She imagined how it would be, the slow, drifting life with the sound of lapping water always in her ears and the boat rocking gently. It would feel safe and enclosed. Once when she was little, her mother had gone away and a Mrs Oliver had come to look after them. Mrs Oliver was kind and fat and never seemed to mind about anything. It rained all the time that she was with them and on wet wash days she used to let Kitty play houses inside the clothes-horse. It was a huge wooden thing draped with damp sheets and made a lovely little house all for herself. She took toys in there and was allowed to have something to eat and drink at mid-morning. The kitchen fire was built high to dry the sheets so it was warm and steamy. She could remember the feel of it all, the smell of damp sheets and the taste of digestive biscuits and cocoa and the feeling of being enclosed and alone and safe. Being in a houseboat would be a bit like that.

They walked for a while without talking, the river on their left, trees on the right and fields beyond. She could feel the slow up and down of his walk, hear the quiet, regular tap of his stick on the tow path.

'So you like staying with Gwendolen and Arthur?' he said at last.

'Oh, yes, it's lovely. You know, I'm so glad she married someone like Arthur. I was always afraid she might marry someone brilliant that I'd be frightened of.'

He looked at her for a moment and did not reply. She sensed that she had surprised some disappointment that he was trying to hide. Then he said, 'I think she has chosen wisely. Arthur has given her security and she likes to get good value.'

It was an odd remark, she thought. Certainly Gwendolen did have everything; the things Arthur provided complemented what she already had.

But it was odd about Arthur, all the same. She asked, as casually as she could, 'To take a degree, you do have to be rather clever, don't you? And to be a solicitor, you need to be clever, I expect?'

The wry, sideways smile appeared and was hastily suppressed; she wished she hadn't asked.

'Oh yes,' he said very seriously. 'You certainly have to be very clever to do that.'

'What are his parents like?' she asked to change the conversation. 'They're coming over tomorrow.'

'Very nice, very kind and friendly,' he said, as if it was a relief to be able to be enthusiastic. 'Like Arthur—naturally enough. They're very rich but not in the least pretentious.'

'Being rich makes people seem very strong, doesn't it?' she said, remembering how she had felt this of Arthur and Gwendolen.

'All things are possible to him that has the means.'

'*All* things?'

'Well, some of them.' He laughed. 'All the things that don't really matter. But you'll like them, Kitty. They'll make splendid grandparents. They're very kind people,' he said again.

There was silence as they walked between the trees and the

river and then he said, 'When you're young, you value intelligence very highly, you know. As you get older, kindness seems more important. Arthur and his family are very kind people. Never underestimate kindness, Kitty. It's beyond price.'

He spoke so sadly, so simply. She thought how banal the words might sound from somebody else. A silly generalization it would have been from somebody looking for an excuse not to use their brains but from him it was wisdom distilled from years of bearing humiliation and loneliness and unkindness. She could not answer, but just held his arm and tried to keep in step with his difficult up and down walk.

'I'm going to take you to a little place where I once took Gwendolen when she was a Fresher,' he said cheerfully. 'They give you something or other with chips, outside in the garden by the river.'

They crossed a bridge and walked a little way along a road at the other side. The trees which bordered the road arched and met overhead. She walked with her head tilted back, looking at the pattern the sky made through the branches. They seemed to be walking through a tunnel of leaves, damp, mossy and mysterious. Then they came out into the evening sunlight and her father pointed out a little path down through the trees to the left. It was steep and slippery and her sandals skidded. She knew that he would find it difficult; she pretended to have more trouble keeping her feet than she really did, hanging on to tree trunks and exclaiming at the steepness of the path and going so slowly and with so much fuss that his awkward descent went unremarked. It was the first time she had ever felt self-conscious for him.

There was a sharp bend at the bottom of the path so that they came suddenly upon the cottage. 'Hansel and Gretel,' she exclaimed, surprised by the unexpected appearance of its thatched roof, pink walls, white shutters and window boxes. It seemed to her quite wonderful and totally unreal.

The path led round the side of the house to the garden where wooden tables and benches basked in the setting sun which was now low enough in the sky to shine directly into what seemed like an outside room made only of pergolas and climbing roses, honeysuckle and other plants which rambled and intertwined and smelled sweet.

'Here will we sit,' he said, sinking gratefully into a chair and stretching his long legs out in front of him.

'Is it allowed?' she asked, almost in a whisper.

He laughed. 'I should think so. It's a tea shoppe really and wants customers.'

She flushed and looked away.

He took her hand. 'I'm sorry, Kitty. It isn't that I want you to lose your sense of wonder; everything would look so ordinary if you did. Anyway what is reality? Maybe yours matters more than what most people see on the surface. But sometimes I do feel afraid for you, that you'll be let down with such a bump. So that's why I said it isn't a magical, fairy tale cottage, just a tea shoppe prettified to attract the customers, like many others. But I'm probably quite wrong: now we shall sit back and dream in our arbour and you'll know for sure that I am.'

'Here's proof that you are,' she replied, nodding in the direction of the house. Coming towards them was a little round lady, in a skirt which almost reached to the ground, a big white apron and a face as round and pleasant as a doughnut.

'I'm sorry. We're closed,' she said.

They looked at each other. She saw the sideways smile hastily suppressed and was afraid she was going to giggle.

'We were very much hoping for something; we've walked especially over from Oxford,' he said.

'Half day today, you see, being Saturday. Nothing after four o'clock. That's why I took the board down from the top of the road.'

'I'm afraid I didn't notice that—I just recognized the path from my last visit.'

'Oh, well, if you've been before. I thought I remembered your face.'

They waited hopefully.

'Perhaps you could come back tomorrow,' she concluded.

'I'm afraid not. And the next day I return to London.'

'I'd have to charge extra,' she said. 'It's more expensive when it's just one off.'

'That's all right. Do you still have cider?'

'Yes, I'll bring a flagon, shall I? Mixed grill for two then?'

They watched her walk back up the path to the cottage, round and solid yet unreal in her old-fashioned clothes.

'Mrs Tiggywinkle,' Kitty said. 'Who won?'

'It was a draw, I think. A suitable compromise between romance and reality. Learn from it, Kitty.'

'No.'

'Obstinate little devil, aren't you?'

It was not until they had finished eating that he said casually, 'No news from your mother, I suppose?'

She thought how long it had taken to get round to the major topic this time. The sun was almost setting, the arbour was warm and sleepy. She had a nice full feeling and the cider was potent.

'No, but Gwendolen says she has everything under control.'

She hesitated and he waited for her to go on, but she decided to say nothing of her mother's visit to Oxford; it would be better for Gwendolen to tell him about that.

'Well, as Gwendolen says, your mother does listen to her and will obviously do so more now that she's married. She thinks that Arthur is a sensible chap, too. She's always liked solicitors, your mother, you know. When we were first married she wanted me to be articled rather than go to the Bar. She couldn't understand why I should be so absurd as to want to be a barrister when I could have had a nice respectable job as a solicitor. Poor Martha,' he said thoughtfully, squinting at the sun through his cider glass, 'she's always found me very perverse.'

Kitty banged her own glass down. 'Well, I think you're jolly perverse, too,' she said.

He looked at her in surprise.

'You're so jolly forgiving,' she said. 'You just don't fight back. You let her do all the hurting,' she added, and her voice trembled. 'And now you haven't even got the Bar left.'

He took her hand. 'Look, Kitty, I know it hasn't had the advantages I expected and I maybe wouldn't have done it if I'd known that Gwendolen would be off so soon and have a home of her own.'

'Any chance of going back?' she asked as matter-of-factly as she could.

'No. I must abide by my decision.'

'Do you ever go into court?' she asked, partly to make normal conversation.

'No; we don't handle that kind of work. Perhaps it's just as well.'

'Whiff of grapeshot to an old soldier?'

'That's it.'

He drank some cider and put his glass down thoughtfully. 'You know,' he said in the voice he used when he forgot that she was not a grown-up. 'Maybe even if I'd never left the Bar I should never have got quite to the top. After I was so taken in by your mother and Wally Deedes over the divorce, I was talking to an old solicitor friend about it and he said, "You're very trusting for a barrister, aren't you?" I thought a lot about that remark afterwards. Maybe I was. Perhaps there's a bit of iron missing from my make-up.'

She looked at his hand on the table, at the long tapering fingers, at the thoughtful, resigned face, the philosophical set of the eyes, the funny, sensitive mouth. It was the sort of face that sees both sides, not the face of a fighter.

'I think there's too much iron around anyway,' she said lamely.

'You're a loyal little object, aren't you?'

'Is that altogether bad?'

'Well, it's not altogether good. You won't compromise. In a storm Gwendolen would bend. You would break.'

'Then I'll just have to keep out of the storms.'

'That's not in your nature either.'

CHAPTER TWENTY-EIGHT

'RUN and open the gates for them, will you Kitty?' Gwendolen said. 'They should be here soon.'

Kitty walked slowly down the drive, for it was hot and sultry this afternoon. Dust rose from the gravel, even though it was weeded over with patches of grass. Bees were buzzing purposefully in the hedge as if preparing to swarm. The wooden gates were heavy and had to be lifted or else they stuck in the ruts which they had already made in the drive. Arthur insisted that they should be closed every night and although it seemed to Kitty that burglars could easily climb over them, she sympathized with the pleasure he clearly felt when he shut himself into his domain every evening. Like a camper tying his tent flaps, like a caveman rolling a stone in front of his cave, Arthur dragged his gates closed and fastened the latch, and looked well pleased that his property was secured, his sense of possession satisfied. For some reason it was usually Kitty's task to tug them open again the next morning.

She tugged and heaved at them now, but still smiled as she remembered the satisfaction with which Arthur closed them at night; like a child playing at houses was Arthur with his gates. She had felt like that when she closed the chinks between the sheets in her clothes-horse house by the kitchen fire.

She was back in the house when she heard a car coming down the drive, then the engine being turned off and a door slammed. She stood back and watched as Gwendolen went to greet them. A woman in a big floppy hat got out. She wore a cotton frock and a cardigan, thick stockings and sandals. With her was a big, bronzed man in a Panama hat.

'Gwendolen, my dear,' Arthur's mother was saying as she embraced her daughter-in-law and then held her at arm's length.

'You look quite, quite radiant. A real picture, isn't she, Duncan? I hope you are as well as you look, dear?'

'Quite, thank you.'

'You know you have a touch of greenfly? I noticed it on that red pillar rose as I came in at the gate.'

'No, I hadn't noticed that,' Gwendolen said without surprise.

'Spray it; soap will do. I know they talk a lot about expensive chemicals, but I find sudsy water from the washing just as effective. Duncan, dear, doesn't Gwendolen look splendid?'

'How are you, my dear?' he asked in a rich, fruity voice, as he kissed Gwendolen's cheek. 'Did I hear my Eliza say you had a touch of the greenfly? If so, it suits you.'

'Now then, Father,' his wife said in automatic rebuke.

'This is my sister, Kitty,' Gwendolen said. Kitty who had been standing awkwardly by, shook hands.

Arthur's mother looked at her kindly. 'You're not at all alike,' she said with, Kitty thought, a touch of compassion in her voice.

'I should hope not,' Arthur's father put in. 'Gwendolen's expectant.'

'Now then, Father,' his wife rebuked him again.

Arthur, who had been working on the conservatory, now joined them, holding a hammer in one hand and a small saw in the other. He took a large nail out of his mouth and kissed his mother.

'Well, dear, quite the busy handyman,' she said approvingly. 'Go carefully, won't you? We don't want any nasty accidents.'

'Don't worry, Mother,' Arthur said and shook hands with his father. 'Now come and inspect the property. We've done a lot since you were here last. Not much in the garden though, Mother. We're going to have to leave that until the winter.'

'Albertine has mildew, I'm afraid, Gwendolen,' Arthur's mother remarked as they walked under the archway into the back garden.

Kitty wondered if Albertine was Arthur's cousin or perhaps the maid, but Gwendolen replied, 'Yes, I did know about that one. We got some stuff for it, but I'm afraid I haven't got round to spraying it yet.'

'You won't get rid of it easily. It's the one disadvantage of Albertines. But really greenfly is the greatest pest.' She stood and addressed them all. 'I was reading about it the other day in my gardening magazine. Quite extraordinary. They procreate at the most amazing rate. They reproduce by virgin birth, you know.'

'Serve 'em right,' said Arthur's father. 'Now let's go and look inside.'

Later, as they stood in the model kitchen having toured the rest of the house, Gwendolen said, 'Well, Mother, do you like it?'

'It's all perfectly splendid, dear,' her mother-in-law said. 'You've both worked so hard. Just one thing worries me, though, where will you keep your preserves?'

Kitty did not know what preserves were and was fairly sure that Gwendolen did not either.

'Where do you suggest?' Gwendolen asked.

'Well, dear, I don't want to interfere, of course, but I should think in that big cupboard off the kitchen. The cellar is too damp and those attic stores will be too hot in the summer. It gets very hot under the eaves, you know.'

'I can easily move things out of that kitchen cupboard. Thank you so much, Mother. I'd be quite lost without your advice.'

Arthur's mother smiled. 'You must always tell me if I interfere,' she said. 'I'm very fortunate in the wife my son has chosen,' she added, taking Gwendolen's hand for a moment. 'I'm a very lucky old woman.'

Kitty followed them out into the garden.

Throughout tea she marvelled at the way Gwendolen handled people. It was going to be quite a bore for Gwendolen emptying out that cupboard all arranged with hooks from which hung strings of onions and garlic, but she hadn't shown a trace of resentment. Of course, she scarcely needed to, for Arthur's parents clearly weren't going to interfere and be bossy, but Gwendolen seemed able to identify with them, take on their assumptions and even suspend her sense of humour in the process.

'Well, where are you going on holiday this autumn, Mother?' Arthur asked, handing her a second cup of tea. 'Have you decided yet?'

'Well, dear, I rather fancied Jamaica, you know. We did book to go last year but then it clashed with the flower show. I'd so much like to go to the United States on the way back. Duncan tells me it's fascinating. I'd have gone with him this spring if it hadn't been for the Guides' fete. He's been three times, you know, and I've never managed it.' She paused to sip her tea and then said, 'But I don't know: there seem to be so many problems abroad nowadays, so I think we will go to Torquay instead.'

Kitty glanced across at Gwendolen, but she was concentrating on stirring her tea.

'That's a nice rose—Ophelia, I think,' Arthur's mother said suddenly, getting up to make sure.

'Yes, Ophelia it is,' she said as she returned and lowered herself carefully into her deck chair again. 'But so badly pruned. Everything has been very neglected; we really shall have to set about this garden next spring.'

'We thought we would do just that. We hope to get the house finished this autumn and then start on the garden.'

'There are plenty of good things in it,' Arthur's mother conceded, 'and quite a few roses which have a second flush of bloom, which is such a good idea as August can be a very colourless month. But everything has been let go. I hate to say it, Gwendolen,' she went on apologetically, 'but nature really has got the upper hand in this garden.'

'There are certainly plenty of weeds.'

'It's not just that, everything is so overgrown. Just look at that great patch of phlox! All the herbaceous things must be lifted and divided into manageable clumps. I could bring Simpkin over to lend a hand for the odd day.'

'Oh, could you? How kind. I'm afraid I don't know anything about gardening.'

'You're willing to learn, dear,' Arthur's mother assured her, 'and that's the main thing.'

She began explaining the principles of pruning to Gwendolen, using her fingers, which were rough and stained, to demonstrate how and where the branches should be cut.

Kitty listened rather sadly as Gwendolen and Arthur's mother discussed the garden, planning to tame and clip and tidy this lovely, overgrown, sweet-scented wilderness.

'And are you looking forward to going back to school, Kitty?' Arthur's father asked her suddenly.

'No.'

They all laughed.

'Speaking of schools,' Arthur's mother said, 'you ought to be thinking about entering the baby for school. One hears such terrible stories about waiting lists nowadays.'

'I think we'll wait until after it's born, Mother,' Arthur said, smiling.

'It does no harm to be in good time with these things,' his mother told him. 'Promise me that you won't delay.'

'We'll do it as soon as we know which sex it is,' Arthur assured her.

'Well, of course, if it's a girl it doesn't matter so much,' his mother replied.

For a moment Kitty thought Gwendolen would be drawn, but she only said, 'Would you like me to show you the sketches I've done for the conservatory?'

'Thank you, dear,' Arthur's mother said, taking them and holding them on her lap. 'Tomatoes would do well in there, I should think.'

'Actually, Gwendolen is planning to have flowers, Mother,' Arthur put in firmly. 'Pots and tubs, you know, and she's got a lovely bit of marble to fix on top of that old sewing machine stand we found in the attic, so we can have meals out there in the evening next summer.'

'Well, it sounds nice, but it does seem a bit of a waste of space, when you could fit in about fifty tomato plants, but you know best, of course. Did I tell you how scandalously Simpkin has neglected ours?' she said with sudden feeling, leaning forward so that some of the drawings slid off her lap. 'Let them get bottom end rot, he has.'

Gwendolen and Kitty both dived to pick up the papers and she thanked them, rebuking Gwendolen for stooping.

'You must take care, dear,' she said. 'How are you going to manage for help when baby is born? You can't go on like this, of course.'

'Oh, I expect I shall. There isn't much help to be had nowadays, you know.'

'I know. It's so trying. How young people manage I just don't know; when I think of the staff people used to have to bring up a family. And even so there was never a spare moment. Leisured classes indeed! Well, now, I just have my faithful old Mrs Mopp.'

'I thought I might try and get a daily help for the rough work.'

'You must, dear, of course, but you'll need more than that. It's marvellous what can be done if you try. Father!'

Arthur and his father were deep in conversation about stocks and shares and both looked at her vaguely.

'Yes, dear?'

'Did I tell you about Mary Poulter?'

'What about Mary Poulter?' her husband enquired, taking off his glasses and rubbing his eyes.

But she looked away from him and explained to Gwendolen and Kitty. 'The Poulters are such keen evangelists in our church. At least they were at our church but didn't quite see eye to eye with the vicar. Well, Duncan,' she said, turning back to her husband, 'she was telling me the other day that she's got a real maid at last. Just like they used to be, she said, and wears a little black dress and a white starched apron and frilly white headband, exactly like they all used to be before the war when they were ten shillings a week. I remember my mother-in-law being quite shocked because I paid mine twelve and six. Where was I?'

'You were going to tell us how Mary Poulter got this phenomenon,' her husband explained patiently.

'She prayed,' Arthur's mother said simply.

There was silence.

'Well, she does need her mostly to help serve coffee after the prayer meetings,' Arthur's mother said defensively. 'So it was quite fair really.'

Her father joined them for dinner; Kitty was surprised how easily they all mixed. It had seemed to her that they inhabited different worlds; the Chathams always talked about things, about cars and holidays, boats and jobs. Even when they talked about schools and maids they talked as if they were things to be bought and used. Her father, on the other hand, rarely talked of things but of people, situations and problems. If ever he did talk of things, it was to probe and analyse and theorize. She had never heard him talk about stocks and shares in her life.

Yet they all talked easily together, and it was a very happy sort of evening; perhaps it was this catalysing kindliness that he had been talking about last night.

Afterwards they took their coffee out into the garden where the air was still warm and soft. They were sitting now talking. A big patch of night-scented stock in the overgrown herbaceous border sweetened the air. The light in the sky was fading to silver and the flowers were turning pale. Only the big clump of white phlox took on a translucent glow as night began to fall.

'You'll have to watch Ophelia,' Mrs Chatham said. 'I do believe she has damp rot up her stalk.'

Gwendolen murmured something in reply; they were both lying back in deck chairs, speaking only intermittently. The men were doing most of the talking.

'Looking back, I admire the stand you took,' Mr Chatham was saying to her father. 'Myself, I was a Chamberlain man. But then I have always left politics to the politicians.'

'Well, he seemed such a peace-loving man, dear,' his wife put in, 'and our paper supported him.'

'So did they all—or nearly.'

'Then tell me, Charles,' Mrs Chatham went on, 'how did you know?'

'Know what?'

'Well, I mean, we try to do the right thing, you know, and what with our paper supporting Chamberlain and that nice Lord Dunglass visiting Hitler and so on with him, it all seemed so respectable. All our friends thought so too. And then Czechoslovakia was so very far away. I mean, how did you *know*? Of course, we all know better now, but what I mean is, how did you know *then*?'

Her father hesitated. 'I suppose because in the last resort what we did would have been a very shameful thing for one man to do to another.

'Oh,' she said and there was unmistakable disappointment in her voice. 'I thought there might have been some secret reason which ordinary people didn't know about.'

'No,' her father said, and Kitty could tell by his voice that he was smiling. 'There rarely is. It's just that there comes a time when self-interest has to be discarded as a guide. The bigger political issues are all moral ones, though it is unfashionable to say so, I know, and sounds priggish. There are times when one has to stand up and be counted and that was one of them, but believe me, it wasn't pleasant at the time.' There was an edge of bitterness in his voice. Then it softened and he added, 'However, for some reason or other there just happen to be enough people in this country to do so whenever there's a real need, though they usually leave it to the last possible moment.'

He talked on, he talked well, simply, convincingly, and they listened with respect as night fell in the garden. She thought of the other times she had listened to him talking, holding everyone captive, and her pleasure in hearing him merged with her quiet joy in the evening. It was twilight and the flowers were now quite drained of colour. Kitty lay back in her chair entranced by it all, breathing in the scent, absorbing the sound of grown-up conversation, reassuring, droning. It seemed impossible to believe in quarrels, or wars or hunger or evil; everything was so peaceful in Arthur and Gwendolen's garden.

It was slowly turning into a ghost garden, she thought, watching as the colour drained out of the flowers and trees. If she turned her head to one side she could just catch the scent of some creamy-white flowers that straggled all over the walls of a shed; summer jasmine, Arthur's mother had called it. If she turned her head back again the smell of the night-scented stock drifted towards her. It was lovely just to lie back and gaze up at the silvery sky, able to absorb it all and not required to do anything. Usually she resented the way that being a child cut her off from the grown-up world, so that she couldn't do anything to alter the course things took, but now she was glad of it. It was as if she was in a marvellously privileged position to savour and enjoy without having to take any part, make any effort. A wonderful production was being staged, and she did not have to do anything about it, just lie back and watch the stars appear in the darkening sky.

As she listened to them asking him questions, deferring to him and heard his answers, she marvelled at it all. As always when he was at his best, he answered simply and often amusingly, but always with this quiet authority and conviction. It was strange that the rich Chathams, the happily-married Chathams, the secure Chathams, should listen with such deference to her father, who was always worried about money and had no proper home, who was lonely and knew no peace. It showed that there was justice somewhere in the world, even if only for one evening in a north Oxford garden. She caught the scent of the flowers and listened to his voice and watched the stars appearing one by one and knew that she would remember this evening for ever.

CHAPTER TWENTY-NINE

'FANCY being allowed to stay with her all the summer holidays. Honestly, Kitty, you are lucky having a married sister. Does she tell you anything?'

'Well, she taught me how to cook.'

'I mean anything *useful*, silly.'

The two sixth-formers had left, but the rest of the dormitory remained unchanged this year. Two new third formers had joined them, but it was early in the term so they were still shy and homesick and always pretended to be asleep before the others came up.

'But isn't it beastly,' Jill interrupted, 'to have your sister go away and get married? It must break up the whole family. I just couldn't bear my sister to do it.'

'But I thought you hated her?'

'Of course I do. That doesn't make any difference.'

'Hate your own sister?' Felicity said in horror. 'Oh, how dreadful. I mean. I couldn't bear it if Philip . . .' she broke off and picked up the photograph in the little leather case and stared at it intently.

Polly looked at her. 'You look quite mad staring like that,' she remarked casually. 'But, Kitty, when Gwendolen's baby's born, you'll be an aunt.'

'I had worked that out.'

'What will it call you? Aunt Catherine? How about Auntie Kitty?'

'It sounds like a cats' home.'

'Actually,' Kitty said slowly, 'it's not one baby. I heard from Gwendolen this morning and she's had an X-ray and it's going to be twins.'

They all stared in appalled silence.

'But how *awful*,' Felicity exclaimed, 'to have it all *twice*.'

'You don't,' Sue said knowledgeably. 'Twins are no problem now. I have often heard my father speak of it. You only have one placenta for the two of them.'

'Oh, I'm so glad,' Felicity breathed in relief at this obviously economical and presumably less painful arrangement.

'My father,' Sue went on, 'has a fine team of midwives.'

Kitty imagined them, streaming out of the stable, harnessed together, their heads back, whinnying, pork-pie hats at rakish angles, Sue's father with a whip . . .

'What are you sniggering for?' Sue asked.

'Nothing. I was just thinking about the twins.'

'There's nothing funny about childbirth,' Sue said as she went out of the bedroom.

'She's ever so bossy now that she's in the sixth form,' Amanda said. 'I wish they'd put her somewhere else. I do think it's a rotten idea of the Head's to keep the same bedrooms as last year.'

'It's only an experiment; she's going to review it at half term, so perhaps Sue will get shifted then.'

'Oh, I do hope they won't take her away from us,' Felicity said. 'She knows so much about everything. I like having a G.P. in the bedroom. Well, you know what I mean.'

'Polly's father's an accountant, so you could forget about sex and concentrate on money for a bit.'

'Kitty's father's a barrister, so you can sort out your legal problems.'

'But I don't have any legal problems,' Felicity persisted, her eyes filling with tears.

'Never mind,' Kitty said kindly. 'Perhaps you will when you're older.'

'I tell you what,' Polly said. 'We'll try to find someone else with a father who's a doctor to take Sue's place if she's moved.'

'Oh, yes please, Polly. I do think it's so important to have a doctor in the dormitory.'

'We might even get you a gynaecologist. Isn't Hannah's father one?'

'Better still, we could have Jane Thimble,' Amanda said. 'Her father's a pederast.'

Gwendolen's twins were born a month early. The Head, who

seemed to have taken leave of her senses, actually suggested that Kitty should go and visit them for a weekend, to make up for missing the wedding. It was an astonishing weekend. Looking back on it, Kitty realized that she had really been excited at the prospect of travelling alone, crossing London with her father, seeing Gwendolen again: the advent of the twins had been no more than a happy excuse for the excursion. In fact they had overshadowed all the rest. She had never expected that they could be so special and that every single thing about them should be so extraordinary.

When she arrived, Gwendolen was sitting up in bed, a twin on each arm. Timothy and Sarah, they were called. Gwendolen had told her that, although they had been born early, they were a good size, so she had not been prepared for the sheer tininess of them. They had minute little mauve hands which seemed to have been left soaking in water for too long, and tiny little screwed up faces and hair like wet feathers. They were like newly-hatched birds. They had a marvellously sweet, powdery smell and were quite unbelievably light to hold. Gwendolen said that Sarah was a good size and Timothy small but likely to catch up in no time, but Kitty could not distinguish between their smallness.

During the day there were crowds of visitors and Gwendolen, looking radiant, held court. They brought offerings of cards and flowers and knitted things in tissue paper. 'She's fantastic,' they said. 'Who but Gwendolen could have taken a B.Litt. and got married and had twins all in eighteen months and still look like this? She really is fantastic, your sister.'

A nurse was staying for a month. She was tiny and moved quietly around like a little mouse, glancing up every now and then as if to make sure that nobody was going to tread on her. She seemed quite overawed by Gwendolen and treated her like a being from a different planet, though Gwendolen was very gracious to her. There was a new queenliness in Gwendolen's demeanour since she had had the twins.

Night times were best of all. Everything was put ready in Gwendolen's room and the twins were brought in for feeding and Kitty stayed and watched. They had their eyes shut as they sucked and seemed like little animals. Everything about them was in fascinating miniature, even their finger nails scaled down to a perfect but tiny copy of a proper person. Only their crying was louder than human.

It all seemed like magic, the first evening: magic and Christmas and fairyland all in one, at once peaceful and astonishing and utterly removed from everyday existence. Before she left on Sunday she crept into the room where they were sleeping and looked at them and could have gazed for ever. She thought about it all on the train going back to school. She still felt as if she were in a dream, for it had been an astonishing experience, this first encounter with new babies. She tried to analyse what it was that was so surprising about them and why it was impossible to look at them without being filled with wonder. It was so strange that real life, new life, should be so remote from ordinary, everyday life. She tried to make herself realize that they would grow up into two ordinary people with their own separate lives just like anybody else, but gave up.

She knew better than to try to describe this phenomenon to anyone at school.

'Tell us about Gwendolen's twins, Kitty,' somebody asked in the dormitory on Sunday night.

'Oh, they're all right. Similar, you know.'

'Naturally.'

'What do they look like?'

'Lobster-coloured prunes.'

'I mean do they look like Gwendolen or Arthur, silly.'

'They take after their aunt.'

'Poor little devils.'

Altogether it had been a marvellous term, Kitty thought, as she put on her hat in front of the big looking glass in the cloakroom, pushing her hair back under the brim. After the perfect summer holidays this perfect term, for even apart from the visit to the astonishing twins, everything was going remarkably well at school. The prospect of Christmas at Arthur and Gwendolen's house cast a warm glow which spread back into early December.

For it was the first Saturday in December now and she was going out with her father for the afternoon. She savoured the thought as she sat down on a bench in the cloakroom and leaned back among the overcoats. She still had a few minutes to wait, but she did not feel her usual unbearable impatience. She thought about the twins. It was very odd the way they were so important; everything revolved around them and yet they couldn't even speak. She was worried about what to give them for Christmas. She could not knit: when she was little at school in Beckgate, Miss Timms had set her to knitting a khaki scarf for the war effort. The needles were khaki-coloured too which made it even more difficult to keep the right number of stitches. They kept slipping off so that as the scarf grew longer it also grew narrower until one awful day it dwindled to one stitch and she found she had knitted a triangle.

Until then she had gone on knitting and hoping, but now she had to show it to Miss Timms. Miss Timms had been very angry and said Kitty should be ashamed of herself for letting the army down when they were fighting so hard for her. She had held up the dreadful thing for ridicule so that even now Kitty felt again the flush of shame as she remembered it and heard the sycophantic sniggers of the class. That night she had had a nightmare in which soldiers were trying to march through mud and rocks dreadfully hampered by her triangular woollen scarf.

Somehow after that she had never taken to knitting. She had learned to weave at school but even if she managed to finish the rather stiff blue and grey skirt length she was working on, it would hardly be suitable material to make into anything that two-month old babies would enjoy wearing.

She might make them soft toys; there had been a craze for making them recently and next term classes were going to be held on Wednesday afternoons, when they were free to do hobbies. She could go and learn to make them properly and have something ready for the twins' birthday. Or she might go to woodwork, which was taught down in the basement by little old Mr Flynn, who had a limp and only three and a half fingers on his left hand. She had been once to try it and liked the stone-floored room with the sawdust and wood shavings and the little pot of carpenter's glue bubbling on a gas flame in the corner, filling the air with the smell of old bones. Occasionally Mr Flynn terrified them all by shouting, 'It's not plumb!' in his broad Yorkshire voice at some poor girl struggling to make a coffee table. The twins were perhaps a bit young to be given furniture or even wooden toys. Now that she came to think of it, Mr Flynn's pupils seemed to turn out an awful lot of rather boring table napkin rings.

She walked slowly down Silence Corridor concentrating on the problem of the twins' presents and then laughed aloud as she suddenly remembered those other twins at Mrs Deedes at Christmas standing on the stairs holding their fluffy lambs. Then she remembered Wally and stopped smiling. Too many episodes like that might be enough to embitter anyone, she thought, as she walked across the sandstone flags, each worn in the centre by the tread of many feet. Then she stood at the reception-room door, feeling the big knob in her hand and turned it.

The room was empty. She stood and stared round it in surprise and was still standing there when she heard her father's voice behind her. The Head and he had walked up together from the Head's study and were talking to each other as if the Head were an ordinary human being.

'Catherine is waiting for you, I see. Good-bye, Mr Langdon,' the Head said, holding out her hand. They shook hands, the Head smiled graciously at him, glanced at Kitty and walked back to her study.

'Please God don't let him kiss me in case she turns round,' Kitty prayed, walking quickly to the front door.

He followed her out of the door and down the steps, tucking her arm under his when they reached the road.

'Going off by yourself? Or can I come too?' he asked, looking down with the funny sideways smile.

'Didn't want to hang around in the hall,' she muttered, feeling stupid.

'I came early and had a chat with Miss Ainsworth.'

'Golly.'

Parents—even marvellous ones—just didn't understand. You didn't chat with the Head. Confer, communicate perhaps, even debate, but not *chat*.

'We were talking over your future.'

'Did she ask to see you?' Kitty asked, now thoroughly alarmed.

'No, it just seemed sensible now that I'm here. It's all right, you needn't look so worried. Whatever have you got on your conscience?'

'Nothing.'

'I don't think you want your two worlds mixed up, do you?'

'I suppose not.'

'Well, nothing subversive was said. She's still very pleased with you. You go from strength to strength, it seems.' Kitty wasn't sure if the quote was conscious or not. 'You might one day end up at the university like Gwendolen.'

I might end up at the university, she thought, but not like Gwendolen.

'Neither is likely,' she said.

'We'll see, but that's the way she's thinking about you just now.'

'You mean it's what *you'd* like to think?'

'I'd be delighted. The prospect of paying three years' university fees when I've finished paying school fees fills me with unadulterated joy.'

She burst out laughing and took his arm again and they walked together down into the town, his stick swinging regularly in time with the up and down of his walk.

'How did you like your niece and nephew?' he asked.

She paused, not knowing what to say or where to start. Then, 'They're perfect,' she said. 'Daddy, don't you think they're just, well, perfect?'

'Yes, but then I've seen new babies before so it's not quite such a miracle to me. It's like the first time abroad; it's never quite so astonishing again.'

Miracle, yes, that was it. 'I don't know what to give them for Christmas,' she said. 'They're a bit young for calendars and table napkin rings and I'm not much good at knitting.'

'Would you like to buy them something this afternoon?'

'Oh, could we?' She stopped and looked up at him. Of course it would solve everything. She had never thought of *buying* them something.

The toy shop was warm and crowded. There was a feeling of Christmas and suppressed excitement. On the floor in one corner an elderly, anxious-looking assistant was rather inexpertly demonstrating how an engine worked to a very knowledgeable small boy. It was an old-fashioned shop with an overhead railway system by which money, put into a little wooden container, ran along wires and out of sight.

'You had a teddy bear just like that,' he said, pointing to one.

'I don't know what became of it. At least, it started life like that but then lost an ear.'

'I ate it. I remember.'

'You were only one year old at the time.'

'I can remember earlier than that. I remember going somewhere and lying on top of the world and everything smelled oily and something was put on my head and people made kind, laughing noises.'

'That would be sunray treatment when you weren't much older than Gwendolen's twins.'

She looked at him gratefully. Any other grown-up would have laughed and disbelieved. It was the oily smell she could remember best, a smell like green lint.

The assistant was waiting, tapping impatiently with her pencil on the pad.

'Can I help you, sir?' she said in a voice that suggested that she had asked once already.

'This little girl wants to buy two soft toys,' he explained. Kitty was disappointed: she had had to speak to him before about not calling her 'this little girl' in shops.

The assistant brought out all sorts of soft toys; smooth ones, furry ones, hairy ones, funny ones, white ones, coloured ones. Her father looked at the labels and asked surprisingly practical questions about such things as how their eyes were fixed in and if they could be washed. Finally they chose two teddy bears that were like the one she had had when she was little. She was worried because they were alike but he said babies always knew the difference. All the same, she decided she would give them each a differently coloured ribbon. He gave the assistant a note which she put into the little wooden container with the bill. She was short and had to stand on tiptoe to reach up and screw the little round box into its lid which was suspended from the wire over her head. Having done so, she fired it off by pulling a cord and the little box went speeding across the ceiling and out of sight. It made a fascinating swooshing sound as it raced along. There was something magical about it, inexplicably like new babies and Christmas. A few minutes later it sped back with the change neatly wrapped in the bill.

'I'm not your little girl, you know,' she said as they left the shop.

'Sorry, I realized as soon as I'd said it. But honestly "this girl" sounds awful and "this young lady" sounds as if I'm being sarcastic.'

'Well, "this little girl" sounds worse than either, as if I were a toddler or something.'

'There are problems about being half grown up. You tell me what you'd like me to say and I promise to try to remember.'

'Couldn't you just say "she"?'

He laughed. 'I promise,' he said, 'if that's what she wants. Now I'll take her out for some tea.'

'She'd like that.'

It was only after she had eaten her way through a large tea and sat back comfortably that she was suddenly aware that he was watching her in a calculating sort of way. It was a shock, after she had been relaxing in all the pleasantness of thinking about Christmas and knowing that all would be well, to feel his eyes on her as if he were weighing her up.

'You're wondering whether to tell me something,' she said.

He looked away. Then he looked at her again and his hand went up to the inner pocket of his jacket.

'I had a letter from your mother,' he said.

She could sense the menace even as she took the letter from him. It was written in the small, neat, slightly back-hand writing, every word carefully chosen to hurt.

It was nonsense all the same and that was a relief. In it Martha wrote that she had decided not to go to Ireland for Christmas but to go instead to Gwendolen, who would need help with the babies. Gwendolen needed a mother now, she said, and understood the situation much better since she had become a wife and mother herself.

'Goodness,' Kitty exclaimed. 'But Gwendolen would be furious if she knew Mummy had written this. She'd be livid. She was telling me herself that Arthur had said how important it was for you not to be under the same roof or it might stop the divorce. You didn't think Gwendolen *knew* about this letter, did you?'

'Well, no, not really,' he said, looking rather shame-faced. 'I didn't quite know what to think. It arrived just as I was leaving for the station and I read it and began to wonder. She's clever, your mother. You see, there's an element of truth in it: a young wife needs a mother's help.'

She stared at him. '*Needs*,' she repeated. 'What do you mean *needs*?'

'I'm sorry, I'm philosophizing too much as usual.'

'You're always so busy seeing both sides: more like a judge than a barrister, you are.'

He laughed. 'I promise I'll forget all about it.'

'You do that.'

She took his hand and leant forward intently. 'If Gwendolen knew that Mummy had worried you with that beastly letter she'd be furious. She'd think you were absolutely potty to believe it, absolutely stark-staring mad.'

'All right. I've said I'm sorry. I know I have two very loyal daughters. It was quite wrong of me to doubt it for a single moment. I should have realized that Gwendolen had never been consulted before that letter was written. Now let's forget all about the wretched letter.'

'Burn it, go on, burn it.'

'Dramatic little object. How on earth do you think I can burn a letter in the middle of a crowded restaurant?' He put it back in his pocket. 'Now let's get on with planning Christmas. Are you going to take these bears back to school, or shall I take them to London and keep them for you?'

'I do love your new dressing gown,' Polly said enviously to Felicity on the last night of term.

Felicity put it on again, pulling up the frills round the neck so that her anxious little face was almost lost in the frothy material.

'Mummy sent it to me to make up for leaving me behind when she and Daddy take Philip abroad for Christmas,' she said. 'But of course I don't mind.'

'I should think not with that lovely dressing gown to make up for it.'

'Mummy called it a négligée,' Felicity said, going over to look at herself in the long mirror. The dark eyes peered back at her as she surveyed her under-developed little body carefully from head to foot. 'Mummy says it's very seductive,' she said.

'You know my blue bell-bottomed trousers,' Polly said. 'I'll swop them for your new dressing gown.'

'Négligée,' Felicity corrected her, fingering the frills lovingly.
'You know swopping isn't allowed,' Sue said.
'Bossy boots,' Polly muttered under her breath.
'Well, I don't know. Daddy was rather angry when I swopped my new fluffy slippers for your ball-point pen last term,' Felicity said.
'What did your mother say?' Polly enquired anxiously.
'Nothing, I don't think she noticed. But Daddy says he'd write to the Head if I parted with any more of my belongings,' Felicity quoted.
'Well, perhaps we'd better not do anything about your dressing gown then,' Polly said, admitting defeat and preparing to go to wash.
'Négligée—we'll see.'
A little later Kitty came back from washing. 'Thesby's on the prowl,' she said. 'Whatever are you doing, Felicity? Have you got a sore back?'
Felicity was standing in her vest and knickers, her back to the long glass, her head screwed round to get a better view.
'No, thank you, Kitty. I think Polly would really like to swop her bell-bottomed trousers for my new négligée so I was just trying to see if I had a bell bottom.'
Suddenly Miss Theswell was in the doorway.
'Are you aware that there are only five minutes to go until lights out?' she enquired rhetorically and vanished as suddenly as she had appeared.
Kitty jumped into bed, Felicity finished undressing and began putting on her pyjamas.
'Felicity,' Kitty said firmly, 'you must not swop that négligée with anyone. Promise? There'll be a terrible row if you do. Promise now.'
'Oh, I don't mind if Polly really wants it. I'm not really sure that it suits me.'
'Of course it does. You look absolutely ravishing in it.'
'Oh, do I really, Kitty? Then I'll certainly keep it. Mummy said it was seductive.'
'Have you heard that Thesby's having a breakdown?' Polly asked casually as she came back from washing.
'What *here*?'
'Yes, she walked in her sleep last night; the Head caught up

with her trying to weigh herself outside Woolworth's. They walked all around town, Thesby in her nightie and the Head in a dressing gown.'

'Who said so?'

'Melanie told me. Her room overlooks the front door.'

'She must have had binoculars and a periscope to see from there to Woolworth's,' Kitty said.

'She deduced it from the time they were away. But don't believe me if you don't want to. Melanie says Thesby's heading for a nervous breakdown and *her* father runs a loony bin so she ought to know.'

'I believe you, Polly,' Felicity said fervently. 'Truly I do.'

'You'd believe anything,' Sue said coldly. 'Polly you shouldn't stuff her head with such rubbish. Wandering about in nighties indeed! Of course, there is no doubt a lot of psychiatric trouble with Miss Theswell. My father has made a special study of such cases and he says that it is a knife edge between normal and abnormal—a *knife edge*.'

Having delivered herself of what somehow sounded like an ultimatum, she went down to wash.

'I'm sick of hearing about her father,' Polly said. 'I bet he never qualified.'

'He must have—or he wouldn't be able to pay the fees. Our school fees are outrageous, Daddy says.'

'Perhaps he made a lot of money and then did something terrible and got crossed off the scrolls.'

'Isn't it *rolls*?'

'What are they?'

'Oh, honestly, Felicity! It's where they write down the names of all the doctors in the world and then cross them off when they're naughty.'

'Oh, I do see. Yes, it's a very good idea.'

They all seemed so young, Kitty thought, listening to them. Catastrophes had not touched them. They did not know what life could be like. Perhaps they never would. Even Felicity did not understand what was happening to her. She rather envied Felicity: her tragedy would be her own. She would act it out, which was better than watching.

'Isn't it foul of the Head to cut the holidays down? We've always had a month at Christmas,' Amanda grumbled.

'The idea is that we'll have longer in the summer.'

'I bet she forgets by then.'

It was nice having Christmas Day on a Saturday, Kitty thought. They were breaking up late so most of the holiday would be after Christmas, which would give her a long time afterwards with Gwendolen and the twins.

They were always too excited to sleep on the last night of term. 'Someone tell us a story,' Amanda said, after Lights Out. 'Whose turn is it?'

'I've told heaps this term,' Kitty said.

'And I told you about Thesby.'

'And I can't tell stories,' Felicity said.

'There shouldn't be any talking now,' Sue said, but without much conviction.

'But it's the end of term, Sue, and nearly Christmas.'

'So it's Jill's turn. Don't be mean, Jill. You used to tell us marvellous horror stories last year. You must know some more.'

'Well, my mother's old nanny did tell me something quite extraordinary last year, but I don't know if I ought . . .'

'Oh, do go on. Don't be mean.'

'I'm not sure if it's suitable really.'

'Oh, good.'

'Well, you know how hopeless my mother is? Her mother had to keep her own nanny to go on looking after her even when she was grown up, and she lives with us still because Mummy is so useless. She was *her* mother's nanny so you can tell how old she is.'

'Oh, yes, she must be . . .'

'Shut up, Felicity. Go on, Jill. Nobody interrupt.'

'Well, this is something she was told by an old doctor in her village. Outside the village was a thicket. A hermit woman lived alone with just her dog—a huge Alsatian, a savage beast, like a wolf—in an old tumble-down cottage in the middle of this wood. Nobody ever went near her; sometimes the villagers caught a glimpse of her if they happened to go by the thicket, just a wild face through the trees and a ragged body, but then she would vanish away. She feared and hated all human creatures,' Jill went on, her voice now sunk to a whisper. 'And all human creatures feared her.'

'Speak up, I can't hear.'

'Nobody lived near her, nobody visited her. Then one day this old doctor, who told our old Nanny about it afterwards, found a message nailed to his front door. Ill-written it was, on a piece of torn paper, and it said she was ill and he must go to the house in the thicket. He set off with his bag towards the dark wood on a black, dark, wild and windy night. When he reached the cottage there was no light but he could hear a terrible moaning and groaning. He found some candles and began looking around the house by the light of a flickering candle. Everything was rough and filthy. He found her lying groaning on a heap of straw which was all she had for a bed.'

There was silence. Had a pin been dropped in the dormitory it would have seemed a fearful clatter.

'And he delivered her of twelve puppies.'

There was a stunned silence and then Kitty said, 'Did she feed them herself or give them the bottle?'

'Honestly, Kit! Actually, he told my old nanny that he buried them that night by the light of a candle deep in the heart of the thicket where nobody would ever find them. Then he went away and never told a living soul—until he told our nanny, of course.'

'That was lovely, Jill. Thank you very much.'

'Yes, thanks, Jill.'

'Thanks, Jill: it was just right for the end of the Christmas term.'

'Good-night everybody. Time we stopped talking now,' Sue said.

'Yes, or we'll have Mad Thesby in again,' Polly agreed.

They all murmured good-night and one by one fell asleep. Kitty listened to the quiet, slow breathing and then Polly began to snore. She did not mind; it was a companionable sound. She knew that she was too excited to sleep so decided that if she was to lie awake she would at least choose her own thoughts, pleasant ones. She would remember about last holidays. She pictured the big, white-painted house and the overgrown garden, the kindly Mr and Mrs Chatham, friendly, practical, unintentionally funny as people are who think in terms of things and even think of people in a thing way, thereby reducing problems to absurdity. Her father's way of thinking exalted people but it exalted problems too and prepared the ground for tragedy. The Chathams wouldn't have tragedies, just sad things would happen. It would be a refuge for Gwendolen and this made Kitty suddenly uneasy. Gwendolen's way of thinking was really much more akin to theirs. She belonged with them.

How strong they were, the Chathams and Gwendolen together. The combination of her will and their wealth was irresistible. It was being so easy for them to save her father. She herself had struggled and tried and failed. She remembered the failure at the Funnel and shuddered with self-disgust. Now Gwendolen just needed to stretch out her hand to save him without any difficulty at all. She and Arthur just had to talk to Mummy and that was it. It was absurd that she should feel any unease for him, but for a moment she did, feeling again a chill like a passing mist, seeing again in her mind's eye the chess board with the dark king always in check.

It was no good; she tried to keep her wakeful mind on practical, cheerful things and ended like this. Perhaps she did not really want to sleep, but way down wanted to keep on her guard and not surrender to whatever god took over the unconscious mind.

Not that she ruled her mind when it was awake. Even now the garden with the flowers and clothes line was coming into it. A long time ago, towards the end of the war when she was about nine and the news always had reports about Russian salvoes and generals with names like Voroshilov and Vishinsky, they had told of a woman tortured by the Germans to give information. She refused and they told her that they would take her two children and blind them, but still she would not speak. Kitty used to think of the mother watching her children being prepared for blinding, and she always pictured them in a garden with flowers and a clothes line, though she did not remember that they had said anything about that on the news. She never thought about how it must have felt for the children, just the mother.

She tried to think again of real things. She set her mind to thinking of tomorrow when she would catch the train to London, stay a couple of days with her father at Mrs Wedgwood's and then travel with him to Oxford. How different Christmas Eve was going to be from last year. She would help Gwendolen cook and her father and Arthur decorate and there would be no quarrelling and no awful tension and unkind remarks. It would be like Christmas when she was tiny, when it had all seemed perfect. Probably it had been just as bad then, but she had been too little to understand.

She made a last effort to remember something real and pleasant. She pulled the sheet over her head and remembered how it felt inside the big clothes-horse. Rain outside, damp-smelling sheets within and the taste of cocoa and digestive biscuits. She curled up and remembered the peacefulness of it. Or she was floating in the womb, running the ridged cord through her wrinkly fingers. She tried to imagine the millions of years before she was born. People thought so much about what happened to them after they were dead but never bothered about where they were before they were born, but there was no difference. She began to think about the awfulness of eternity.

She had a particular form of torture which she used to inflict upon herself at night when she couldn't sleep which was just that: trying to grasp what it would be like to do anything for ever. To be dead *for ever*. It didn't sound too bad until you really tried to imagine it, really and truly imagine it. Your mind began to grasp it and suddenly you realized that you were cheating and had imagined an end in sight, so you had to kill the hope and remind yourself that there would never, never be an end in sight. Never, never. It made her dizzy and terrified. Terrified because it was a certainty. It wasn't something you could tell yourself not to be silly about because it wouldn't happen, like another war or being tortured. It was an absolute certainty: death—and after that something for ever.

Around her the others were sleeping, six of them breathing quietly and Polly snoring. As the rest of the dormitory slept, Kitty lay awake thinking about death and the even more terrifying prospect of eternal life.

CHAPTER THIRTY

KITTY climbed up the stairs to Mrs Wedgwood's flat. It was a long, steep flight of stairs and her case was bulging and heavy. She stopped half way up to rest and wondered if her father sometimes did the same when he came in tired at the end of the day.

'Well, Miss Kitty,' Mrs Wedgwood said. 'Come along in.'

Kitty liked Mrs Wedgwood. At first she had been embarrassed at being called Miss Kitty but now she enjoyed it, especially when Mrs Wedgwood said, 'Miss Kitty, dear.' It sounded dated and comfortable and made her feel like the daughter of the manse in some old-fashioned children's story book.

The room which she was to have for the night was not much bigger than a cupboard, but that did not matter. What really mattered was being able to go in, look around and then shut the door. After sharing a dormitory at school and never being alone anywhere all day, it was a marvellous feeling, this shutting the door. Even if only for twenty-four hours it was her little space, protected by her own four walls and if anyone wanted to come in they had to knock at the door. She could tell them to go away. She wouldn't, of course, but she could if she wanted to.

Mrs Wedgwood brought her a cup of tea and biscuits and she felt like a princess being waited upon. The little boy, Christopher, followed her, holding his puppy.

'Don't bring him in here, dear,' Mrs Wedgwood said. 'Miss Kitty doesn't want dogs in her room.'

'Oh, that's all right. They can stay while I unpack.'

The hanging cupboard was full of somebody else's clothes and the chest of drawers contained sheets and towels. But it didn't matter; she spread the contents of her case around the room. Last of all she took from her writing case the little photograph frame which she had made out of cardboard in a craft lesson years ago. She had later inserted into it a photograph of her father, removed from a passport which he had given her to play with. She placed it carefully now on the top of the chest of drawers, pulling back the flap of cardboard that propped up the slightly lopsided frame. It wobbled and she steadied it with her hand.

Christopher sat on the bed, gripping the puppy, and watching Kitty.

'Do you go to school yet?' she asked.

'No. Do you?'

'Yes. I went when I was five.'

'I expect I shall go when I am five.'

'Do you live here now?'

'No, I live with my Mummy. Granny may come to live with us.'

'That will be nice, then you'll be all three together.'

'Four,' he said, nodding towards Rags.

'Of course. All four of you.'

She sat on the bed next to him and drank her tea. She gave him the biscuits and he shared them with the puppy. Then he held the plate while the puppy licked the crumbs off it.

'My father died,' he said cheerfully. 'It was very sad.'

'Yes,' she agreed.

'If Granny comes to live with us, it'll be easier for my Mum.'

'Yes,' she said again.

He mused upon this, picking up the larger crumbs of biscuit off the bed and feeding them to the dog.

'Of course, we don't know about Mr Langdon,' he said, running his finger down the folds of the eiderdown in search of more crumbs. 'It's a bit of a nuisance not knowing what he's going to do. Granny doesn't want to push him out, poor chap.'

Kitty felt a cold shock, her stomach contracted, then her face went very hot.

'No, I'm sure she wouldn't,' she said, fumbling among the paper at the bottom of her case and extracting her slippers.

'Well, it will all sort itself out somehow,' he said philosophically, leaning back against the wall at the side of the bed. 'Do you put lipstick on?'

'No, we're not allowed to.'

'My Mum does. And black stuff on her eyes too. She spits

into the black stuff like this and then rubs a brush into it and paints it on her eyelashes like this.'

He demonstrated in front of the mirror, the puppy straddled over his left arm, his right crooked up so that he could hold an imaginary brush in his hand. He pretended to apply it to his eyelashes, keeping his mouth twisted and his eyes screwed up. Kitty laughed in spite of herself.

He glanced at her. 'I like watching her,' he said. 'I wish you did it.'

'I'll do my hair if you like,' she offered and he watched every movement of the brush and comb.

'Can I count your spots?' he asked, licking the index finger of his right hand in anticipation, but his grandmother called him before he had time to make a start.

Kitty lay back on the bed and repeated his words about her father carefully to herself. He had obviously heard an adult say them. Moreover, the adult, granny or mother, had spoken kindly. She must keep reasonable: it was clearly a problem to them. She tried to imagine that she herself was Mrs Wedgwood, needing to remove and yet having a lodger whom she had had for a long time and did not want to upset. Of course it was a problem. Of course she wouldn't want to push anyone out. Of course there was no harm in saying it in front of a little boy. But the awfulness, the loneliness struck her again like a physical blow, so that she curled up on the bed, rocking herself for a moment. It was unbearable that outsiders should see him thus: as a problem, a lodger, a homeless one to be pitied.

She couldn't bear that he should be pitied. What right have people to be so smug that they pity someone better than they are? She thought of the Chathams: ordinary, not too clever, a bit funny, full of goodwill. That they, if they knew, would pity him, sickened her. They had no right to; she must at all costs protect him from sensing it. Then she remembered that she was only fifteen and protecting him wasn't exactly a practical proposition. Besides, why should she feel this about pity, she asked herself. The feeling she herself had for him had compassion in it, a queer kind of recognition of her own misery in his. Compassion must be something between equals. Pity was quite different; it couldn't be felt for an equal; it didn't hurt. Pity always had a bit of contempt in it: in one particular the person pitied was inferior. She could not bear that he should be thought inferior in any particular whatsoever.

She heard his key turn in the lock. She jumped off the bed and ran out into the hall. His coat felt cold and damp as she hugged him. It seemed to her that he held her for a little longer than usual, as if to reassure himself.

'Well,' he said, holding her from him, 'and how's my Kitty? It's nice to come back and find you here. I'll have a wash and then we'll go out and get something to eat.'

'Doesn't Mrs Wedgwood give you supper any more?'

'Well, no. She often has to take the boy back to his mother in the evening so I asked her if she'd rather I went out to save her having to bother with an evening meal. It was obviously a relief to her not to have to cook at night and sometimes she stays with her daughter-in-law or baby-sits for her. I come back for a bit and then I wander off somewhere for a meal. I don't always feel like turning out again but I usually do in the end.'

She thought of him, all these winter evenings when she had been wrapped away in the false security of school, wearily climbing the stairs and coming back to an empty room, sitting or walking about restlessly as he was doing now, nobody to welcome him. Then making himself go out and eat somewhere alone.

'What do you do at weekends?' she asked.

'Mrs Wedgwood will always cook a midday meal for me, or leave something ready. I go out to friends for the day sometimes on Sunday. You remember the Fairhursts at Great Missenden? And I've been to the Braines quite often too and other people you don't know. I get plenty of invitations—don't start feeling sorry for me whatever you do!—but I don't want to land myself on them too much; they've got families of their own and an odd man isn't too easy to fit in.'

'Nonsense. I bet they love having a spare man. Every hostess's dream. You don't read the right magazines.'

He smiled and sat down next to her on the couch, taking her hand. 'That bantering tone is going to stick with you, if you don't watch it,' he said. 'Then, of course, there is the fact that I can't invite them back and can't afford too many outings to restaurants. Apart from that, there's the small point that I just can't be bothered; sometimes I don't feel like making the effort to get out of London to be sociable, so I just relax here and read the papers and potter about and catch up with the weeklies. I'll be fifty in two years' time. Half a century; it's quite an age.'

Half a century! It would be ages before she was even two decades. It seemed that a great abyss separated them. Partly it was this great gap which made daughters not able to help fathers. Just keep their distance and watch.

'It's a beastly night,' he said, 'all drizzle and fog. Shall we go early and then we can settle in properly for the night?'

'I wish I could cook something for you here and bring it in. I got quite good at cooking at Gwendolen's.'

She saw herself carrying in hot tureens and her father sitting, unfolding his napkin, at a beautifully laid table.

'Better not—it's not our kitchen, you know.'

'No.'

She put on her raincoat and they left the flat. She ran downstairs in front of him and then wished she had gone more slowly for he came down stair by stair behind her, leaning heavily on the rail.

'How's your leg?' she asked casually as they walked along the pavement, lightly greased with rain and shining under the street lights.

'Not much worse,' he said equally casually. 'Now where do you fancy we should go to eat?'

'Where do you usually go?'

'There's a place just round a couple of corners,' he said, 'which is very reasonable and quick.'

It was an unusually-shaped restaurant, very long and narrow, with high seats arranged like railway compartments, so that they were cut off from other couples. Not that there were many to be cut off from, for they were early and the place was almost empty.

They hung up their coats and settled down in their seats. He got in rather awkwardly, she noticed, and sat down with a bump, as if his muscles were not working very well. She tried to recapture the festive feeling that going out with him usually gave her, but it wouldn't come. Somehow going out was not quite the same when it was compulsory.

The service was quick and they did not talk much at first. She was hungry and concentrated on the meal. When she had finished her apple pie and custard she sat back with a contented sigh.

'You can have some more,' he said.

'No, thank you.'

'Funny choice—don't you have that sort of thing rather a lot at school?'

'Yes, but they make the custard with water and they don't put any apples in the pie.'

'Coffee?'

'Can't we make it back at Mrs Wedgwood's?'

'Better not; I don't go into the kitchen and it might upset her stores and things.'

'If she had a woman lodger I bet she wouldn't be able to stop her making things for herself.'

'I suspect that's why she doesn't.'

'Tell me all the plans for tomorrow,' she said later, looking at him over the rim of her coffee cup.

He did not answer and she knew immediately that something was wrong. Little things came back into her mind, like the way he had held her when he first came in. She should have realized sooner.

He leaned forward.

'There's been a slight change of plan,' he said quietly.

She did not answer, but her eyes did not leave his face, watching for every sign.

'I'm not staying with Gwendolen,' he said.

A dry sound came out of her throat. He took her podgy, chilblain-scarred hand in his long fingers and said, 'Now I don't want you to be upset. I'm staying at a hotel. You will stay with Gwendolen, that's the main thing.'

It's not the main thing, she thought, it's nothing. You are the main thing.

'Why?' she said.

'Your mother is staying with Gwendolen,' he said.

She had an odd sensation that the blood was being drained out of her body, leaving her cold and weak.

'Don't look like that,' he said. 'Your eyes are filling up all your face. Kitty, love, it's not the end of the world.'

But it is, she thought.

'Why,' she managed to say, making her voice as calm and strong and grown-up as possible, 'has Gwendolen done this?'

'Your mother came to stay and has proved indispensable,' he

said, as if it was all perfectly understandable. The resignation in his voice, the acceptance, was worse than tears of rage, worse than bitterness that he, who had once been so necessary to Gwendolen's way of life, could now be dispensed with.

'Gwendolen told me that I was still very welcome to stay, but I had to explain that I shouldn't stay under the same roof as your mother.'

There was no need to explain, she thought, Gwendolen knew perfectly well already, but she said nothing, wanting him to have the comfort of believing that Gwendolen had perhaps not understood.

'Of course, Gwendolen's had a lot on her mind,' he went on. 'So the best thing is not to make any problems for her, but just stay nearby. That way nothing is lost.'

Everything is lost, she thought. Goneril, oh, Goneril.

The fog met them like a grey wall as they left the restaurant and they made their way slowly through the grey-green fluffiness of the streets, not talking.

'That's better,' he said, shutting the street door behind him. 'What a night! Depressing stuff, fog.'

She followed him upstairs. Half way up he paused to rest. His face, in profile, as he stood leaning on the rail for support, looked thin and drawn. The flesh, which used to seem so firm and fresh and young, was curved in below the cheek bones. They will turn him into an old man, she thought, watching him brace himself to make the effort to go on up the stairs.

She left her coat in her bedroom and followed him into the sitting-room. He was sitting under the centre light. She walked across the room, turning on the two little table lamps and drawing the curtains.

'Homely touches,' he said, 'you're turning into quite a little hausfrau.'

She turned suddenly and then stopped in horror; although his voice had been laughing she saw, as she looked him in the face, that his eyes were full of tears.

She stood, her hands still on the curtain, wondering what to do. If she moved towards him the tears in his eyes might overflow. It would be a terrible humiliation for him in front of a teenage daughter. So she laughed and said, 'That's just what I am,' and began banging about, poofing up the cushions and fidgeting with the ornaments, stooping to pick up imaginary pieces of thread off the carpet, in an inspired burlesque of a fussy housewife. She went on until she was sure he was laughing.

'Oh, Kitty,' he said, 'you ought to go on the stage, really you should.'

She caught a glimpse of herself, as a clown, a masked clown with a white, spotty face and behind the mask all the unshed tears in the world.

'I bet that's what you were talking to the Head about.'

'It wasn't actually, but I think it should have been—it will be next time.'

'She'll tell you about Mrs Worthington's daughter—and anyway I'd rather be gainfully employed as soon as possible.'

The most important thing was to leave school and get qualified as something or other and get a job. Then she could have a flat with him and make him a home, a real home for the first time, so that after work he wouldn't have to come back to emptiness and go out seeking a meal.

'I've got a letter or two to write,' he said. 'Here are the papers.'

She picked up the evening paper and he sat at his desk. He didn't settle, but got up and went off to his bedroom, returned, started writing, sighed, walked over to the window and back again. Soon after that he wandered off into his bedroom again. She watched him as she held the paper in front of her. He seemed so restless, she thought, like a soul in torment.

'Like a game of chess?' she asked, as he crossed the room yet again.

She took the familiar chess box from the table in the corner and set the men out on the board. He turned his chair round and she sat opposite to him on a stool. Soon they were chasing each other's queens round the board, exchanging pawns, clearing the board of almost all the pieces. But it was like a shadow of their usual game: it had no heart in it. She was relieved when he suggested packing it up for the night.

'What will you do with yourself tomorrow?' he asked as he came into her bedroom to say good-night.

'I had planned to go out and buy some ribbon,' she said. 'I need it for the teddy bears.'

'Here's a pound,' he said. 'I'll get the bears for you.'

He came back and put them down on the bed and turned to kiss her good-night. He held her closely, as if seeking, not giving, comfort. It was not paternal. 'Good-night,' she said, drawing away and wishing she was anyone other than herself.

After he had gone she picked the bears off the bed and put them on the chair. They had lost all the glamour and excitement they had had in the shop and looked just like two ordinary, bought toys. She decided to close the window and keep out the fog. She drew back the curtain. In the distance she could hear a rumbling sound—of trains, perhaps, or the underground, or traffic. She stood and listened. Fog blanketed the other sounds of London, but this one, lonely rumbling sound persisted. It might have been the noise of a cattle truck crossing the deserted countryside of Europe during the war, loaded with the homeless, the friendless, the hopeless. The fog was swirling and eddying outside the window. She closed the window, drew the curtain, shutting out alike the sound of the train and the sight of the fog, but the menace remained. The room no longer seemed a refuge. It was only a temporary resting place and its cupboards were filled with other people's belongings.

CHAPTER THIRTY-ONE

THE fog delayed the train, but had lightened to a mist by the time the suburbs of London had given way to the fields of Oxfordshire. It had almost cleared as they crossed and recrossed the river and saw at last the spires and gasworks of Oxford.

Arthur met them at the station. He greeted them cheerfully, brushing aside their apologies for keeping him waiting.

'Well now,' he said. 'I expect you're ready for some tea. We'll drop your case in at the hotel and then go straight on home. I'll run you back to the hotel in the evening,' he said to Charles as if it was the most normal arrangement in the world.

It set the tone: everyone was busy and normal and preparing for Christmas. Gwendolen greeted them at the front door a trifle casually, kissed them both and said, 'Same room as last time, Kitty, come on,' and ran upstairs with her. As Kitty turned to talk to her in the bedroom, she said, 'Can't stop, must fly down and put the kettle on.'

'But Gwendolen, we must talk . . .' Kitty began urgently.

'Of course, darling, heaps to tell,' Gwendolen said, flashing her brilliant smile. 'Gorgeous to see you again. But you look different—you're taller or thinner or something.'

Her father was sitting by the fire with Arthur when she went down. Shortly afterwards Gwendolen pushed in the tea trolley.

'Mummy will be down in a minute,' she said casually. 'She's busy in the nursery just now.'

Kitty stared at her, but Gwendolen just returned the look rather blankly and smiled. 'You can hand round the plates, can't you, Kitty?' she said. 'It's lovely to have an extra pair of hands; we really do need them.'

Her mother entered the room. She was wearing a white overall which rustled importantly. She stood in the doorway for a moment, a look of quiet triumph on her hard grey face as she surveyed them all. Then she spoke rather formally and politely to Gwendolen.

'Do you mind if I keep my overall on? The twins are asleep now but may wake at any moment and when they do I'll go straight up and change them for the six o'clock feed.'

'Of course not,' Gwendolen said. 'Do just what you like.'

'Oh, no. It is your house and we must all do what *you* like,' her mother replied.

Kitty stood still while her mother kissed her and said reprovingly, 'Well, I must say I'm surprised you haven't been up to see your nephew and niece, Kitty.' Then she turned to Charles and said, 'Good afternoon, Charles,' turning on him such a look of quiet, triumphant malice that Kitty, used though she was to her mother, felt suddenly weak with fear for him. She watched them kiss.

'Well, I must say this is very jolly,' Arthur said, putting another log on the fire. He stood and surveyed them, brushing his hands together. 'It's splendid to have the whole family together again like this, eh?'

Nobody spoke.

'You've grown, Kit,' he went on obliviously, 'and you won't know the terrible twins—they've grown even more. It's all the roast beef and Yorkshire pudding that Granny Langdon gives them. Isn't that so, Granny?'

Martha smiled at him tolerantly.

'I'm sure I don't know what we'd do without you, Granny,' he said.

'I'm glad to help, Arthur,' she replied piously. 'It is what we are put into this world for.'

'Well, it's jolly nice for Gwendolen and me that you feel that way about it.'

'No more than you deserve. I never had any help from *my* mother-in-law when *I* had young children.'

She shot a venomous glance at Charles. Kitty instinctively moved over towards him. She wished he would make some acid comment on *his* mother-in-law, she who had left the infant Martha in an orphanage before flitting off to Australia, but of course he remained silent.

Arthur, noticing nothing, talked on.

'My parents have gone away for Christmas again,' he said, helping himself to some more toasted teacake. 'It saves so much work; but you'll see them in the New Year, Granny.'

'I look forward to getting to know your mother better, Arthur,' Martha said, still in the formal voice which Kitty interpreted as meaning that she was the ideal guest and had no intention of putting a foot wrong. 'She is a keen gardener, I believe?'

'Never stops, always at it. (Cake, Gwendolen, darling? Oh, come on, must keep your strength up.) She used to have quite a staff in the garden but now she just has one old man. She prefers it. You know in the old days,' he went on solemnly, 'gardeners used to get the upper hand. It was quite a problem for a lot of our friends. The gardeners always had to grow everything huge and hideous in order to win prizes at shows; they wouldn't let you pick a marrow until it was so big it tasted of seasoned oak.'

They laughed and he talked on and Kitty wondered what it would be like to grow up in a world where the main problem was not to let the gardeners get the upper hand. Suddenly there was an angry cry from upstairs. Martha rose immediately.

'Oh, finish your tea, Mummy,' Gwendolen said. 'It won't hurt them to wait a minute or two.'

'I've had all I need, Gwendolen, thank you,' Martha said. 'I never could sit idle when there was work to be done.'

'Can we bring them down for a little to play on the rug?' Arthur asked, jumping up. 'I'll give you a hand bringing them down.'

'You'd better ask their mother,' Martha said. 'I'm only a guest.'

'Ah, but the most important one,' Arthur assured her. 'What do you think, darling?'

'I think—yes, bring them down.'

Arthur returned holding Timothy who was still asleep, and Martha held Sarah, who was wide awake.

'Good gracious!' Charles exclaimed. 'She's the image of you, Gwendolen, when you were a baby. It's quite uncanny.'

The two-and-a-half-month-old Sarah was lovely; pink-cheeked, fair-haired and blue-eyed. It was easy to imagine that Gwendolen had been the same. Charles looked at her longingly, as if feeling again his love for his first-born child when she was a baby.

Kitty could hardly bear to look at him. She looked instead at Sarah. She tried, and failed, to see in this fair-skinned beauty who could hold her head up properly and look around at them all, the screwed-up crimson little object of last October, which looked as if it had been left in water too long.

Gwendolen was going to put her on the rug and then caught Charles' eye.

'Want her?' she said, holding Sarah out towards him.

'I'd love her,' Charles replied, holding out his arms eagerly towards the baby.

Sarah looked at him. Her expression became aghast, her chin puckered and she began to scream.

'Don't be silly,' Gwendolen said. 'It's only your grandfather.'

'It's all right,' Charles said, dropping his arms. 'Don't force her—she's not used to me.'

'Come to Granny then,' Martha said, picking up Sarah, who looked at the familiar face, relaxed and began to smile. Martha talked to her, quietly, possessively, glancing over the fair head every now and then at Charles, who sat, rejected, by the fire.

'How's the conservatory?' Kitty asked, managing to keep her voice normal, but only just.

'Going slowly,' Arthur said. 'We've been concentrating on the new nursery. Want to see? I'll show you now if you've finished your tea.'

He led her upstairs and then up the second flight to the top floor, talking enthusiastically all the time.

'The through room will be the nursery,' he said, opening the door on the left. 'Then on the right your mother can have a sitting-room and a bedroom. We're going to make a bathroom here out of this huge loo and the broom cupboard next to it, which we don't need. It'll be quite a good size and save her carrying the twins down to the main bathroom.'

'Do you mean she's going to live here?'

'Oh, didn't Gwendolen tell you?' He laughed. 'She's getting quite absent-minded, my Gwen. Well, now that she's set her heart on taking this job next term . . .'

'What, *Gwendolen* has?'

He gave her an understanding, slightly conspiratorial look.

'Well, between you and me, Kitty, I've had a few doubts

about it myself. But the way I look at it now, is this: she's a brilliant girl, your sister, a brilliant girl. Domesticity isn't going to satisfy her. It's a waste of her talents, in a way. I've always felt that if a girl has talent she ought to develop it. I hope I'm as liberal-minded as the next man—I think I am. I'll tell you something, Kitty.'

He paused and looked down at her.

'Yes?'

'I've entered Sarah for public school as well as Timothy.'

His point thus proved, he leaned back against the banisters and nodded at her. She looked up at the big, handsome face; innocent, it looked blissfully unaware of what was going on. It wouldn't be any good trying to get through to Arthur.

'So, you're doing all this altering,' she said, wanting to get it quite clear, 'so that Mummy can have this as a kind of flat and be handy for looking after the twins?'

'Oh, it's nothing,' he said deprecatingly. 'We're glad to do it. Anyway, it adds to the value of the house.'

'Yes, yes, of course. And will she stay for ever?'

'Oh, no. It's just a temporary arrangement until we can find somebody, but there's no hurry, she says. Of course, we wouldn't dream of imposing on her good nature, but if she's happy to be here, that's different. It will be a useful place for a nanny later, or we might even get a married couple one day.'

'Yes. When does Gwendolen start work?'

'Not for a while, but she thought she might as well have your mother here to help at Christmas. It makes a lot of extra work, does Christmas. People coming in and so on, though Gwendolen loves entertaining. She's marvellous at it, she really is fantastic, Kitty.'

'Yes, well, we'll all help,' Kitty heard herself say.

'I'm sure you will,' he said. 'You really are a marvellous family, you Langdons.'

He glanced at his watch. 'Nearly feed time,' he said. 'Must trot.'

It was like that for the rest of the day. Everyone was busy; there seemed to be so many small urgent tasks connected with the babies and everything had to be seen to at once. Gwendolen put up around herself a barrier of cheerful preoccupation. Kitty was aware that this was deliberate and yet somehow flinched from trying to break it down. She never seemed to be able to get Gwendolen to herself anyway. Her mother strode about importantly in the rustling white overall, and sent Kitty on errands.

'Get me another nappy pin,' she would say, balancing a baby expertly across her betowelled knees. 'No, not that sort, a big one. Don't you know a nappy pin when you see one?'

She contrived to keep Kitty always in the wrong, ceaselessly praising the twins in a way which implied that Kitty had failed to notice their virtues for herself.

'Look at those little hands,' she would say as she put on Sarah's nightdress, and Kitty, who had been doing just that, would look away and want to point out that it would have been odd if Sarah had had fully-sized hands. Somehow the magic seemed to have gone out of the twins, now that her mother pointed out all their attributes as if she herself were personally responsible for them.

Gwendolen, the initial excitement of motherhood having worn off, seemed less delighted with the twins. When it was time to feed them she obviously resented having to leave the family downstairs and insisted that Arthur should go upstairs with her to the nursery. He left the tree that he, Charles and Kitty were decorating, and went up immediately.

'It's very lonely being a mother,' he said to Kitty afterwards. 'I think Gwendolen is quite right about putting them on the bottle soon. Then we can take one each and be sociable. Of course, she'll have to have them on bottles before next term anyway. She's done marvellously well to feed them herself until now. You'd never think they were premature. Well, not Sarah anyway. We were a bit bothered about Timmy at first but he's catching up.'

They had dinner late. As they sat at the round table with a twisty candle in the chianti bottle, Kitty tried hard not to remember how it had been in the summer, the idyllic summer. A lump came into her throat and she could hardly eat the concoction that the others were congratulating Gwendolen upon.

'When do you intend changing to bathing the twins in the evening?' Martha asked Gwendolen.

'Oh, I don't know. Do whatever suits you best.'

'Well, I'm arranging to leave the office at half past five after

Christmas, so that I can help with that,' Arthur said. 'I'm looking forward to it when they're older—boats and things.'

'You're lucky to have a man with regular hours,' Martha said. 'I had to put up with irregular hours, sudden journeys to court and then long spells when Charles wanted to work at home and the children had to be kept quiet. Count yourself lucky you didn't marry a barrister.'

Arthur nodded. Gwendolen smiled sympathetically and Charles said nothing.

Lucky, Kitty thought. She spoke as if she hadn't known what his career was likely to be when she married him. As often when her mother carried on about how awful it was being married to a barrister, Kitty opened her mouth to ask her why she had. Charles glanced at her and shook his head imperceptibly. Kitty looked down. So the hard monologue went on uninterrupted. Why did he have to let her win every time, she wondered, as she pushed the rice round her plate. Why were the cruel and insensitive always allowed to have the last word?

'I'd better be getting back to the hotel,' Charles said as they finished their coffee. 'I don't know what time they shut their doors.'

'I'll run you back.'

'There's no need, Arthur, thank you. It's no distance and I'll enjoy the walk. The fog has cleared now. Run and get my coat, will you, Kitty?'

He said good-night and the others drifted away, her mother and Gwendolen up to the nursery, Arthur down to the cellar to check the wine for tomorrow.

They were alone in the hall.

'When did you say you go back to London?' she asked.

'Monday morning. I'm back at work on Tuesday.'

'I'll come back with you,' she said, as casually as she could.

'No, Kitty, we'll keep to what we arranged. Mrs Wedgwood isn't expecting you until next week.'

'But I wouldn't be any bother to her.'

'It might upset Gwendolen and Arthur. They've worked so hard to make Christmas a success.'

'*Please* let me come, oh *please*,' she pleaded, forgetting about sounding grown-up and casual. 'Don't leave me behind.'

'Be a brave lass. There's a good girl.'

He kissed her. For a moment she leaned her face against the cold, rough cloth of his overcoat, swallowing hard in order not to cry. Then she watched him walk down the path, leaning more heavily than usual on his stick. At the gate he turned and waved. Then he went through the gate and crossed the road. He looked neither to the right nor to the left as he did so. He doesn't care any more about safety, she thought. He doesn't care if he lives or dies.

CHAPTER THIRTY-TWO

CHRISTMAS Day passed like Christmas in a nightmare. All the forms were gone through, and the traditions observed. The others—Gwendolen, Arthur and her mother, the Portmans who came in for drinks in the morning and the Tonkins who came in for tea and the Smythes who came for the evening and played games and had supper—all seemed to be living in Christmas. Even her father acted like one who is enjoying himself. She herself seemed to do everything mechanically; she helped to prepare the lunch, she peeled potatoes and washed sprouts, she laid the table and dried the dishes. She gave presents and received presents. She put one teddy bear into the hands of each twin and watched Sarah throw hers down and Timothy hang on to his by one ear, the little hand gripping tightly so that the fingers were hidden in the fur.

All the time these scenes were being enacted, she watched as if frozen, like somebody in a nightmare who cannot move. The danger threatened, the horror of it overwhelmed her but she could not help him, just watch as they destroyed him, celebrating all the while. She saw the innumerable small cruelties of her mother, the single, devastating rejection by her sister. She knew that somehow she must get through to Gwendolen who was acting as if nothing untoward was happening, casually, normally, refusing utterly to admit what she was doing. But every time she approached her, there was this barrier and Gwendolen seemed to slip away or misunderstand or get involved with something so important that Kitty felt herself to be an irritating distraction.

As the day wore on she resigned herself to not being able to get Gwendolen alone until night time. When everyone had gone and she was in bed, Gwendolen came to her room to say goodnight. She sat on the bed and Kitty seized both her hands.

'Gwendolen, I must talk to you,' she said. 'It's urgent.'

Gwendolen looked surprised. 'Anything wrong at school, pet?' she asked in deep concern.

'No, it's *here*. Oh, Gwendolen, how could you?'

'Do what, poppet? You're not making yourself very clear,' Gwendolen said patiently, almost swallowing a yawn.

'Why is she here?'

'Who? Mummy?' Gwendolen laughed. 'Because I couldn't stop her, of course. She just turned up again. I couldn't keep her away; she just stayed on. Of course, she nearly drives me mad always fussing about the twins, especially Timothy, though they're both absolutely as strong as full-term babies now. Don't you think they are?'

'Yes, but that's not the point, it's about Mummy.'

'Well, you know how she adores babies. I can't keep her away, can I?'

'But you said that you . . .'

'Wait a moment—there's Arthur calling. I'm in here, darling,' she called out.

Arthur knocked. 'You can come in,' Gwendolen said. 'Kitty's quite decent. Well, good-night, little one. And don't you worry, do you hear?' she added with a touch of reproof as she bent down, sweet-smelling and soft, and kissed Kitty good-night.

Arthur, who was watching his wife's every movement and was touched by her concern for her little sister, held out his arms and Gwendolen ran into them.

'Let me know if you want anything, Kitty,' Gwendolen said, smiling as she leaned against Arthur in the doorway.

Even when they had gone and her room was in darkness, Kitty could still picture the two of them standing there. Invulnerable, they looked. Somehow she must get through to Gwendolen. It was no good talking to Arthur, the unwitting collaborator, or even to her mother, the very eager collaborator. Both of them were pawns in Gwendolen's game, whatever that was.

She hardly slept at all that night. She had a recurrent waking dream that he was drowning and they were all there watching with other holiday makers on the shore. Arthur kept waving politely back at the drowning man. Gwendolen smiled and wore dark glasses so that she seemed to see nothing. Only her mother watched him openly and in triumph as he drowned. She herself could not move or make a sound and—such is the illogicality of dreams—she could see his face very clearly and it was resigned and patient. Near him, on the water, floated his stick.

'I like Boxing Day,' Arthur said, scraping the last of his grapefruit from its skin. 'Nice holiday feeling and no chores.'

'Speak for yourself, darling,' Gwendolen replied. 'I've got two babies to look after.'

'We'll all help. Many hands and all that,' he said, beginning to eat his scrambled egg.

'Don't forget that it's Sunday,' Martha put in. 'Morning service at eleven.'

'Do you know, Granny, I had forgotten! What's the best plan then, Gwendolen?'

'You take Mummy and Kitty to church. I'll stay here with the twins and get the lunch. Daddy is spending the day at his old college with the Master.'

'Right you are.'

'I'll stay at home and help you,' Kitty offered, seeing her opportunity for a talk at last, with all the family out of the way.

'Yes,' Martha said. 'I don't like you doing all the chores by yourself, Gwendolen. It won't do Kitty any harm to peel a few potatoes for you.'

'Oh, very well,' Gwendolen said with obvious reluctance. 'Do you want to stay at church, Arthur? You could just drop Mummy and come back and then pick her up again later.'

'I won't have that. I'll walk if I'm going alone,' Martha said.

'Oh, no, I'll stay,' Arthur said, to Kitty's relief.

'Very well,' Gwendolen said less graciously than usual. 'Do as you like. I'll go up to the nursery.'

'She's a bit tired,' Arthur explained after she had gone and he and Kitty were clearing the breakfast table. 'It took a lot out of her having the twins, you know.'

Kitty tried not to smile.

'It's an emotional strain,' he went on, knowledgeably. 'Hormone imbalance, don't you know?'

He tied a tea towel around his middle and began to wash the dishes. Kitty stood beside him waiting to dry them.

'We've had a lot of visitors, too,' he said, peering into a long jug to make sure it was clean. 'She's a marvellous hostess is Gwendolen. Could have been an ambassador's wife, I shouldn't wonder. She's such a conversationalist. Just hand back anything that's not quite clean.'

He began to scrape at the scrambled egg pan. 'Of course, your father's a brilliant man, so I suppose it's in the family. One of the best lawyers in the country, my senior partner thinks. Between you and me, Kitty, he thought it was a tragedy the way your father left the Bar: amazing what odd things these brilliant chaps do sometimes. Well, that's the lot. I'll just see if I can give Granny a hand, then I'll get the car out. She'll want the twins out of doors, I expect, to make the most of this sunshine. It's not going to last, the forecast said.'

The twins were duly brought down, well swaddled, and put to rest in the prams. Martha went to her room to get ready for church and Arthur went to get the car out. Kitty felt excitement rising. Now she really would be alone at last with Gwendolen. They would talk and she would find out the reason; there must be a reason.

Her mother came into the kitchen, tall and severe in grey. 'Mind you help Gwendolen now,' she said to Kitty. 'No sitting about dreaming, do you hear?' she added as, tucking her Bible and prayer book under her arm, she went out to join her son-in-law.

'Thank goodness they're off,' Gwendolen said as they heard the car drive away. 'Now you and I can have a bit of peace. Shall we have a cup of coffee before we start on our chores?'

For a moment Kitty was tempted: it seemed as if it would be the nicest thing in the world to agree and sit at the little table over the chunky brown mugs of steaming coffee and laugh and gossip as they would once have done, herself feeling privileged at being allowed to share Gwendolen's grown-up confidences.

'No, thank you,' she said.

'Oh well, later perhaps,' Gwendolen replied casually.

'Gwendolen,' Kitty said firmly, 'we must talk.'

'Well, fire ahead. I'll get on with this cake while you talk,' Gwendolen said, reaching for butter and sugar and getting out the scales.

'It's about Daddy.'

'What about him? He looks all right to me.'

'Oh, Gwendolen, can't you see what you're doing to him? You promised that he could come here. We were all to have Christmas and be happy and . . .'

'Now, Kitty, I never went back on that invitation; he could gladly have stayed. There's an empty room still.'

'But you knew that he couldn't once you'd invited Mummy.'

'Oh, that! I didn't ask her; she just arrived,' she said in the rather defiant voice she used when she was not speaking the truth. Kitty was silent, lacking the courage to call her a liar, knowing that all Gwendolen's lies had the ring of truth. Gwendolen saw the world from her own point of view and somehow created her own truth.

'You see, Kitty,' Gwendolen said, following up her success, and talking very reasonably, 'since they couldn't both stay here, one of them had to go to a hotel and, since it was Daddy who was the one who was bothered about it, he was clearly the one to go. He quite understood, you know.'

'But, Gwendolen, you said you would see to the divorce, you said you could deal with her and arrange everything.'

'Really, what a *child* you are! You can't make people get divorced, just like that. The law needs changing, but at the moment he just can't have one. That's all there is to it. One must be practical. Thousands of other people are in the same boat.'

'Oh, Gwendolen, he *trusted* you so!'

The words just seemed to come out of their own accord. Gwendolen flushed and looked at her. For the first time something seemed to strike home. Then her face hardened.

'Why are you being so critical, Kitty?' she said. 'Why are you trying to cause trouble?'

Kitty felt suddenly younger, a trouble-maker, a bother to the grown-ups.

'I don't want to be critical, Gwendolen,' she said humbly, but obstinately. 'I just want to know why you've done it.'

'Done what?'

'Gone back on everything you said, broken everything you promised. You said, you absolutely said, you'd see about the divorce.'

'That was before I was married myself.'

'No, afterwards, too. Last summer you said the same and you said Arthur understood too and about not being under the same roof and everything and you were quite sure about it.'

Gwendolen put the cake into the oven and began to get out the ingredients for making a sauce. She said nothing, just put a lump of butter in the pan, and, perched on a high stool, watched it melt.

'I can see that you can't make anyone have a divorce,' Kitty went on, 'but you did say you would try to persuade her. You said you wouldn't let her come here until she had agreed. Why have you made it more difficult by asking her here—why do you do the reverse of what you said?'

'Because she's useful to me,' Gwendolen said sharply, as she stirred flour into the butter. 'You don't think I *enjoy* having her here, do you?'

'That's just what I mean. It wouldn't be so bad if you did. I mean if you loved her and wanted her here, I could understand it, but you don't. You've always said we owe everything to him. Gwendolen, the number of times you've told me how she tried to stop you coming up to Oxford and now, now when he needs you, needs your help . . .' she broke off, beginning to stammer.

'Look here, Kitty, I've listened to enough of this nonsense. As far as she is concerned, Arthur and I don't feel we're imposing on her, because she likes work and if she wasn't doing it for us she'd be working herself to the bone for some villager or other. We might as well use her in the family. As for Daddy, I've asked him to stay and it's not my fault if he refuses.'

'You mean you'd rather be disloyal to him than alienate her now that she's useful to you?'

There was a terrible silence: the words hung on it.

Gwendolen drew herself up with dignity, her beautiful Madonna-like face expressing hurt and disappointment.

'I think you must realize, Kitty, that that was a most unkind and unfair thing to say, and I'm sure you regret it. I should make you apologize, I suppose, but I won't. We will not refer to it again—ever.'

She got off the stool and walked out of the kitchen. Kitty thought she had gone for ever but she had only gone to the cellar to get some brandy for the sauce.

As she returned she smiled forgivingly at Kitty. 'Now, dear, no hard feelings. How about a coffee or even a drop of brandy and then we'll forget all about it?'

She took Kitty's hand. 'How are the chilblains?' she asked.

Kitty hesitated. Only desperation made her withdraw her hand.

'Gwendolen, we have to go on about it,' she insisted. 'It's breaking his heart.'

Gwendolen laughed, a hateful, hard laugh.

'I'm sorry, pet,' she said, glancing at Kitty's stricken face. 'But really you are so absurd and melodramatic. Hearts don't break—it's just not scientifically possible.'

'Yes, they do. The life sort of goes out of people and then they die of a broken heart because they don't want to live any more.'

Gwendolen laughed again, 'It's adolescence gives you all these funny feelings, pet,' she said. 'You'll grow out of it.'

'Gwendolen, *please* help him. You must. I promise you it's the last chance. Just believe me.'

Gwendolen did not reply. Encouraged by her silence Kitty went on, 'You said Arthur understood, so you and he only need to talk to her—like you said you would last summer.'

'No,' Gwendolen said shortly. 'We're happy, Arthur and I, and it suits us to have things this way and if you are going to cause trouble, Kitty, you will have to go. I'm not having you upset things.'

'I don't mind going, Gwendolen. I'd manage. We're talking about him.'

'Then he can go, too,' Gwendolen said, a note of hysteria edging its way into her voice. 'Arthur's used to a happy marriage at home and expects one himself and I won't let anybody upset my marriage.'

'But nobody is. Arthur understands. It's got nothing to do with your own marriage to him.'

'Oh, yes it has,' Gwendolen said, her voice rising. 'He told me that if my parents argue here he'll leave me. That's what he'd do—leave me.'

'Gwendolen! You know that's not true.'

'Oh yes, it is.'

'No, it's not—it's just not like Arthur.'

'Not like Arthur! How do you know? What do you know of men? You don't know what they say to their wives alone in the bedroom, do you? Well, do you?' her voice rose almost to a shout.

Kitty shook her head, tears silencing her voice. So now here she was trying to save him and succeeding only in wrecking Gwendolen's marriage. She had been so sure of her ground, sure she was right, but Gwendolen was so knowledgeable now that she was married and absolutely invincible when she was angry.

Worse was to come: Gwendolen's voice began to break as if she was near to tears.

'I'm sure you don't mean any harm, Kitty,' she said in a tired, bewildered voice. 'I did just want to do the best for everyone and give you all a happy Christmas, but if you keep causing trouble I really don't know how I shall keep going, really and truly I don't. It's been no picnic having the twins and I do get so tired sometimes and if you upset me you'll stop my milk.'

Kitty was about to reply that the twins were going on the bottle anyway, but bit the words back.

'I don't think,' Gwendolen went on, 'that Daddy would really thank you for causing trouble between Arthur and me.'

Her voice trembled and for one awful moment Kitty was sure she was going to cry. It was true: Daddy would never forgive her for upsetting Gwendolen's marriage and making her cry.

'I'm sorry, Gwendolen,' she said.

'That's all right, poppet,' Gwendolen replied, her voice suddenly strong and cheerful again. 'Now let's make that coffee, shall we? And I really don't think that a drop out of that brandy bottle would do either of us any harm. Come on—it's medicine.'

They made the coffee together in that curiously relaxed way that comes of being reconciled after an argument. This feeling was increased for Kitty by the sharp, warm tingling that filled her when the brandy had burned its way down her throat and made her choke. It was true, she thought, as they sat side by side on stools in the kitchen. This was what he wanted for them: that they should be friends. He desperately wanted the golden Gwendolen to be happy and would be horrified at the thought of doing anything that might hurt her marriage. He had often said to her that she must not let her own eventual marriage be harmed by her experience of her parents' unhappy one. He must surely have said the same sort of thing to Gwendolen.

So there was no reason for her to feel that she had surrendered and that in accepting the coffee she was committing treachery, she told herself as she sat on the stool alongside Gwendolen. Alongside Goneril.

He rejoined them after tea for the last evening of his holiday. Some friends of Arthur and Gwendolen called and they talked around the fire and played games and he was in high spirits and had them all laughing, so that Kitty felt that perhaps she had been a bit melodramatic. She knew that her fears were not melodramatic but maybe her way of expressing them to Gwendolen had been. The trouble was that Gwendolen always seemed to have reason on her side so was bound to win any argument, especially as she could always produce the right facts at the right moment too.

Kitty already regretted giving in to Gwendolen this morning. She despised herself for the way she always fell under Gwendolen's spell when they were alone. Watching her like this she could be more detached. She observed the three of them coldly and clearly: Gwendolen coaxing Arthur, being sweet to her mother. Martha, triumphant, cunning yet stupid. For it was stupid of her not to realize that if Gwendolen was encouraged to do this to her father, to whom she owed everything, she would not hesitate to do the same to her mother one day when she found she was dispensable. Kitty watched Arthur too and felt sorry for him. She had a queer presentiment that, having tasted blood, Gwendolen would one day destroy Arthur as well. Poor Arthur, he would be a willing victim, she thought. She checked herself suddenly, quite consciously reining in her thoughts. This was nonsense, she told herself; it was much more likely that Gwendolen had spoken the truth. It was pitiable that Gwendolen had felt compelled to act like this through fear of losing Arthur, but it made more sense. It was human. It was easier to believe in than evil. It was better to believe it too. If once you accepted evil, pure motiveless evil, in ordinary everyday people there would be terror and madness all round. But it was all supposition, it was all too difficult, she thought as she watched them talking, playing games, enjoying Christmas.

'It's ten o'clock,' her mother said, as the guests left. 'I'll go up to the nursery. You others can stay a bit longer by the fire.'

Her father glanced at his watch. 'Time I was going,' he said.

'I'll certainly run you back tonight. It's beastly again. The fog is thicker than ever,' Arthur said, looking through the drawing-room curtains. 'I'll go round and get the car out.'

'I'll get your coat,' Kitty said, leaving him alone in the drawing-room. She went and brought it from the cloakroom and watched him put it on. The happy Christmas mask which he had worn all the evening had slipped away, leaving his face drawn and sad.

'Gwendolen,' she called upstairs, 'Daddy's going.'

'All right,' Gwendolen called back. 'I'll be down soon.'

'Don't bother her,' he said. 'I'll ring her tomorrow to say good-bye before I leave for the station.'

They went together to the back door. From upstairs, faintly, they could hear sounds of laughter as Gwendolen and her mother roused the twins.

She was filled with dread for him. 'Please, can't I come too?'

'No, you just keep on smiling here. I'll meet you at the station next week. It may be easier for you once I've gone.'

She knew that he was forcing his voice to sound cheerful.

He opened the back door. They could hear Arthur reversing the car out of the garage.

'Well, good-bye, little one. Thank you for everything.'

She clung to him, suddenly terrified of letting him go out alone in the fog. If only it hadn't been so foggy, it wouldn't have seemed so bad. Her head reached just to his shoulder, which seemed colder, thinner. She dared not look at his face as he said good-bye. He moved away and she stood at the door, watching.

The light from the kitchen made orange patches in the swirling yellow-green of the fog. Slowly he made his way down the steps, stood at the bottom for a moment and then began to walk away. It was an awkward, lurching kind of walk. She watched him move from the orange light to the paler yellow and finally disappear into the fog.

She shut the door and leaned back against the wall of the kitchen, shaken with silent, dry sobs. He was doomed, she knew it. Nobody would see, they thought she was just fussing. Nobody would save him and she, who would, could not.

'If the fog lifts I'll shove the twins in the Parks this morning,' Arthur said after breakfast.

'I'll take them, Arthur,' Martha said. 'It's the last day of your holiday. Put your feet up and read the paper. Time you had a bit of rest and spoiling in your own house.'

Kitty had noticed before how her mother was always keen to spoil any man other than her own.

'Oh, let him go, Mummy. Kitty can go too and you and I will get the lunch.'

'Very well. You're a splendid father, Arthur. Always ready to help. They're not all like that; I can tell you that from experience.'

'Well, I enjoy it. I've got time to lend a hand. Hot water bottles, Gwendolen?'

'They're in the bathroom,' Martha said. 'You run and get them, Kitty. Don't just stand there.'

They filled bottles, found rugs and blankets while Gwendolen and her mother got the twins ready.

The telephone rang. 'Take it, will you, Kitty?' Arthur called from the back door. 'I expect it's for me; I'll be there in a minute.'

She picked it up.

'Hello. Is that you, Kitty?' her father's voice said. 'I'm just off to the station, so I thought I'd give Gwendolen a ring to say good-bye.'

'Yes, of course. Are you sure I can't come? Anyway a bit sooner?'

'Quite sure. You're very useful where you are. I'll meet you at the station on Thursday. Gwendolen will be glad of your help.'

'Arthur and I are just going to take the twins out now in the Parks.'

'Splendid. That's the way.'

'I'll call Gwendolen then.'

'Thank you.'

She went to the foot of the stairs and called up.

'Who did you say?' Gwendolen asked, appearing with her mother at the head of the stairs.

'Daddy's on the phone to say good-bye.'

'I'm changing the twins. Say good-bye for me,' Gwendolen said, moving away.

'But, Gwendolen, he's waiting to say good-bye to you.'

'Tell him I'm busy.'

'But, Gwendolen . . .'

'Kitty,' her mother called down. 'Will you do as your sister says? Can't you see that we're busy?'

'You could take it from your bedroom,' she begged. 'He's rung specially. It's just for a minute.'

Gwendolen's bedroom was at the head of the stairs. She only had to walk a few steps to pick up the receiver by the bed.

'Say good-bye for me,' she said, and walked back into the nursery. Her mother followed her, her very back triumphant, and shut the door behind them.

Kitty went slowly back to the telephone.

'Gwendolen?' her father asked as he heard the receiver being picked up.

'I'm afraid it's only me again,' she said.

'Oh yes.' His voice was quiet.

'Gwendolen has both twins on her knee and bottles everywhere and she's partly undressed and it is very awkward, but she sent you all her love and told me to say she's awfully sorry not to say good-bye properly and will write when she's a spare moment.'

'Thank you, Kitty. Good-bye, my little love.'

'Good-bye. Good-bye.'

CHAPTER THIRTY-THREE

IN the afternoon Gwendolen went to lie down, Arthur was painting the new top floor nursery and her mother was resting. Kitty went into the drawing-room to write thank you letters.

At least she meant to write thank you letters but decided to write to her father instead. She wasn't much good at saying things, she thought; Gwendolen had always been much better at assuring him of her affection, but she would write it. She could at least write and say she wanted to be with him soon, tell him that she wanted to leave school and have a house with him and learn how to cook. That was it, she thought, she must leave school and get a job as soon as possible. It came into her mind that she might marry very young and have a baby girl that would smile at him and run to him when he came into the room.

In the end she wrote a long letter and said none of these things, but told him instead about the walk in the Parks and asked him again if she could come back sooner. She did not tell him that the walk in the Parks had been a turning point in her life, a moment of complete disillusion. For as they walked, she and Arthur, pushing the prams along the gravel paths under the leafless trees, she had by casual but precise questioning, elicited from the unwitting Arthur that there was no truth in what Gwendolen had said. Kitty now despised herself for even half believing Gwendolen when she had said Arthur had threatened to leave her. She had been won over against all her common sense. She had known all the time that Arthur was totally, irretrievably in Gwendolen's thrall and asked nothing more of life than to remain so.

She addressed the envelope and stuck it down, giving it a thump with her clenched fist as if in confirmation of her disillusionment and of her resolve never to be deceived again.

Henceforward she would accept nothing and rely on nobody but herself.

The telephone rang. She went to answer it.

'Is that Mrs Chatham's house?' a rather nervous voice asked.

'No,' she said, thinking of Arthur's mother. Then, 'I mean, yes, yes, it is,' she corrected herself.

'Am I speaking to Mrs Chatham then?' the voice inquired.

'No, this is her sister, Catherine Langdon.'

'Oh, Miss Kitty. It's Mrs Wedgwood here.'

'Oh, what is it?'

'Miss Kitty, I can hardly tell you, not on the phone like this. It's—I'm afraid it is very bad news.'

'Please tell me what it is.'

'It's your father; he's dead.'

'But I've just written a letter to him,' Kitty said.

'It's a dreadful shock, I know. I've never had to do such a thing before. I'm sorry. Really I am.'

'You shouldn't say things like that just because it's Christmas. It's a silly game,' Kitty heard herself say severely.

'But it's true, Miss Kitty.'

'Who said so?'

'The police came—he just stepped off the pavement, they said, and was struck on the side of the head. They didn't think he was badly hurt, but when he got to the hospital—he died. It must have been a hard blow in some vital spot, I don't know; it doesn't seem possible. Not damaged at all, they said he wasn't.'

She saw Arthur come in. He was holding a paint brush.

'They found a letter addressed to him in his pocket so they came round to see me here. They asked me what to do and I thought it best to ring you myself and not have the police do it.'

'Thank you. It was kind of you.'

Kitty laid the receiver down and stood quite still by the telephone.

Arthur picked it up and they talked, Mrs Wedgwood and Arthur, for several minutes. Then he put the receiver down. She was aware that Gwendolen and her mother were standing by.

'What is it?' Gwendolen asked.

'What's wrong with Kitty? Look at her face!'

'He is dead,' she heard her own voice say.

'Nonsense,' her mother said. 'I've just seen him in his cot.'

She ran upstairs to make sure. Nobody moved while she was away or spoke a word. 'He's perfectly all right, you silly girl.'

'Not Timothy—Charles,' Arthur said.

'Oh, *him*—I thought you meant the baby.'

'My poor Gwendolen,' Arthur said, turning to his wife. 'Come away, darling,' and he led her away upstairs.

Kitty stood and faced her mother.

'Well, it's his own fault,' Martha began. 'He could have had a perfectly happy time staying here with the rest of us, just one happy family. Never could fit in and . . .'

Kitty was aware of nothing except the need to stop her, stop the hard, cruel voice ravaging his body. She put her hands around the throat that was producing the voice.

'If you say one more word against him,' she said, 'I'll kill you.' She could do it so easily, now that it was too late. For a moment they looked into each other's eyes. She saw fear in her mother's face. She released her. Martha said nothing, just turned and walked away. At the door she paused. 'Well, I've got a clear conscience,' she said. 'I've kept my vows.' She was going to say more, but thought better of it and left the room.

Kitty stood quite still. It could be a mistake, she thought. Mrs Wedgwood might have been mistaken, nothing deliberate, just a misunderstanding. She must go to him at once. Alive or dead, she must find him. She went upstairs to her room, pulled out the case from under her bed and packed everything into it, remembering only just in time to take her pyjamas from under the pillow.

She looked in her purse: she had her return ticket and thirty shillings. So that was all right. She would go to the station and catch the first train.

The door opened slowly and Gwendolen stood in the doorway. Tears were rolling down her face. She held her arms dramatically open. 'Oh, Kitty,' she said, 'we must comfort each other.'

Kitty looked impatiently at this hindrance which might delay her departure and said nothing.

'Oh, Kitty, don't be unkind, not in the face of this tragedy. You'll break my heart.'

'You told me yesterday that hearts don't break.'

'Oh, Kitty, I hope you won't remember anything I said yesterday. We were both overwrought.'

'I wasn't. I shall always remember everything. I'm going now.'

'But I mean, you won't sort of, well, go round saying . . .'

'If you mean will I tell people, no, it wouldn't do any good. It is too late now.'

'I didn't do anything. I just wanted everyone to have a happy Christmas,' Gwendolen said, starting to cry again with relief.

Kitty left her there and went downstairs. Arthur met her in the hall.

'I'll come with you to London,' he said. 'Your mother will look after things here. There's a train in half an hour.'

Her letter was lying by the telephone in the hall. She must have had it in her hand when she went to answer the telephone. She picked it up automatically, thinking to post it in London.

She followed Arthur to the garage, though she would really rather have gone alone. It was sunny as they drove through the deserted streets of the town. They did not speak; Arthur was relieved that she seemed so little upset, quite dry-eyed the child was, not like his poor Gwendolen who was so very upset. Of course, being the older one she had always been closer to him and would feel it more, Arthur reflected. It was a shame that he had to leave her. Still, widow and child would comfort each other.

Arthur parked the car at the station and helped her out, making little remarks like, 'Here we are, then,' and 'Well, well, splendid,' which she heard, but did not answer. She was astonished to see a tree with coloured lights at the station and decorations everywhere and for a terrible moment thought that the station had gone mad and was celebrating his death. Then she remembered that it was Christmas.

The train was in and Arthur found them an empty compartment. She sat in the corner and stared out of the window. A porter was standing outside the window scratching his head very slowly and methodically. Somebody came and asked him a question and he paused to answer. Then the passenger moved on and he resumed his careful scratching.

'We're off,' Arthur said, as they jerked forward, stopped and started again.

She was aware of him sitting opposite to her. She was aware of being cold. She was aware, with detachment, that they were travelling to London. There had been that news—a great raw area of pain—which was not to be thought about. It might be true or it might not. Except that it was true, of course. With terrible certainty it had forewarned her. It had cast its shadow before. Why had she known? It must just be that, that it had cast its shadow before.

Arthur looked at the white face and staring eyes.

'I say,' he said. 'I do believe that this train has a restaurant car. I'll nip up and get you a cup of tea, Kitty. Do you good. You'd like one, wouldn't you?'

'Yes, please,' she said, out of pity for him. It would be easier for him to have something to do. She stared out of the window after he had gone. Fields and trees flew past, telegraph wires moved up and down, up and down, poles blipped by.

'Well, well,' Arthur said as he returned. 'There you are. Sorry to be so long. Nothing like a hot drink.'

She gulped some down. Poor Arthur, she felt in a queer, detached way that she could see his life ahead. He was not born for this. He should have married somebody like his parents, matter-of-fact, kindly, easy going, comfort-lovers. He had married a killer.

She understood it all: too late. She had stood by and let them crucify her father. Suddenly she felt a surge of joy that they could not hurt him any more. He was free, out of their power, he had escaped them. The constant worry of what move would next be made against him, what hope raised in him in order to be dashed, what bitter unkindness spoken to him, written to him, was no more. Her mother, the Deedes, Gwendolen, were powerless with no victim left to torture. Never again would Wally Deedes humiliate him, or Grace deceive him; he was beyond the reach of a wife's harshness or a daughter's betrayal. Suddenly she began to cry and Arthur leant forward to comfort her, not understanding that they were tears of joy.

CHAPTER THIRTY-FOUR

'NO, really, we can't go tonight, Kitty.'
'But it's what we came for; please can't we go and see him tonight?'

'But really, Kitty, there's no urgency. It isn't as if we can do anything to help him now. We'll see to it all tomorrow.'

It was no good; she would never be able to make him understand how she wanted just to see him and that everything else was just waiting.

'I'll tell you what, Kitty, we'll ring up from Mrs Wedgwood's just to make sure. But the best thing is to get a good night's rest and then see to everything tomorrow.'

There was a queue for taxis but he had a word with a policeman standing nearby who led them to the front of the queue. It seemed that death had made them important.

Mrs Wedgwood greeted them nervously, so that Kitty did not know what to say. They stood together waiting while Arthur telephoned.

'I'm sorry,' Mrs Wedgwood said.
'That's all right,' Kitty replied awkwardly.

Arthur returned, evidently relieved. She had known that the conversation would go his way so was not surprised when he said, 'As I thought, Kitty. They'd rather we went along tomorrow. So now for a bit of rest; it will be a tiring day.'

'I've put you in Mr Langdon's room,' Mrs Wedgwood said to Arthur, more relaxed now that she had something to do. 'I didn't think Miss Kitty would like to be in there somehow. She is in the little room again. Now what about something to eat?'

Since she could not see him, the next best thing was to see his room. While Arthur was in the bathroom she crept into the bedroom. It was just the same: the same smell, the same few belongings. She opened the cupboard door: all his suits. Behind the bedroom door his striped dressing gown. She ran her hand down it; he had worn it as long as she could remember, dear striped thing. She had never noticed before how thin it had worn.

She heard Arthur coming out of the bathroom and made guiltily for the door.

'Just forgot something,' she mumbled.

'You're all right, aren't you, Kitty? Like an aspirin or something?'

'No, thank you. Good-night.'

'Good-night, sleep well and don't worry. Remember, I'm used to these formalities; I'll see to everything tomorrow.'

When he had gone she went quietly into the sitting-room. The curtains were not drawn and it looked bleak, as it must have looked many times this winter when he came back from work. She drew the curtains and turned on the lamps. That was better; more welcoming and homely.

She walked very slowly about the room, touching things; his desk, his books, the chair he usually sat in, the chess box. All part of him. He lived in them. She would look after them for him. She would keep them for him as long as she lived, these things which had shared his life.

She went back into her bedroom. She shut the door behind her and turned to find herself looking at the photograph of him, which she had left on the chest of drawers. She looked into his eyes; he smiled back at her. She stood staring, too shocked to move. Then she reached out blindly and turned the frame round so that she could not see his face. It was no longer bearable to look at the familiar photograph in its home-made frame. She did not know why but it had become a monstrous thing. It was like seeing the shadow of somebody who is not there. It had no right to exist now that he was gone.

Would it always be like this, she wondered, as she prepared for bed? Would she never again be able to bear to look upon his likeness? She was afraid of the night that lay ahead. But for the first time for years, her mind seemed to become blank the moment she lay down and she slept immediately and did not dream.

To awake and remember, that was much worse. Somehow she got up and dressed and responded to Arthur's remarks and ate a little breakfast to please Mrs Wedgwood.

'There's one thing I ought to mention,' Arthur said apologetically, as he helped himself to some more toast. 'I hope it won't upset you.'

'It's all right.'

'Well, you see, the driver of that wretched lorry said your father just seemed to step in front of his wheels. He couldn't understand how your father had failed to see him, so of course it raises the possibility—in some minds, not ours, of course—that he *did* see it.'

'You mean that the police might think he committed suicide?'

'Well, yes, it's possible. If there was any doubt it might make things difficult. There'll have to be an inquest, anyway. It was fortunate that he lived for a while in hospital, that always simplifies things.'

She smiled at him vaguely, having no words.

'Just a quick look at the headlines,' Arthur said, picking up the paper. 'You don't mind?'

She was relieved; it saved her having to find words. He had been unhappy enough to have killed himself, that was all that mattered and that was a certain fact. Yet it didn't seem to matter to anybody else; they were all concerned about trivia like whether he had walked in front of a lorry by accident, because he was careless of his life, or on purpose because he wanted to end it. Such an unimportant little distinction.

If only he had had a few years' happiness, she thought, or even been free for a few precious months or weeks, it would have been all right to die. But to die now, without knowing happiness, that was intolerable. The pity of it, the pity of it. The words went through her head.

I'm glad she takes it so calmly, Arthur thought. Of course, she wasn't as attached to him as Gwendolen was. Gwendolen would be—will be—very upset at the idea of anybody suggesting that her father would do such a thing.

An attendant took them from the hospital to the mortuary. It seemed like a store room, all dust covers and screens. He led them to a kind of partition and in it there was a thing like a stretcher with someone lying on it under a sheet. The attendant drew back the sheet, Arthur looked down and nodded. The attendant withdrew and Arthur glanced at Kitty. She moved forward and Arthur followed the attendant to the door.

So she had reached him at last.

Kitty looked down at him. It was so strange not to say hello or to see his expression change to a smile as he saw her approach. They had said good-bye at Gwendolen's back door, expecting to meet at the station next week, not in this strange place. He looked rather serious, his mouth not smiling as it usually did when she approached, not a trace of the funny sideways smile or even of the pretend one that she had observed so often recently.

He did look solemn though, as if he were saying, it's a serious business, death. His skin seemed thicker, too, she thought, stroking his forehead. It was true about marble death. Only his hair seemed exactly the same, irreverently bouncy, thick and alive. She ran her fingers through it. Now more than ever it seemed odd that his expression did not change, for often, as he had sat back in a chair, she had run her fingers through his hair like that and he had always looked up and smiled, even if he was tired and his eyes were closed.

The pity of it, the pity of it, she thought again and his face began to lose its outlines and become blurred as her tears fell into the thick, dark hair. Some rolled down on to his face and she rubbed them off his cheek with her fingers. It looked as if he were crying, she thought, and remembered the evening at the flat before Christmas. 'I'm sorry,' she said, 'I'm sorry.'

She felt Arthur take her arm. The attendant appeared from nowhere, pulled up the sheet as if to show that this was hospital property, and she walked away from him for ever.

'I'm sorry you had to go through that ordeal,' Arthur said, when they got outside. 'Very upsetting, the first time you see someone who has passed on.'

They were led to a little room and she was given a cup of

'A cup of coffee will do you good, Kitty. We can get one back at the hospital, the sister told me.'

They were led to a little room and she was given a cup of coffee while Arthur and a nurse signed papers in an annexe.

She could hear odd phrases: the nurse's voice seemed to come and go in waves. 'Of course . . . puzzling; still alive when he came in . . . wouldn't have thought it was lethal blow . . . damage not extensive . . . shock . . . not much resistance, perhaps . . . can't tell . . . sometimes miracles . . . will to live . . . very sad . . . daughter . . . tut tut . . . nice to have met . . . sad circumstances . . . next time . . . his things . . . almost forgetting . . .'

She rang and another nurse brought in a parcel which she put on the desk. Next to it she placed a pair of shoes and his watch. Kitty stared, shocked. Yes, of course, his clothes. They would be here. Arthur signed again and picked up the watch and parcel. Kitty took the shoes. She had not noticed before how much they were moulded to his feet; the toes turned up slightly. The nurse said, 'Wait a minute; that won't do,' and gave her a piece of brown paper which she wrapped round them.

Outside it was very cold. The wind seemed to cut her face and buffet her body as they walked to the police station. The brown paper was not big enough and the shoes kept slipping out. She held them closely to her.

'Don't worry,' Arthur said, as they went up the steps. 'I'm quite used to these things, remember, law courts and so on. The police are always marvellous on these occasions, very considerate.'

They were taken into a little side room and left. The police turned out to be a little less marvellous than Arthur had predicted; they kept them waiting, talked curtly and asked rather suspicious questions. They kept going away and returning and asking for more details and dates and then saying they would be back shortly and staying away for a very long time. The room in which they sat on a bench was unheated. She was glad in a way, for she was aware now of absolutely nothing except the cold. She was waiting, waiting, and was quite numb.

'You see, they have to establish cause of death, make sure no blame attached to the driver, or if there is any grounds for postponing the funeral—these things can't be settled in a minute or two.'

'Rome wasn't built in a day,' she offered helpfully.

'That's the spirit,' Arthur said.

At last they were allowed to go.

'We'll find a spot of lunch,' Arthur said, 'before we go to the undertaker's. This calls for a celebration.'

She looked at him in surprise. They were all mad, of course, but surely not that mad.

'You did understand that the police are satisfied that there is no cause to delay the funeral or make further enquiries and that it was just an accident?'

'Oh, did they? That's good.'

Poor Kitty, Arthur thought, she just didn't have Gwendolen's quick mind.

It was warm and steamy in the restaurant but she carried the cold with her and remained numb. She could hardly manage to make herself eat anything; she felt as if she was eating his body.

Arthur took a piece of paper out of his pocket as he got up to pay the bill. 'Very helpful that almoner at the hospital,' he said. 'Gave me the name of some reputable undertakers in the locality; here we are—Mumbly and Snoggins they're called.'

Kitty burst out laughing.

'He'd have loved that,' she said.

'Well, yes,' Arthur said, trying to hide his distaste. Being brave and cheerful was one thing—indeed he had been trying to cheer her up ever since they heard about her father's death—but to laugh like that! Again he thought how different she was from Gwendolen. Gwendolen would bear her grief like a queen. He longed for her.

He led the way to the cash desk and Kitty followed him out into the cold.

Mumbly and Snoggins were all that anyone could wish a reputable undertakers to be. Again and again Kitty found herself thinking how he would have enjoyed them. Mr Mumbly who, as the receptionist had promised, dealt with them personally, was a tall, yellow-coloured man with a stoop which, at the end of every sentence, he extended into a kind of half bow. He had a small triangular-shaped face which swayed about on the end of his long neck, so that as he bowed and swayed he looked like a praying mantis. He referred to the 'deceased' with reverence, always pausing slightly before the word as if in apology. He was most concerned to make the disposal of the deceased as comfortable and as seemly as possible, he said, inclining his angular body towards the ground. They spent a long time making innumerable small decisions which were very important to Mr Mumbly and Arthur, such as the quality of the wood in the coffin and the material for the lining.

It was all so entirely removed from him and from reality, from grief and even from death. At first she thought how he would have enjoyed the irony of it all; all this fuss about things which were less than unimportant, that were nothing. It was all quite, quite irrelevant, but all being done so seriously and even in his name. For at one point she heard Arthur say, 'Funeral expenses come out of the estate, of course,' and again wanted to laugh; it was a bit of cheek, Mr Mumbly and Arthur choosing all these things and then sending him the bill. But gradually she grew more and more tired as the discussion went on and gave up even pretending to take an intelligent interest.

'That will be very nice, very suitable,' Mr Mumbly was saying, making his half bow and rubbing his hands together in approval of his own arrangements. 'Now we have a little ante-room here, of course, and will be glad for the—er—deceased to make use of it while awaiting the journey to the crematorium. Some flowers perhaps? Thank you, it shall be seen to.' He bowed again and rubbed his hands.

'And arrangements for getting the—er—for getting from the mortuary to here?' Arthur queried.

'I see to all that; I'm well known at the hospital, leave everything to me, Mr Chatham.'

'Why can't we take him home to Mrs Wedgwood's?' Kitty asked suddenly.

She was immediately aware that she had said something embarrassing.

'More suitable here,' Mr Mumbly began.

'Very awkward those stairs,' Arthur said.

'Can assure you that everything here will be very comfortable, very seemly for the—er—deceased,' Mr Mumbly concluded, bending again from the waist and rubbing his hands.

It was over at last and he led them to the door, genuflecting as he went. Arthur called a taxi and they said good-bye to Mr Mumbly on the pavement outside his shop. As they drove away Kitty caught a glimpse of him: perhaps the cold had numbed him but he was standing quite still, frozen in a half bow, his praying mantis eyes fixed upon them and his hands devoutly clasped as he stood in the doorway of his shop and watched them go.

In the taxi home, Arthur said rather awkwardly, 'You see,

Kitty, it is only a body, after all. You must not attach too much importance to it.'

Gwendolen, he felt sure, would understand the spiritual side. Kitty was perhaps too young to go beyond the merely physical.

'Yes,' Kitty said humbly, 'but it is *his* body. I mean it's all that's left now.'

'Well, we don't know that, do we? All that's left down here, maybe.'

'I meant here.'

Mrs Wedgwood had left some tea for them on a tray. Kitty could see that Arthur wanted to say something, but feared to upset her.

'I don't mind if you go back to Oxford,' she volunteered.

'Oh, don't you, Kitty? I have been wondering, you know. Of course, I want to help you in every way I can, but my poor Gwendolen needs me too. She'll be so upset and perhaps her need is greater now that everything here is seen to. Of course, you can come back too . . .'

'No, I'd rather stay here if Mrs Wedgwood doesn't mind.'

'Well, if there is any problem over the arrangements for Thursday and so on, just ring up. Mumbly may run into some snag or other and need advice. I'll ring him and give him my Oxford number. But he seems a very competent chap. Just ring me if you have any worries.'

'Yes, I'll do that.'

'There'll probably be more letters. You open them but keep them safely for your mother and Gwendolen to see, won't you?'

'Yes, I'll do that.'

People had already written to the flat, thinking it was his family home. She had been surprised to find how much he was respected and admired by people she did not know. It was almost as if they were writing about a stranger, an important man, somehow more powerful and secure than her father. But they were wonderfully comforting, those letters, because they told her something new about him and so made him live longer.

'Well, I'll be off then,' Arthur said. 'There's a train at six o'clock. Sure you won't come? You don't mind being left alone?'

'I'd rather stay here,' she said, longing for him to go, wanting only to be left alone in the flat.

'Right you are then. I told you that the chap rang up from the men's home, didn't I? They'll send up a sack, but if you don't want to put the clothes in, I know Mrs Wedgwood won't mind seeing to it for you.'

'It's all right. I'll do it.'

'And don't worry about the arrangements for Thursday. Mumbly will see to everything. Nothing much to go wrong, really.'

When Arthur had gone it all seemed suddenly still. She went into the drawing-room and sat on the couch looking at all his things in the room. They still looked the same, that was what was so odd; the way nothing changed when everything had changed.

She stared at the chess box. She got up, intending to take it into her bedroom for safe keeping, but found that she could not bear to take it from the little table in the corner where he had always kept it. Instead, she stood stroking the lid of the box. Perhaps one day it would be bearable to open it and look at the pieces inside, the pieces that had moved across the board under his hand.

She still had the feeling that she was waiting, waiting for something to happen. It was the same kind of feeling she had about imagining eternity; for ever waiting for the infinite to stop, for ever waiting for him to return.

There was a tap at the door and she jumped.

'Would you like a little supper?' Mrs Wedgwood said. 'Christopher will be going home soon and then I'll get you something. Do you fancy anything special? Meanwhile I've brought you a cup of tea and a few biscuits.'

As she poured it out, Christopher followed her into the room.

'Hello,' he said to Kitty. 'I don't mind eating your biscuits for you if you're not hungry.'

'Thank you very much.'

'Funny Mr Langdon dying like that,' he said casually. Then with more feeling he added, 'And poor Rags getting killed, too. Very sad about both of them.'

'Christopher!' Mrs Wedgwood said sharply. 'I told you to stay downstairs. Go back at once.'

'I am sorry, Miss Kitty, really I am. He meant no harm,' she said when he had gone.

'I don't mind,' Kitty said, surprised that Mrs Wedgwood

should think that it mattered. 'My father would have been very flattered to be classed with the puppy. It's a great compliment when you think how Christopher loved poor Rags. Really, he would have been very touched.'

'Well, I don't know. I daresay he might.' She shook her head. 'There's the doorbell, that'll be my daughter-in-law come to get Christopher. I'll get on with making a bit of supper when he's gone. We'll have it together in my place, shall we?'

'Thank you; it would be nice.'

'But don't let me interefere with you if you'd rather be alone. I tried never to interrupt your father,' she said, as she paused in the doorway, her hand on the knob. 'I used to see him, you know, and wish I could help him.' Then she said quietly, almost to herself, 'For he was the loneliest man I have ever met.'

The following afternoon a sack was delivered from the men's home. When they had said they would send one of their sacks, Kitty had imagined a hairy old brown thing, but this was new and orange and smooth like leather.

She carried it into his bedroom in the evening and laid it on the bed. She took out the suits and coats, one by one, carefully emptying out pockets. There was so little: he had travelled light. Perhaps only happy people acquire bits and pieces, she thought, as she made a little pile at the bedside of diaries, notebooks, keys. She seemed to feel his hand on all of them. She felt very guilty, opening the cupboard doors and taking his clothes out, and did it all as quietly as she could, so that the door seemed to squeak unnaturally loudly and when a pair of socks, rolled together into a ball, fell down, she jumped and nearly cried out.

It was absurd to feel guilty, she knew. It was just that it felt wrong for a daughter to be going through all his things. 'I'm sorry,' she kept saying to him. 'I'm not meaning to poke around.' It would have been different for a wife; she would be used to this private side of him. 'Please God let there be nothing he wouldn't want me to see,' she said.

Mrs Wedgwood's words kept running through her head. 'He was the loneliest man I have ever met.' He was, of course, but it was somehow worse that outsiders had known it. It made it seem official.

Soon all the clothes were in the sack and she had put the oddments like keys and diaries, which she had so often seen in his hands, into a box. She left the sack on the bed and was going out of the door to take the box into the sitting-room when she noticed the dressing gown hanging behind the door.

She stared at it. Not the dressing gown, she couldn't put it into the sack and send it to the home. She had somehow turned her mind off as she had folded up the suits and said firmly, 'He would have wanted someone to use them,' but the dressing gown was different. It was old and worn, as old as herself at least. Suddenly she fell against it, held it close in her arms and began to cry.

She did not cry because he was dead; she cried for what his life had been, for his loneliness and despair. She cried all the unshed tears of all the years she had been able to understand. She cried for the years before that, when she had believed that he did not love them and had even been afraid to be alone with him when he came on leave. She cried for all that they had done to him and for her own failure to stop them, for all her inadequacy. She cried because she knew that the comfort she had had from the letters people had written was meaningless; the love of friends had not been enough to keep him alive, for he was a very private man, intensely needing the love of a particular person to whom in return he would have given endlessly, richly. Martha had known this and had made sure that he was deprived of it. She herself had known it, but had not saved him. She cried for what his life might have been. She cried because she had not helped him to gain the freedom he longed for and remembered how he had paced the rooms like a caged animal. She cried because she had failed him, because her kind of love was not enough and never could be.

She cried until she was too exhausted to cry any more and then lay on his bed, holding the dressing gown close and feeling strangely relaxed. So that was why nature arranged for tears, she thought. Then she realized that Mrs Wedgwood was calling.

'I'm here,' she said, suddenly ashamed and embarrassed. 'Just sorting out a few things.'

'Oh, you did have me worried; couldn't think where you'd got to,' Mrs Wedgwood said, and then stopped at the sight of Kitty's face.

'I'm all right,' Kitty said.

'There now—come and have some tea. It's all ready,' Mrs Wedgwood said, and took her into the kitchen which was warm and comfortable.

'I'm glad you've had a good cry,' she said matter-of-factly. 'I didn't like the look of you before.'

It was strange, Kitty thought, that she should be getting to know Mrs Wedgwood now, now that he wasn't here any more.

'I'd like to live here,' she said.

Mrs Wedgwood smiled. 'It's a nice enough place,' she said, 'but it's up for sale now; I'm moving in with my daughter-in-law.'

'Oh. When I leave school and have a job, I'm going to find a little flat like this to live in and put all his things in it.' It had suddenly become easy to talk. 'I shall arrange it all just as it is now and look after everything for him. I can't do anything else for him now, but I can look after all the things that were his.'

'Well, you can store them until you're ready. I'll arrange it for you if you like—I shall have to store some of my things, so I can see to it all at the same time. But it's a lot for you to see to, Miss Kitty. Won't your mother or sister arrange things? He never talked about his troubles but I imagine that your mother and he . . .'

She broke off. Kitty nodded.

'Miss Gwendolen?'

'A bit busy, you know, babies, job and so on.'

She stopped suddenly. She could not fob Mrs Wedgwood off with talk about the twins and a job. So she told her the truth. She told her everything, amazed at the ease with which it poured out almost involuntarily; the whole saga, Gwendolen's betrayal, all of it. Their quarrel came out almost verbatim. It came out in a great rush, but it was very accurate, each word must have been lying fresh in her mind. She ended by telling her how he had rung up to say good-bye and Gwendolen would not even walk the little distance to the telephone in her bedroom. Then she stopped.

Mrs Wedgwood had not spoken throughout, but listened very attentively. Now she said, 'But if what you tell me is true, Kitty dear, your poor sister must have a terrible conscience. We must pity her.'

Then Kitty knew that she should not have spoken, must not do so again. Mrs Wedgwood had not understood a word. It really was all too unlikely; no wonder she had said, 'If what you say is true,' unable to believe it. It did not sound true because it was not what a normal person would do. Gwendolen was not a normal person. The way Mrs Wedgwood referred to Gwendolen's conscience showed more than anything that she had not understood. The whole point was that Gwendolen did not have a conscience. She was a beautiful, clever, evil person. In time they would all realize it. Now Kitty was the only one that did and nobody would believe her. She must never speak to anybody about it again. He would live in her until she died, but as far as the rest of the world was concerned his life would be buried in silence.

CHAPTER THIRTY-FIVE

THEY all came to the funeral: her mother, Gwendolen, Arthur and his parents. The Deedes came all the way from Yorkshire to pay their last respects. They brought the Bishop with them because, as Grace Deedes said, it was nice to have a Bishop. There were many other people, too, faces vaguely remembered from the past, looking solemn now. There were some she did not know and some she discovered later were official people, representing other people.

It was very cold as they waited outside the crematorium. She always seemed to be waiting, waiting for something to happen. Ever since Mrs Wedgwood had rung her up and told her, she had been waiting for some special moment, a significant, isolated point in time, which would explain it all. Surely something must happen at his funeral to bring to an end this feeling of waiting?

They moved inside and she seemed to stand for a very long time in the front row next to Gwendolen. Gwendolen had on a new dark blue coat with a fur collar and was crying. Next to her was her mother, dressed from head to foot in black. She even had black stockings, her gloves and shoes were black and she had a black-edged handkerchief. Grim indeed she looked and sombre in her widowhood.

'In the morning it is green and groweth up,' they were singing, 'but in the evening it is cut down, dried up and withered.' It was inappropriate; he had not lived to be withered. 'The days of our age are three score years and ten,' but he was in his forties and had known no happiness. He was the loneliest man that Mrs Wedgwood had ever known. The loneliest man that anybody had ever known.

The coffin was beginning to move; perhaps this was the moment which she had been waiting for, she thought. His body was sliding away to be burned. It was not the moment. It would have been better to have lowered it into the ground and cast lumps of soil upon it. There was something surreptitious about the way it slid away.

Afterwards they walked outside and looked at the wreaths, her mother stooping to read the labels, sometimes having to turn them over. The faces from the past became individuals, some even talked to her, but mostly they talked to Gwendolen and her mother. There was something kind but oddly condescending, she observed, about the way people talk about a friend who has died. As if by dying he had failed, and it was up to the rest of us to be nice about it. They seemed to be saying that death was not an event in his life, but his last and final failure. Sad but a bit embarrassing, like all failures.

Not everyone came back to the flat afterwards—just the family, and the Deedes and the Bishop, because they had a long journey. Mrs Wedgwood had prepared food for them and they stood in the drawing-room eating and talking as if it was a party. Kitty tried to eat a ham sandwich but again felt with horror that she was eating his body.

It was not a very big room. As she stood in the corner, by the dormer window, she could hear Mrs Deedes talking to Arthur's mother as they sat on the couch in front of her.

'Poor Gwendolen will feel it dreadfully, so close to her father she always was. He was so proud of her.'

'Yes, so Arthur tells me. She can lean on us now, of course.'

'Indeed, yes. What a blessing she has you all.'

'We're lucky to have her. She's a lovely girl.'

'Do you know, Mrs Chatham, as I stood behind her at the service I thought she had the most lovely profile I have ever seen. Distressed though she was, she could still gaze up, and still sing, obviously inspired by those marvellous, comforting words of the psalm, and she looked like a Madonna. I found it an inspiration just to look at her.'

Arthur's mother turned and saw her.

'Well, Kitty,' she said kindly. 'You've been staying here, I gather. What will you do now?'

Martha came up.

'School on Wednesday,' she said briskly. 'We don't need to upset Kitty's plans at all; she needn't be affected.'

'No, of course not, Mrs Langdon. Come and sit down; you must be very tired.'

Martha went and sat down next to her.

'I hear that you and Gwendolen are going to give a dozen rose trees in his memory to the Garden of Rest,' Mrs Chatham continued. 'What a lovely idea!'

They went on talking and Kitty moved away. They did not give him one flower when he was alive, she thought, but now that they have destroyed him they will give him whole trees.

A picture came into her mind of a bowlful of anemones, purple and blue and powdery black. If she could only slip back to the time when those anemones were alive, play one more game of chess. She clenched her fists; she would not think like that, she would not cry.

'Make yourself useful,' Martha called after her. 'Hand things round.'

Kitty took a plate and moved towards the window.

Gwendolen, Arthur and his father were standing by the desk. Arthur was leaning on it.

'I think we'll store the furniture,' Gwendolen was saying in reply to something her father-in-law had said. 'It would be useful if Arthur and I decided to have a little *pied-à-terre* in London.'

'Yes,' Arthur said. 'We were thinking, Father, that it would be nice to have a little place to stay after a late party or meeting in London; it's such a business getting into an hotel, especially in the summer.'

'It's a good idea; I've often said to your mother that we should do that.'

'You'd be very welcome to use ours at any time,' Gwendolen said, 'once we've got it all arranged. Of course, it won't be easy to get exactly what we want in the right place. If we can't find anything we like, we'll just sell the furniture; it's not worth paying for storage for too long. We might take one or two of the better pieces to Oxford. We'll sell most of the books, of course—except a few legal ones which Arthur says he might find useful.'

'Don't forget,' Arthur said knowledgeably, 'that it will all have to be valued for probate. Frankly, in most of these cases it is simpler to get an independent valuation done and divide the money between the beneficiaries.'

Probate, valuation, beneficiaries. Once it had seemed funny, the way they thought of everything in terms of things; now it enabled them to lay unclean hands on all his possessions, everything he had used and touched and made part of himself. Everything which she was going to keep and look after, they would take and destroy because they understood nothing.

'Now don't you go worrying yourself too much about it,' Arthur's father told Gwendolen. 'We can't have you overdoing it. This business will have tired you. These emotional upsets take more out of you than any amount of work.'

Gwendolen sighed.

'That's very true,' she said.

'I've got a surprise for you,' Arthur told her to cheer her up. 'I've bought a lovely silver frame and we'll get an enlargement done of a photograph of your father and put it in. There's bound to be a photograph among his papers somewhere. If not we could ask *The Times*—they had a good one. It's a big frame; at least twelve by eight.'

'Oh, Arthur, how lovely. There's nothing I'd like better. I'll keep it on my dressing table always.'

You should put it in the hall, Kitty thought. More people would see it there.

'Eat up now, Gwendolen,' Arthur's father said. 'Keep your strength up. Let's see what Kitty has on that plate.'

Gwendolen flashed him a brave smile and reached for the plate without looking at Kitty. Kitty watched as the even white teeth bit into the flesh of the ham sandwich.

Arthur was gazing at her with devotion; Gwendolen certainly was exquisite in her grief. Poor Arthur, Kitty thought. He stood, proud, confident, leaning on her father's desk, and Kitty watched him and thought that the day of his disillusionment would be terrible indeed.

'I've nothing to blame myself for, my conscience is quite clear,' Martha said to Grace Deedes.

'Of course it is, Martha dear, you mustn't blame yourself for any little misunderstandings you may have had in the past. Married people tend to do that. I find this in my work to help them. It's always the nicest and best of wives who forget the lifelong devotion they have given their husbands and remember only one little unkind word they said the day before he died, that he probably never noticed anyway.'

'Well, he understands everything better now,' Martha said, glancing upwards as if challenging a denial. 'He sees things in a clearer light now that he is with his Maker.'

He saw everything clearly before, Kitty thought, alas too clearly. It was her mother whose vision had become so clouded by emotion and hatred that she could not see what was happening and had fallen in with Gwendolen's plans, thinking that she was in control when really she was only a pawn. She stared at Martha, fascinated by the movement of her lips. Suddenly the room seemed to be filled with mouths uttering falsehoods about him. All around her they were talking to each other, these people who had killed him. It was no good thinking that she could not bear it; she had no choice. She listened to them with a kind of numbed endurance.

Later she heard Martha saying again, 'I've nothing to blame myself for, my conscience is quite clear. I kept my vows.' This time she was speaking to the Bishop, who made soothing, fruity sounds in return.

You protest too much, Kitty thought. That's the third time I've heard you say that. She reflected, with some satisfaction, that her mother was going to have to battle against a bad conscience for the rest of her life.

'Gwendolen, my dear,' Grace Deedes said, 'I must have a little word with you before we go.'

Her great brown eyes were moist and cowlike. 'I know how much he meant to you and we are—so sorry.'

'Thank you, Mrs Deedes.'

'Of course, it is a terrible loss to your mother, too. We all know that, but perhaps *in the circumstances,* you know, less of a blow than it is to you.'

'Yes, I think perhaps you are right,' Gwendolen said and sighed. 'But you know it gives me the greatest possible comfort to think that he had Christmas with us and saw my little ones and was part of our home just before he died.'

'I am sure it must, dear. Everyone has been saying how nice it was that he had a last happy Christmas with you. It must have rejoiced his heart to see you so happily settled.'

'And a marvellous way for him to go, Mrs Deedes, without

suffering or anticipation. I try to think of that all the time.'

'I'm sure you do; how like you to think only of him. It is the best way to go, of course, but such a shock to the ones who are left behind.'

'Indeed, yes,' Gwendolen said in a little voice and took a handkerchief out of her new blue bag and wiped her eyes.

'I hope you weren't too upset, dear, about those shocking suggestions in some of the papers that he did it on purpose. All of us who were his friends know that any such idea is absurd.'

'Naturally, I was very annoyed. As if *my father* would even think of such a thing.'

Kitty listened to them, numbed endurance turning to anger. If he wanted to, why shouldn't he? It was his life to do as he wanted with. After they had taken away the job he loved and all chance of a home and happiness, it was all they had left him. Now they would even deprive him of the right to do as he chose with that.

She leaned against the wall, watching them. They were here because of him, in his honour and yet ignoring the reality of his life, as if to inflict one last insult on the guest of honour who was not there.

They had killed him, they would take away all that had belonged to him. There was nothing left of him for her. For the first time she thought of herself and how her life would be. Only one thing she knew: she would guard his memory. They would try to destroy it, but as long as she lived, he would live.

She looked about the room: at Gwendolen talking to Grace Deedes with a kind of martyred cheerfulness, at Wally Deedes, down-trodden, sinister and spider-like, saying something to her mother. She looked at her mother, nodding to Wally while a quiet, triumphant smile worried the corners of her hard, grey mouth.

Unobserved, ignored, Kitty stood by the couch and watched them as they celebrated the death of her father. Her anger fixed itself into a single determination: I shall hate them, she vowed, until I die. Then, with a little smile as she pictured her own coffin slipping surreptitiously away, she added: and even after that, if it can be arranged.